seat of mars

Seat of Mars

Jason Heppenstall

Seat of Mars

© 2016 Jason Heppenstall

Original cover art by Pernille Christensen

Publication date: 2016-11-24

ISBN-13: 978-1540631176

ISBN-10: 1540631176

Club Orlov Press

http://ClubOrlovPress.blogspot.com

cluborlovpress@gmail.com

1

This royal throne of kings, this sceptered isle,
This earth of majesty, this seat of Mars,
This other Eden, demi-paradise,
This fortress built by Nature for herself
Against infection and the hand of war...

—William Shakespeare, *Richard II*

It was a quarter past ten and the pitch of the engine had risen to a tinny whine as the old van struggled up the seemingly never-ending hill. Cat, her face half-lit by the screen, cursed quietly. Her boyfriend shot her a cursory glance but remained silent. Reflector lights set into the tarmac glowed green in the twilight as they floated past like will-o'-the-wisps. The young man stepped down hard on the clutch, dropping another gear. There was a slight jerk in the forward trajectory of the vehicle and the engine pitch went up another half octave. He glanced nervously at the temperature gauge just as she looked up from the screen. She frowned and looked out of the window at the moorland they were travelling through.

"Where the bloody hell are we?"

Willie Nelson crooned faintly on the van's stereo, hardly audible behind the noise of the engine.

"Bodmin Moor," said Jack. "Not too far now. The traffic's all behind us."

Cat had been sleeping for most of the journey. In her just-awoken state the scenery outside gave her an uneasy feeling in the pit of her stomach and she half-considered telling Jack to turn round and take them back to the bright lights of London. Ahead of them a faint halo crowned the silhouette of a distant hill, suggesting a rising moon. She looked down at her phone again and frowned.

"There's no signal."

She was sat with her knees up under her chin, bare feet on the vinyl seat cover as she pawed away at the tiny screen. Jack sighed inwardly. "I doubt there are any transmitters up here on the moor."

Cat took this in. The last time she had been somewhere with no signal was that holiday in Greece. She thought back to that time, remembered seeing the old man and the donkey walking down the street, taking pictures of him with her phone. She hadn't known there were places in England with no signal. That holiday had been with someone else. It hadn't worked out. Perhaps it was some kind of omen.

"We'll be over the moor soon enough and then it's all downhill from there. Should be a signal soon." Jack tried to sound reassuring, although even he was starting to feel that this journey was taking forever.

Earlier on, as they were leaving London, she had been engaged in a group chat with a clutch of friends strung out in various bars around London, Madrid and other places too. Tina, who worked in the finance department, had just taken a picture of herself with a waiter, who looked Italian or maybe Spanish. It remained there on the screen, static, right

2

underneath the 'no signal' icon. She looked out of the window but saw only a fading light and her own reflection. In the distance, high up on the moor, a single light hovered. Perhaps it was a lone farmhouse. "Who'd want to live there?" she thought. This sparked another thought.

"There *will* be a signal where we're going, won't there?"

"'Course there will," scoffed Jack. "It's got Wi-Fi and everything." But even as he said these words a flicker of doubt crossed his mind. He tried to remember whether the place would indeed have Wi-Fi, or whether he had just made that assumption. Would she be angry if there wasn't? He sensed problems, even now. This week was supposed to be about getting away from London and their full-on lives. The two kayaks strapped to the roof of the VW attested to that. *You don't just drive for eight hours from London and expect everything to be the same*, he thought.

"What is that white stuff?" said the young woman.

"Crap," said Jack, easing off the accelerator. The fog was like a wall and they drove straight into it. It cloaked them, muffling the sound of the engine—a blankness so sudden and all-enclosing that for a moment it felt as if the wheels of the vehicle had left the road and they were now sailing up through the clouds. Cat pulled her heels further behind her on the seat and wrapped her arms around herself.

"When will we be there?"

Jack glanced at the clock on the dash. "About an hour," he said, even though he knew it would be more like ninety minutes and then some. This was their first time away together. Unless you counted that night in Brighton, but that was with friends and most of it had been lost in an alcohol blackout. He liked Cat. They'd been together for four months and people at the company said they made a good couple: He, the slightly dreamy one who worked in Communications, and she the exotic catch from Buenos Aires.

She was stationed in the HR department of the global marketing agency they both worked for. In the short time she'd been there she had already climbed several rungs up the ladder to success, and senior management were treating her well lest she be headhunted by a rival. He wondered what he had done to deserve such a head-turner. In his estimation, whenever he looked in a mirror, all he saw was a slightly dorky young man, unable to shake off the provincial blandness that his Midlands upbringing had instilled in him. Despite six years in London and his best efforts, his accent still retained a slight Midland twang that reasserted itself every time he went home to visit whatever friends had not managed to escape. His parents were both long gone. There really wasn't much point visiting his hometown any more, he thought.

Escape. Maybe that's what this week was about. Getting out on the water with Cat. Eating mussels overlooking the bay in St Ives. Evening walks on the cliffs watching the sunset over the Atlantic, perhaps with a sundowner or two.

He caught her reflection in the whiteness of the windscreen. She was frowning, and looked tired. Her smallish face sat between curtains of tangled dark hair; the dark shadows in the van's interior emphasising the pout of her lips and her long curled eyelashes. He turned back and focused on the road and the whiteness. He had slowed almost to a crawl for fear of cars backing up on the single carriage road. It felt as if they were not moving at all.

There were so many things that had puzzled Caterina Ana Gutierrez about this country in the two years since she had landed at Heathrow with a suitcase full of clothes and a head full of plans. Her father, whose firm designed steel rigs for the Brazilian oil sector, had made sure she would not have to worry about money while she was away. A year's rent was paid up front in cash to secure an apartment near Hyde Park, and before she left he had put in her hand a credit card and folded her fingers around it. "Just for you, *mi preciosa*," he had said. It was there in case of trouble, and the limit on it was sufficiently high that it could be used to get on a plane "to anywhere" if the need arose.

She loved her life in London. Loved the restaurants, the parties, her flat, her friends. She was equally as comfortable shopping for cast-off jeans at Camden Lock on a Sunday morning as she was picking out cocktail dresses at Harrods or engaging sales staff in the Louis Vuitton store. She kept fit by jogging around the park most mornings, spent weekends clubbing and was on a mission to dine at as many different ethnic fusion restaurants as one life would permit. Just the previous evening she had been at a Rwandan/Ethiopian place eating *gored gored* and *kifto* with her friends, one of whom was doing well for herself as a foodie blogger. Life had never tasted so sweet.

Spending a week in Cornwall was something she'd had to be talked into. She had been with Jack long enough to realise that he didn't feel the same way about London as she did. When she'd asked him what he wanted for his birthday, a week in Cornwall had been his reply. *Fine*, she'd thought. She looked it up online. It looked nice enough. Lots of beaches and pictures of stone cottages and boats. It looked a bit *primitiva*, in her own words, and she wasn't sure why anyone would want to spend so long away from London—wouldn't a long weekend be enough—but there *was* a Tate gallery there, as well as a smattering of Michelin-starred eateries, so maybe it would be able to hold her interest for a week if she lowered her expectations a little.

All of a sudden the fog cleared, revealing the landscape around them. It was a clear night, and the stars in the darkening sky seemed close. One star shone brighter than the rest in the western sky. "Mars," said Jack, pointing through the windscreen. "You can tell it's not Venus because it's slightly orangey."

She looked. It didn't look that orangey to her. She wondered if he was mansplaining. Perhaps leaving London hadn't been a good idea—that he was de-evolving into something primitive. She stared at the bright dot in the sky again and a thought occurred to her. *Typical of a man to say that Venus is Mars.* She gave him a sideways glance, trying to gauge his intentions. He shifted up a couple of gears and the sound of the engine steadied and quieted, revealing Willie Nelson once more. "I'd rather see you up than down," he sang to a sliding steel guitar and harmonica accompaniment. "So leave me if you need to, I will still remember angel flying too close to the ground."

Cat stared at the stereo. "Jesus Christ, can we turn this depressing crap off?" she exclaimed, punching the on/off knob. Jack felt a spike of resentment once more. "*She's just tired,*" he told himself. The road levelled off and they began to descend. The feeling of getting over the moor was usually a natural mood lifter for him. It was as if a liminal threshold had been passed, a severing of some invisible line that had reached out from London and held the old VW in a tractor beam since the M25. They had crested the moor and the A30 began to angle down into a descent. A truck passed by, going in the opposite direction, its headlights picking out the white forms of a few sheep sleeping in a field amongst spiky tufts of marsh grass.

But something wasn't quite right. At first it was just a feeling; Jack's intuition told him that something was amiss. They continued to drive along in silence. Cat fumbled with her phone. "Still nothing," she said after a few minutes. They rounded a bend and approached the town of Redruth. Jack knew this route well, had done more after-work night drives down here than he cared to remember. The cars became more numerous as the road turned into a dual carriageway, and some appeared to be going too fast. *Friday night boy racers,* thought Jack.

Cat, restless, leaned forward and punched on the stereo again. Willie had only a moment to croon a few syllables before he was ejected, the CD flung unceremoniously into the glove box. She turned the radio tuner and watched as the little digital display raced up the frequencies looking for something to latch onto. After a moment it halted and the sound of static came from the speakers. There was a voice somewhere in the background but it was speaking French. She pressed it again and it ran all the way through without finding anything. She tried AM but that just resulted in an eerie looping noise that sounded like something from a cheap 1950s alien movie.

"Don't they have radio here either?" Giving up, she punched the off button once again and settled back in her seat.

The main road, which had taken them over the moor, and would take them all the way to Land's End if they continued on it, brushed against the outskirts of the town. More cars. They passed under the grey concrete shape of a bridge. The moon had risen above the distant hill and was casting a pale light onto the cuboid outlines of a housing estate. It connected all at once in Jack's mind.

"The lights," he said. "There's a power cut."

2

Arthek "Art" Gwavas was in a hurry. And he was frustrated. If only he could remember where he'd put his keys he wouldn't be late for the party. He checked the pockets in his faded combat trousers for the twentieth time, rummaged through the unkempt bedclothes and finally issued a curse so loud his cat, which had been sunning itself on a window ledge, ran for cover under the bed. It was by no means the first time he'd lost the keys to the pickup, and each time he'd eventually found them he'd promised himself to take better care of them and even get a spare set cut. But he never did, and this time it seemed like they were lost for good.

"Fuck!" he bellowed, kicking out at a small wooden table and sending a half-drunk cup of tea, several empty cans of Old Rosie and a small pottery ashtray crashing down onto the stone floor. He'd turned over half the cottage looking for the keys since he got back from work, and the chances of finding them were looking increasingly dim. The cat scowled at him from beneath the bed and considered making a break for the half-open door. Art sat down on the bed and put his head in his hands. Grimy black fingernails dug into the mop of dread-locks that hung down lank obscuring a tanned and weather-beaten face with a wispy beard. "Think, *think!*" he implored himself. When was the last time he'd had them? The last few days were a bit of a haze, if he was honest. He remembered driving into town to pick up his chainsaw from the repair shop. *Had that been yesterday or two days ago?* He couldn't remember. This lack of clarity in his recollection made him anxious. *What if it had been a week ago?* He just couldn't remember.

The cat came out from under the bed and, having decided that his master didn't represent a threat, rubbed its head against his inner calf. Art looked down at the cat, noticing a half-smoked joint that had fallen out of the ashtray onto the floor. He picked it up and lit it, drawing the sweet smoke deep into his lungs and exhaling slowly through his nose. "Thanks Buster," he said to the cat, reaching down to scratch him on the neck behind his ears. The cat purred in response and Art suddenly remembered where he'd put the keys. He'd been over at a nearby farm all day in one of the lower fields planted up with maize. It was one of the fields Peck leased off someone or other and it was always full of weeds blown in from old Patrick's land, which had gone to rack and ruin of late. The day had started off cloudy and Art had worn his favourite hoodie—the one with the faded marijuana leaf on it—to keep him warm. Two acres of docks and thistles needed to be scythed and Peck was only paying *dreckly* wages, so Art hadn't felt much need to be punctual or to work too hard. By mid-morning the sun had appeared and it had become hot, and so he'd taken off the hoodie, stashing it by a granite gatepost beside the millstream. And that's precisely where it still lay, with a bunch of keys in the pocket.

He stood up and walked out of the cottage into the warm evening air. Midsummer and everyone would already be down at the beach, he mused. Art had said he'd bring along a load of old pallets for the fire, but that didn't seem like it was going to happen without the pickup so they'd just have to burn driftwood or whatever else they could find. He weighed up his options. It would take at least half an hour to walk back to where he'd left the keys in the hoodie by the gate-post. Perhaps he should just cut his losses and walk to the beach. It was a good four and a half miles cross-country, down lanes and across town, but he could do it in an hour and a half if he walked fast. He had no precise idea of what the time was and squinted up at the sun through the leaves of the huge oak tree that grew beside the cottage. Probably about half six, he reckoned. No hurry—there'd be a few more hours of light, and the party wouldn't even get started until much later. He began to relax, but even as he did so another worrying thought crossed his mind. He had no money. Peck, the miserly skinflint, hadn't even had the decency to pay him his *dreckly* wages, and had left him a note saying there'd been a problem at the bank and he couldn't get any money out. *Bullshit*. The man was full of lies and would say anything to wriggle out of paying Art for the work he did. *That's why worms like him are rich and decent folk like me live like peasants in rat-infested cottages without so much as an electricity connection*, he reasoned. When he considered this for a moment—and he very often did consider this—thoughts arose within him that could only be described as murderous. He imagined Peck wriggling on the sharp end of a pitchfork, using his last re-maining breath to beg for mercy and apologise for five hun-dred years of villainy and sin.

With this comforting thought in mind Art sucked the last out of the joint, pulled shut the front door to the cottage and set off in the direction of the coast. The first part of the jour-ney took him through an area of woodland filled with dappled light. He passed beneath great oaks and sycamores, beside beeches and ash trees, eventually climbing over a rock stile to emerge in a field of industrially planted cabbages. He walked straight through Peck's field, kicking the occasional cabbage head off its stalk and whistling quietly to himself. He could see the town in the distance and observed the way its spreading estates were creeping over the hills. He stopped for a moment to look at something. On the edge of town, where there should have been a patch of trees there was, instead, the yellow outlines of construction machinery. "More bleddy houses!" he exclaimed. "Like we don't have enough already."

The sun was still hot and sweat trickled from his brow as he strode purposely onwards towards town. When he reached the main road he walked alongside it with his thumb out. There were plenty of cars this evening but nobody was willing to stop for a shambling figure with combat trousers and dreadlocks. It didn't matter, Art reasoned, he wasn't banking on a lift anyway. Nobody stopped these days. *Miserable selfish feckers!* Twenty minutes later he was knocking on the door of an old school friend who owed him a favour or two, if memory served. Perhaps Zippo would lend him a twenty and he'd be able to get an eight pack of tinnies from the supermarket. He'd buy a stick of bread as well, and some Rizlas and tobacco. That'd be enough to sort him out for the night. He could always blag extra booze and weed once he was there, but it was bad form to turn up empty-handed from the outset, especially since he'd let them down with the fire-wood.

But there was no answer at the door. Zippo, it seemed, wasn't in. Art sighed and walked away from the house. He continued on his way into town, running through various options in his head. There was always his ex. Perhaps Janey had forgiven him enough by now to bung him a tenner or more. And if not her, there was always her mother—she was always a sucker for a sob story. These were the things that ran through his mind as he walked and he was all but lost in thought as he passed the supermarket car park and might easily have missed the commotion occurring outside. Indeed, if it hadn't been for the man shouting into a megaphone he might not have noticed anything out of the ordinary at all. "Please," the man's amplified voice rang out, "we are only able to accept cash at the moment. As you must be aware we are unable to process card payments, and we do apologise for your inconvenience."

A crowd of Saturday shoppers were milling around outside the supermarket's automatic doors, which had been propped open with a shopping trolley. The sign above the store was usually lit up yellow but was now dark. Art's curiosity was piqued and he walked over to investigate. A sweaty man, stripped to the waist, was berating the harangued-looking store manager. "What am I supposed to do?" he was shouting. "My daughter's sat in the car and she's been at tennis all afternoon and you're telling me I can't even buy some water for her. What kind of place is this?" Others chipped in with their disapproval and the store manager protested his innocence in the situation. His tie was undone and his shirt pulled out of his trousers as he held up the palm of his hand to the angry shirtless man. The manager suggested the shoppers try a larger store in a neighbouring town: perhaps they have a backup system in place. A few people wandered off shaking their heads and Art saw his chance. He pushed through the crowd and entered the store. The manager grabbed his arm. "Cash only, Sir."

"Do I look like the kind of person with a credit card?" asked Art. The store manager gave him a quick once over and let him go.

Inside it was a scene of chaos. Six lines of people snaked to the back of the store as the confused-looking teenagers manning the tills attempted to add up figures using pocket calculators that had clearly just been taken from the "*Back to skool*" promotional display, and were writing out receipts with ballpoint pens. Their colleagues were rushing around holding items aloft and shouting out prices above the general din of raised voices and shuffling shoppers. Art got a basket and wandered past shelves that were half-empty. He tossed in some peanuts, and a bag of crisps. Most of the fresh meat had disappeared, but the freezer cabinets were still half-full. He leaned in and took out a frozen steak, which was already showing signs of thawing. As he squeezed it a drop of blood fell onto the shiny supermarket floor. He looked around. Only one security guard and he was occupied with a distressed-looking mother who was jabbing a finger at his face and yelling something as her child sucked on its dummy thoughtfully.

In a moment the steak was down the front of his combat trousers. An icy sensation began to spread immediately. *Better get out of here fast*, he thought. Art moved swiftly through the store, randomly tossing items into the basket to make it look like he was shopping. He walked longingly past the cider section, knowing there'd be no way of getting much of that smuggled out. But rum was another matter. His eyes scanned the different labels, settling on the Navy Rum—not because he favoured that particular brand but because the rounded bottles looked more pocket-friendly. He picked up two half-litre bottles and placed them in the basket. Art then joined one of the lines, avoiding eye contact with any of the other shoppers and keeping his face downcast. As he queued he listened in on the conversations around him. Some people were chirpy, happy even. An old man was regaling a group of bored-looking youngsters with stories about the war and all the deprivations he had suffered and how this was "a walk in the park" compared to those times. Art took the bottles and slipped one into each pocket, glancing down to make sure the tops were not poking out.

"You don't know about rationing," went on the old man. "And why should you?"

The youngsters carried on looking bored and the staff continued to run around holding items aloft and shouting out prices from one end of the store to the other. Art glanced at the security guard, seeing that the woman with the pointy finger was still distracting him.

"Excuse me," said Art, leaning forward and tapping the old man on the shoulder. "I've just realised I forgot to get the ketchup ... would you mind keeping my place?"

"Of course," said the old man, and Art flashed him a smile. "Manners and trust go a long way when things don't work like they're supposed to," continued the old man, turning back to the kids.

"Thanks," said Art. "I'll be right back." He walked away to the back of the store and then made his way round again to the front down a different aisle. He had to push his way through the lines of shoppers queuing up to get past the till. "'Scuse me, sorry," he said, as he shouldered his way though. The manager was still standing in the door apologising, and Art slipped past him and out into the car park. He didn't dare turn around, and fixed his eyes on the ground as he made good his escape. He was almost at the exit to the carpark and thought he had got away with it when he heard it.

"You," bellowed the manager. Art froze, and it wasn't due to the steak in his underpants. He turned around and saw the sweaty-faced manager staring at him, along with about two-dozen shoppers.

"Show me your receipt."

The man began to push his way past the shoppers, who stood there mutely. "Don't go any further!" he shouted, breaking into a jog. Art looked down at his trousers, seeing the two bottle tops poking clear out of the side pockets. After a moment's consideration he made his decision about what to do: he ran.

It wasn't easy running, encumbered as he was, and he had to do so by holding onto his outer thighs to prevent the bottles from jumping out. He ran out into the road, weaving between the cars, and carried on sprinting into the town, dodging down an alley that passed between two rows of red brick cottages. The manager was still following him, yelling at him to stop and threatening to call the police. But the flabby man in his restrictive polyester suit was no match for the lanky young Art, who had extensive experience of being chased. He sprinted down the maze of alleys, emerging in the yard of a coal merchant, and quickly climbed over a low mesh fence. Once over it he bounded off down a muddy hog-weed-chocked track and eventually came to rest behind the graffiti-covered wall of a decrepit parking garage. With his heart pounding he leaned against the wall, alert for any sign of the manager.

After a while it became clear that Art had lost him. Reaching down he felt the reassuring form of the bottles in his trouser pockets. He pulled one out and unscrewed the lid. The liquid lit up his throat as it made its fiery way down inside him. He took another swig and began to laugh. *"You fat moron!"* he cried out loud. Feeling down further, he pulled out the lump of steak. Holding it aloft, he saluted the bloody chunk of meat with his other hand. "Here's to power cuts!" he said, and took another swig of the rum. The alcohol mixed with the endorphins in his blood, creating a feeling of wild euphoria. *What a perfect end to the week,* he thought. "Peck can go screw himself," he said to the meat. "I've got some wild partying to do and nothing's gonna stop me now."

But in actual fact, although he could scarcely have known it, Art was entirely wrong, and something was most definitely going to thwart his plans for the midsummer party. Because in only a few hours' time, he would be lying in a pool of blood, rum and broken glass, and a young woman would be standing over his body and shrieking.

3

~ The Mournful Tale of Rose O'Keefe ~

Decades later, when Rose used her powers of recall, she found she could run old memories in her head as if she were watching a film in a cinema. She would take to going on lonely walks along the cliff tops as the orange ball of the sun sank down low over the western horizon at the end of each day. It was much quieter these days, she would reflect, thinking of all those turbulent years that had passed by. Often, sitting by her favourite rock, she would select a particular episode from her long and eventful life and play it over again in her mind. It was a curious thing, this power of recollection, and she was sure that few others possessed it. Nevertheless she was grateful that she could use it to peer back into the past and assemble some kind of narrative out of the chaotic jumble.

There were a lot of memories to choose from, and not all of them were memories as such. True, there were memories of things that had happened to her and to the world, and these stood out the clearest, but much of what was stored in her mind could not be neatly categorised as a "memory."

Much of this was far more ephemeral, and might include snatches of feeling or the upwelling of emotion sparked by a piece of music heard years before. All of these thoughts and feelings and memories jostled inside her head, sometimes making her tired. There was so much to recall, *so much.*

No doubt about it, there were downsides to having made it this far, but generally she enjoyed reviewing her life in retrospect. They say that one's life passes before your eyes at the moment of death and so, by Rose's reckoning she was experiencing a long and drawn-out death due to some malfunction of the cerebral cortex, quite possibly as a result of what had happened to her around the time the Tribulations had begun and the old ways had been so abruptly taken away in the first part of this tired old century.

Rose had grown up in Liverpool, a fourth generation immigrant from Ireland and the brightest girl in her class. The youngest of four siblings, at school Rose was teased and called names on account of her short stature and dumpy physique. Even at four years old she'd had to wear thick prescription glasses and because of this she was called 'four eyes' and was always last to be picked for games. When she was ten years old her schoolmates put slugs in her schoolbag, dipped her pigtails in paint pots and, once, wrote her a poisonous letter saying she would soon develop cancer and die. Worse things happened, too, and some of those things she kept secret from the teachers and her parents.

Remarkably, though, Rose brushed all of this aside. As she grew from a dumpy bespectacled child into a dumpy bespectacled teenager with acne, she could barely care less what her contemporaries thought of her. Because while her tormenters' earthbound heads were filled with pop songs and boys, Rose's was lit up with something of far greater substance: astrophysics. At first her parents were happy to have such a bright daughter but they became concerned when she began using all of her pocket money to buy thick books with titles such as *In Search of Schrödinger's Cat* and *Hyperspace: A Scientific Odyssey through Parallel Universes, Time Warps and the Tenth Dimension.* Moreover, weekends and evenings were spent hunched over the family computer scrolling through page after page of comments on web forums for the terminally geeky.

"I blame him in the wheelchair with the funny voice," said her concerned mother. "He should only be on TV after the watershed, if you ask me." Once, noticing that her fourteen-year-old daughter had worn a troubled look on her face all day, Roisin O'Keefe had sat her down and asked her what was wrong and if she wanted to talk about it.

"You don't want to know," Rose had replied.

"Tell me about it," said her mother, thinking—perhaps hoping—that, finally she might be having boyfriend problems.

"Okay," said Rose, after a pause. "I'm just confused."

"We all get confused from time to time, Poppet," said her mother, caressing her hand.

"I'm worried about dark matter," said Rose, raising a worried face to her mother's. "I mean if the multiverse model is true—isn't it possible that gravity might be, you know, leaking out into other universes and that some kind of threshold will be reached and that we'll all just kind of blink out of existence without warning?"

When she recalled this conversation seventy years later Rose realised that this was undoubtedly an inflection point; the point at which she had realised she was indeed alone in the universe and that even her parents could not be relied upon to understand her. Her father had taken away her books and given them to Oxfam. Shelves were swept of Carl Sagan, Stephen Hawking and Brian Greene and all their elegant theories of superstrings, black holes, trans-Planckian physics, Calabi Yau manifolds and quantum mechanics were bundled into the back of the family Ford Focus never to be seen again.

After this disaster Rose had taken stock of her predicament and decided the best way forward was to attempt engaging with the type of reality her parents insisted was important. To that end she saved up her wages from a weekend job in a shoe shop, and spent them on getting herself a new look. The look she chose could be described in one word: black. She wore tight black jeans, a black leather jacket, dyed her hair jet black, and wore black eye liner and black Doctor Marten boots.

"That's more like it," said her father, a little uncertainly, when she appeared from the bathroom after her transformation. "Now you just need to go and make some friends."

Rose found this simple aesthetic makeover worked wonders with her social life. The other emos and goths at school suddenly wanted to be her friend and she was invited to parties every weekend. *"How shallow people are."* Rose thought. *"They are like simple machines!"*

Her new friends drank premium strength cider and smoked dope, and Rose found out that she liked these things too. It amused her that the more she modelled her behaviour on the standard issue template of rebelliousness, the more respect she garnered from her contemporaries. She devised a hypothesis which she called the *Ratio Theory of Inebriation to Social Acceptance Equilibrium*.

She didn't tell anyone about this.

But when her father discovered a tab of acid poking out of a packet of Marlboro Lights in her jacket pocket he didn't say "That's more like it." In fact, to Rose's dismay, he grounded her.

"You can't do that," she snarled. "I'm almost seventeen."

But he did. Rose put up a fight and gained some important concessions. She felt quietly happy, in a Brer Rabbit kind of way. And so she stayed in her bedroom for the rest of the year, emerging only to go to her classes at sixth form college.

She painted the walls of her room black and played loud music at all hours of the day and night. The Sisters of Mercy, Alien Sex Fiend, The Damned, The Cult, Joy Division, The Jesus and Mary Chain and Fields of the Nephilim boomed and wailed out from behind the locked door day and night. Her brother Liam shook his head in wonderment. "Weirdo."

Inside her 'black hole' Rose was hardly physically present at all. Part of the plea bargain around being grounded had involved getting a laptop computer, through which she conducted the major part of her life. Her parents, who had grown tired of the battle, left her alone in the hope that it was all just a phase. All they saw was a bedraggled and pale-faced teenager who never seemed to eat anything except margarita pizza and Spicy Nik Naks. They had no idea that, online, their progeny went by the handle AstroQueen and wrote a blog followed by thousands of people around the world. They had no idea that the moment she hit the "post" button on her website, legions of geeks across the planet eagerly consumed her latest prognostications and theories, and scrambled to be the first to reply, bowing and scraping like medieval courtiers. They had no idea, in fact, what a blog was at all.

Rose felt happier than ever. It was only when she ventured out into the physical world that she felt exposed and vulnerable. The teachers at sixth form, she felt, were condescending and narrow-minded. They urged her to study hard for her A Levels and to make something of herself. But Rose found it difficult to concentrate during lectures and nurtured a gnawing sense of approaching doom whenever there was any talk of career pathways. Consequently, she did poorly in her exams, managing only to scrape enough grades for a place at one of the less salubrious institutions of higher education. Still, it was a means of escape.

Her mother and father drove her down to London in the Ford Focus and helped her move her few things into the tiny bedsit they had managed to find in the city's ramshackle inner suburbs. Her mother wept uncontrollably at their parting, promising to send food parcels and love.

On that day, after they had left, Rose sat down on her bed, took out a notepad and did some calculations. Her student loan was mostly eaten up by the rent and the tuition fees, she worked out, leaving only a few pounds left over for other necessities. Internet connection was a necessity, as was electricity. There was no gas connection, and water was included in the rent. That left only about a few pounds a week for food. This was unfortunate, she told herself, but it would have to do. Next she worked out how many calories she would need to survive and set about devising a simple weekly menu that would allow her to subsist without the horror of having to find a part-time job.

She had already decided that socialising was something she would not do at university. She had a whole universe of high-minded friends to communicate with, even if they mostly went by aliases and, in one case, a string of alphanumeric characters. It was good enough for her. She placed adverts on her blog and was pleased to find they brought in a trickle of money in the form of click-throughs. It was enough to survive.

But university turned out to be a disappointment: not that she had high expectations in the first place. The tutors seemed stale and dusty, like relics, and most of the students just wanted to hang around the bar. She was studying applied mathematics and physics, which wasn't ideal, but it was the best course she could find that would accept her unimpressive grades. Every day she walked the four or so miles between her bedsit and the faculty, returning the moment she was no longer required there any longer. She found a book on urban foraging in a charity shop and put what she learned to practice, often coming back from college with a carrier bag filled with apples, berries, nuts and weeds. It was surprising what you could get for free, even in a city like this, she thought.

The area in which she found herself living alarmed her. She could not see any redeeming features of Tottenham: to her it was a concrete hinterland filled with potentially harmful people. Indeed, she felt, there was the sense of something waiting to happen at any moment, and every night her tiny flat shook as cars passed by booming out gangsta rap, often followed by the wail of police sirens and ambulances. Gangs of youths stood on street corners and called out to her whenever she passed. She flattened her hair and stopped wearing black, instead buying a baggy shapeless brown coat from Age Concern which she would wear when out walking. And when she walked she did so with her eyes averted down to the pavement. The bright lights of the West End, the Houses of Parliament, the big houses of the rich and famous beside Regents Park—all of the things that London might be known for could well have been a million miles away, as far as Rose was concerned. Three weeks after she moved in a man was shot in the street outside her bedsit and the police came and drew chalk outlines of where the bullet casings landed. She decided she had better spend as much time in other parts of the city, and maybe find somewhere safer to live.

On three consecutive Sundays she bought an unlimited travel card and ventured out to see the iconic sights, ticking them off one-by-one on a list she had drawn up. She had hoped to get a grip on the city but instead the scale of it engulfed her and made her feel anxious. She had thought Liverpool was big, but London was clearly in a different league altogether. The more she saw, the more her mind grappled with the immensity of the human warren she found herself living in and for that reason she decided henceforth to only venture out in a limited one-mile circumference from her dismal bedsit just off the North Circular Road. It amused her, when she thought about it, that she was far more comfortable with the immensity of the cosmos than she was with this relatively insignificant concrete crust filled with random people doing random things.

For the next three months, with the aid of a London A-Z, she walked assiduously down every street, alley and cul-de-sac within the mile-radius circle, until her mind was satisfied that the mental model in her head corresponded tolerably well with the physical reality outside her front door. She made a note of patches of waste ground and abandoned plots of land where forlorn trees wept ripened fruit onto patches of scabby tarmac littered with broken glass, food wrappers and the decaying bodies of poisoned rats. This, she thought with sadness, was now her home. She bought extra locks for the door on her first floor bedsit, took lessons in street defence provided by the Women's Union at college, and did her best to block out the outside world.

Remarkably, though, Rose didn't live in Tottenham for long, and her life was about to take a strange and unexpected turn. In fact, only some nine months later she found herself sitting in a hushed room with the Prime Minister, his eyes shifting nervously in his sweaty pink face as the city erupted in violence around them. *How strange my life has been!* Rose chuckled to herself that evening as she sat back on her rock and watched the sun light up the underbelly of the clouds as it passed into the west.

4

Jack opened his eyes and stared at the ceiling. The room was bright, with white-painted walls and was well-lit by the morning sun which slanted through the blinds and fell in contoured stripes on the duvet covers. Beside him lay Cat, still asleep and lying on her side with her back to him. He watched her as she slept, seeing the gentle rise and fall of her shoulder as she breathed. From outside the house came the faint cry of the gulls, carried on the breeze above the low murmur of the surf on the beach. He gazed out of the window, seeing only blue. The light seemed brighter here than in London, he thought. It wasn't a harsh light but it did seem to glow in a way that he thought unusual. He lay there for a while wondering if other people noticed such things, or whether it was just him. Pondering whether to stay in bed a while longer, he reached out and touched his girlfriend on the shoulder. His hand slid down her tee shirt to the curve of her hips and rested there. She didn't move, and continued with the soft breathing that Jack knew meant she was in a deep sleep. He rolled over onto his back once more and fixed his gaze on a circular LED light set into the ceiling. As he lay there he considered what to do with the day ahead. Maybe he would take Cat down to the little café by the beach for breakfast or brunch. After that maybe they'd get the kayaks out or perhaps do a bit of surfing. With such thoughts in mind he rose from the bed and padded softly out of the room.

Down in the kitchen he filled the kettle and flicked the switch. There was no reassuring red light to indicate that it was working. "Still?" said Jack out loud. He tried a light switch. Nothing. They had arrived shortly before midnight and the power cut had still not been rectified. If Jack hadn't once before rented this house, they might never have found the small village sitting in darkness at the end of a road that was not much wider than the van. The key had been in the key safe and they had fumbled with a pocket torch to open the door. The old granite fisherman's cottage had been modernised and done out with blonde wooden floors, quartz kitchen tops and designer furniture from Stockton's. Of course, none of this had been visible in the dark. "Let's go to bed," Cat had said. "I will show you what we do in Argentina when the power is down."

And she had.

Now, staring at the cold kettle, Jack was puzzled. He was well aware that other countries experienced power cuts and blackouts, but as far as he could remember he had never experienced one before in his own country. He went and stood at the bay window looking out over a neat patio space edged by fuchsia filled borders dripping with red flowers. The manicured yard ended in a triangle of blue sea flecked with small white waves that twinkled in and out of existence moment by moment. Jack's suitcase still lay in the hallway. He unzipped it, flipping open the lid to reveal a jumble of hastily packed clothing and toiletries. Selecting a pair of shorts and a fresh tee shirt he slipped on some sandals and, pausing briefly to check his hair in a mirror and grab his wallet, turned the handle of the front door and stepped out.

The village street was quiet but for the sound of the gulls and the frenetic chirps of a group of sparrows squabbling in a bush. Hollyhocks drooped down over the sides of the road, shedding their purple petals on the tarmac as bumble bees lumbered unsteadily through the air. Jack walked down the hill in the direction of the beach. A few family estate cars were blocking the narrow lane and Jack glanced back at his own vehicle, checking that he had managed to park it considerately in the darkness the night before. At that moment a jaunty-looking couple of retirees appeared as if from nowhere and walked quickly past him, uttering the obligatory "morning" as they passed by. "Morning," Jack replied, and with a swish of Gore-Tex they were gone.

Further on down, on a bluff overlooking the beach and the bay, stood the café. It was a glorified summerhouse, adorned with driftwood to make it look like a beach cabin. Outside it a daily menu was written on a surfboard fixed into a square of concrete. Jack could see people sitting on benches in the garden drinking tea. As he got closer he could hear the chug of an engine and smelled diesel fumes mingling with the salty smell of the ocean. A woman wearing a black apron and a baseball cap stood behind the counter and greeted him. "Morning—what can I get you today?"

"I'll have a coffee," said Jack, and then scrutinising the menu board added "and can you do me a full English?"

The woman glanced back and called out to a teenage girl cooking in the open kitchen behind her on a gas stove. "Can we do a full English?" she asked. "Yes," said the girl. "We don't have any sausages though."

"We haven't got no sausages," conveyed the woman, smiling broadly to reveal a gold tooth. "All out of them for now, but I can fry up some extra rashers of bacon."

"No worries," said Jack. "That sounds great."

The woman looked over at the surfboard menu and tapped the keys on the cash register. "That'll be six forty-five, my lovely. Milk and sugar are over there and we'll bring it over when it's ready."

"Thanks," he said, and paused to turn. "What's going on with the power? We just arrived last night."

"No idea!" said the woman, leaning forward on the counter, her hands splayed out. "We haven't heard nothing since half-seven last night when it went off. Not a dickybird on the radio either other than some BBC sounding fella saying over and over that they're working to get it back again. Sounds like a recording, if you ask me, and that's exactly what I said to Steve, and he said it probably is and it'll be up and running again soon enough. If it wasn't for Ted over there and his gennie there'd have been no way we'd be open right now, I tell you."

"Oh," said Jack, looking around at the fridge and the lights and the coffee machine. "Is it just round here, do you know; the power cut, I mean?"

"We're just as in the dark as you are, my lover. Far as I know it's just round here, but then if that was so then you'd expect the telly to be working wouldn't you?" she nodded at a small television set in the corner of the café. "Nothing, just black. Very odd, I says." As she said this she handed over a cup of coffee on a porcelain saucer. "And like I said about the radio, there's this fella comes on every half hour or so and says they're working on it and that we shouldn't go panicking or nothing, and then they keep playing God Save the Queen over and over. It's downright creepy, I says to Jade, innit?"

The girl in the kitchen looked up and nodded. "Well creepy."

Jack took the coffee and sat on a bench by a low stone wall. He could see down onto the beach below where a few people were already lying on towels and a man with a windsurfing board was pulling on a wetsuit. His eyes rose to the horizon, where he could make out the long form of a cargo

28

ship in the far distance. He watched it while he drank his coffee but it was impossible to tell whether it was moving or not.

"Full English?" It was the girl from the kitchen holding up a large plate, thumb-deep in assorted greasy food items.

"Thanks," said Jack as she placed it down in front of him. "Anything special going on round here today?"

The girl looked slightly bashful, as if the question was a prelude to something else; she'd had men like Jack from upcountry asking her out in the past. "Well, Golowan's still going on in Penzance, you can catch that." And, seeing the nonplussed look on Jack's face added, "it's the midsummer festival. Parades, music, that kind of thing. Oh, and lots of drinking. Gets bigger every year. It's a right laugh if you've never seen it before, but don't think you'll get a parking place easily."

"Great," he said. "Maybe we'll check it out."

After he had eaten he went down to the beach and walked by the water. The tide was going out, leaving an unmarked sandy beach in its retreat. The sea was calm and conditions would be perfect for kayaking. He tossed a couple of pebbles into the water and held his hand up against the glare of the sun, hoping to spot a dolphin or a shark. He knew the basking sharks came in at this time of year, although he had never seen one on any of his previous visits. Failing to spot anything larger than a seagull, he walked back to the cottage and let himself in. Inside, Cat was still asleep. He brushed his teeth in the en suite, trying to be as quiet as he could. In this weather he was eager to get his kayak down off the top of the van and get out onto the water.

"Where have you been?" asked Cat, one sleepy eye open. "I woke up and you were gone. Thought you had left me."

"I've been down to the café by the beach. The power's still off, otherwise I'd have made you a coffee." As he said the words he hoped they didn't sounded too apologetic.

"Power still off?" said Cat, her voice husky from sleep. "What is wrong with your country? Sometimes I think we should go back and live in my country. My *first world* country, and leave your cold, unfriendly country, with your funny-shaped people and your funny food behind." She snorted a little, as though the idea amused her.

Jack knew she was teasing him. She was always teasing him. One of these days he was going to tell her that it annoyed him when she did so. But not today. "I'm going to get down the kayak. The water's perfect for it and there's not a cloud in the sky. You can get some breakfast at the café while I get ready."

Cat eyed Jack for a minute and sighed. "No, no, no," she said chastising him. She switched to a mock cave-woman voice. "Boy can play with his toy when girlfriend not here. Right now, girlfriend here and in bed." She pulled back the covers and beckoned him over. He did as she asked, although she detected a hint of reluctance in his manner.

"Now," she said, lying back on the bed, "prove to me that not all Englishmen are wimps."

5

As the girl in the café had warned, it was difficult finding anywhere to park when they drove the short distance up the coast to the old port town of Penzance. Cars were pouring in from all directions and queuing up in long lines on the approach roads. "Jesus," said Cat, wafting her face with a sheaf of papers she had brought from work, "it'd be quicker if we walked." As they neared it became clear that it was not just the volume of traffic that was causing problems: traffic lights were out of action and drivers were having to take turns letting one another in. "Oh God," groaned Cat.

Eventually Jack managed to park the van down a side street and the two of them walked the remaining ten minutes into the town. Cat looked about with interest. It didn't look like any of the other places she had been to in this country. Walls and houses were quite clearly made from rock, and huge blooms of flowers seemed to sprout from every crack and gap. There were palm trees and giant purple flowers ten feet tall. Some gardens had small squat cacti growing in gravelly beds, and the glare of the sun reflecting off the whitewashed houses made her half think she was somewhere in the Mediterranean, rather than down at the bottom end of the soggy British isles. The crowds became thicker as they got closer to the centre of the town, and everyone seemed jovial and spirited.

"It's because it sticks out so far into the sea," explained Jack, noting Cat's curiosity. "It's always mild here, never too cold."

The streets were thronging with people. There were tents in which food was being prepared: Thai, Mexican, Chinese. A glazed pig rotated slowly over half an oil drum filled with glowing charcoal as a man, sweat dripping down his neck, turned a crank.

"I want some of that," said Cat, tugging on Jack's arm.

They both got a paper plate with trimmings of roast pork, a half-stale white bun and some apple sauce. The crowds became tighter and the sounds of a Samba band swirled around them as they walked along with their plates of food. Shrill whistles pierced the air and the streets reverberated to the sounds of drumming and singing. Huge figures appeared above the heads of the revellers and the crowd began to cheer. The monstrous tentacled face of a movie pirate appeared—twenty feet tall and with a mechanical arm that raised an oversized bottle of rum to its lips over and over. Cat squeezed her way through to the front of the crowd to get a closer look. The effigy was being borne on a bamboo palanquin by a dozen schoolchildren, their teachers all wearing plastic pirate hats. Next came a giant tin man, followed by a Cyclops, followed by a red-skinned devil with smoke pouring out of his nostrils. She laughed. *What kind of crazy place has Jack brought me to?* she thought.

The sound of the samba band receded and as the parade passed people poured back onto the roads, which had been blocked off from cars. Jack spotted Cat and came over to her. "Let's go down to the seafront and get a drink," he said.

They walked down a narrow street past a house that had been turned into an Egyptian folly, through a churchyard and down a hill that led to the sea. Strung out along the promenade was a funfair, the cries and whoops of teenagers rising above the drone of the diesel generators that powered the rides. There was a tent selling beer and Jack went in and ordered drinks. He emerged a couple of minutes later holding two plastic glasses containing frothy Cornish beer. "Been ages since I had a pint of Doom," he said, handing one of them to Cat, who eyed it suspiciously before taking a small sip. They sat on a low wall together and watched the revellers. Mostly it was families, strolling along with buggies and candyfloss. Gaggles of teenagers charged about, unable to contain their restless energy. And behind this human scene of fun and frivolity lay the sea, blue and implacable, glinting in the sun.

"There are a lot of drunks here," stated Cat matter-of-factly. Jack looked around. It was true. They stood outside the beer tent, men with sun-reddened noses, softly bulging beer bellies and raucous laughs, gabbled loudly with one another. Close by, a particularly large woman with faded shoulder tattoos was holding court with a group of them, causing them to bend over with laughter at something she said. A muscular man with a shaved head and a dog tied to a piece of string staggered past holding a bottle of vodka, followed by his equally plastered girlfriend who was hurling insults at him. Cat sipped her drink and tried not to stare.

"These people are strange," she said quietly to Jack. "Let's go somewhere else."

They walked down the promenade, past some shabby-looking guesthouses and a darkened amusement arcade, emerging by a grassy park beside a beach. Families were barbecuing and sitting on deck chairs on the grass, while nearby a group of ragged-looking young people were blasting techno music from an old ambulance they had driven onto the beach. They had piled up a load of old packing pallets, pieces of driftwood and the rotting hull of a rowing boat, and it was clear they intended to set the pile alight at some point. One of them, a woman wearing baggy Indian clothing, was dancing with some pieces of fabric tied onto the ends of ropes. As Cat watched her gyrate to the music she found the effect somewhat hypnotic, if not entirely to her liking.

"Let's not sit near them," she said, breaking away.

Thus the afternoon was spent by the beach. Cat read a book she had brought with her and Jack, who could never sit still for long, walked up and down the beach looking in rock pools or skipping stones on the placid sea. Eventually, having exhausted all the obvious possibilities for distraction, he came back to Cat and stretched out on the grass for a siesta.

It was early evening when the tide came in and the families began to drift away. "I am hungry," announced Cat, prodding Jack awake.

Jack knew a place. It was an old beachside tavern, redone as a bistro and with a star chef from London. He knew Cat would approve and he wasn't wrong. They ate Newlyn crab and fresh mussels for starters, and beer battered pollock with monkfish tail and wild mushrooms for the main. The waiter suggested a wine pairing for the crab, saying the lightness and acidity of a bottle of Domaine Chandon Brut would "elevate the crab's sweetness and purify your palates."

"I could get used to this," said Cat, thinking it would please Jack to hear it.

When it came to paying it was already getting late and candles had been lit at each table. The waiter took Jack's credit card and wrote down the details, getting him to sign a receipt. The manager came out and spoke to the diners one table at a time. When he got to Cat and Jack's he said "We will take payment when the system comes back online."

The pair returned to the town centre, walking beside the sea as the light faded. The beach revellers had set fire to their pile of debris and the techno music pulsed across the bay as sparks rose into the darkening sky. In the centre of the town once more the pair came across a troupe of well-lubricated Morris dancers who were leaping about, bashing their sticks together and waving handkerchiefs. A heavily bearded man with a black top hat squeezed an accordion and a thin woman with grey hair played a tin whistle as the dancers performed their ancient fertility rite. "I'll just use the bathroom," said Jack, disappearing into a nearby pub and leaving Cat by herself. She carried on watching the dancers as she waited, getting out her mobile and taking some pictures of them. She was about to tweet it with a suitably sarcastic message when she remembered. "Still no signal," she said out loud to nobody but herself.

"And neither will there be for a very long time," interjected a man standing next to her. Cat looked up at him. He was a smooth-faced and overweight man in late middle age, and he appeared to be slightly unsteady on his feet.

"What do you mean?" said Cat. "When will the signal come back?"

"Problems upcountry is what I can tell you," he replied. "Power's out all over the place, they say. Motorways at a standstill, shops shut everywhere, no word from anyone as to what's going on. For all we know it could be a nuclear war's 'appened and they forgot to tell us."

Cat stared at him in horror. "How do you know this? My boyfriend says the television and radio is not working."

The man looked at her for a moment and took a swig of beer. "Driver, I am. Been in haulage since '84 and never seen anything as bad as this. Got a radio in the rig and I's been on it 'alf the night speaking with our boys all over. Pumps stopped working, they say, and one of 'em's got a load of dairy and he's stuck on the M5. 'Parently there's some sort of tyre depot fire near Bristol, he says, black smoke billowing all over the place and nobody to put it out."

"But why?" said Cat. "What's happening?"

"Your guess is as good as mine. Seems there's some sort of power outage, though nobody's saying why. Army's out on the streets of London, trying to stop what 'appened the last time, what with all them riots and all." The man paused for thought for a second, as if something had just occurred to him. "You wouldn't be down from London would you?"

At that moment Jack reappeared, another couple of pints in his hand. He smiled at Cat sheepishly. "I couldn't just walk past the bar, could I?"

Cat ignored him. "Jack, we have to leave this place and get back home. We need to leave right away."

Jack looked confused. He had only been gone for a few minutes and now his girlfriend was talking with another man and saying they had to leave. "Huh?"

"Jack, this man is a truck driver. He says the electricity grid has gone down all over the country. We don't want to end up stuck here, do we?"

The man, hearing this, said. "If I was you, you'd better get a move on if you're planning to go anywhere. Couple of petrol stations off the A30 still got some backup, so I 'ear, but if this carries on much longer they'll be out just like the rest of 'em. I can write down where you'll find 'em. A bit secret, they are, if you don't know where to look."

Twenty minutes later Jack and Cat were driving out of Penzance and back to the holiday cottage to pick up their belongings. Neither of them said a word. It had been a short, fierce argument, and one that Cat had won. Jack, out of protest, had necked the beer down in one, and then drunk Cat's for good measure. His holiday ruined before it had even begun.

"Drive faster," said Cat.

Back at the holiday cottage they packed in silence. Jack's head was swimming with the beer and the wine and, if it was true what the man had said, he worried about the journey ahead. Getting stuck somewhere without any petrol was not his idea of a good way to end the holiday.

"You sure you can drive?" said Cat. "I saw you, you been drinking like a fish."

"I drove us here alright, didn't I?"

When they were packed up Jack started up the van. The fuel needle rose slowly, settling on the halfway mark. "What are we waiting for?" said Cat.

"GPS," said Jack. "That bloke said we had to avoid the motorways if we want to get back." He sat there fiddling with it for a couple of minutes before placing it in its holder on the windscreen. "At least that still works."

They drove. The lane they had come in on was pitch dark and the van's headlights made the blooms of the wildflowers appear white as they passed by. "Faster," said Cat, once more. Jack glanced at her. Sudden anger arose in him.

"For Pete's sake." He put his foot down to the floor. If there was another car coming round one of the bends he'd have to slam the brakes on. They'd probably skid, maybe even crash. That'd show her.

But it wasn't a car that was around the bend. There was only a split second to react. Jack slammed his foot on the brake as hard as he could, but that didn't prevent the sickening crack of something hard hitting the windscreen and the crunch of imploding safety glass. Cat screamed and the van came skidding to a halt. They both jumped out. On the road lay a dark shape. "Get in the van and reverse," yelled Cat, "I can't see anything." Jack got back in the van and slowly reversed it until the headlights illuminated whatever it was that was lying on the road.

"I think it was a deer," said Jack. But it wasn't a deer: the figure was all too human-looking. The both peered down at the body, which lay there completely still. A tangle of dreadlocks splayed out on the asphalt around a bloodied face and the two watched in horror as a dark liquid began to spread around it. Jack felt sick and sunk to his knees. "Oh God..."

Cat stood over him in silence. All of a sudden she began to wail. It was a high-pitched banshee-like scream that rent the night air.

"You've killed him, you stupid idiot! You've killed him!"

6

~ The Mournful Tale of Rose O'Keefe ~

The sun had slipped below the rim of the horizon illuminating an underbelly of the clouds in a last gasp burst of crimson and purple. Gulls wheeled below on air currents thrown up by the sea as it crashed against the rocks in great foamy claps, and the end of the day was marked by the *carrach carrach* call of the black rooks flapping lazily inland for the night. Rose breathed in the salty air and closed her eyes. A most unusual sensation had taken hold of the old woman. *I have been here before*, she thought. The feeling was so profound that her eyes flicked open. She had, of course, experienced déjà vu before, rationalising that it was merely the random stimulation of past memories in one part of the brain by another, unrelated, experience or thought. But this didn't feel like déjà vu to her, it felt more like a message in a bottle floating on the sea of time and washing up here, in the mind of an eighty-something Liverpool Irish woman in the quietening years of the twenty-first century.

This is my saga, tell me yours, it seemed to say.

Rose let the strange message wash over her. She saw a young woman in a ship on the high seas. She seemed to be searching for something, or someone. The young woman had clear green eyes and dark hair that fell about her shoulders and she seemed somehow familiar. She allowed this strange vision to linger a while in her mind and then observed as it faded away to nothingness. *This is my saga, tell me yours.* What could it mean? She pulled her woollen shawl tighter around her shoulders against the cool breeze and gazed towards the darkening horizon.

All of a sudden she felt very cold. Perhaps it was the vision of the young woman but Rose found herself being flung back in time to her own youth. A knot of emotion and longing welled up within her. She let it stay for a moment, regarding it tenderly before dismissing it. Knowing how to banish loss was one of the skills that had kept her alive for so long. Life was full of simple but hidden rules like that, she figured. Either you worked them out for yourself and lived, or you played by other people's rules, and died.

She chuckled and rose from the rock on which she had been sitting. It was a short walk back to her home along the well-worn cliff top path. Not many people were out on this November evening, when the stirrings of autumn were making themselves felt. To Rose this was the best time of year. The heat and the languor of summer had faded to be replaced by the promise of the season of reflection. Autumn was a time of new beginnings and fresh energy, she thought, a time to set off on soul journeys, to revel in the sacred spirit that was all around, to connect with the subtle energies of the universe. Maybe that's what the message was about. Soon, she would visit her friend the charcoal man, who lived on the hill, and put in her order for the winter.

Rose walked slowly up a rise between two granite outcrops that were furnished with ferns and the twisted shapes of wind-dwarfed hawthorns. Catching her breath, she leaned against the granite, pausing as her heart caught up with her. Yes, she thought, I will tell them all about those first few years. About the confusion and the sense of shock, the dislocation from one narrative to another. About how it had felt like standing on one of those moving floors they used to have at fun fairs where you try to walk but the floor keeps moving up and down, side to side, spinning round.

She carried on up the hill, catching sight of her home nestled in a sheltered hollow by a bend in the road further up. *I will start right now*, she thought. *I will make myself a pot of tea, take out my pen and write until the electricity runs low and the light fails me.*

The house wasn't much by the standards of the first part of the twenty-first century. Indeed, it was more of a shelter than a house, but it nevertheless had all the necessities a person could ask for. She remembered choosing this spot by the side of the road, hacking away at the gorse and burning it afterwards in a ceremony. The man who had built it for her was tall and sinewy, with large hands and dark curly hair. He had spoken little of her language and was perhaps from Spain or Romania or somewhere—she had never found out and it didn't do to press people too much on where they might be from. His name was Zian, or Zittan, if she remembered right, and he had known how to strike a good deal in his favour even with only a few words of English. He had set to work the morning after she had handed over the first purse of her money. She'd parked her wagon not too far away and watched in wonder as this quiet, rugged man built an entire house over the course of one season. The man had possessed nothing more than a horse, a buggy and a bag of old tools. For the first few days she observed him set off early each morning, returning periodically with a full-length tree trunk dragging along the road behind his muscular horse. Then she had watched him debark the trunk, watched him dig out foundation holes with an iron bar, watched him haul

41

stones up on his bronzed shoulders from the beach, and watched him dig up earth and mix it with water and dung and the sun-dried foliage he had cut with a scythe. The man had worked from dawn to dusk, seven days a week, never complaining or falling ill or saying he had to take a day off to take care of other business.

Every month she handed over another purse of coins, which he took wordlessly, the only gesture of acceptance being a quick touch to his forehead and a slight forward bow. Occasionally he went off for a day or two to speak with salvage merchants who traded the materials he couldn't get for himself, returning with these finds on the crude wooden buggy fitted with the wheels and tyres from an old car. In this way he would come back with windows, a sunlight panel and a battery for the electricity, sacks of lime mortar, and an old cast iron wood burner. Whenever she asked him if he had enough money for such purchases he always replied in the affirmative: "Yes, my lady." Other than that, he rarely spoke, ate on his own with his horse, and slept in a hammock on the other side of the house to where Rose's wagon was parked.

To her it seemed like a miracle that an entire house could be built in this way by one man, but at the end of those three months Rose found herself in possession of a comfortable and well-constructed little house with straw and cob walls and a roof thatched with the type of reeds that grew down in the murky and brackish mudflat that had once been series of flat fields on a low cliff. There were real plastic-sheathed wires in the walls that carried a faint current from the sun panel on the roof to a single lightbulb hanging in the centre of the house's only room. What's more, there was also an automotive cigarette lighter wall socket for powering Rose's collection of antique tablets, laptops and other nostalgic gadgets she had collected and stored in a wooden pine chest at the back of her wagon, her prized possession being a small black device no bigger than one of the chestnut shingles that clad the southern wall of the house and protected the mud and lime render from the worst of the Atlantic storms. On this ancient gadget was the electronic imprint of thousands of books from the Old Times, and she would take it out from time to time and rub the screen with her thumb as the words flashed by.

When the house was finished the man—Zian or Zittan—had left, leaving Rose on her own. How many years had it been since she had lived in a proper house? At least twenty-five, she considered, maybe more. There was hot water in the stove and she turned a small brass tap to fill a chipped mug. Rummaging in a drawer she pulled out a box of powdered herbs and sprinkled some into the cup, which she then set on the side to brew. *Pen or computer*, she thought. Computer would be easier and she wouldn't need ink. But then there was the electricity to consider, and the old battery was growing as feeble as she was. What's more, who would be able to read it? *Not many*, she thought.

She settled at the small table by the window that gave a view out to the west. On a wad of already yellowing paper she doodled the pen in a corner, licking the nib to get it going. When the ink began to flow she put the pen aside and fetched her tea. *It's getting too dark*, she thought, and went to get a candle. There was, after all, no point in wasting the electricity just yet. She sat down again, took a sip of the tea and closed her eyes. Memories and stories boiled up in her mind unbidden. *Calm down*, she scolded herself, *try to think straight.*

This is my saga, tell me yours.

It had all been so chaotic. *Where do I even begin?*

Doubts began to surface. She'd never before considered writing her own story: *Everyone* had their own story so who'd be interested? She tried to stand back from the memories of her own travails, put them against a wider backdrop. But it was hard. There had been so much confusion, especially in the early days, right before the time of the big break. There had been so much information back then: so many words written and spoken, so many screens, and so many speakers. Back then there had been a whole industry dedicated to providing a universal view of what was important and what was not. *Too much information!* Now, there was nobody to say 'this is how it is' or 'you must be concerned about that'— everything had become so subjective and open to interpretation. How did historians of the past organise their thoughts and their writings?

Rose O'Keefe closed her eyes and once more tried to calm her mind. *This is my saga, tell me yours.* This time it was a voice. It was a female voice, a woman not unlike herself, with a voice soft and wise. It spoke a language she had never heard before but she could nevertheless understand it perfectly well. "But where do I start?" she asked out loud. There came no reply.

Rose sighed and put the pen to the paper. After a minute of stillness the memories began to flood her mind. They came thick and fast; clear as the day they happened. She smiled. *That's more like it.* The old woman began to write.

My life became interesting shortly after I left home and went to study in London. I was not much of a student. Life at university was too shallow for my liking and I craved something more fulfilling. That is why, when I was offered a paid job as a science writer for one of the newspapers, I didn't even hesitate. I have learned to be modest over the years, but back then I was so young, and my head was in a spin, because all of a sudden I found I was famous. Well, in a way. Fame, you see, was what everyone hankered after back then. We all had enough food, we had places to live, entertainment, there was peace of sorts – but it was easy to get lost in all this, and to feel that your life was of little value. So what we hankered after was recognition – recognition that we were individuals with talents and not just faceless bodies on an overcrowded planet. I didn't seek it out, though: Fame found me, instead of the other way around. I was only doing what I enjoyed and felt drawn to. That's how I found myself about the one thing that interested me above all else – I wrote about what made the universe tick. And people loved it.

The old woman looked at the words she had just written on the page. Her writing was cramped and untidy, lacking in any style or finesse. What's more, it all seemed a bit random and she felt she was jumping in at the deep end. It had been years since she had written prose. Would anyone actually be able to read it? She considered what to write next. Should she go into detail about her time as a star astrophysics blogger, about the fan mail she received (and the hate mail from the poisonous trolls)? No, she thought. These things were no longer understandable. Let us cut to the chase. She continued.

I had been working at the newspaper for only six months when the Old World fell apart and we found ourselves living in a situation none could have predicted, or even understood. Normal, everyday people were suddenly thrust into an alternate reality, and I was one of them. One moment I was a shy 19-year-old of no consequence, and the next I was sitting in a room with the Prime Minister as he sweated and shook and tried to pretend he was not a traitor who had the blood of millions on his hands.

She put the pen down and rubbed her eyes. *Where am I going with this?* Sometimes she couldn't quite believe her story herself.

7

"He's not dead," said Jack.

The figure lying on the asphalt in a pool of light and blood groaned a little. One hand spasmed and some fingers began to feel around the road surface as though they were looking for something. There was another groan and a faint cough. Jack, who was crouching down beside the man whose skull had just spider-webbed the van's windscreen, exchanged a horrified glance with his girlfriend Cat, who stood aghast with one hand half covering her mouth, the other tucked under her armpit. "I think he's trying to say something," she whispered.

He leaned in closer. The glare of the van's lights made the man's skin china white and turned the blood surrounding his head into a puddle of deep blackness. Even lying face-up on the road it was clear that he was tall and wiry, built like a scarecrow and with knotty limbs that poked out of combat fatigues and a skin-tight tee shirt. All of a sudden the man sat up, spitting blood out of his mouth.

"Jesus," cried Jack, almost falling over backwards.

The man sitting up in the road wore a dazed look as he turned his head towards first Jack and then Cat, before looking down at his own body. He gave a deep sigh, muttered something unintelligible and then tried to get to his feet. Those long gangly limbs unfolded themselves and Arthek Gwavas rose to his feet in the ungainly manner of a stork standing up in its nest prior to taking off. He stood, unsteadily, wiping saliva and blood off his chin with the back of his hand.

"Steady on, mate," said Jack. "You'd better sit down." He moved towards the man but was stopped by a palm suddenly thrust into his face.

"Feckers," said the man with hot animosity. "Feckin' ruined my evening have you?" His voice was slurred and he continued to sway from side to side as he spoke. He lowered his hand and began to kick around at some shards of broken glass at his feet. "Where's me pipe? You made me drop me pipe."

"Look at his head," said Cat. "He is bleeding a lot." She didn't like the sight of blood, having seen too much of it once in Argentina as a child. The cars had been piled up on the highway, the bodies lined up beside them. "We have to get him to the hospital."

"You ern't gettin' me to no doctors," said Art. "You help me find my puff pipe and I'll be on my way, thank you." As he said this his centre of gravity shifted backwards and his feet couldn't move fast enough to compensate. He took one staggering backwards step into the front bumper of the van and then fell down hard on his backside with a groan.

"What are we going to do?" said Jack, turning to his girlfriend. "We can't just leave him here, he'll just get run over again. And that head wound." Cat glared at him. This day was getting worse by the minute. First there was the power cut. Then the man who had told them about the problems on the roads, and now... this! All she wanted was to get back to her flat in London, make herself a cup of chai latte and shut the curtains until the power came on again. Except, of course, she wouldn't be able to make that chai latte until the power came on again—but at least she would be surrounded by people who knew how to behave in a civilised manner—people whose idea of fun wasn't to get legless in public and dress up like medieval peasants and pirates. Her phone hadn't worked for over twenty-four hours. She had no clue what her friends were up to, or what was going on in the wider world. She did not want to be standing in a dark country lane miles away from what she considered proper civilisation and remonstrating with a drunken bumpkin who had damaged her only means of transport with his thick head. "Right," she said, marching towards him. "You are coming with us and then we will be on our way."

Art winced as he was hauled to his feet by one arm. "Watcher doin'?" he protested as Cat bent his arm behind his back and pushed him cop-style into the side of the van. "Let go of me you bint."

"Open the door," she snapped at Jack, who immediately complied, sliding it open. She shoved Art into the rear seat, noting the mess the van's windscreen had made of his face. The nose was broken, that was for sure, and as for the rest of the face... she could barely make out what was what in the tangle of blood-soaked dreadlocks, dirt and bits of twigs. "Sit there and don't move until we get you to the 'ospital."

"Here," said Jack, placing a small silver pipe into a side pocket of Art's trousers. "I found it on the road."

It seemed to take an eternity to drive down those dark country lanes before they emerged onto the equally dark main road. Jack drove slowly, partly from fear of running over someone else and partly because he couldn't see properly through the spiderweb of concentric cracks. Art groaned in the back causing Cat to turn around and eye him. He was curled up on the seat, the fabric of which was now liberally smeared with blood and dirt. "You must not be sick," she said curtly before turning to face forwards again.

When they reached the town they drove around for some ten minutes looking for the hospital. "There," said Cat, pointing at a sign that read 'A&E Admissions'. Jack drove the van into the car park and pulled into a bay right outside the main doors.

"Lights," said Cat looking at the illuminated interior of the emergency wing. "The power has come on again."

"No," said Jack. "Emergency backup. All hospitals have it." He jumped out of the vehicle and slid open the side door. Art was still lying curled up on the seat. "He's out cold again. Help me get him out."

"Wait," said Cat, looking disdainfully at the crumpled specimen of a man bleeding into the upholstery. "Maybe they have stretchers or something. Go and talk to them and I'll wait here."

Jack walked into the hospital through the main doors which glided open on his approach. It had only been a day since the power cut but already he appreciated this simple reminder of a functional daily life. The waiting room was not large, consisting of a dozen or so yellow plastic seats under some strip lighting and a low table covered in well-thumbed magazines. Seven people sat around, none of them apparently in any mortal danger except, perhaps, a large middle-aged man dressed in shorts and a muscle top who was sitting with his head bowed between his legs and breathing heavily.

"Can I help you?" said a woman from behind a Plexiglass screen. She was around sixty years old and wore huge oval glasses, which made her neat face seem small.

Jack hesitated a little, wondering how he should put it. "I've got a guy in the back of my van. He was hit by a vehicle —erm, my vehicle. Lots of blood—quite a mess."

The woman looked shocked. "Is he breathing?"

"Last time I checked."

She punched some numbers into a phone, waited for a few seconds as she held the receiver to her ear, and then hung up. "Stay right there," she said. "I'm going to fetch a paramedic."

Jack stood and waited. He looked around at the others in the waiting room. Under the strip lights they looked pallid and diseased. A clock on the wall said 11:43. None of the patients moved or spoke. He thought: *this could be the start of a zombie movie.*

The silence was broken when a pair of double doors suddenly swung open and the efficient-looking woman with the small-looking head appeared. Behind her strode a stocky man in a green uniform with silver stubble covering his head. He was carrying a bag of medical supplies and his round face was sweaty and tired-looking. "Where is he?" he said simply.

Jack led him outside and the medic immediately set to work examining the man slumped in the back of the van. "Hello my friend, can you hear me?" He was lifting Art's eyelids up and peering inside with a tiny torch.

Art groaned a little and replied in the affirmative. The medic's thin beam of light made his eyes grow wide, each white surrounded by a pink ring of skin. "Argh, stop it, man, you're blindin' me!" The medic clicked off the torch and placed it in a pocket in his uniform. Next he bent down and took some latex gloves from his kit bag and pulled them on before taking some swabs that he wetted with clear liquid from a bottle. Gently at first, and then more vigorously, he proceeded to wipe away at Art's face, tossing the dirtied swabs into the foot wells of the van. Art uttered a curse and pawed at the medic's busy hand. "Stop it will you?"

"Been out drinking?" asked the medic.

"I think so," said Jack. "He just kind of came out of nowhere on this dark road. No warning. He spoke a bit after with us, certainly seemed pissed."

"I didn't mean him," said the medic, turning around and looking at Jack. His eyes glinted in his sweaty face as he stared at the young man. Cat put a hand nervously to her hair. *Jesus, this is the last thing we need,* she thought.

"Are you going to help him or what?" she interjected, pointing at the figure in the van.

The medic pulled off his gloves and sighed. "Well, he's got a broken nose, a gash on his head the size of small ravine, some blood loss, probable concussion and he's going to have one hell of a headache come tomorrow. But he'll live."

"Thank God for that," said Cat. "Can you get him out and put him on a stretcher or something? We really have to get going."

The medic was shaking his head. "He's not staying here, that's for sure. Not a bed in the whole hospital. Do you know how many admittances we've had today? We've got an entire ward full of piss artists with broken arms who can't seem to walk around without street lights, as well as three carbon monoxide cases—why people think they can cook on a barbecue indoors is beyond me—and that's not even counting the traffic accidents. I ask you, how did people survive before traffic lights?"

Jack butted in. "Are you saying he can't stay here? We don't know who he is or where to take him."

"I'd have thought the least you could do is take this fine young gentleman back to wherever it is that people like him call home," replied the medic. Jack thought he detected a hint of sarcasm, or perhaps even animosity in his voice.

"Impossible," snapped Cat. "We don't know where he lives. As far as we know he could be a homeless."

"A homeless?" repeated the medic, staring at Cat intently. "You're not from round here are you?"

"Listen," said Jack, "we have to get back home tonight. Back to London."

The medic looked at the two of them and then at the figure of Art on the back seat of the van. He bent down and clicked his medical bag shut before standing up and walking over to Jack until the two men were eye to eye. "Of course, if you'd like to indulge me in a breath test I'd be willing to bet that at least *you'll* be getting a place to stay tonight, Sir."

Jack backed away, his eyes shifting uncertainly. "We'll look after him until tomorrow. It's the least we can do."

"What?" said Cat.

"That's more like it," said the medic. "Now if you'll excuse me, there's plenty more to be done tonight before they'll let me go home." With that he walked back into the hospital, the doors sliding shut behind him as he disappeared into the rectangle of light, leaving the young couple staring at one another in disbelief. Neither of them could have known then what an effect they had set in motion that night, and the part the crumpled man lying on the back seat would play in it.

8

On the morning of the fourth day of the outage some-thing amazing happened. All of a sudden, as if by magic, the power came back on again. Fans and pumps leapt to life, room-temperature fridges and freezers hummed as they got back to work, and microwave ovens beeped to show they were still alive. Mobile phones with batteries that had not yet run down spat out dozens of messages all at once, most of which said "Where r u?" or "How r u?" or "What is happen-ing?" and people from the four corners of Britain reached for their television remotes.

What they discovered when they turned on their TV sets was what seemed to be a live feed from a packed room. The camera had been set at the back of the room and you could see people's heads from behind as they sat in rows whisper-ing to one another and occasionally coughing. The room was filled by a general low-level murmur that was picked up and amplified by the sound equipment. Facing them, at a long table, sat a group of men and women. Some of them were re-cognisable as members of the government, and all of them wore a sombre look that spoke of anxiety and sleepless nights. At the middle of the table there was an empty chair in front of which were a microphone on a stand and a glass of water. To the left of the empty chair sat a silver-haired man wearing combat fatigues hung with medals. This was General Sir Michael Fossbury, Chief of Defence Staff. Those who took an interest in military matters would know that he made his mark as a commanding officer during the Troubles in Northern Ireland, and later as a Deputy Commanding General during the first Gulf War. Sir Michael sat there with his hands clasped in a relaxed manner on the table in front of him and exuded an air of military authority and calm.

By contrast, seated on the other side of the empty chair, was a man who could scarcely have possessed less natural authority. With a head that looked like a piece of rawhide stretched over a skull, and a body that seemed too feeble to support it, Ignatius Pope was the Prime Minister's director of communications. Only thirty years old and with a face that could have belonged to a sixteen-year-old, Pope looked like an awkward public schoolboy in a room full of grown-ups. The hair on his almost perfectly spherical head was closely cropped, adding to his grotesque appearance, and he wore a pair of small round spectacles perched on a nose that jutted out sharply from this disagreeable arrangement. Everyone in the room knew who this man was. Pope was universally unpopular, and endured endless mockery on social media and at the hands of satirists on late-night TV shows. But the respectable media, for the most part, dared not indulge too deeply in the fun-making. True, there *were* some in the tabloid end of the print media who dared to make fun of his jerky movements and his frequent public meltdowns, but most dared not for fear of being cut out of the information access loop. Pope, it was said, had them on a rope. Right now this unusually unpleasant specimen of a man sat there thrumming his fingers impatiently on the table and occasionally mouthing something silently to someone off screen to the side.

All of a sudden the murmuring stopped and the backs of the people sitting at the table visibly stiffened. The Prime Minister strode into the room behind the assembled cabinet members and took the empty seat. Despite his considerable girth, he moved fast and his body language spoke of control. Both of his sleeves were rolled up to the elbows and his tieless collar was open. As he took his seat the camera zoomed in and the crowd of people fell silent. He stared silently and intently into the lens, and if you looked closely you could see the sweat beading up on his face and neck and beginning to darken the cotton fabric of his shirt. When he spoke he came straight to the point.

"Our country is under attack. We do not have all the details of what is still a fluid situation but I can tell you this. On Friday a number of power stations and other crucial elements of our infrastructure were hit by a coordinated and premeditated attack. What we now know is that the assailants used cars and, in one case, a small plane packed with explosives, to hit their targets. This resulted in a power outage across the whole electrical grid and brought Britain to a standstill."

At this the Prime Minister paused, his lip quivering a little. He continued.

"Our engineers have worked day and night to restore power. What they report is that the level of damage is unprecedented but that they are moving heaven and earth to restore system integrity. For this reason I would urge everyone to be patient as there are likely to be further disruptions to the power supply as we try to repair the damage. At this moment I am unable to tell you how long it will be before our power production and distribution systems are back to full capacity again, but you have my word that I will personally keep you updated at every step along the way."

The PM took a sip of water, cleared his throat a little and re-fixed his gaze on the camera.

"Let me be honest with you. This is the moment that any Prime Minister dreads. Not only has our country come under attack but it appears that those who would cause so much destruction and misery walk among us."

When he said this there was a stifled gasp from the assembled people. The PM took a moment to look around at the faces in the audience before he continued.

"Britain is a liberal democracy. We pride ourselves on our openness, our standards of parliamentary discourse and our ability to tolerate dissenting voices. For one and a half decades since that fateful day in New York we have been the victims of but one major act of terror. As terrible as that day was, there were many others that were thwarted, countless lives saved. We have grown our economy, making it the envy of the world, and thanks to the dynamism and hard work of the British people we have broken away from the pack and created a prosperous, modern state. For that we should be proud. Furthermore, we are resolute in our traditions, proud upholders of our heritage and unflinching in our moral duty. I am proud to call myself the Prime Minister of this great country, to humbly serve it and to revel in its successes.

But there are those who do not see it that way. These people have hearts filled with bitterness. They sneer from the sidelines and complain from their positions of privilege, even as hardworking Britons toil to build a better tomorrow for us all. For them, our efforts and toil are anathema to their poisonous outlook and they want to turn back the clock to the misery and failed policies of the past. To them our prosperity is an affront, our freedom an insult to their warped ideology. In short, they hate us because of our success."

Absolute silence filled the room. The Prime Minister's face was growing red as he spoke, as if anger were welling up from inside him. His eyes became steely and his voice rose in timbre as he spoke.

"For too long we have appeased them. We have listened to their concerns and we have used the tactics of soft love to try and bring them round. We have offered them the chance to protest, to express their opinions, and to air their grievances, no matter how offensive their point of view might be to many of us. I myself have always adhered to Churchill's mantra when he stated so nobly 'I might disagree with you but I will defend to the death your right to say it.' I suspect most of us would agree with such a lofty sentiment and, as members of a wealthy and tolerant country like Great Britain, they should expect no less. There are healthy expressions of dissent in any mature democracy, and it is values such as these that we have spread around the world.

And yet.

We could never have anticipated this act of violence against us. Who could have guessed that there were those walking amongst us who would take up arms against their own kin? That they would stab their fellow men, women and children in the back?"

The PM took another sip of water and knitted his hands together in front of him. His Adam's apple went up and down in his throat as if he were fighting back emotion. Adopting a softer tone he continued.

"I could never have expected, even in my worst nightmares, to have seen what I saw yesterday at Great Ormond Street Hospital for children. For there, right before my very eyes, I saw babies gasping for air because their ventilators lacked the necessary power to function. I saw innocent children stricken with cancer, unable to understand why their operations had been cancelled, their pain-relieving medication unavailable. I saw a young girl who was just two years old, her life stolen away before it had even begun."

A few cries went up as he said this and one woman in the front row drew out a handkerchief and pressed it to her face. The PM himself appeared to wipe a tear from his eye before he continued in a voice choked with emotion.

"I never again want to have to see what I saw yesterday. I never again want to have to answer to heartbroken parents who ask me how this could have been allowed to happen in this country. I never again want to look out over this great city and see nothing but darkness."

The PM raised a forefinger and pointed directly at the camera.

"To those who would wish to destroy our way of life I have this to say to you:

We will hunt you down.

We will dig you out of your foxholes.

We will bring you to justice.

I will never let you attack the British people again."

The PM lowered his hand and with his eyes still fixed on the camera, which was slowly panning in so that people's TV screens filled with his face, he continued in a flat voice that was devoid of all emotion.

"Make no mistake, the spectre of radical environmentalism is haunting the free world. We have for so long tolerated the protests against fracking and the building of our new nuclear power stations. We let ourselves believe that these were good-hearted people: people who allowed themselves to be guided by emotion and sentimentality rather than reason and logic; people who would rather we all lived in the cruel times of an earlier age, an age in which prosperity and progress are sacrificed on the altar of fear and superstition. But this time they have gone too far. They have bitten the hand that feeds them. But let me tell you this: they will soon find out that this hand can transform itself into an iron fist."

As the PM said those last words he slammed his own fist down on the table, upsetting the glass of water. He then stood up sharply and strode out of the room. The assembly exploded into a raucous discussion and hands shot up as the press conference commenced. The TV cut back to a studio. It was a BBC studio and people were glad to see something so familiar after four days of dark screens. Some changed the channel but the BBC feed was on every frequency and every station was carrying the same picture. The studio set and graphics were familiar but the presenters were new. Across the bottom of the screen scrolled a ticker tape dispensing official advice: fill baths and containers with water while the power is on. Call family members and friends and agree on rallying points. Do not attempt to syphon petrol at home. Keep mobile phones on charge at all times. Call 0-800-999999 or visit www.crisis.gov.uk for further information.

A female anchor with straight hair and a suitably mournful black outfit spoke. "Powerful words there from the Prime Minister who looked visibly upset as he detailed that visit to a children's hospital. I'm joined now by the BBC's security affairs editor, Greg Humphries. What do you make of it, Greg?"

The camera panned out to show a stocky man across the desk wearing a grey suit.

"Indeed Angela. What we do know is that a group calling itself Gaia First has claimed responsibility for the attacks, which left twenty-six people dead and dozens injured. The attacks caused the entire electrical network to fail, plunging people into darkness and shutting down essential services."

"Do we know who or what Gaia First is and why they might have launched such an unprovoked attack?"

"Well, Angela, they are something of a shady group and not an awful lot is known about them. We know they are headed by a man called John Breatnacht, who is known within the group by the moniker John Barleycorn. They do have a website and on there we can find a rambling and somewhat incoherent manifesto that Breatnacht himself wrote in which he calls for the modern world to be 'brought to its knees'. Other than that we don't know a huge amount about why they did it or whether they might have had help from entities that might be considered unfriendly to the UK.

What we do know is that there have been several arrests across the country, although Breatnacht is still at large. I'm sure we'll know more soon."

A picture of a young man with short hair and a long double-pointed beard came up on the screen. Underneath was the caption: "John 'Barleycorn' Breatnacht, wanted for domestic terrorism."

"So, what you're saying is there are suspicions there may be affiliations with other radical groups?"

"Clearly, Angela, nobody can make those connections with any certainty at the moment but the unspoken fear is that some of the young people who often make up these groups may have been radicalised, and once that happens they can easily be influenced to commit atrocities on behalf of other groups, no matter how loose the affiliation."

"Are you saying that some of these anti-fracking groups may have becomes allies of Islamic terrorists?"

"It's too early to say for sure Angela, but what we do know is that Gaia First might be acting as an umbrella organisation for some of the more well-known groups, and that a lot of their funding comes indirectly from groups who are opposed to fracking, as well as so-called animal welfare charities and other direct action and pressure groups. Many of the supporters of those groups may have been unwittingly funding the purchase of weapons and explosives, which have now clearly been used with such tragic consequences."

The camera cut back to the woman again.

"Thanks Greg, and we'll be coming back to you later. But now we have some live images from the Humber Estuary, where the worst of the attacks took place. We now know that two major power stations were knocked out, along with an oil refinery, a key gas onshore delivery terminal and a gas pipeline. We're getting word that around a dozen large power transformers were similarly targeted around the country, and that several lorries were set alight, blocking motorways and causing gridlock. Up to thirty people still remain unaccounted for, rescue services say, although operations are ongoing."

The screen filled with a video taken from a helicopter. It was an apocalyptic scene of craters blackened from explosions and dense billowing smoke filling the horizon.

"Dramatic scenes there from one of the two gas-fired power stations hit on the Humber Estuary and we can only pray that the number of casualties will not rise today, the day that the Prime Minister said he would respond to those who caused this outrage with an 'iron fist'. Thanks for watching, we'll be back in twenty minutes after this special message on what you and your loved ones can do to stay safe."

Across the land people looked away from their TV sets and turned to one another. There was fear, to be sure. But masking the fear there was something else far more ugly and dishonest.

Twelve hours later, as the sun was sinking into the Atlantic and twilight swept across the skies over the British Isles, the power went off again. It had been on just long enough for phones to fully recharge, for freezers to re-freeze their ready-meals, and for a thousand conspiracy theories to bloom on social media.

In the dead of the night millions of mobile phones lit up as a new message came in. The message was simple and clear and it was the same for everyone who received it. It started with a twelve-digit string of alphanumeric characters followed by a message which stated:

This is the Unique Identifying Number (UIN) for you and your family. Write it down immediately and keep it safe. Do not reveal your UIN to anyone. Your UIN is not transferable. Failure to comply with requests by the Ministry of the Interior will be treated as a serious offence. Await further instructions.

9

~ The Mournful Tale of Rose O'Keefe ~

I suppose I had a way with words. How else could I explain the popularity of what I wrote? It's true I had a fascination with a particular realm of science that had become fashionable, but I was hardly original in what I wrote. And yet all those long nights hunched over the keyboard led one day to a message from a commissioning editor at *The Shield* asking me if I'd like to work for them. At the time, everyone at the university read *The Shield*, because they thought it was somehow better and fairer than the others. Of course, it was a lot more complex than that but I didn't know it at the time. The kind of people that read it called themselves "progressives," even though they had no real idea of what they were progressing towards. As a matter of fact it was these people who turned out to be the most soul-broken when the bad times came, and many chose to end it all and start their next life early rather than continue to live with such bitter disappointment.

Anyway, in the email, which came up on my computer screen, this woman from *The Shield* said she liked my style.

Don't forget, I called myself AstroQueen in this virtual computer world, rather than my dowdy real name, and the picture of me that my readers saw was one of a spiky-haired girl with rather too much makeup on. Really, I was quite a fake! But the commissioning editor was enthusiastic: "The boss loves it!" she said. They asked if I would be interested in writing a weekly column about physics and computers and said I could have a position as an intern in their swanky office near Euston Station. "We can't verify how good your material is," she said "but we just want you to write *sassy*. Your job is to be a kick-ass girl in a male-dominated field. Do you think you can do that?" Of course, I said yes.

I didn't exactly quit my course. Many of the students skipped lectures, sometimes for weeks or months on end, so I decided to do the same. It helped to remain a student and keep my entitlements, and I could carry on living in my small bedsit in Tottenham. I showed my face every few weeks, dropping in to attend a lecture or seminar, and once, when my tutor asked about the long absence, I explained that I had personal issues and pulled a face. He never asked me again. You have to understand, it was like that in those days: you could get away with a lot of things because the systems in which we lived were so complex and easy to manipulate to your own advantage. A little white lie here and there—everyone was at it. That's just how life was back then.

At *The Shield* I was given my own desk and computer. The newspaper was run from a five-story building made completely out of steel and glass. When you were inside it felt like being in a greenhouse and everyone on the outside could see you. The idea of the architects who designed it was to covey the idea of transparency: *"We've got nothing to hide!"* said the building. Furthermore, each floor was open-plan, meaning that there were no walls anywhere and everyone could see and hear one another. The ground floor was for administration staff, while the next two were taken up with salespeople. That's how the newspaper managed to stay in business: by selling advertising space for foreign holidays, cars and other things. The next floor—the one on which I worked—was filled with editorial staff and reporters. You might assume that it would have been a lively and noisy place but the reality was that it was quite a glum setting with row upon row of workers quietly tapping on keys or clicking on computer mouse buttons. The floor above us was the top floor, and this is where the most important staff worked. The editor spent most of his time up there. They had a restaurant on the top floor where important visitors such as politicians, businessmen and celebrities were treated to grape wine and cow steaks. I only saw it a couple of times but it was truly splendid.

Splendid or not, I soon found out that *The Shield* was an unfriendly and competitive place to work. Few of my colleagues smiled or greeted me when I came in to work. Indeed, a lot of them wore earplugs that played music right into their ears, so it was impossible to talk with them anyway. I had been born and brought up in the North, and I found this coldness odd. On the other hand, I was not exactly a social person, so did my best to ignore them and simply kept my head down and got on with my work. This would have suited me fine but unfortunately there is always at least one fly in the ointment, as my mother used to say. This particular fly was called Chloe Scarlett, and she was my boss. Chloe was the editor of *The Shield*'s travel supplement and she took an immediate dislike to me. She was everything that I was not: tall, glamorous, well connected and confident. She spoke with an upper-class home counties accent and everything about her spelled privilege. When she met people she pressed her cheek against theirs and made a kind of *mwah* sound—one for each cheek—and she called everyone 'dahling'. She could only have been in her late twenties, but ambition and school connections had propelled her to the top.

I was employed as an intern, meaning that I worked without getting paid. The reward for doing so was measured in experience, so the theory went, but if that were so then my experience did not add up to much. In theory I was supposed to be learning how to be a journalist, but in practice I was given the most basic of tasks to do. Quite often I felt as if I were merely Chloe's personal assistant. I spent hours each day scheduling her diary and booking her flights and restaurant tables. If I wasn't doing that then I was tasked with helping do the layout for the travel section, which was a fiddly and thankless chore involving resizing boxes, nudging images around and clipping words out of articles so that they would fit in the space allocated to them. More often than not my clipping incurred the wrath of whoever wrote the article, and on many occasions I was blamed for "ruining" their work. Usually, after spending hours getting this annoying multi-dimensional puzzle just right there would be a change of plan at the last minute and I would have to re-do the whole lot with half the office breathing down the back of my neck and telling me to hurry up. It really was a thankless task.

Of course, I was also permitted to spend some time writing my own column each week, and I was sometimes invited to attend editorial meetings. From my readers I received messages by the hundred, and spent a lot of time answering them. Some, however, were messages of hatred and violence directed at me. The intensity of some people's anger puzzled and worried me. I received threats, many of them explicit. But then you have to remember that many people were mentally ill in those times, and that a computer in a private room was often the only outlet by which these anonymous people could project their brain spew. When I think about them now, I feel a deep pity for them. It was hardly their fault they felt so trapped.

Within the newspaper, round-robin emails would be sent out to all the writers asking us to conform to the house style and informing us of upcoming events and anniversaries that we should try and tie into our pieces. More blatantly, we were reminded to comply with the "editorial direction."

Closely following "editorial direction," I soon learned, was how you rose up in the organisation. *The Shield*, which had been founded in Sheffield during the nineteenth century, prided itself on being progressive, and that, as I mentioned before, meant that its readers believed that the human race was heading towards a glorious future where everything was fair and peaceful, if only we worked at it. It's hard to comprehend that attitude these days, but you must remember that back then things had reached such a level of unfairness that only the most privileged could remain inside a bubble of ignorance where they could convince themselves things were getting better. Remember, I was still only a very young woman back then, but even I had picked up on how bad things were getting in our world. It was as if all that oil and technology meant that just a small handful of rich countries could take resources from the rest of the world at will, and say at the same time they were doing it for the greater good—and hardly anyone seemed to care.

And there was a reason for this. People—especially those with nice homes and from comfortable backgrounds—didn't want to be reminded of how harsh and cruel the world was. And so it was the editor's job to comfort them and whisper sweet lullabies to keep them sleeping. The last thing they wanted to be told was that they were actually making the world a *worse* place to live. So, for example, in the travel and motoring sections it was not allowed to mention global warming, and in the food section it was not allowed to mention the way we treated animals in factories or how we poisoned and killed almost every last fish in the sea, and in the business section there was no mention of the slave labour

69

that was used to make the latest gadgets they insisted we should buy. And so everyone just carried on doing all those things that made them feel good without a thought for the future and that is how the world ended up as it is today. That's right, I'm not making this up. Is it any wonder that so many of them lost their minds when the props were kicked out from under them and they were exposed to the full glare of the actual reality of the world?

Yes, there were many things that couldn't be mentioned in the newspaper—but there were plenty of things you were *expected* to mention—and by doing so you could earn yourself points for a promotion. Again, I may need to explain. In those times many people worked in jobs within larger organisations. You generally started off near the bottom and over the course of your career worked your way higher up. The word "career" simply meant the trajectory of your time within an organisation or sector. In other words, you gave over your life to the institution, so that you could afford to buy all the luxuries that were available back then. At *The Shield*, with its crusades—to raise people out of poverty or give women the same rights as men in the industrial system—we were expected to go above and beyond merely not mentioning inconvenient truths. Those at the top had got there by reinforcing the system.

I knew none of this when I worked there. Only later, as you will see, did I experience an awakening that opened my eyes to what I am writing about now. At the time, I was as clueless as everyone else.

Few realised it at the time but we were living through the greatest theft in the history of the human race. We had stolen from other nations, we had stolen from the Earth, we had stolen from the future—all that was left was for the powerful to steal from the weak within their own nations. The future was being bundled out of the back door—and it was our job in the mass media to make sure nobody noticed.

So instead of trying to inform and educate, the news organisation I worked for filled the readers' heads with fantasies and trivia about the most ridiculous matters. "That is what they want to hear, so it is our job to provide it," said the editorial directives. It remains a puzzle to me how people let this happen, and to this day I still have not fully decided whether all the lies and distractions were part of some cruel plan or whether it was merely some self-assembling system of willing blindness that had hypnotised people like a magic spell. Nevertheless, whatever had caused us to look the wrong way until it was too late was an enigma that may never be solved, and its importance has now been lost.

For my part, during that critical time I was but a small cog in the great machinery of that evil system. The machine was so large and so all encompassing that it was no wonder those trapped inside it had little idea how they might escape it. In my case, I think it was blind luck that saved me. Most of those less fortunate than I now lie in unmarked graves across the land, having remained clueless to their last breath. Oh, how I wish I had been able to do something to avert what had happened!

We might have been guilty, but at the same time we were bewildered and innocent. I still remember the day when the computer screens went black in that great big office, and a great cry of despair arose up from those working on my floor. It was the start of a bad dream: a nightmare from which many would never wake up.

10

Three days after the Prime Minister had appeared on television a great number of Army trucks and delivery vans rolled out of the small town of Broxbourne situated just to the north of London. It had been the largest single job ever taken on by the print works, which covered an area the size of thirteen football fields. Shift workers had laboured day and night to ensure that the order of twenty million copies was met before the deadline. Local residents, having endured living with no electricity for seven out of the previous eight days, were puzzled as to how the plant could operate. But they didn't need to wonder long because it was right there on Page 2 of *Fortitude*—for that is what this new publication was called—under the heading "Emergency National Infrastructure Recovery Plan (NIRP) Agreed Upon." The short article explained that the nation's reduced energy capacity would be directed at critical infrastructure, without which the nation would not be able to defend itself. This was to be a temporary measure until the damage to the network was repaired, it explained. A small asterisk was placed after the words "critical infrastructure" directing the reader to a full-page list on the last page in small print italics. The list was no means exhaustive but there was a definition at the top which read "As defined by the government, those facilities, systems, sites and networks necessary for the functioning of the country and the delivery of the essential services upon which daily life in the UK depends." The obvious entries included military bases, naval yards and airports, but there were less obvious ones as well, such as communication hubs, critical industries and financial centres.

On the facing page of the inside cover there was an explanation of the mysterious numbers that had been sent out to millions of Britons by SMS. "Have you received a UIN?" asked the headline. It continued: "If you have received a Unique Identifying Number this means you have been identified as being of critical importance to the National Emergency Plan (NEP). Please study and memorise your number as you may need to repeat it to a member of the security services upon demand. If your number ends in the letter Y you should report to work as normal, as far as this is possible under the circumstances. If your UIN ends in an X this means your skills are needed at one of the centralised Critical Response headquarters (CRHQ). The primary CRHQ is situated in London. Please pack a suitcase as soon as possible with enough clothes to last for up to a month and identify yourself to your local military forward response team who will convey you to your allocated centre. Do not attempt to make your own way there as motorways are now closed to all but military traffic, and the rail network has been suspended until further notice. Due to the nature of the security situation, anyone travelling by bicycle, on foot or by horseback will be stopped and may be subject to arrest if unable to prove their identity. Please be aware that under the NEP your cooperation is mandatory.

Compensation for lost income and expenditures will be awarded once the current state of national emergency has been lifted. The Prime Minister thanks each and every one of you for helping Britain get back on its feet."

Copies of *Fortitude* were driven the length and breadth of the country and delivered in bundles to every population centre worthy of a name on an Ordnance Survey map. Fishing boats were commandeered by the Army to take copies to over a hundred different islands, some of which had not even noticed the electricity outage. In this way people across the land got to learn about the declared state of emergency, and how it was being dealt with. The front page, which, like the rest of the publication, employed an austere black and white style, showed a picture of a serious-looking Prime Minister under the headline "PM: We're All in This Together." The accompanying article was a reprint of his televised speech, with a few extra points added for clarity. Much of the inside of the paper printed news articles of national relevance, including the outbreak of violence and looting in the inner cities and a spate of copycat attacks on transformers and electrical substations in the regions. Saboteurs had derailed a west coast train, it was reported, by damaging a section of track using angle grinders, and flames had engulfed a block of flats in York, with many feared dead.

Most of the rest of the publication was filled with advice on how to stay safe, with the back page featuring a photo of the wanted man John Barleycorn, which readers were encouraged to cut out and affix to their windows. There was an international news section informing readers how offers of help were pouring in from several countries. German and Japanese engineers were working on manufacturing and installing new turbines and large power transformers, to replace the ones destroyed or damaged by the attacks and the resultant catastrophic unplanned shutdowns. Ireland, including Ulster, which had not been affected by the power outage, was sending medicine and machinery. France was sending trucks filled with milk and beef, America was sending a ship filled with grain, and the Red Cross was mobilising to distribute medical resources to the most needy. None of this was of much use to the majority of the population, which by that point had not eaten for several days. Shops and stores were either empty or barricaded, and only the luckiest or best-prepared people had cupboards filled with cans of baked beans or packets of cup-a-soups.

Water, in most places, had at first dribbled from the taps and then stopped altogether, and the unholy smell of backed-up toilets had begun to cast a stench across towns and cities. In the larger of these the Army was handing out bottled water and packets of dried food—although the lines were very long and demand was nowhere near met. The sick and the frail were left to sit in their homes, often alone, awaiting help that in many cases would not come.

Nothing worked. The banks were closed, the streetlights were off, there was no television or radio or Internet. A few people who had their own means of making electricity by way of generators stood out from everyone else in the first few days, but even they were forced to turn them off, or at least conceal their good fortune for fear of attracting untoward attention. Some people, driven crazy by hunger, sat in the streets begging, while others went door-to-door with their children and pets seeking goodwill from neighbours. There was an air of disbelief about what had happened. "How could everything have gone so wrong in just a little over a week?" they asked. "It'll all be back to normal in a few days," some said, and everyone hoped they were right.

Some 300 miles from London, down at the tail end of Britain where a narrow peninsula juts out into the Atlantic Ocean, three people and a cat sat in room staring at one another in uneasy silence. On the night that Arthek Gwavas' intoxicated head encountered the windshield of Jack's restored classic VW Kombi, three people had been thrown together in an unlikely fashion that would certainly not have endured beyond a few hours under normal circumstances. But these circumstances were, of course, far from normal. For a start, there was the fact that Jack, and his girlfriend Cat, had been unable to escape from Cornwall and head back to London. A lack of fuel and a duty of care had held them up for the first few days, and now they were being told the motorways were closed to all but military vehicles. "It says it right here," said Jack, waving the crumpled copy of *Fortitude* at Art.

Art considered this from his position slumped deep in an old armchair with his cat Buster, a piebald black and white tom with a crooked door-slammed tail and a scarred face. It had been an unusual few days, thought Art, even by his standards. These people had been living with him for a week now, and he was almost starting to like them. On the night of the accident he remembered getting hold of the rum in the supermarket, remembered being chased down an alley and remembered sitting in the crook of an old sycamore and enjoying the first of the bottles. After that it was all patchy images and sensations. And that was all he remembered until the next day when he'd awoken lying on an unfamiliar sofa in an unfamiliar house.

Holiday home, he'd thought. *Rich upcountry feckers—that must be it.* The pain in his head had been intense—much worse than a normal hangover—and he had lain there for some time trying to remember a beach party that he had not in actual fact managed to attend. His fingers had explored his head and discovered the gash there causing him to gingerly rise and examine the damage in a mirror on the wall. The mirror also showed him a broken nose sitting in the middle of a face spattered with dried blood. *Just whose place was this?* As far as he was aware he didn't have any friends who might own a pad like this. Most of them lived in old caravans, ambulances, tin sheds, benders or ex-Army trucks. One or two lived in council houses, but this place was far too posh, like something out of a magazine.

He'd peered out of a window. Outside he could see a purple camper van parked up beside the cottage. It was one of those vintage VW types that moneyed urban yuppies lavished unspeakable sums of money on. Strapped on top of it was a couple of sea kayaks, but the thing that was really noticeable about the vehicle was that the front window was smashed in as if it had been hit with a cannon ball. *Curiouser and curiouser*, thought Art.

He saw Cat's reflection appear behind him in the mirror. She was standing at the bottom of the stairs wearing a white terry-towel dressing gown and staring at him. Art turned to face her, his mind racing. Had he actually scored the night before? There was an outside possibility, unlikely as it may seem. She was a real looker—far better than he thought himself capable of. Perhaps he had met her at the beach party and they had come back here, wherever *here* was. *Yes, that must be what had happened*; it was all starting to make sense to him now. He stood up and walked towards her. "Morning love," he said cheerily. "What a night, eh? I'll just be getting the kettle on for us. Think I was just havin' a little snooze down here for a while, but I'll be right back up."

The young woman's eyes widened. "Jack," she called out nervously. "He's awake."

A young man with ruffled hair and wearing boxer shorts appeared at the top of the stairs. He looked down on Art with something that looked like guarded disdain.

Bugger, thought Art, although he didn't say it. "So that'll be three teas will it?"

Jack and Cat hesitated, as if Art was some kind of alien speaking another language. "There's, er, no electricity," said Cat. "Don't you remember?"

"Remember?" said Art. A slight frown crossed his brow. "Seems there's plenty I don't remember today." He sat down on the sofa again and touched the wound on his head gently. "Like 'ow's I got this one 'ere."

How strangely he speaks, thought Cat, *a proper country bumpkin.*

Jack and Cat exchanged glances. "I think I'd better explain," said Jack, and walked down the stairs to sit opposite him on one of the sofa chairs.

As Jack spoke Art fingered his wispy beard, taking it all in. He told him everything that had happened, and everything they had learned from the truck driver and the paramedic. He left out the bit about drinking the expensive wine and the pints of Doom Bar ale. When he had finished his edited account of events, the ragged-looking young man on the expensive-looking couch seemed pensive. At length he said "Seems you owe me an apology then."

"Sorry," said Jack, looking down at his hands. "We were in a bit of a hurry, I admit."

"Sorry?" exploded Cat, who was still standing on the stairs. "Sorry for what? *You* were the one who ran out in front of us. You're lucky to be alive you bloody idiot!" Her Latin accent made "bloody" sound like "bladdy."

Art looked up at her. He liked feisty women. "That's a fair point you have there, lady," he said. "Ordinarily, I might agree with you on that one, and I'm sure a careful examination of the forensic evidence would go in your favour, although I do believe it was *me* that got run over and your good husband here who was behind the wheel of the offending vehicle. So from a moral perspective I'd say it was *you* who'd best be doing the apologising and not me." He folded his arms across his chest and nodded his head slightly.

"He's not my husband," Cat blurted. *Was he deliberately trying to goad them, or was this what passed for sarcasm around here?* She pursed her lips and glared at him, consoling herself with the idea that he seemed well enough to now leave their lives, and that Jack would shortly return him to whichever particular hedge he lived in. "He's just my boyfriend."

"Apologies," said Art, returned her stare with a casually arched eyebrow. "And what might I be calling you in that case? Can't call you lady, nor missus, can I?"

She regarded his sarcastic-looking face, framed by filthy-looking twists of brown hair and half-covered in darkly congealed blood. "Cat," she said coolly. "You can call me Cat."

"Cat?" said Art, a smile breaking on his lips. "As in meow?"

Cat did not smile back.

"Arthek Gwavas at your service Miss Cat, though those who know me tend to call me Art." He stood up and proffered an outstretched hand, which Cat studiously ignored.

"What kind of a name is that?" she said, digging her hands under her armpits. "Does everyone around here have silly names like you?"

"Only the best of them," quipped Art. "Now if you'll forgive me I'll have to be on my way. That's unless, of course, you'd like to make a fellow some breakfast. Don't worry, I'm not a vegetarian. Just some good old-fashioned bacon and eggs should do it. Black pudding maybe, with a cup of your finest tea, not forgetting the toast, of course."

Jack held a finger up. "As I was saying about the electricity..."

"Ah yes," Art interrupted, "but it's heartening to see that you city slickers had the good sense to come down in a fully-equipped camper van. And I did happen to notice there's all we want for a good feed in the little fridge you've got in there. We shan't starve today!"

"When did you see that?" exclaimed Cat hotly. "Have you been snooping around?"

"Last night," said Art. "Selective amnesia, it seems." He tapped the side of his head knowingly. "There might be more where that came from too!"

Cat uttered an oath in Spanish under her breath and stomped back up the stairs to the bedroom, leaving Art and

Jack staring at one another.

"Women, eh?" said Art, with a shrug. Jack stared at him, wondering what else he might know.

Twenty minutes later the smell of frying bacon came drifting through the door of the cottage. Art sipped his mug of tea and smiled inwardly. *Selective amnesia! These bleeding emmets always came down stocked up with food from Waitrose as if they were heading off for a week in North Korea. Talk about predictable!*

Then he thought about what Jack had said about the electricity grid going down, and his mind set to work on this as he waited for his breakfast. *Is this it? Is this when the fun starts?*

If it was, he'd been waiting for it for a long time.

11

The Prime Minister of Great Britain and Northern Ireland was furious. A generally peaceable fellow most of the time, he was now striding up and down the central aisle of the BA Boeing 777 with a mobile phone clamped to the side of his head. "Answer the bloody phone will you." But instead, all he heard was the crackle of static over the top of a faint ring tone. His left hand fingered longingly the packet of Benson and Hedges in the pocket of his suit jacket. *Just one won't do any harm*, he told himself before remembering that he was 25,000 feet above God-knows-where and that they didn't allow smoking on planes anymore, even for heads of state.

He removed the phone from his ear and stared at it. "Fuck you Pope," he spat, and turned it off. He looked around at the interior of the plane. It was big enough for 450 people, yet apart from the flight crew it was just himself, a scrum of officials plucked from the Department of Trade and Industry, a handful of trusted hacks and his wife. Sitting back down in his seat beside her he leaned over and slid the window blind up. Outside the skies were dark. He looked at his watch, frowned a little, and sighed.

Where the hell was that wretched man and what was he up to? In the last week, since his audacious plan had been put into action, Pope had gone practically AWOL. Nobody had actually seen the fellow for three days and this alone had caused the PM's peptic ulcer to flare up. He wasn't answering his emails or texts, and whenever he'd tried to contact the skinny Evian-supping Saffer all he'd got was a fob-off from his obsequious private secretary. He closed his eyes and tried to relax. *Blood pressure, remember your blood pressure.* To the forefront of his mind he tried to force images of tranquil seas, of trees rustling in a late spring breeze. The face of his mindfulness tutor, Suzanne, was there too, cooing quietly and saying "As you breathe out you feel yourself slip deeper into a state of relaxation and bliss." He exhaled and tried to focus on his bliss. But it was no good. Instead of waves breaking gently on a tropical paradise all he saw was the purple-faced general screaming at him. "What game are you playing?" The words repeated over and over like a loop, and in the background, standing behind the general, was the polished grinning head of Pope.

"Fuck you, Pope," said the PM out loud once more. He opened his eyes and stared at the seat in front of him. Pope was good, he told himself. Pope won us both elections. Pope was the cleverest son-of-a-bitch this side of Timbuktu and he was the only one bold enough to contemplate what all of his other spineless advisors were too scared to say. Pope had *vision*.

He took out his iPhone and looked at his reflection in the darkened screen. The angle was unflattering and emphasised his double chin so he raised it higher until his visage was satisfactory. He turned his head in profile a little, affecting a more statesman-like look. No, not serious enough. He furrowed his brow just a little and removed all traces of what might be mistaken for warmth from his face. That was it. Commanding. Resolute. Perhaps even a little imperious—the adjectives flattered him, and even if only he spoke them, surely others would see it too. That would be the portrait he wanted on the wall at Number 10. An idea crossed his mind. He turned on the iPhone and began to fiddle with it. How did other people do it; they made it look so easy? He went into settings. No, that wasn't it. Camera—yes, that was more like it. The screen filled with a close-up of his pink thumb. *Result.* He raised the phone once more and affected the pose from a minute earlier. He'd just about got it when his wife stirred, the heavy lids of her eyes half open.

"Aren't you a bit old for selfies?" she said quizzically. The PM hastily lowered the phone and glared at her, effecting incredulity.

"They need a new picture for Twitter," he lied. "Anyway, go back to sleep, dear. We won't be in Beijing for another seven hours."

"Terribly burdensome, this job of yours," she purred sarcastically and turned over a little so that her face was to the window. After a few moments she began to emit the soft sounds of sleep. The PM too closed his eyes, but once again all he saw was the barking general and the hideous shiny face of Pope. It was as if the two of them were waiting there behind his eyelids; a couple of scary clowns, jeering and mocking. He opened his eyes and looked around at the white plastic interior of the plane. Business class. *Business class!* Weren't heads of state supposed to travel in grand style or had that gone out the window too?

He closed his eyes again, this time concentrating with all his might on seeing that white sandy beach, and the blue sea and the coconuts. It worked. Suzanne appeared on the beach —and she wasn't wearing any clothes. She walked over to the PM holding a couple of drinks in her hands. "Feel your bliss rising," she whispered in his mind. His eyes blinked open like a startled puppy.

After he had checked that his wife had not somehow been able to tune into his vision the PM sighed and reached for his briefcase. From it he took out a sheaf of papers and, with his gold-nibbed Visconti, began the meditative task of scribbling his signature on a pile of executive orders. After a while he paused in his task and allowed a feeling of glumness to arise within him. All of a sudden he felt very alone, as if everyone was against him. Of course, this was nothing new to him. He'd endured the taunts of the Opposition and the public for so long that he was unbothered by it. But recently it seemed as if *everyone* had it in for him. When he'd finally, after many months, consented to follow Pope's outrageous plan, he'd known that he would be acting almost alone. One doesn't go into politics to make friends, but still, he'd also hoped that there would be at least *some* support from his inner circle. How naïve he had been. He tried to think of a single person aside from Pope who wasn't after his blood. A line of hecklers and accusers rose up before him. There was Defence, of course, as well as the Opposition, and captains of industry. World leaders had been on the phone demanding to know what was going on, as had the Secretary General of the UN, the head of NATO, an alphabet soup of Washington Consensus bureaucrats and NGOs—hell, even the Queen was demanding to know what was going on and what he was doing to fix it. And Pope with all his well-laid plans just disappears into thin air!

To top it all now he was being summoned to Beijing as if he were some kind of errant schoolboy suspected of wrongdoing. Summoned! If that wasn't humiliating then what was? Time was when it was London who summoned people from Beijing, but now he was on a mad dash across half the world to assure investors that their assets were safe. After Beijing it was Delhi and after Delhi it was Riyadh and Qatar. From there he would have to fly to Washington by way of Brussels, and then he'd be back in London—that cauldron of hellfire where everyone seemed to be holding a dagger behind their backs.

He called to mind one of his favourite Churchill quotes: *"When you find yourself going through hell, keep going."*

But Pope was right. Of that he was sure.

His hand reached for a file in the compartment at the back of his briefcase. It was of the manila variety and entitled TRANSITION 3.1.3 UK – FOR PM's EYES ONLY. That was all it said, there was not even a CLASSIFIED or a TOP SECRET on it. He opened it and thumbed through it, as he had done so many times before. Each time he read it a deep shiver went all the way down to his bowels. He looked at the charts, the graphs and the executive summary. There was no denying that Pope had done his homework on this one. The original report had been over 500 pages long but he'd asked him to condense it into something a tenth of the size, which had caused one of Pope's very rare laughs. He flicked to the opening executive summary and ran his eyes over it, as he had found himself doing several times a day lately. As he took in the words a kind of neediness took charge of his brain. He needed to again convince himself—reassure himself—that the course of action, however painful it might be, would be remembered as an act of reformation that saved the country.

The report was blunt and to the point. It spoke directly to the PM in a no-nonsense kind of way. The words, lines and paragraphs seemed to be addressing *him*, and him alone.

* * *

Précis: The UK faces numerous threats which have grown in number and magnitude over the course of the last three decades. These dangers are economic, political and ecological in basis, with conditions of scarcity and overshoot threatening the basis of the continuation of a civilised society within these shores. Current off-record debt projections are unsustainable in the medium to long term relative to committed expenditures, despite the assurances to the contrary of economists, while real, off-record GDP growth remains to the downside, exhibiting anaemic tendencies at best and undermining the tax base. Although quantitative easing, negative interest rates and the financialisation of valueless assets has provided short-term relief, the Treasury and the Bank are rapidly running out of options for further stimulating an economy that is weighed down by too much unproductive capital and awash in debt. Because of this, we face a situation where the next recessionary relapse will initiate unwelcome feedback loops in the spheres of energy, resource availability and, ultimately, population.

As these feedbacks become established, the probability that political power will swing away from the Party is a given. If this were to happen, it is likely that the UK's wealth-earning sectors would come under sustained attack as new legislation is drafted by ideological extremists, forcing the productive classes to flee. At this present time, neither of the main parties understands the true gravity of the situation we face. Nobody in any position of authority is able to demonstrate an understanding of the dynamics of energy and the financial sector, and the ephemeral nature of how these give us privileged access to world markets in the context of a shifting geopolitical environment. The reality of the predicament facing this country as well as the other advanced industrialised nations is one of utmost seriousness.

At this late stage there is little that can be realistically achieved in terms of saving the nation's wider socio-economic culture as a whole, but there is much that can be done to preserve the most productive and valuable parts of it. Following the next financial seizure, of which there is a now near-certain probability, there will be a corresponding collapse in world trade. The UK is able to produce less than half of its food needs, and much of what it can produce is dependent upon imported nitrogen and potassium fertilisers, petroleum and farm equipment. This figure is dwindling rapidly as other nations take a larger slice of the pie, yet current policies assume a permanent abundance and availability of both fuel and fertiliser. Our models show that even in a best-case scenario this is both unrealistic and complacent.

This paper sets out the case for a series of measures involving the controlled demolition of the non-productive sectors within our society. There will be nothing easy about such a destructive process, but a carefully planned and executed winnowing of non-productive social overhang —"deadwood"—is far preferable to a chaotic and messy descent into chaos. Our advanced economic and population dynamics model shows that robust preemptive action will, in the long term, permit the UK to emerge stronger and with a greater per capita wealth relative to nations which lack the political will to follow such a path.

Yet the window of opportunity for such action is fast closing, and history shows us that reformers have but one chance to act. Deep reformation will take the kinetic work of a bold and decisive leader to initiate and drive the process, and there will be risks along the way. Such a leader, who is willing to demonstrate the resolve to tackle the deep-seated problems threatening to overwhelm this once-great nation, and to restore it to its fated place in the world, would likely be a leader remembered by future historians as the one who rose to the challenge of saving his country from destruction.

The UK **must** transition from a low-production, high population nation, to a high-production, low population one. At this stage to do nothing would be to accept defeat.

Main points of paper in summary:

Threats
• Financial sector no longer able to support the weight of a stalling economy

• Serious near-term risk of simultaneous collapses in global trade, oil production and food availability

• Cascading collapse to hit supply chains, with a 90% chance of severe food shortage in the UK. This would be sharply at odds with the expectations of the population as a whole

• Above factors would likely lead to conditions of civil unrest in which the productive sectors would be destroyed, further hindering the possibility of recovery for the nation

• Weakened nation likely subject to hostile takeover bids from great powers

Action Points

• Diminishing the population overburden is the only way to avoid all-out collapse

• Preemptively degrading the reactive potential of the civilian mass is the only realistic option to achieve this goal

• Reduced load on system and unhindered exploitation of untapped domestic energy sources will allow for the long-term preservation of the productive sector and the nation as a whole

• Nation to remain fully armed for the duration (including adhering to NATO commitments) with increased resources devoted to military and security sectors throughout the transition period

• Short-term hit to markets and industry will be a price worth paying for reestablishing long-term equilibrium

• Rapidly closing window of opportunity which must be exploited to prevent full-scale catastrophe

Timing and Transitional Tranches

Implementation of controlled clearance of non-productive sectors to proceed in a series of tranches:

Tranche 1. *Casus belli.* Initial "hit" and restructuring of apparatus of state and private sectors. Timescale 3 months.

Tranche 2. Population rebalancing process using tools of energy, nutrition and direct intervention. Timescale 3 years.

Tranche 3. Consolidation of productive sector, including energy exploration/exploitation for long-term prosperity relative to competitor nations. Timescale ongoing.

65 million civilians to be separated into three tiers as follows:

Tier 1. Highest executive level. Approximately 50,000 individuals.

Tier 2. Lower level executive and managerial staff, including debt-bonded individuals, who will make up the seed group for a reformed middle class. Individuals to be heavily vetted for suitability, including assessment of genetic traits and history of political activity. Any likely subversives and/or those with undesirable features not conducive to the national reformulation (see appendix 7) will be removed to **Tier X** (see below). Approximately 3 million individuals.

Tier 3. Operational and security personnel, including police and armed forces, needed to maintain order, implement Tranches and protect capital investments and infrastructure during transition period. Approximately 5 million individuals.

Two further unofficial Tiers to be defined, including **Tier 1A**, to include the executive branch and royals, as well as a number of carefully selected business leaders; and **Tier X**, to comprise of those excluded from all other Tiers i.e. the target reduction population.

Population dynamics modelling indicates that within 36 months **Tier X** will have been reduced from 58 million to around 20 million—a level considered as being sustainable within the national carrying capacity. **Thus, over a 3 year period, the population will be reduced to 1/3 of its currently unsustainable level, hence 3.1.3 nomenclature.** This process is to be catalysed by seeding unrest and disharmony, as well as providing the means to self-reduce in the form of access to small arms and addictive drugs. Those who have managed to survive outside of the protected zones for 3 years will be offered gainful employment working in the newly reformed agricultural and mining sectors. They will likely consider themselves lucky to be alive at the start of a new Golden Era for the nation and will, it is hoped, be more productive and efficient as a result. Those that work the hardest will be offered the chance of rising to a Tier 3 position, as and when places become available.

* * *

The PM closed the report, placed it back in its manila folder and stowed it in the briefcase. Agreeing to the plan had been the price of his reelection. It had been four years in the planning, and building the infrastructure and the command hierarchy to execute it had been a costly exercise to say the least. The operations centre alone—disguised as a new air traffic control hub—had cost over two billion, and that didn't even include the staff or the vastly expensive installation of smart meters across the nation. Immense warehouses at Grangemouth had been filled with food and supplies for the top three Tiers, and the nation's emergency oil stocks and strategic petroleum reserves were filled to overflowing.

Several rows behind him a junior trade minister snored and turned over.

The PM turned on his phone and looked at the picture he had taken. The statesman-like demeanour, the no-nonsense look in the eye, the steely countenance—he saw none of this. Instead he saw a weak and dithery man with a double chin. The eyes were sallow and unsure of themselves, the jowls flaccid and the nose too small for the puffy face that surrounded it. He saw, in this unattractive visage, the faint echo of a young boy.

Why me? he thought. *I didn't ask to be born into this wretched world.*

12

~ The Mournful Tale of Rose O'Keefe ~

It was a Friday afternoon in late June. I'd filed my copy for the week and my boss was making me do the layout for her precious travel section. It was some feature about weddings on Caribbean islands, and it had been written by one of her friends, who could barely string a coherent sentence together, let alone a whole article. Every line had a gushy superlative in it; the most *incredible* pool, a wedding suite *to die for*, a resort that was *out of this world*. That was the way they used to write in those days. Honestly, I had to correct almost everything she wrote, so I was just as annoyed as everyone else when the power went off and I lost all my careful work.

It wasn't just the screens going blank; everything went dead. Lights went off, phones stopped working, and the hum of the air conditioning went quiet. When people realised what was happening they were either angry or happy. One man, whose desk was near mine, hit his computer keyboard so hard it almost broke in two. Power cuts were so uncommon, you see, people just didn't expect them to happen. More than a few put on their coats and quietly slipped out—it was, after all, already late afternoon. Me, I waited around to see if the power would come back on again.

Chloe, my boss, was furious when she realised she was going to miss her deadline. She went storming off looking for the facilities manager, shouting about "backup" and "imbeciles." But there was no backup, we were to learn; not in the office, not in London, and not in the whole country—at least not for most people. That was it. Nothing would ever be the same again.

Of course, it wasn't as simple as that. It never is.

I hung around in the office until the early evening. We kicked our heels and waited for the electricity to restart. After a while the editor came down to our floor and stood on a desk so everyone could hear him. He had received word, he said, that a substation had suffered a blowout and that the power would not be on again until at least the following day. We should all go home, he urged, and those of us who turned up the next day would get paid double time.

And so I put on my thin summer jumper and took my bag and walked down the stairs and out of the building. Outside, on the busy streets of London, you couldn't tell the power was out. The roads were still filled with buses and cabs spewing diesel fumes from their exhausts, and black-leathered motorcycle couriers continued to weave between them as they hurried to deliver their urgent packages. Groups of tourists were still milling around outside St Pancras station taking pictures of it with their phones, and pigeons still sat around on window ledges pluming their feathers. In fact, the only sign that something wasn't right was the darkened traffic lights at the top of Tottenham Court Road and the silent gridlock that surrounded them.

I knew that no power meant no Tube. Or maybe it would mean a terribly overcrowded Tube filled with angry sweating commuters. Either way I wasn't keen to find out, and so I began walking home. I knew it was a long way and would likely take several hours, but I was in no hurry and had nothing planned for that evening other than reading a book. I thought to myself that maybe I would watch a film on my laptop computer if the power came on again. I walked up the Hampstead Road in the direction of Camden, slipping on my headphones to drown out the din of the traffic. I spun the little touch sensitive dial that selected the music, settling on The Cure's *Head on the Door*.

I've waited hours for this
I've made myself so sick
I wish I'd stayed asleep today
I never thought that this day would end
I never thought that tonight could ever be
This close to me

Those were the words; I can still remember them to this day. The singer's plaintive voice carried me all the way to Camden and I continued on my journey home, turning east through Holloway and Haringey. It always amazed me how different London was from street to street. It was as if all these little galaxies were pressed together like individual cells making up an organism. One minute you would be walking past great white-stuccoed houses with huge black gates and brass plaques, and then the next you would be walking through shabby areas filled with car body shops, kebab stalls and booze stores with metal bars over the windows. There were streets upon streets of terrace houses, all jammed together like teeth, and then there were private roads with tall gates and metal bollards that rose up out of the road. Somehow all of these places managed to coexist together, and it was like everyone was an atom: alone and with their own purpose, but in aggregate making up something much bigger. I felt like an outsider: my purpose unknown. I kept my head down and hurried along.

Even with no electricity in the grid the city hummed with energy. It was Friday evening and high spirits abounded. People crowded outside pubs, sipping glasses of lager and wine beneath hanging baskets filled with flowers. It seemed like the power cut had given rise to more jollity than was normal even for the Friday after-work drinks crowd.

By the time I reached the streets of Tottenham it was dusk and the buildings were dark inside. I was scared to be out after dark, so I was really hurrying by this point. There were youths standing around on the street outside where I lived, and I recognised some of them. It felt as if they were waiting for something to happen, or maybe they were waiting to cause something to happen. I didn't want to be outside for a moment longer and I fumbled with my front door key, feeling their eyes on me. A bus went past and its headlights lit up the door and my unsteady hand. I pushed in the key and turned it. Once inside I shut the door behind me and put the security chain on. There was a deadbolt too and I slid it into position. The door was shared with Mr Singh, a man who ran a mobile phone repair shop with his teenage son Kiran, and my bedsit was on the floor above this. He was also my landlord, although he didn't live in the property. When I moved in he'd had told me to always remember to lock the door at night.

There was a letter for me on the mat. I picked it up but couldn't make out the writing on it in the half-light. Another key opened the door to my flat and I trudged up the stairs, absent-mindedly flicking on the light switch out of habit, forgetting that it didn't work.

My bedsit was a single room that served as a bedroom, a kitchen and a lounge. There was a narrow bed, a countertop with a gas stove and a fraying old armchair next to the window. A small door led into what had once been a cloakroom but was now a tiny bathroom with a toilet and a dribbling shower. It wasn't much, but it was my home in this unfathomable city, and I could be myself there. I kicked off my shoes and slumped down in the chair by the window. My feet ached from the long walk and I was hungry. I stood up and opened the fridge, which reminded me once more about the electricity situation by failing to illuminate. Inside was a soggy cardboard packet of veggie burgers, three-quarters empty. I took the remaining burger out and placed it in my small frying pan on top of the stove. Turning the knob on the cooker I half-expected there to be no gas. But I need not have worried as gas came from a butane cylinder under the sink. That kind of setup was no doubt illegal in those days when there was a branch of bureaucracy called "health and safety," but I don't think Mr Singh was overly worried by it.

I sparked a match and lit the gas. Pretty soon the veggie burger was frying in the oil, spitting a little and filling the bedsit with the smells of cooking. I didn't eat meat back then, but there was a lot of food to choose from and it was easy to live as a vegetarian—which is what somebody like me would have been called. I went over and yanked open the stiff window, sliding it up in its frame so the cooking smells had somewhere to escape. On a plate I cut a slice of cheese and chopped a tomato in two.

When the burger was done I sat down in the scruffy but comfy chair to eat my meal. I've never been much of a drinker but I had a can of beer in the fridge and I decided to open it before it got warm. I think it was a Budweiser, or maybe Heineken. They had funny names back then, you know, and they were nothing like the kinds of beer people make these days. I ate the burger and sipped the beer. Outside in the street people were shouting and the occasional jarring bass of a car stereo made the building shudder. In this way it was no different from any other weekend night, and I had grown used to living there.

It was getting dark inside the flat and I suddenly realised that reading would be out of the question. There were no candles, I was pretty sure of that. I got my laptop computer out of my bag and flipped open the screen. The room was bathed in its blue light and I searched on the hard drive for a film to watch. Oh dear; hard drives, laptops, mice and MP3 players—please don't ask me to explain all these things—it would take up many extra pages and you would not see the point of it! It's all you need to know that back in those days you could press a few buttons on a computer and whatever film you fancied watching would appear on the screen. The kinds of films I was interested in were the classics. Maybe it was all part of my carefully crafted persona. At the time I associated with an *avant garde* movement that called itself *Steampunk*. It's very hard to explain this adequately but some of us thought aspects of the modern age to be vulgar and the entertainment crass. Perhaps we were right: so much time has passed and so many matters of great import have occurred it's difficult to remember how I felt in such minor matters of style. But the upshot of it was that I was more interested in the type of films my grandparents might have watched rather than anything that was made in the 21st century.

Two films tickled my fancy that evening, both of them old even back then. One of them was called the *Wizard of Oz*, and it was about an American girl whose house gets blown away and she ends up in a magical land with talking scarecrows and witches. It was a children's film, but back then adults also watched children's films, so this kind of behaviour was culturally acceptable. Nevertheless, I decided to watch another film instead. *Metropolis* was a film made almost a century before, and it was about a city of the future where some of the people were slaves to machines. The film included special effects that made you feel like you were living inside it, and they were quite good for their time. I always felt a peculiar fascination whenever I watched it. Is that really how people thought the future would be like?

Whenever I saw it, it made me think about how the future you think you'll get always turns out different from the one you get. In *Metropolis* there's a utopia, where the privileged class of people lived. These people didn't need to work and they were all fit and healthy and had good food; it was all the other people, living under the ground and enslaved by the machines, that had the bad deal.

I don't know, perhaps that night the universe was trying to send me a warning signal as I watched that crazy old black and white film on that small computer screen. Maybe the cosmos does have a sense of humour after all, because who'd have thought that not more than a few miles away from where I was sitting there *were* real-life crazy people scheming up ways to make their own version of *Metropolis*? People who would consign most of their fellows to misery and death so that they could continue to enjoy privilege and wealth and live like the gods on Mount Olympus. Of course, I didn't know that at the time; you always get to learn important things after the point at which they would have been useful.

I think the beer and the long walk must have made me fall asleep, because I awoke later on, half-slumped in my chair. The computer screen had died and the room was in darkness. All was silent, yet something had woken me up with a start. The net curtain hanging over the window was blowing in a breeze; a faint moonlight illuminated it as it billowed silently inwards. I stood up and went over to close the window, thinking in my half-asleep state that I was perhaps in some quiet cottage in the countryside and that my parents were surely sleeping in the room next door. As I put my hands on the sash to push it down there was a bright flash followed by the sound of shattering glass. I fell backwards onto the floor as an orange light burned through the gossamer fabric of the curtain. There came the blood-curdling sound of a man screaming from the street below and more crashing sounds followed by shouts. I lay on the floor stiff with shock as the orange light was supplanted by a suffocating blackness and the room began to fill with smoke.

Yes, my nightmare had begun.

13

The sun had already risen high into the sky even at this ungodly hour, softly illuminating the rounded hills, wooded valleys and green fields of west Cornwall with a sepia light that made anyone who was awake think it was going to be a hot day. A light mist clung to the ground as the dawn chorus started up and another extraordinary day began. Cornwall. To some it was not much more than a peninsula dangling off the southern end of Britain and jutting out into the Atlantic —more of an island that you could get to in your car. To them it was ice creams and surfboards and the smell of pasties drifting from bakeries hidden down narrow cobbled alleys. These people—who outnumbered the residents tenfold— came and went every summer. The money they brought to the economy was tolerated, if not entirely welcomed, although their habit of picking up a cottage or two as an investment was something of a sore point among the locals.

Yet for others it was the one of the six Celtic nations, its language and heritage done away with, its pixie-lore and ancient magic Disneyfied, its contributions to the human project barely even a footnote in the history books. Those who kept the flame alive saw it as only a matter of time and opportunity before the spirits of the land manifested themselves once more and the slumbering populace awoke. One of those people was Art Gwavas.

Inside the little keeper's cottage that lay nestled in a crook by a gravelly path running alongside a lazy stream the young man opened one eye. He'd been awake for most of the night scribbling on a pad of A4 paper which had slipped down to the floor some time around four. The cat, sensing his master's awakened state, rose from his spot of sunlight on the windowsill, stretching first one back leg and then the other. Art sat up in bed and rubbed his eyes. His first thought was the same one that had run through his head upon awakening for the last five days, namely: *Is this all a dream?* He looked around the cottage, which was illuminated with soft morning light and, noticing the pad of paper on the floor, recalled everything. He leaned over and picked it up. On the top-most page was jotted a list of names stretching to about twenty individuals. Some had been crossed out with black ink and others had been added in the margins. A question mark was placed after many of them, and some had an addendum in brackets detailing a particular skill or asset. Those names that were higher up the page had obvious skills or assets and seemed to have come to mind sooner than the ones below, who may have possessed less tangible qualities. Thus we had Zippo (metal/electrics) and Jago (meat) near the top along with Linda (herbs etc.) and Sharkey (fish). Further down the list was Dragoş (hard man/security) and Mankell (builder), and right at the very bottom, seemingly added as an afterthought, were the names Cat and Jack. The former of these two names had a string of dollar signs after it and a question mark, and the second had the words 'scrounger/driver' added.

The second page in was headed "NEEDED" in large black letters. Beneath it, and stretching over the next seven or eight pages was a hand-drawn table featuring headings that included *Item, Quantity* and *Where?* The list was extensive and featured everything from garden tools (as many as possible) and seeds (ditto) to generators (3 at least), lighters (500) and crossbows/guns (several). Under the heading "Where?" was a list of names, most of which were the names of shops and chain stores, but also included the names of people and farms.

Separate to the pad was a larger sheet of paper on which Art had drawn out a crude sketch of the land around him. The diagram would not have been immediately recognisable to Donald Peck, the legal owner of the land, because instead of expansive fields filled with neat rows of cabbages, daffodils and cauliflowers there were numerous blocky outlines, swirly patterns and shaded-in areas, each with its own label. Thus, there were clusters of caravans and vegetable plots, ponds labelled "aquaculture," orchards stretching down to the banks of the stream and child-like depictions of strutting chickens and pigs with curly tails. The main field itself had been divided into about twenty smaller plots and beside this was a list of vegetables, grain crops and fruits, along with a picture of a marijuana leaf. A smaller field was labelled "Herbs (Linda)" and adjacent to this were some domed buildings that had animals standing outside them, which could have been sheep but might also have been alpacas. The whole map was surrounded with the stubby outlines of trees and Art had written "Forest" here just for clarity.

Art gazed with satisfaction at all he had dreamed up in the night. It was all too good to be true. This is what he'd been talking about and dreaming of for years, not that anyone would listen to him unless they were past their fifth pint. But *he* knew what he was talking about, even if they called him a conspiracy theorist, a doomer or a prepper. *Nothing wrong with being prepared*, thought Art, but then most of the folks in the circles he moved in would agree, even if half of them were too lazy to actually do anything about it. The other half of them would talk about chemtrails in the sky, a CIA plot to start a war using robots or other Illuminati stuff that he had neither time nor patience for. Baz, who wore tin-foil inside his hat to protect against MI5's brainwashing microwaves, was a case in point. Baz had never met a conspiracy theory he didn't like and Art regarded him as the kind of person who gave a bad name to *truth* theorists, such as himself. That's why Baz, despite being a drinking buddy, wasn't on the list on Page 1. Art liked to think that his understanding of the world was a little more finessed than Baz's and considered himself as having dodged the bullet of the CIA's cultural conditioning experiment that in his opinion had turned most citizens into sheep. That was the curious thing about Art, because in his case outward appearances were misleading. Despite having left school at the age of sixteen with only a couple of GCSEs under his belt, Art Gwavas had educated himself in matters he considered far more important than the rigid must-compete-with-the-Chinese fare served up by the national curriculum. He'd always been an avid reader and had developed an appetite for thrillers. When their local celebrity writer John le Carré had come to give a talk at his school about espionage and the deep state, Art, for once, paid attention. Spy novels replaced pulp fiction, which in turn sparked an interest in geopolitics. From there it was only a short fleshing-out-the-background journey to an interest in history and onwards to the history of ideas, economics and politics. Now, at the age of 28, he was one of the very few people in the area who could not only hold forth in the pub on the topic of, say, the Austrian school of economics and its contribution to the decline of Western hegemony, but also leave everyone else looking blank and not knowing what the *hell* he was talking about.

Besides being an expert truth theorist, doomer and prepper, Art also possessed considerable natural flair and ability when it came to growing things. His if-it-can-be-grown-I'll-grow-it attitude had earned him a career—if you could call it that—in horticulture. Yet despite this early promise Art had managed to go off the rails at a young age. There was no man in the house for him to look up to, his father having never existed as far as he was concerned. His mother had tried to hold things together as best she could, but with a fondness for bottles of pills and a long string of false starts and failed relationships it came as little surprise to many when she decided to walk out in front of a train. For several years prior to that fateful rainy February night she'd been working on and off as a pole dancer in a bar down on the harbour. The bar, which in actual fact was a sticky-carpeted pub frequented by horny fishermen—deceived itself to be a gentlemen's club. And pole dancing, it turned out, was something that Tracey Gwavas was rather good at on account of her being double-jointed. There were certain routines and contortions that she could perform that brought "gentlemen" from as far away as Exeter to witness. And although the job itself paid lousy wages, she'd been allowed to keep the tips, making it the most well-paid employment she'd ever undertaken. When the place was eventually shut down by the police, who were investigating an illegal amphetamine and crab racket, she found out she had become dependent on her high earnings to fuel her own narcotics habit. From that point on she spiralled downwards, going through a variety of dismal jobs and taking out payday loans to make up the difference between her earnings and her habit. It was only a question of time before she hit rock bottom, although no one could say exactly how long she'd be able to hold out...

The answer, it turned out, was about six months. When fifteen-year-old Art's up-to-the-eyeballs-in-payday-loans mother stepped out in front of the Paddington Express it seemed that his world would fall apart. There followed a year of living on people's sofas, smoking home-grown in bongs and watching conspiracy videos on YouTube. Nobody seemed to be able to get through to him until Peck, having seemingly heard about his green thumb, stepped forward and offered the young drifter a place to live and a desultory wage in return for working on his farm. The conditions were medieval, but it offered Art a chance to pull himself out of the downward spiral. At the very least it put a roof over his and Buster's heads and afforded a bit of stability after life with his chaotic mother and a year spent couch-surfing. At first Peck had treated him with a certain gentlemanly fairness, almost as an equal. Art got on with the planting and harvesting, keeping the hedges in order and doing whatever needed doing around Twin Oaks Farm, which included raising, slaughtering and processing the farm's collection of Gloucestershire old spots. The work was hard but at least Art got a place to live, a wad of money in his pocket each Friday and some experience under his belt.

Yes, Art considered, old Peck had been all right in those early days: he'd been the kind of jovial businessman who might be a bit of a swine but you could almost forgive him for it on account of his occasional generosity and his affable nature after a pint or two. All of that changed when his wife died. Art knew that Glenda wasn't well, but it had been another couple of years before breast cancer took the increasingly gaunt woman away. Peck had reacted badly to losing her. Not a Cornishman by breeding, he was originally from Surrey and had moved down in the late 1970s to marry. The farm had almost been a dowry, although Peck, an accountant by profession, wasn't much interested in it. The place had been co-owned with Glenda's brother Paul, who had lived in the cottage until he fell into a baler in '89 and came out all back to front like something out of a Picasso painting. After this, hired help was brought in, and part of the farm was sold off to pay for it. Still, with forty acres remaining, Glenda and Donald could live comfortable lives, made all the more comfortable by Peck's income as an accountant and his investment portfolio. Having made a killing letting out student accommodation in Bristol, Peck could be forgiven for thinking that he would never have to endure hard times.

Yet hard times had followed hot on the heels of his wife's death. The couple had never had children and Peck, wondering what to do with the small fortune he had amassed, placed his bets on the dot-com boom just before it nosedived. Soon after the margin calls began to come in from his broker, he found himself highly over-leveraged and was forced to cash in his property chips at a major loss just to cover his debts. To numb the pain he began to drink, and Art had a front-row seat watching this formerly agreeable man transform Jekyll-and-Hyde-like into an irascible, red-faced pig-beater. Many were the days when Peck would emerge from his farmhouse on the hill, whisky-breathed and stick in hand, to enter the sty. When all the squealing was done, more often than not Peck would come looking for Art shouting "Show yourself boy," although by then Art knew all the paces to hide offered by the farm.

One evening—and this was something he would never forget—Peck, so drunk he could barely stand up, came into the cottage holding a 12-bore. The old man pointed it at him and told him to get down on his hands and knees. Peck had then fitted him with a dog's choke chain and lead, and proceeded to walk him around the farm like a dog, shouting instruction at him. "*Sit! Beg! Play dead!*" Finally, when he had become bored with this charade he used the choke chain to tie Art's hands together behind his back around a six-foot granite gatepost, blindfolded him and told him to say his last words. Art, pleading for his life and expecting his brain to be filled with lead any second, heard the shotgun blast, followed by the feeling of a warm glow spreading across his groin area. Thinking perhaps that it was blood he had listened to Peck laughing uncontrollably, expecting the pain to kick in at any moment. Instead the blindfold was ripped off and Peck stood there with his member exposed, still dripping urine. "You filthy Cornish loser!" cackled Peck through tears of laughter. "Look what you made me do!"

The next day life had carried on as normal and Peck seemed to have no recollection of the incident. The dysfunctional man, hung-over and dishevelled, greeted Art as if nothing had happened. Art, however, never forgot or forgave, and had since been plotting ways to exact a suitable revenge on the man he called "Donald Pig." Being somewhat unemployable and forever penniless, however, Art had conceded that, for the time being, he needed to stay at Twin Oaks Farm until something better came along, which it never did.

Peck's problems had worsened as the years progressed. Whatever fortune he had once possessed was now mostly gone and one night he came home the worse for wear from the Royal Cornwall Show, not remembering that he'd been talked into borrowing money for a new high-tech combine and John Deere tractor. Practically bankrupt, he was forced to let out the farm to the agricultural conglomerate, Green Hills plc.—which had sold him the combine and tractor in the first place—and it was only a couple of growing seasons before they came and forced him to sign an agreement. Before the ink was dry they took away the new farm equipment, along with various land deeds to cover the bad debt, and the next year they came back and ripped up most of the hedges to make the fields more amenable to large-scale production. They took whatever machinery they could from the farm and auctioned it off, and Art found out that his services as a tied worker had been thrown into the deal too. Two static caravans arrived and within a week eight Romanians, six Poles and a couple from Lithuania occupied them. Art suddenly found himself promoted to the role of farm manager, although there wasn't an accompanying pay rise, and was charged with maintaining the bits of the farm in which Green

Hills had no interest—meaning the margins or the areas too steep for a tractor.

He had to help out at harvest time too, cutting the cauliflowers and supervising the workers, and on occasion he had to scythe a meadow that had been left to pasture due to its difficult access. For this he got to stay in the cottage and received a weekly pittance from Peck, whom he was sure was paid somewhat more by Green Hills for his labour. The old man himself retreated to the farmhouse or went on lengthy foreign holidays, sometimes for months at a time, leaving Art to look after the farm.

Despite not having any farming sense to speak of, Peck knew that with four crops a year, deep ploughing and such an intensive use of chemicals, the land on his farm would be good for nothing within a few short years. He didn't care. He had plans to sell it off for development, and already had an investor interested. Converting the land use from agricultural to urban would not be a problem as he'd done the work buttering up the parish council planning committee, one of whom was an old friend who'd been sympathetic to him following the loss of his wife. "This county's got to house all those blow-ins somewhere," the man had said when they met, giving him a slap on the back and a knowing wink. Peck already knew what to do with the money. He had a place in Spain in mind—a place where he could end his days in a soft alcohol haze under the blazing sun. These were the plans that Donald Peck turned over in his mind as he wiled away the last of his days in his farmhouse.

And it was this farmhouse that was pictured at the centre of Art's map. Sticking its head out of the window of the old stone building was a tweed-wearing cartoon pig with a large question mark hanging over it. Art stared at the pig and the map. After a moment a wide grin spread across his face and he reached for the pencil. Beside the farmhouse he drew another animal: a cartoon wolf with puffed-out cheeks.

He then put the pencil down and turned to Buster, who looked at him expectantly. From the cupboard Art took out the last tin of cat food and Buster rubbed himself against his master's legs in appreciation. "Looks like nothing but rabbits and pigeons for you from now on my friend," he said to the dusty black and white cat with the scarred face. He put the food in a bowl and placed it on the floor. The old cat went to it immediately, gobbling up the chunks of jellied meat hungrily. Art stroked his back. "Who's afraid of the big bad wolf?" he said, still smiling, and then began to whistle the accompanying tune.

14

The Sikorsky S-76 had reached maximum cruising speed and was nosing its way northwards through a band of heavy cloud lying over the Pennines. The helicopter's single passenger, a thin bald man in a grey suit, was holding a pair of binoculars and fidgeting. "Can we take her a bit lower," he said into a mouthpiece.

"Right you are, boss," came the static-distorted reply from the pilot. There was an instant sinking feeling as the aircraft lurched downwards. They came down out of the belly of the cloud and it took a moment or two for Ignatius Pope to scan the horizons of the land below and locate his target. There, just beyond the sober green of the Yorkshire Dales, a greyish blur spread across the land. "What's that place up ahead?" he said into the mouthpiece.

"What's what, Sir?"

"There. Eleven O'Clock. City of some sort."

Through the door to the cockpit Pope could see the pilot conferring with his co-pilot for a moment. "That'd be Leeds, Sir."

The thin man pursed his lips and raised the binoculars to his face for a closer look. Raindrops streaked across the cabin windows as Pope tried to focus on the distant city. After a few moments he asked "How low can we go?"

"How low would you like, Sir?"

Pope thought for a moment. It had been six weeks. By now the useless eaters should really be feeling the pinch. Curiosity burned in his chest making him slightly breathless. He felt reckless.

"As low as you can get without it being a danger."

"Right you are, Sir," said the pilot in his chirpy Geordie accent.

Pope put down the binoculars and spread out his hands on the white leather seat next to him. Two nights at Big Bear's place and then he'd be back. A lump rose in his throat as he considered the nature of their meeting. All eyes would be on him. He'd have to to keep his wits about him. Pope didn't like Big Bear one bit. Detested him, in fact. Could he trust him? No. Trust no one. At least he'd be able to get some running in. But they'd be impressed, that was for sure. Pope was the pioneer in all of this. He'd be lauded. He needed something to show them: a photograph.

"Here we go, Sir." The helicopter was now moving stealthily over the rain-streaked suburbs, its alignment angling front forwards as the altitude dropped. Pope raised the binoculars again and scanned the streets for signs of life. His eye was drawn to some movement along a main road. An Army truck on patrol, nothing more than that. Impatience rose up.

"Can we speed up the descent? We don't want to be late in Aberdeen."

The pilot didn't answer but Pope felt a noticeable acceleration. He gazed from the window. There. It looked like a group of people—not quite enough to be a crowd but large enough for a dispersal order. They were standing in a park, perhaps twenty of them, looking up at the helicopter.

"Get closer to that group there," said Pope.

"How close, Sir?"

Pope stared at them. They didn't look dangerous. He could make out a buggy—and was that a couple of old people sitting under blankets? "Take us down as low as you can, Jimmy. I want to see the whites of their eyes."

The helicopter began a vertical descent, as if it was landing. Pope gazed at the people through the binoculars, taking note of their appearance. He studied them as a biologist would study bacteria on a plate of agar jelly. They didn't appear as ragged as he imagined, but there was a definite neediness about them. The group was a mixture of men, women and children. The two old people were in wheelchairs under blankets, and they didn't seem to be moving. There was a boy among them too, his foot resting on a ball, and next to him a young girl wearing a ragged floral dress—his little sister?—was holding a puppy and staring up at the helicopter.

Pope felt the excitement rising in him. He had been on safari plenty of times back home, but he'd never been much interested in animals. Now, on a human safari, he could sense the thrill that others got from it. He grabbed his camera, which was sitting on the seat opposite him, and turned it on. Focusing the Pentax's 700mm zoom he trained the lens on the group of people below. They began to wave excitedly at him as the down current from the executive copter's rotary blades played havoc with their hair and clothes. Snap, went the lens shutter.

"Are we to pick them up, Sir? asked the pilot. Pope ignored him and pressed the shutter release once more.

"Bring her around a bit," he shouted into the intercom. The people turned as the vehicle manoeuvred above them. Everyone seemed excited—everyone, that is, except for the small girl with the dirty floral dress and the puppy, who stared up sadly. Pope zoomed in until her dirty tear-streaked face filled the shot. *Excellent*, he thought. *Big Bear is going to love this.*

In this way they hovered for several minutes as Pope snapped away. The group was joined by more people who came running out of houses and from across the park. Two people were carrying a stretcher with a man on it. They put it down next to the crowd and joined in with the full-arm waving that the others were doing. Pope zoomed in on the face of the man in the stretcher, which was ashen and white. "Not bad," he said to himself, reviewing the image on the miniature screen.

"Okay, get us out of here," he said into the intercom.

The copter rose once more. Pope stared at the people in the park. They had stopped waving and were standing still once again. "Adios, vermin!" mouthed Pope out of the window. He realised the hairs on his arms were standing on end. "How's it feel to be without your Big Macs and your Xboxes now?" he said out loud. A smirk played on his lips as he marvelled at his own cunning. An idea popped into his mind from somewhere. It involved Big Macs and rat poison. *Could you open the windows on these things?* It would be hilarious watching them fight one another: to see them shoving the poisoned food into their mouths. *How quickly would the poison take effect? Maybe there was something that was faster acting.* He then wondered if his staff had had the foresight to include a few McDonalds' restaurants in the critical infrastructure protection plan. He would find out as soon as he got back to London.

"I wouldn't say no, Sir," said the pilot.

Pope came back to reality. "Huh?"

"You said something about a Big Mac, I believe, Sir."

Pope pursed his lips and kept silent. *Damned northern fool.*

"But anyway, Sir, you have to feel for those folks down there don't you?" continued the pilot. "I mean, it looks like they're starving, like."

Again, Pope chose not to reply. Instead he turned off the intercom and looked through the pictures he had just taken on the Pentax.

It was another two hours' flight time before they landed in Aberdeen. Pope took his bag and got out of the helicopter, which had come to rest on the tarmac beside the sleek form of a Cessna Citation X executive jet. Minutes later they were taking off and setting a northeast course for Iceland. The plane—a gift from Big Bear—was equipped with every feature a modern billionaire could desire and even had a staff of two pilots, an air hostess and a masseuse—all of whom Pope purposefully ignored as he seated himself.

The flight was smooth and uneventful. Pope went over in his head the scenes he had observed in Leeds. He checked his phone. There was no signal, of course, but a collection of frustrated calls from the PM had piled up in the voicemail. He listened to a few of them before becoming bored and turning off the device. *Idiot.* Instead, he got out his laptop and once more went over his PowerPoint presentation. The images on the Pentax were the icing on the cake, he thought, and he played around with them until he was happy with the result.

By the time they began their descent, it was already evening, and a bright twilight lit up the sky. Peering out of the window, there was nothing as far as the eye could see in any direction, save for a harsh flat landscape fringed by the ice-tipped cones of mountains and volcanoes. The landing strip was little more than a streak of tarmac in this vast wilderness, and it always impressed him the way the pilot could touch down on it given the lack of lights or markers. Beside the strip, clusters of dark-windowed four-by-fours were parked here and there, but other than these there were no signs that they had arrived at the home of one of the world's richest men.

The Cessna came to a stop and a set of stairs extended to the ground. Pope, emerging from the plane with his bag, was immediately led away by two bull-necked security guards who walked him over to the BMW X5 that was waiting, engine running. Behind them the Cessna taxied and took off again, disappearing into the twilit sky. "How was your flight?" asked the security guard, holding a door open for him. The accent was American, with a Texan drawl. Big Bear always employed Texans, claimed they were the only people he could trust.

"Uneventful," said Pope. "Have I got time for a run before our meeting?"

The security guard shook his stubbly head. "No, Sir. Bear wants to convene at twenty hundred. Just time to freshen up first, Sir."

Pope got into the car with the two minders. He knew the drill, and Bear's place was only a few minutes from here. The guard who had done the speaking reached for the microphone bud that extended towards his mouth and spoke into it. "He's here, Sir. Repeat, Oryx has landed. All World Patriots now present and accounted for."

15

~ The Mournful Tale of Rose O'Keefe ~

I must have blacked out for a few moments following the explosion. It was the shouting in the street below that brought me round again. The first thing I noticed was the smoke. For a moment I thought the flat was on fire but then I realised it was just the curtains. There was also smoke coming in through the window from outside—the kind of thick, chemical smoke you get from burning plastic or rubber. I jumped up and grabbed a broom that was propped against the wall and with this I beat the curtains. They were thin and made of nylon and as they burned they dripped little droplets of burning plastic onto the carpet. To stop the carpet from catching fire I had to stamp on these little spots of flame—it was lucky I was still wearing my work shoes. The bedsit was lit up by an eerie orange glow and I now realised that there was something burning fiercely in the street just outside. I used the broom to jab the rest of the flaming curtains out of the window and then made sure the carpet was not on fire.

The smoke in the flat was suffocating. It was terrible, and I held my sleeve up to my mouth and tried to breathe through it. But whatever was burning outside was so hot I could feel the heat coming in through the window. Many different voices were shouting and I struggled to look down into the street. Immediately I could see what was on fire. It was a parked car. Flames were leaping out of the windows and it was burning with a white-hot intensity. I guessed that the fuel tank had exploded because there was a large hole in the rear body and smoke was pouring out. People were running around and yelling and I thought they were the youths I had seen earlier, although now they mostly had bandanas pulled up over their faces so it was impossible to say. They were shouting and yelling at one another and I counted around twenty or thirty of them. The glare from the car fire lit them up and made their shadows dance on the road.

What happened next was so shocking I can still replay it in my mind as though it happened yesterday, because right then a car came screeching round the corner. At first I thought it was going to fly past the burning car but it accelerated and changed course. Some of the youths realised too late what was going to happen next and had no time to get away. The car knocked them like ninepins, throwing one of them high into the air. There were screams and the car skidded to a halt. I stood there watching in horror, unable to move. The door of the car opened and two men got out. It was right then I realised the car was a police car. It had been driving without its headlights on and in the general darkness I hadn't seen the marking until right then. But the two policemen didn't rush to the aid of the injured. Instead they just stood there and fiddled with something on their belts. I should have known what would happen next; the shots rang out, sharp cracks in the darkness. Those who were able to ran for their lives. I saw a bullet strike one of them, dropping him on the road where he lay motionless. Four or five others, who had been injured by the car, were lying on the ground. One of them tried to crawl away and I watched in frozen fear as one of the two police officers walked casually over to him and shot him in cold blood. His companion walked over to the other injured youths and administered the same fate, killing them all.

By the time they had finished, five young men lay lifeless in the street below. The policemen calmly holstered their weapons and surveyed the scene of carnage they had created. Instinct told me to duck out of sight and so I lay curled up in a ball under the open window, my heart in my mouth. I can't have been the only witness to this crime; surely, numerous others were looking out of their windows too. I hoped—and prayed—that some higher authority would turn up and stop what was happening. But none did.

I sat there on the smouldering carpet for several long minutes before there came the sound of a car starting. There was a brief revving of the engine and then a tremendous crashing sound. An alarm went off—it must have been wired up to its own battery because there was still no electricity supply—and its pulsing electronic shriek filled the night air. There were more shouts and then another couple of shots. Despite my fear, curiosity got the better of me and I raised my head above the window frame just high enough to be able to peer out. I saw one of the officers, a burly uniformed man with a shaved head. He was carrying a large flatscreen television and I watched as he threw it down with a crash onto the road next to the body of one of the youths. The other officer stood hands on hips in the window of Microland Electronics, the computer and electronics store across the street. I watched as his colleague walked back and forth, collecting computers and televisions and throwing them down into the street around the inert bodies lying there. After a couple of minutes of this the scene was one of complete devastation— the bodies of the youths and the smashed electronics and broken glass all lit up by the flare of the burning car.

At a signal from one of the men a rear door in the police car opened and a figure stepped out. It was impossible to tell if it was a man or a woman but they took out a phone and began walking around and filming the scene. Someone began screaming from an upstairs window and one of the officers pulled out his weapon and released a volley of shots in their direction. "Anyone else want to take a look?" he shouted out loud at the dark windows. I ducked out of sight again, terrified of being shot at—I had never even seen a real gun before, let alone seen anyone shot by one. After a few moments there was the sound of a bottle smashing and another flash of light illuminated the walls inside the flat. Finally, doors slammed and with a squeak of tyres I could hear the car speed away. When I was sure it was safe to do so I slowly rose and peeped out of the window. Curtains twitched and doors slowly opened as the frightened residents emerged into the scene of destruction and soon the street was full of people.

In all the confusion everyone seemed to be trying to help the victims lying on the ground. People supported one another and wept. A woman was wailing loudly as she knelt over the body of a young man, her hands clasped over her face. She bent down to hug the blood-spattered body and I caught a glimpse of her face. In horror I realised it was Mrs Singh, my landlord's wife. The young man she was kneeling over must have been their son, Kiran.

"There's nothing that can be done for them," said a man's voice from only a few feet away. My legs almost turned to jelly and I must have yelled out in shock. Someone had managed to get into my bedsit—I could just make out his form, sitting on the bed in the gloom.

"Who the hell are you?" I managed to stammer. My voice must have sounded weak and fearful. I wanted to scream out in terror. "Get out of my flat or..."

The man chuckled slightly, his voice deep and calm. "Or you'll do what?"

I didn't know what to say. He wasn't much more than a silhouette, sitting there in the gloom. He leaned forwards slightly and his face came out of the shadows. He was older than me, but not by many years. The soft features of his face were topped by a crew cut and he wore dark, tight-fitting clothes. There was something familiar about him.

"Do I know you?"

He considered this for a moment and then replied. "We have never met face to face before but we have spoken many times."

That was when it clicked. I recognised his face from his screen avatar. He was usually one of the first to write comments on anything that I published online. Of course, what I wrote about had to do with physics and astronomy, but usually I injected a bit of something extra to spice up the prose and keep people's attention from straying. It was my shtick: the thing that probably got me the job at *The Shield*. Occasionally I talked about aspects of my own life although I was always careful not to reveal too much. Revealing too much to strangers could get you in trouble. I couldn't recall this man's real or made-up name, but did remember that he was knowledgeable about computer systems and that he often took me to task over perceived inaccuracies. "Why are you here?" I asked.

"To give you a warning," he said.

"A warning?"

He paused for a moment as if to think of how he should frame his reply. "In a few hours it will get light. Various people from the media will be here taking pictures, and asking questions about what happened and what they saw. My advice to you is to say that you saw and heard nothing. Say that you were asleep the whole time and only woke up when it was all over."

"But I can't say that," I protested. "I saw those policemen shoot those kids. I saw them smash up the shop and throw things around."

The man on the sofa sighed. "The situation is far too dangerous right now for you to expose yourself like that," he said. "The police will be here too. The actual police. Do you really want to tell them that two of their kind are murderers? What you saw tonight is just a scene being set for a wider narrative. Forces are at play and you will serve yourself far better by saying nothing."

I thought about this. Why was he telling me this? I didn't like it one bit. He continued.

"In the morning, you will recognise one of the journalists taking pictures. Approach him in the street as though you know him well. Greet him and talk to him as though you were expecting him to be there. Pack a small bag with everything that is important to you and he will drive you back to your office at *The Shield* when he has finished his assignment. When you get there, sit at your desk and wait."

"Wait for what?" I said.

"Wait for you to be called. The editor will appear around mid-morning, looking for your boss."

"My boss?"

"Yes, your boss. She will not be there tomorrow. She's got enough connections both here and abroad to escape this mess right at the start—just as others are doing right now—and so you will take her place."

"And do what?" I spluttered. I had heard the rumours about the editor. *Bad* rumours.

"You will accompany him to a press conference with the Prime Minister. It is a very important press conference so make sure you are there. And don't forget your security clearance."

"But I don't have any security clearance," I protested. "I'm an intern blogger who helps with the layout for the travel section, not some political correspondent in and out of Downing Street, you know."

"That's why I brought you this," he said leaning forward. "Don't lose it."

It was a plastic card. On it was a picture of me accompanied by some biometric data along with the word "MEDIA" in block capitals. I turned it over in my hand and on the back there was a photograph of a green-irised eye.

"Is that my eye?" I asked incredulously.

"Yes it is," he replied curtly. "Hold the card up like this when you are asked to." He held up a similar card beside his head, level with his eyes. "It works only for you, so it's useless to anyone else."

My head was swimming. I was still in shock from what I had witnessed in the street below and this was almost too much to take in. "How did you get that image of my eye?"

The man on the sofa shrugged. "We have images of almost everyone's eyes. Everyone who's ever got a passport or spent time looking into a computer screen or used a smart phone to make a Skype call. I thought you'd know that."

What he was saying chilled me. Questions swam around in my mind. Who was he? Who did he work for? Why was I being given security clearance and asked to go to a press conference? He must have seen my look of confusion.

"I know you'll have a lot of questions but they must wait until later. For now, the best thing you can do is try to get some sleep and then pack your bag. You won't be coming back here, it'll be too dangerous by tomorrow night." He stood up, as if to leave.

"What...?" I stuttered. "But I live here. This is my home."

"Don't worry," he said. "You'll be given secure accommodation. And it'll likely be a lot nicer than this place." He glanced around at the shadowy interior of the bedsit, which was almost dark now that the flames outside the window had died down. I slumped down on the chair by the window; this was all too much for me. He looked down at me and smiled as he reached for the door handle. "Just remember, you saw nothing tonight. This is an easy test—your first—and I expect you to pass it."

I was confused but I nodded all the same. Before he left I had one last question. "How will I know the journalist I am supposed to go with—the one who will take me back to the office?"

"Oh, you'll recognise him," he said. "It'll be me."

And with that he slipped out of the door and closed it behind him. There was a click as he locked it again from the outside and then it was just me, alone in the dark bedsit with a racing heart and a mind full of foreboding.

16

In future times it would come to be known as the Great Shock. When the power went off most of the people of Great Britain simply did not know what to do with themselves. At first they joked about it, but as one day without power turned into two, and then three, uneasy thoughts began to surface. To begin with, people were angry about missing their favourite TV shows, but such fripperies were soon replaced by fears over where their next meal would come from. When hunger began to stalk the nation, people became angry and demanded to know who was to blame.

Then, as if by some miracle, on the morning of the fourth day the electricity began to flow freely again from wall sockets everywhere. The nation collectively breathed a sigh of relief. Phones became hot from overuse, fridges once more emitted a reassuring hum, and people everywhere hunched over computer screens hungry for knowledge and reassurance. TV screens across the land all displayed the puffy-faced Prime Minister as he addressed the nation and identified a target for their fear and wrath. SMS messages and emails went out by the million informing people of their duty to turn in anyone they suspected of being involved with Gaia

First and citizens were asked to do their bit by conserving electricity, water and food as much as possible.

And then, after this brief respite, the power went off once again.

This time people worried not about missing soap operas or baking shows; instead, they wondered what they were going to eat. Those with cash to spare queued up for hours at shops and supermarkets to buy what they could, but after only a week the shelves were empty. The perennially underpaid shelf stackers, checkout staff and security guards suddenly found themselves in positions of power as tins of food, pet food, sugar and eggs—which had sky-rocketed in value in only a week—mysteriously disappeared from shelves across the land.

Great lines also formed at petrol stations, even though the signs read "closed" and the staff had walked away. The pumps no longer worked, but that didn't matter to the swarthy men with diesel generators and garden hoses who were on hand to suck out the precious fuel and apportion it out to frustrated drivers who handed over their watches, iPhones and jewellery. Eventually, even the generators ran out of fuel and were left dumped on the forecourts along with the lines of idle cars. Some drivers stayed with their vehicles for a number of days, fearing they would be vandalised or stolen, until hunger and thirst forced them to walk away.

In less than two weeks a black market had come out of nowhere and established itself as the only source of basic supplies for a desperate nation. Pharmacies were raided during the night and local police forces—who in most areas had lost both radio communication and fuel for their vehicles—were powerless to intervene. In some cases they found themselves being confronted by gangs openly brandishing pistols and sawn-off shotguns, and there was little they could do but retreat as fast as they could.

Fights broke out everywhere. Whether they were over a loaf of bread, a can of petrol or a chocolate bar, they were usually vicious and sometimes fatal. But thirst was the true scourge. An area of stationary high pressure had settled over the British Isles, forcing temperatures up into the low thirties and driving up the demand for water. The taps in most areas, which continued to flow freely for days after the power went, began to slowly dry up as the water towers, no longer replenished by electric pumps, started to run dry. First the water turned brown, then it stopped flowing altogether, and that's when the great thirst took hold of everyone. Some drank the water from their toilets, swimming pools and fish tanks, while others made the fatal mistake of draining radiators and drinking that. In London and other large cities, people flocked to the rivers and ornamental lakes and drank the water directly. Cholera made a comeback in no time, adding to the extent of the emergency. Only those with the correct identifying codes were allowed access into the various warehouses and storage depots across the land where they were allowed to eat and drink freely of what they found therein. Nobody thus permitted inside was allowed to take so much as a glass of water away with them, and many simply gravitated to these distribution centres and stayed there, awaiting further instructions.

But the lack of fresh flowing water caused other problems for the people. It came as something of a shock to most people that the sewage system—for so long unseen and unsmelled—did not function all by itself. Toilets, with no water to flush them, became blocked with wads of tissue paper and excrement, as did a great many underground pipes, which had been constructed with a narrow diameter under the assumption that there would always be a powerful diesel pump at hand should they become blocked. The old brick sewers beneath the streets of London, built by the Victorians, stopped flowing and became clogged with a great mess of

127

faeces, sanitary products, plastic junk and fat. "Rats," said the people. "It's only a matter of time."

And the hunger—how could this have happened? In the space of a few weeks the country went from a land of plenty to a zone of famine. When they looked in their cupboards and pantries, most found that they had only enough food for a few days. Some had none at all. There was nothing to cook on, either. Gas and electric cookers had stopped working, and people heated up food on whatever they could find that would burn. Furniture was broken up and burned in barbecues, and people learned the hard way what was flammable and what was not. Soon enough the smell of burning plastic permeated the air in most towns and cities as trash was burned in piles, along with clothes, rugs and anything else that would catch fire. A great fear fell upon the people that they would starve.

And it wasn't just food that was lacking. With all the pharmacies closed, there was no way the chronically ill could obtain supplies of whatever drugs they needed. The black market soon ran out as well. Some of the more unscrupulous operators mixed up pills and sold fake ones, with predictably fatal results.

The psychological shock alone was too much for some. After only a couple of weeks of maddening hunger, thirst and uncertainty some could no longer cope with the situation and sought a quick exit. They used the last few litres of petrol in their cars to asphyxiate themselves, taking the lengths of hosepipe from others who had gone before them, using them to pipe exhaust into their cars. Whole families jumped from bridges and cliffs, clinging to one another as they fell. Many more simply sat on their sofas staring at the dark television screens until they themselves faded away—and in the years that followed it became common to enter abandoned houses and find blackened couches encrusted with the mouldering remains of human beings.

The Army came. They spread out across the land, handing out parcels of food, bottles of water and copies of *Fortitude*. Mostly they were young men and women, full of courage and sympathy to begin with, but as the situation continued to deteriorate they soon became weary and wary of the crowds. The Army personnel had food and fuel and clean water supplies, because without these things they could not function. Initially they went after the black marketers, the thugs selling cans of petrol and bottles of painkillers, and the store raiders and the gangs of youthful burglars who had spilled out from the council estates and into the wealthy parts of the towns and cities. The soldiers dug latrines, tried their best to unblock the pipes, put corpses in body bags. They stood on street corners chewing gum and holding their guns. They set up mobile field hospitals in which Army doctors and surgeons attended to those most in need, and they drilled boreholes into the ground and pumped up water.

But the armed forces could only do so much. Little did they know that they were a mere public relations exercise for the benefit of foreign observers. As the weeks rolled by with no sign of the power being restored, even the Army began to run low on supplies and was forced to reduce rations. Confrontations with the lawless became increasingly ugly, with numerous instances of gunfire being exchanged. The soldiers commandeered town halls, putting up barricades and razor wire outside them, and great snaking lines—sometimes miles long—began to form outside them. Desperate people held out their hands like beggars and pleaded with the tired soldiers to be given more rations for their sick relative or their bedridden child. Every now and again one of the people would get to the front of the line and quote a number to the duty officer. They would then be taken away and led to a hall or a school gymnasium, where they would join others awaiting the next convoy to take them away to their assigned position. They didn't know where they were going but they reasoned that anywhere would be better than the hell they had found themselves in. Many were inwardly ashamed, knowing that they were leaving others behind, although they each had justifications for escaping the misery and reassured one another that they were contributing to something greater than themselves. "It'll all be over by Halloween," they said.

And then there were the animals. With no food to feed them, people began to turn their pets loose on the streets in the vague hope that nature would provide. In most instances, it didn't. Dogs fell back on their wolf-like instincts and formed large packs that howled and barked throughout the dark starlit nights. The howling and the darkness awoke a deep primeval fear in the people, a fear that had lain buried in the crawlspaces of their minds for so long. Then the Army began to shoot the dogs, and there were few who complained, even if they were their erstwhile owners. There were fewer still who questioned the meat that began to appear on the black market; chunks of fur-lined flesh wrapped in plastic bags and passed discreetly between buyer and seller. Rabbits, said the sellers, or perhaps squirrel, pigeon or pheasant, although some of the "rabbit" seemed to have remarkably long tails, and who'd ever seen such large-boned squirrels?

A few lucky places were visited by the Red Cross and other international aid agencies, who set up scores of tents in farmland and provided a basic level of subsistence for a few thousand families at a time. But most were not so lucky, and anyone with the means to get away did so. With airports on emergency backup power, international flights only came to evacuate foreign tourists and businesspeople. It was possible for others to get a seat on one of these departing planes, but the price was high and immigration officials demanded to see proof of adequate funds before allowing British citizens to board their planes. For anybody lacking the funds to get away by air, a relationship of convenience sprang up between the nation's fishermen and those who wanted to get out.

Finding themselves able to refuel in neighbouring countries, trawler crews and those with private pleasure craft were tempted by the easy and profitable business of smuggling goods and people. It was easy enough to conduct this type of business, and on any given day many a UK-flagged boat left port in Holland, France, Belgium or Ireland, their holds filled with food, alcohol and a miscellany of everyday consumer products, returning the very next day with a number of suitcase-carrying passengers. It wasn't long before foreign vessels got in on the act too, picking up passengers from a variety of small ports along the coasts.

Word soon spread and camps began to appear, many of which were filled with Europeans wanting to get back to their own countries. It was a dangerous business, and there were quite a few instances of drowning, but the money was too tempting and there was a continuous supply of people wanting to get out. The vessels were sometimes boarded by the Coast Guard and impounded if contraband was found, but the smugglers knew that the British maritime forces would do nothing to halt the flow of people wanting to leave. If anything, they seemed to encourage it.

It was under these conditions of austerity and misery that Art Gwavas and his small band found themselves living. They, and others like them, holed up in similar situations throughout the land, sought to pick the seed of triumph from between the teeth of adversity. Whether or not they would succeed was to be decided by the hand of fate.

17

Caterina Ana Gutierrez—known to her friends simply as Cat—sat down by the stream and sighed. If an observer had been hiding in one of the nearby willows, secretly spying on the young Argentinian woman from a position of concealment, they would have seen her close her eyes and cross herself as her lips silently mouthed the Trinity. After this they would have observed her sitting in quiet contemplation or prayer for some minutes before her eventual reanimation, whereupon she would sit with slumped shoulders by the little brook, breaking off twigs from an overhanging branch and tossing them into the water.

Despite her peaceful attitude, Cat's inner world was in turmoil. It felt as if the hand of God had reached down from above, taken her by the scruff of the neck and dumped her into a colder version of hell. She had, after all, only come down to Cornwall for a short break from her fully-lived life in London, and now she found herself almost two months later living in a van parked under a tree and eating a revoltingly unhealthy diet of tinned food and Pot Noodles. Yet the only alternative to this food was a disgusting vegetable and bean slop cooked up in a huge pot each day by a woman with hairy legs and no front teeth. Cat's boyfriend Jack, who only a few weeks ago had been a respectable if a bit boring middle manager with a nice set of wheels, now seemed to have fallen under the spell of the straggly-haired human weed who called himself Art Gwavas. This bad impression of a pirate would take her formerly-respectable boyfriend out each night raiding local shops, warehouses and abandoned vehicles. What had her life come to?

There were now about forty of them living on the farm together. Cat and Jack had been the first to arrive—although it was only supposed to have been for a few days. A week later the others began to turn up. Caravans arrived. Not the kind of well looked-after caravans you saw pitched up at Caravan Club sites, but the kind of ramshackle tin boxes that looked home-made and had blackened chimneys poking through their mouldy roofs. Others turned up in cars packed to the ceiling with possessions, and it wasn't long before there was a whole collection of ragged-looking young people, some with dogs and babies, infesting the place. At first Cat didn't care. She gave them wan smiles when they spoke to her and accepted the food they made for her when she was hungry. She was focused on getting out of the situation as fast as she could and was willing to put of with the social discomfort as long as it didn't last too long. Of course, she kept hearing about all the problems upcountry—after all, people talked about little else—but she felt that, for all the panic, things would soon sort themselves out and get back to normal. She imagined Jack coming back one day to tell her how the lights had come on again and the petrol stations were filled once more. In her mind she pictured the drive back to London, her key unlocking the front door to her flat and the long, long hot shower she would take to wash off all the filth and weariness of these last few nightmarish weeks.

But Jack never came home and said these things. Instead he said things that disturbed her and gave her sleepless nights. He told her about stores that had been ransacked and about people wandering around in the night begging for food. He told her about howling dogs silenced by soldiers' bullets, and about seeing a burning house with a family trapped inside as people looked on helplessly. Once, he came home bruised and covered in blood. "There was at least ten of 'em," explained Art, describing how their paths had crossed with a gang of young men looting a big box hardware store in the small hours. "We was lucky to get away like we did," he added.

Whenever Cat challenged Jack about his nightly excursions, he would get defensive. "We have to eat," he would say, or "Art's got a plan—you'll see soon enough." She hated him for it, but he was all she had and she was frightened too. Sometimes "the boys" went off on foot, dressed all in black like a band of ninjas. But more often they would go off in Art's pickup truck, crawling off slowly into the night with the headlights off.

Petrol, in those first few weeks, wasn't a problem. They would head off with some syphoning tubes and a dozen empty jerricans and come home with a dozen full ones. But they could only store so much petrol at a time, even though they stole more jerricans as time went by. In any case, petrol trips became less frequent as the number of cars with any fuel left in their tanks petered out. Mostly they came back with food and building supplies. Large pits were dug in the woodland and lined with roofing membrane. Into these was stowed whatever booty had been liberated in the night. There were thousands of tins of food and great sacks of pasta, rice and beans, as well as a great miscellany of random food-stuffs including everything from fresh vanilla pods and birthday cake icing, to dried vegetarian sausage mix and carrier bags filled with little glass jars of spices.

As the numbers on the farm grew, so too did the numbers of those who went off on these raids. Soon there were up to ten men going off each night (Art forbade women to come along, saying it was "men's work") and the amount of goods began to pile up. Before long there was half a DIY store of tools and materials stowed in the old barn, along with dozens of pieces of corrugated steel, hundreds of bags of cement and lime plaster, electrical cable, car batteries and solar panels. The old red-faced man who lived in the farmhouse would occasionally come out and stride around their camp bellowing for Art. Cat called it a camp, because in her eyes it looked like a refugee camp. In the centre stood the little stone cottage where Art lived. Radiating out from it was an ever-expanding shantytown of caravans, cars and stick-built shacks with tarps for roofing. The old man, who always wore black Wellingtons and the same threadbare tweed suit, would wander around and regard the squalor with clear distaste until Art could be located. On these occasions, Cat noted, Art would disappear inside the cottage to return with a cardboard box loaded with food and bottles. There would then be some discussion and the old man would walk back to the farmhouse not to be seen again for the next three or four days; and then the scene would repeat.

In general, Cat and Art warily avoided one another the way cats and dogs living under the same roof do. Cat disliked practically everything about this sinewy Cornishman who had entered her life so dramatically, and yet, if she were to be completely honest, she harboured a certain grudging admiration for him. It was an admiration buried deep, never to be revealed, but it was fascinating to watch him execute his haphazard plans. The fascination ran deeper: how could such an anarchic-looking individual—one who existed in an ever-present haze of marijuana smoke—achieve so much with so little? Yes, he had a certain devil-may-care attitude that seemed to attract followers, and yes, she could even admit that he was possessed of a certain *unusual* intelligence, but how could this add up to anything useful in the world? Art, it seemed to her, was lit by some kind of inner fire that she couldn't fathom. He seemed to have as many projects on the go as there were dreadlocks on his head. How on earth, she wondered, could he be out for most of the night breaking into and raiding shops and burgling holiday homes, and then find the energy during the daylight hours to dig latrines, erect buildings and chop wood, before spending most of each evening knocking back bottles of cider and rum and talking with endless enthusiasm about some "glorious future" he seemed to think was coming? There was no doubt about it, the man was an enigma to her, but as long as he was allowing them to stay there and was providing food for them, she would just have to learn to put up with him.

Which is more than you could say of the way the others viewed Cat. Gemma, who cooked the evening "slop," was one of the first to articulate the growing communal unease about the scowling Latina who rarely helped out. "I mean, what can she actually do?" she said in exasperation one evening as several of them sat around the campfire. "She sits in that van or by the stream most of the day, she doesn't help out with the digging or the building. I'm just wondering how long we have to put up with her."

"You're right," said Zippo, a young balding man with a thoughtful face. "I could do with some help making that waterwheel work. And someone with nimbler fingers than mine would probably be better at doing the wiring jobs."

"Yeah. Or even just some cleaning would be nice. This place is a shit hole," added Linda the herbalist. "I say we make her clean the compost toilets."

"Or else chuck her in them," said Gemma, making everyone laugh.

Cat retreated into the shadows when she heard this. That night she lay awake tossing and turning. By about three in the morning she found herself whispering "*Querido Dios, ayuadame!*" She whispered the words until her face was streaked with tears. *Why is this happening to me?* Her tears were not tears of sadness, they were tears of anger and frustration. Why was she talking to God, she demanded of herself. Why was she asking for His help when she told herself she did not believe in Him? Hadn't she left all that nonsense behind at convent school? She bit her lip and tried not to think about God. But it was no use. He was testing her. Pushing her to her limit. How would she react to His challenge?

She got up. She was hungry. Starving, in fact. She wasn't sure she could face another day of the revolting stew that hairy-legged witch cooked up in her cauldron every day. The grey dawn arrived and she shivered. Autumn was coming. Jack, sweaty and exhausted, lurched into the van and fell onto the bed. He was asleep in moments. As he slept Cat gazed at his face. He looked so innocent. Even the beard he had started to grow made him look cherubic, like a young Che Guevara. *Would he make a good father?* she asked herself. And then, *When should I tell him?*

She went outside and walked over to the campfire, which was smouldering weakly. A couple of figures were sleeping beside it and she went over and took a blanket from the ground, placing it around her shoulders. Taking a bundle of dry sticks she threw them onto the embers and watched as the fire began to kindle once more. She walked over to the stream and half-filled the large copper kettle and then took it back to the fire and placed it on the iron hook that hung above the flames. *I will show them*, she thought. *But first I must make tea.* With these thoughts Cat went over to sit silently beside the little stream that ran down from the hills, past the farmhouse and through the farm where there had once been a water mill. She gazed at the water flowing past over the stones and around the gentle bends on its ceaseless journey to the sea. *I must be like the stream.* She looked over to the fire and saw one of the figures stir a little. From the broad shoulders and blonde beard she recognised the figure of Jago.

Jago, the son of a local butcher, would often come back from the fields with rabbits and pigeons and pheasants. She went over and shook his shoulder. "Jago, wake up. I need you to do me a favour."

Later that day, the occupants of the farm returned from their daily labours to hear a great crashing of pans and an almost continuous stream of low-level invective in fast Spanish. They saw a great long trestle table made from sheets of plywood and with sawn logs for seats, and on it were a great many plates and dishes, along with a motley collection of cutlery, chipped mugs and bottles of wine. The campfire had grown in size during the day and now included a number of smaller pits filled with glowing embers, and on each of them was a pan with something bubbling in it. Beside the main fire stood the figure of Jago, who was wearing a bloodied apron and a toothy grin. With both hands he was turning a giant spit, and on the spit above the coals was the glazed carcass of a pig.

Soon people came to watch and gawp at the dervish-like figure of Cat who was running around stirring a pot here, adding something to another there, and issuing short, sharp orders to Jago who grinned back at her and said "¡Sí, señorita!" Nearby, one of the large trapdoor lids that hid a food stash lay open and a mass of foodstuffs had been rummaged through and removed. "Sit down, please!" Cat snapped at her observers, and they did as she said. "Here," she said, slamming down plates of hot pan-cooked bread. "Eat!" She poured each person a mug of wine. "Drink!"

As the sun set over the copse that lay to the west of the small farm, all forty of them had assembled, lured by the smell of roasting pork and the growing sound of voices raised in increasing merriment. Art Gwavas appeared and slid quietly onto a stool at one end of the great table, his eyes wide in silent wonder. Cat was a blur of activity, placing huge slices of roast pork in piles on the platters and serving them up with hot apple sauce. There were baked potatoes stuffed with morsels of meat, bowls of steaming soup, three different pots of food: one with stewed rabbit, one with beans, nuts and berries and one with a hearty mix of sausages and mushrooms cooked in red wine. There were braised fresh crayfish, pulled out of the stream, and chestnuts roasted on the open fire, all served up with shots of apple brandy. Everyone tucked in and ate until they could eat no more.

All in all it was the best meal that anyone could remember—not least because it was the first proper meal they had eaten for two months. When most had eaten their fill Art stood up and proposed a toast in the chef's honour, which included a lengthy and slurred retelling of how they had first met. When he had finished, everyone cheered and raised their glasses once again in the direction of Cat, who had by now sat down to enjoy the fruits of her labour. "Speech," someone cried and Cat stood up, wiping her mouth and blushing in the firelight. "I don't have much to say," she began, uncertainly. "But what I will say is that when I came here I thought it was only going to be for a few days. Now I can see that we are probably going to be together here a lot longer. So I think we all have to get along." Everyone became silent and the only sound was the crackling of the fire.

"If I'm honest, I don't really want to be here," she continued. Jack looked up at his girlfriend and gulped. "In fact, I'm used to living in a spacious apartment in a big city, not a refugee camp. I'm used to having clean bathrooms and not being cold. I'm used to having things done the way I want them to be done." She paused for effect and looked at the collection of faces around the table. "Now, I can put up with not having any of that. But what I can't put up with is your *shit food!*" She pointed her finger at the assembled crowd who stared at her uncertainly. "If I *ever* see a bowl of slime being served up with a lump of turnip it will be you lot turning on that spit over there. Got it?"

140

Cat gazed at them with mock ferocity, but she couldn't prevent the faintest smile turning up the corner of her lips. And then someone, seeing this, began to laugh, and the laughter was infective and rippled through everyone present. Cat began to smile and waved her finger at them like a prissy schoolmistress. "So if you ever start serving me your *shit food* again I am out of here and you can cook for yourselves again forever!" There came more laughter and cries of "Never!"

"Wait 'till Peck sees what you've done to his pig!" shouted someone, pointing at the rack of empty ribs hanging forlornly from the spit.

Cat grabbed a carving knife off the table and raised it in the air. "Then you tell him where he can find me!" she shouted, and the night air was filled with the commotion of forty wine-addled men and women—and more than a couple of children—cheering and thumping the table. Some Romanian pickers, seizing the moment, pulled out fiddles and began to dance around the fire and sing. One of them—the wife of the first fiddler—leaped on the table and began to stamp out a beat and clap her hands. It wasn't long before everyone else joined in, even though nobody knew the words. Art struggled into the circle of dancers holding a wooden crate. He slammed it down on the table and the lid flew open, revealing the bottles of rum inside.

"Drink yer fill everyone, let's party like it's 1999!"

That night there was no raiding mission. In fact, precious little got done the next morning either.

18

~ The Mournful Tale of Rose O'Keefe ~

It was just like he said. I managed to get a couple of hours' sleep but no more than that. When daylight came and I looked down from the window of my flat, all I saw was ruin. It was like something out of a war zone—there was broken glass everywhere, smashed electronics and two burned-out cars. People were standing around in shock. I looked over to where I had seen Kiran Singh bleeding out his life and saw a dark stain of congealed blood on the road. I packed my bag.

Soon the street was filled with journalists and people wearing suits. The Mayor of London was there, flanked by police officers, and he was talking to a group of journalists, some of whom were filming him. I caught a few phrases of what he was saying: "Nip it in the bud"; "unacceptable behaviour by a violent minority." Then I saw my visitor from the night. He was photographing the darkening bloodstains and talking to some of the residents.

A journalist from a rival newspaper came up to me. "Hey, I've seen you around before," he said. "Don't you work with Chloe?" I replied that I did. "So, you must have seen all this last night then," he said, gesturing at the carnage. "I mean, you live right here, don't you?"

I had no idea how he knew where I lived but I played dumb. "I didn't see it at all," I lied. "I was so tired last night after walking all the way back from the office and I went to sleep with my iPod on shuffle—it must have been playing all night."

"Oh, I see," he said, looking slightly disappointed. "Let me know if anything comes back to you." Then he spotted someone else he knew and moved on.

I hung around in the background until my night visitor was ready to leave. He had a motorbike—one of the powerful ones high-speed parcel couriers used back then—and he handed me a helmet. "Put this on and hold on tight." The ride was exhilarating. We sped through the streets of London and I hung onto him to avoid falling off backwards when the bike accelerated. I'd never ridden on a motorbike before, and I liked it. There was almost no other traffic apart from the occasional police car prowling around. We sped over a bridge that crossed over the North Circular Road—a great arterial road that snaked like an asphalt collar all around London— and I was shocked to see a great convoy of Army vehicles moving along it. There were tanks and troop carriers, as well as cammouflaged Land Rovers and pretty much every other sort of military vehicle you could imagine. The motorbike skidded to a halt and my mysterious abductor gazed intently at the convoy as it passed. "What are you doing?" I asked. "Why have we stopped?"

He pointed at his head without diverting his gaze. "Helmet cam," he replied. "We're trying to build up a picture of movements." The convoy passed and we were off again, accelerating through the weirdly deserted streets.

I realised we were not going south towards the office, but in the other direction towards the northern suburbs. I tapped the man on his back, but he either didn't feel it through the thick leather jacket he was wearing, or chose to ignore me. I wondered if I was being taken somewhere where something bad would happen to me. The thought worried me. Pretty soon we were heading up a steep hill past rows of shops and houses, and then the bike slowed and we mounted the pavement. Next thing I knew we were speeding across a grassy park and heading towards a huge monolithic building that looked like a sprawling palace with a giant Eiffel Tower-like transmitter pointing out of it. We cruised up to it and stopped.

"Get off," said the man. I did as he said, and pulled off the helmet as well, which was quite suffocating. He did the same, cutting the engine and putting the motorbike on its stand. I looked around at the view, trying to figure out where we were. From our position one could see most of London spread out before us in the morning sun.

"Why have you brought me here?" I asked. "I thought we were going straight to the office."

"I brought you here to tell you something important."

He sat down on the grass, which was still wet from the morning dew, and motioned for me to do the same. "You've passed the first test I set you, which was to act dumb about what happened last night and come with me, however now you have a much more important task ahead of you. But first I must tell you something of what is afoot."

"What is it?" is asked innocently. "What's happening?"

The man turned to face me and fixed me with his eyes. "It's complicated," he said, "and I'm not going to overload you with information just yet. I'll tell you what you need to know, but no more than that. We must be quick."

And then he told me things that I could scarcely believe. He told me that the nation was under attack, and that from now on I would have to question everything I heard or saw. He said I should believe no one, and that if he himself should suddenly disappear then I should use my intuition in deciding what was right and what was wrong and should never mention this encounter to anyone.

"But who are you?" I said. "And why should I trust you?"

He smiled at this. That was the first time I noticed he was quite good-looking. When his face was not looking so serious he had a warm, shy smile and soft brown eyes. With all that leather gear on and the head camera and radios hanging off him he looked like some kind of space trooper from the kind of low-budget television science fiction programmes they used to make back then. His dark hair was cropped short and he had on a pair of sunglasses that he'd pushed up above his forehead so that I could see his eyes as we spoke. "My name is Robin," he said, "and I'm one of the very few people you can trust from now on."

But did I trust him? Well, if what he was saying was true —and it turned out that it was—then I had very little choice. Everything that he said would happen did happen. He told me that I was scheduled to be screened and that I had better get my act together. I should repeat, whenever given the chance, that I loved my country and hated those who wanted to attack it. Other than that I should not express any opinions at all. If asked what I was interested in I should say "science" and if asked "Would you do anything that went against your principles if it was for the greater good of the nation?" I should answer "Yes" without hesitation.

"What's the most upsetting thing you've ever seen?" he asked me. "A thing that shocked you and made you angry."

I frowned. "Why do you want to know?"

"Just think of it. It's important for you to tell me."

I thought for a moment. I'd led a pretty sheltered life up to that point and couldn't think of anything I'd seen that was truly shocking.

"There must be something," he said.

I closed my eyes and thought harder. A memory came to me. There was the time was I was ten or eleven and had seen

146

our neighbour beating his dog in the back yard. I'd seen the stick rise and fall and heard the whining and the yelps. I'd tried to stop it and had called out, but my father had held me back and locked me in the house: "It's none of your business, Rosie!" The dog had later died from its injuries. That had made me angry. I told Robin.

"Good."

"And now, think of something that made you happy and calm. Try and picture it in your mind, let the feeling of it sweep over you."

That was easy. I imagined sitting by the fireside at Auntie Susan's, shelling chestnuts and sipping hot chocolate with marshmallows as some cheesy Christmas programme ran on the TV. I loved being at my aunt's house. She wasn't ever judgmental and she was forever interested in what I thought or said. Being there over Christmas was the best. It had been one of those cosy moments that I felt could have lasted forever.

"Good," he said. "Now when you are shown images of or asked about anything to do with protestors or the kind of people we might for want of a better word call "hippies" or "crusties," I want you to think of the dog. Think of it yelping in pain, the stick rising and falling. Feel the anger flow through you. Practise it now."

I had a few misgivings but I screwed up my eyes and did what he said. Reliving the scene brought back all those feelings of anger mixed up with helplessness and sorrow. I saw the stick rising and falling, heard the vile man shouting at the poor dog, which was chained up and unable to defend itself as the blows rained down. The memory was vivid: *too* vivid. I was ten years old again and I began to cry like that little girl I had been.

"Excellent," said Robin.

"What?" I said, wiping the corners of me eyes. "It was horrible."

Robin continued unperturbed by my distress. "Now, I want you to forget the dog and the stick. I want you to think of the calming scene in your aunt's living room that Christmas. Feel the warmth and the love surrounding you. There is nothing bad in the world right now as you remember. Take your time and let the feeling wash over you."

Again, I did as he said. After a minute or so I really felt like I was there in Aunt Susan's house, shelling chestnuts and drinking hot chocolate with little pink and white marshmallows floating on top. I opened my eyes to see if Robin was still there. He was.

"Now, I want you to bring that thought and those feelings to mind every time you are reminded of Britain. It might seem weird and counter-intuitive but even if it is pictures of nuclear missiles, or police attacking miners, or an image of Winston Churchill or Margaret Thatcher I want you to recall those feelings of warmth and safety."

We practiced this a few times, with him slowly saying strings of unrelated words and me trying to feel either anger or love when one came up that related to the two "hot topics," as he called them. It wasn't long before I felt emotional and exhausted. "I've had enough of this game," I said. "I don't want to do it anymore."

"You're not ready yet," he sighed "but you get the idea and it'll have to do. Just remember how important this is, but try to relax and you'll be okay."

We got back on the motorbike and he drove me across the city to the office. I sat there at my desk, bag at my feet, staring at the black computer screen. The editor appeared right on cue and asked where Chloe was—just like Robin had said he would—and I said she hadn't turned up. It was true, she hadn't. "Do you have security clearance?" he asked. I raised my card so he could see it. And that's how I ended up being brought along to my first and last press conference instead of my boss.

I don't remember where that press conference took place. All I remember is that it was in some kind of anonymous concrete building in a nondescript part of the city. We were driven there in a big black car with a police motorcycle escort, and when we got there I showed my pass and they let me in. The room was a sea of faces. Most were journalists, some of them recognisable from newspapers and television. There was a long table with some important-looking dignitaries seated at it, waiting for the Prime Minister to appear. Robin was there too. I remember seeing his face in the scrum of photographers in front of where the PM would soon speak. He spotted me too and gave me a kind of half-wink across the crowded room. TV cameras were rolling, and I wondered how they got the electricity for all the lighting. The whole thing was being recorded.

When the PM came into the room, everyone went silent. I remember looking at him and thinking how shiny-faced and worn-down he looked. It was odd seeing someone in the flesh who you'd seen countless times on TV before—it made them look human and frail. The Prime Minister made his speech and I tried to write down notes on a pad I had taken from the office. But it was hard to do as I found my hand was trembling and my notes came out all spidery and unreadable. I felt like a child in a room full of grown-ups and I didn't feel comfortable at all. Having watched this sweaty man bang his fist on the table at the end of his speech and then stride angrily out of the room, it seemed as if the world was going crazy and I had accidentally been placed in the middle of the storm. There was so much I didn't understand back then, I was so young and green.

Afterwards most of the journalists and dignitaries dispersed, but the editor told me to sit and wait for a moment while he went and spoke with one of the officials at the table. I could see him pointing at me as he spoke, and presently a lower-ranking official touched me on the arm and asked me to come with him. I was led into a quiet back room and told to wait. The room was small and uncomfortably warm, and there was only a single grimy window letting in light. There was a cheap table in the room with a plastic chair on either side of it. The man told me to sit on one of the plastic chairs and wait. Again, I was worried. I wondered if I had been seen talking to Robin that morning up on the hill, and considered that I might be in trouble. I sat and waited and fretted.

After some time a woman came in holding a folder spilling out papers. "Miss O'Keefe?" she asked, and I nodded. "Good," she said. "Thank you for being here." She had one of those fake plastic smiles that you can see right through. She asked me if I was okay and whether I wanted a drink of water. When I said I was fine she again said "Good," and sat down opposite me across the table. She gave me a broad smile that revealed her very white teeth and then opened the folder. Thus began my interrogation.

It went on for about an hour and I got the impression that she was rushing through the questions as if I were one of many. The questions were strange to me, but I did my best to answer them as dishonestly as I could just as Robin had advised. At one point the woman got up and left me to fill out some sheets of multiple-choice questions about ethics. They were designed to wrong-foot me by asking the same basic questions over and over with slightly different wording and it was easy for me to see through the system that lay behind. After that, a computer was brought in and I was asked to watch a video. A cable was plugged into the USB port that was connected to sensors which were taped around one of my fingers, as well as a blood pressure monitor cuff that was attached to my forearm. "Don't worry about this, just relax and watch the video," said the woman.

The "film" was merely a series of still images with some soft classical music playing in the background. It was just as Robin had said. The images slowly faded in and out before my eyes. Houses, sheep, the Moon, a cup of coffee, a game of cricket, a group of muddy protestors sitting in a tree holding a banner... I froze. In my mind I tried to picture the dog; the brutal man next door and his cruel stick; the yelps of the dog —not much more than a puppy—my father pulling me away: "It's not your business, Rosie!" When I opened my eyes the image was fading to be replaced by a baby wearing an all-in-one costume. There was a cat stalking a bird in a garden, a man wearing a bow tie and playing a piano, a pile of springs sitting outside a factory, a cartoon mouse, a British soldier in a desert training a gun on a man in a turban... again I shut my eyes and forced the image of Auntie Susan and her living room at Christmas. It came easily—I could taste the hot chocolate with the marshmallows floating in it, feel the warmth from the coal fire, hear my aunt singing gently in the kitchen next door.

I opened my eyes once again and the image had changed to a beach with a bucket and spade on it. And on it went. By the end of it I felt as emotionally drained as I had in the morning. I wasn't sure I could keep summoning up feelings at will. The door opened and the woman came in again. "Let me just take that off you," she said in a soft voice, and there was the sound of Velcro being ripped open. "I'll be back in a few minutes, she said, taking the computer with her.

I sat there feeling lonely and timid. *Just what was going on?* I kept asking myself. I wanted to be back home with my family, for all their faults; wished I had never come to London in the first place. The door opened and the woman came in. She sat down again and placed some documents between us, as well as a pen. The smile was gone. Fixing me with a pair of cold blue eyes she said "Rose O'Keefe, I want to offer you a position working for us."

"Who is 'us'?" I managed to splutter.

"The Ministry of Information," replied the woman coldly. "Right now, your country needs you."

Ministry of Information? I thought. I had never heard of such a thing before. But what else could I say? I had to accept. And that was how I ended up being pulled deeper into the spider's web.

19

As summer slipped into the melancholy tidings of autumn, the people began once more to learn about darkness. With no more electric lights to keep away their fears, or soap operas and sports to numb them, they stumbled blindly in this new darkness and learned who they truly were. To keep warm, they stood around oil drum fires at night, watching as sparks rose from burning furniture into the dark velvet sky to mingle with the stars that so few of them had ever seen. The sudden lack of illumination caused terrors and nightmares; it seemed as if a million demons had been let loose on a defenceless world. Once the plug had been pulled on their thousand-Watt lifestyle, the TV screens had darkened, the Internet had fallen silent, there was nothing left to distract them from what they had done to the world, and from that realisation many of them simply lost their minds. There was no terror on Earth so great as the fear that struck at their hearts and reminded them of their lowly place in the natural order of things. Hunger, the threat of violence, shivering nights of cold—these were as nothing compared to the death of the artificial world they had once inhabited. Only a few embraced this new darkness and saw within it a sense of marvel and a new kind of hope. The rest, paralysed by fear, were already dead.

Yet it was not dark everywhere. A thin web of concentrated light persisted in bright clusters and nodes as the tide of electrical power retreated to only those places considered necessary for the continued survival of the privileged few. Military bases remained powered, as did some ports, airfields, power stations and urban centres. One such centre was the old financial district of the City of London and its environs. Here, in the great glass and steel towers, the light shone brighter than ever. Rooms in offices and houses were still illuminated at the flick of a switch, computers, espresso machines and hoovers all functioned as before, and even the television sets worked, although there was precious little to watch. At ground level the streets were filled with pedestrians pulling suitcases as a great reorganisation was being worked out. To say that chaos ruled would be to misunderstand the deep forces that were at work reconfiguring society, redesigning and rewiring it. People shuffled and queued and argued with one another as they attempted to find out their function and insert themselves into this new paradigm. Police officers blew whistles and conducted the traffic—because here there were still taxis and ministerial vehicles, delivery vans and cycle couriers, Army jeeps and motorbikes.

And although much of modern life in Britain had ground to a halt, the same could not be said of the rest of the world. Anchored offshore were dozens of cargo ships that had arrived from China, Brazil and elsewhere. They waited patiently while their agents and middlemen screamed into telephones at one another across continents attempting to collect payments and transfer funds. Supplies from smaller vessels streamed in from ships unloading at Tilbury Docks, and on lorries from continental Europe aboard the freight trains that still ran through the dark tunnels beneath the English Channel.

"We must make everything feel as normal as possible for those on the inside," said Ignatius Pope as he looked down from his new office on the 40th floor of 31 St Mary's Axe. The Prime Minister put down his coffee cup and grunted. He was seated on a spacious red leather sofa, sitting with his legs crossed and gazing at the back of Pope's silhouette as he stood against the window. The two men were alone in the room, save for a white cockatiel in a cage in the corner. The PM cleared his throat.

"We were bloody lucky, Pope, you can't deny that. We've only been downgraded one notch, although I had to sweat blood to secure that."

"Luck had nothing to do with it," replied Pope. "Thanks to your energetic reassurances and the Bank's opening up the spigots we've got a nice little rally on our hands. Interest rates will continue to remain low and—again, thanks to your statesmanship—the pound is even courting safe haven status once more. All in all, I'd say we should be congratulating ourselves on a job well done."

The PM stared at Pope venomously. How could he be so blasé about this? "It's all just number crunching to you, isn't it?"

Pope turned to face the PM, one eyebrow arched as if in incomprehension. "Are you unhappy with our progress in some way, Sir?"

"Unhappy?" spluttered the PM, rising to his feet. "They're dying out there. I'm up to my eyeballs in reports of dead people in hospitals piled up in corridors, of yobs running around smashing up shops and burning cars, and of people—good, honest people with jobs and families and pet cats—looking like fucking concentration camp survivors."

"With respect, Sir, you already knew the likelihood of this in advance. You didn't think they would just melt away quietly, did you?"

The PM glared at him again. "No, but neither did I expect it to be all so... messy."

"I see," said Pope.

"And what do you actually do when you're not gallivanting around in your helicopter? What do you *do*? All you can do is pull out charts and talk about figures and economics and financial crap. But it's me —*me*—who has to stand up in front of Parliament day after day and lie about what's really going on. It's me who has to meet up with families pleading for power to be switched on in whatever godforsaken hole they come from, and it's me that has to get down on my hands and knees and kiss whatever Chinese or American arse that's hovering in front of my nose at any given time of the day or night. So—yes—you could say I'm unhappy. I'm pretty. Fucking. Unhappy."

Pope stared at the PM, taking note of his goggling eyes, the bulging veins in his temple and the way sweat had formed on his forehead. At this rate he'd probably be gone from a cardiac arrest in a few months. Who would replace him? He had a few ideas but considered that this was a weak area in his strategy and one that would need some careful attention over the coming weeks. He adopted a tone of reconciliation as he addressed the PM. "I'm sorry you feel that way," he began. "We could suspend Parliament, if that would make you feel better. I believe it is possible if the circumstances are sufficiently extenuating—which they most certainly are. And although both of us knew that this situation wouldn't be easy, I completely understand how hard it must be for you at the moment."

He eyed the man a little to see if his words were having an effect. They didn't seem to be, so he made his way across the room and sat down on the sofa beside him. "Sometimes we can't see the forest for the trees, you know. We get too close up to things and it doesn't make any sense anymore."

156

The PM shot him a suspicious glance. "What do you mean?"

"You came into power on the ticket of reform. You're a reformer through and through, and that's what you'll be remembered for. And being a reformer isn't easy. What about your man Oliver Cornwell?"

"Cromwell," corrected the PM.

"Yes, that's him. How do you think he dealt with it all? How did it feel for him taking on the Irish? Did he lose sleep over the royals and those uppity Protestants?"

"Catholics," interjected the PM once again, shooting him a glance. "History is not your strong point, Pope."

"Catholics, Protestants—whatever. The point is that he had the resolve to see it through. He wasn't afraid to break a few eggs to make an omelette. And God knows we've got a few eggs to break to make our omelette."

The PM looked at Pope's imploring eyes, softening a little. He hated this shiny-headed South African. Called him a nerd and a freak and lots of other things beside. But, boy, there was some brain in there inside that bony cranium.

"Come over here a minute," said Pope, standing up and beckoning the PM over to a spot beside the floor-to-ceiling window. "Look out there and tell me what you see."

The PM looked for half a minute before replying. "It's England," he said. "Britain."

"Exactly," said Pope. "It's England. It's the country that forged the greatest empire ever known. When we were fighting the Boers it was to England we looked, and it was England that dragged India, as well as half the world, away from superstition and black magic and brought them development. It was England that kicked Abo butt in Australia, and it was England that made America what it is. It's cricket and football and tennis and cups of tea. It's Blake's Jerusalem—the promised land."

The PM felt a lump rising in his throat and the hairs on the back of his neck stand on end.

"And Shakespeare too. What was that line in Richard the Second again—how does it go? 'This land of little princes, this other Eden, this demi paradise...' you know the one?"

"This sceptered isle, this happy breed of men," continued the PM, remembering Eton. "This seat of Mars."

"Yes, yes, exactly!" said Pope animatedly. "Mars—the god of war! This is the country that stood up to Hitler, the country that brought enlightenment and progress and technology to so much of the world—that's what I see out of this window."

"That's what I see too," said the PM.

"But I see something else too."

"What?"

Pope turned to face him. "Eaters," he whispered. "They're like the woodworm in the throne. Like fleas in the coat of a majestic lion. Parasites. There are so many of them. How many, no one knows. Gobbling and eating and breeding and spreading across the face of this country like bacteria. Eating, breeding, demanding more. They are ignorant of their own history, and they have no love for civilisation or learning or military glory—all they can think about is how much they can milk the system. They don't work. They sit around all day in front of their television screens and they whine and complain and shove fast food down their throats. Everything about them spells ignorance and entitlement, but they are not grateful to those who feed them. And they, Sir, are killing this country, just as surely as termites will undermine the grandest of houses."

The PM nodded and gulped, making his Adam's apple move up and down in his throat.

"With the Luftwaffe we knew how to kill them," continued Pope in the same vein. "We knew that if you shot them down, they died. End of. If only it were that simple with those who threaten this great nation today. Or should I say once-great nation?"

The PM shot him a wounded glance.

"Think of them," whispered Pope. "Think of them when you are reading those reports. Think that with the death of every welfare sponge, that's one less ungrateful eater to feed. With every slob that perishes, that's one less unemployed, unemployable gutbucket raiding the nation's coffers as he putrefies on his sofa playing on his Xbox and stuffing his mouth with fried chicken and chips. With every nose-ringed peacenik who throws herself off a bridge, that's one less person voting for the socialists, one less ungrateful toad squatting on the graves of your ancestors."

The PM was silent. He looked out at the vast sweep of land stretching to the horizon. Yes! Like moths infesting a tapestry, they were invisible to the naked eye. Yet they were there. Hidden. Munching. Mocking. He turned to Pope. "I'm sorry," he said. "I didn't mean to appear like I was wobbling. It's just the pressure gets to me every now and again."

And with that he turned and left the office, leaving Pope alone but for the cockatiel in its cage. Pope turned to the bird and winked. "Too easy. Just too easy."

20

The scavenging party set off in the old blue pickup truck just after dawn on a cold and clear December morning. Art, Jack and the four others each had in their minds what was needed. More plywood, corrugated steel, bricks and other building materials; all of these things were required for the huts that were being built on the farm. There were also re-quests for medicine to relieve the symptoms of the flu that had gripped around a quarter of the community, leaving people coughing and shivering beneath blankets. Zippo, who sat beside Art in the cab, was on the hunt for electrical wire, and the two Romanians sitting in the back would spend the day stripping tiles off the roof of a farmhouse that they reckoned was abandoned. Dragoş, the larger of the two, was a fierce-looking man with a gentle soul. Tribal tattoos curled around his biceps, and his sledgehammer-like fists had been put to good use more than once during their recent salvage operations. His friend, Petru, was an altogether more wily character who held a degree in law but had been working picking cabbages in order to save up the twenty thousand euros demanded by the Bucharest mafia for a permit to prac-tice law. Apart from Jack, the final member of the salvage crew was the butcher's son, Jago, who needed to get a parcel of food to his parents who were sitting things out in their council home in Penzance and hoping that normality would be restored one day soon.

On a good day, it was only fifteen minutes to Penzance from Twin Oaks Farm, but taking the back roads allowed them to avoid the checkpoints and to scout out potential salvage sites along the way. Thus the journey was more like an hour. With the windows wound down, Bob Marley's *One Love* spilled out into the still morning air as this ragged band of opportunists needled their way down country lanes and sent rabbits fleeing at every turn.

Jack felt good; giddy, even. He couldn't quite understand why he felt so good but his rational mind no longer seemed to be in control and he was just happy to let the feelings flow forth. Not six months earlier he had been tied to a life that was beginning to slowly suffocate him. Friends were getting married, taking out mortgages and resigning themselves to a life of compromise and self-imposed repression, and it seemed Jack would soon follow them. He'd seen it again and again: friends had got married and turned into walking corpses almost overnight. It was as if someone had put a spell on them. And his job, with its never-ending rounds of meetings and team-building events, seemed pointless and stifling to him even though he had recently been promoted to an easy managerial position within Corporate Communications. Perhaps it was his subconscious fighting back, but Jack had found himself dreaming of escape. It felt to him as if the walls were closing in on him, like that scene in the trash compactor in Star Wars, and he had sought a kind of measured escape at weekends, setting off in the van with his sea kayak on the roof. Cat had added a bit of spice to the bland reality of his life. And though most would have seen a successful young man with a bright future, Jack regarded his destiny with a sense of impending dread. *"Is this all there is to life?"* he would ask himself on a regular basis, and the answer society offered back was "Yes." *"Then I must be happy after all,"* he concluded reluctantly.

Except that he wasn't. With no parents to advise him, no joy in his work and no discernible ambition in the sphere of career development, it had seemed to Jack that he was on a treadmill to nowhere. Seasons passed and birthdays came and went. Holidays to far-flung places were undertaken, work targets were met in a timely manner and gifts were dutifully purchased for friends' weddings as he watched his friends shuffle off one-by-one into married life. His own life had become dull and two-dimensional and, like a piece of white bread, lacking in fibre and nutritional value. "This is as good as it'll ever get," people said, as if reading his fears, and deep down he feared they were right. He had reached the stage in many a young person's life where they must entertain the thought that they must let go of their dreams, abandon any notion that free will would play anything more than a cameo role from now on, and contemplate the sober reality of an existence inside an elaborately gilded cage.

And then the lights had gone out.

It was as if a switch had been thrown that extinguished one reality and illuminated another wholly different one. In this new reality Jack was cast as a different character on a different stage. No longer was he the clean-shaven suit sitting in a meeting about marketing strategies; instead, he was the hirsute raider wearing a dirty baseball cap and living in a van with a Latina girlfriend. He was the fisherman of the tribe, heading out into the bay to catch bass and mackerel, hauling them aboard as the setting sun illuminated the impossibly romantic scene in which he suddenly found himself living. And for the first time in his life he felt as if he were part of something: that by working with the others to build shelter, catch food, salvage materials—all of this added up to something, whereas before there had been nothing.

The pickup came to a halt and Jack was brought out of his reverie. They had pulled up at a farmhouse that lay down a gravelled drive. It was an old stone building, half-obscured by a row of evergreen oaks, and a slate sign beside the gate gave the place's name as Chy Pengersick. Bob Marley was silenced and Art leaned out of the window, craning his neck to speak to the men in the back. "This is the place I was telling you about. Let's go and give 'em a knock."

The pickup crawled slowly down the drive and pulled up beside a large wire-framed sculpture of a dragon placed on an overgrown lawn. Art cut the engine and got out, stretching his body and yawning. The others hopped out of the back of the pickup, leaving Zippo sitting in the front seat engrossed in some paperback he had picked up. "Right," said Art, "let's see if anyone's at home."

The five men walked up the path to the front door, their feet crunching on the gravel as they went. From the outside the house looked neat and well kept. Clearly it had once been a small farmhouse, bought and renovated by the type of comfortably well-off people wanting nothing more than some peace and quiet and a place to practice their creative talents in retirement. The door was painted a sparrow egg blue and there was a brass knocker cast as a stylised dolphin. Art put his hand on this and rapped three times. They all stood there in breathless silence waiting for some sign of life from inside. There was none. Art rapped the brass dolphin again, this time much harder. When again there was no reply he pushed open the letterbox and shouted through it. "Hello. Anyone there?"

There was a faint sound of movement, followed by a crash, as if an ornament had fallen. "There," said Jack. "Did you hear that?"

Art pushed open the letterbox again and put his lips to it. "We've got some food, if you'd care to open the door. Just asking if you've got any materials or tools you'd want to barter with us."

There was movement at the curtains of an upstairs window and a pair of frightened eyes looked down. It took a moment for them to notice the pointed ears and the whiskers.

"Just a cat!" laughed Jack.

Art turned to the others. "Doesn't look like anyone's at home then. Right, Dragoş you know what to do." The heavyset man walked back to the pickup and returned with a sledgehammer.

"Health and safety say stand back," grinned the Romanian as he swung the twenty-pound head at the blue wooden door. A single blow was enough to splinter it, sending it flying open and half slamming shut again. The men looked at one another nervously.

"Zippo, you coming or what?" shouted Art to his friend who was still sitting in the car with his nose buried in the book. He replied with a blank stare and a noncommittal grunt. "Feckin' lazy tosser," shouted Art back at him. "Okay boys, let's have a look around," he said, addressing the others. They stepped inside the house. The ground floor was mostly open plan, with a large lounge and kitchen off to the side. One wall was lined with bookshelves, and Art went straight over to them. He scanned the spines of the books, pulling a few out, examined them and then tossed them onto the floor in a pile. "Modern art," he said, sounding disappointed. "Pages are too shiny to wipe your arse on, but they'll burn okay."

Jack looked around, unsure whether what they were doing could be classed as burglary. Up until then it had been just shops and warehouses, but now those places had all either run dry or were too risky. With each passing week there seemed to be more soldiers and thugs patrolling the area, making the art of scavenging more difficult and risky. Houses were the second tier stores of value, Art had said, and the more tucked away and remote the better.

The room he stood in was sparsely furnished. Abstract paintings hung on the walls and glass figurines occupied niches that were thick with dust. There was a fireplace with an inglenook and a large iron wood burner sitting on slate flagstones. Near it, on an end table, there rested a framed photograph. Jack picked it up and examined it. The picture showed a grey-haired couple flanking a young woman wearing a graduate's cap and gown. The three of them stood in a sandstone arch, with bright sunlight making their faces seem radiant with joy. Jack knew just by looking at them that they were the residents of the house and that the young woman was their daughter. He placed the picture back on the table and moved into the kitchen.

Where the lounge space had been neat and tidy the kitchen was a different matter entirely. Dirty dishes covered every surface and the floor was a mass of broken crockery and glass. A bin in the corner overflowed with empty tins and other food packaging, and dead flies littered the floor. The cupboards were all open and all empty. Everything had been eaten—right down to some jars of English mustard and tartar sauce. *This is what it looks like to starve,* thought Jack.

"Watch out for all the cat shit," called Art from the living room. "It stinks." And right then the cat they had seen at the upstairs window came running down the stairs and dashed straight out of the front door. It was a black and white thing, skinny as could be and with matted fur.

"He was in a hurry," said Petru. "Let's see what he was getting away from."

Jack didn't want to go upstairs, but followed the others reluctantly. Art, as ever, went first, calling out a tentative "Hello?" Jack was no more than halfway up the wooden staircase when there came a cry and Jago, who had been right behind Art, came flying down the stairs again with his hand over his mouth, almost knocking Jack over in his rush. "Oh man," said Art in a low voice.

Jack could already smell the bodies as he reached the top of the steps. The two elderly artists were lying beside one another on the bed, their skeletal hands entwined beside them. On the female cadaver, bony black-fleshed legs poked out from under the hem of a floral dress—the same dress Jack had seen only a few moments earlier in the picture downstairs. The woman's eyes were closed and the mouldering skin around her mouth was pulled back in a rictus grin, making her teeth protrude. Around her head, long grey hair spread out on the pillow. The mouth remained slightly open and Jack was horrified to see large black flies buzzing in and out of it.

Alongside the body of the woman lay what remained of her husband. The picture on the mantel had showed a jovial-looking bearded man with round glasses and a round belly. It was difficult to reconcile the man in the photograph with what remained of him now. Although he was wearing a dark suit, all of the flesh below the waist had been stripped away, leaving a collection of gnawed bones that ended in a pair of leather shoes with the laces still primly tied. Of his head, nothing much remained except a bearded lower jaw and a blackened strip of side-head, with the rest of the man's skull and brains embedded in the oak headboard behind him. The shotgun he had used in his last moment had fallen from the bed and lay on the floor. Maggots crawled in the cavity where the man's tongue should have been; pulsating and moving over one another in a way that made Jack want to retch. Arrayed around the two cadavers on the bed was a collection of objects, including a crucifix, some crystals and more pictures of their daughter. Art walked gingerly over to the other side of the bed and reached down to get the shotgun. "Fellow won't be needing this any more, will he?"

Jack felt dizzy and nauseous. He had seen plenty of other dead bodies in recent month—mostly on his trips into town—but nothing like this. Usually they were wrapped up neatly in sheets and placed by the roadsides for incineration by the Army. He'd only seen a few that had been left out for the seagulls and the rats, and there'd been the one of the woman half-eaten by crabs on the beach. But these people... it was too easy to relate to them. All of the positive feelings he had felt that morning had been replaced in an instant by a mounting sense of gnawing horror. It was only by an act of will that he managed not to buckle at the knees and fall over. "I check the other room," said Petru quietly.

They left the bedroom and closed the door. Art was wandering around the house and muttering things to himself. "Roof tiles, cooking stuff, windows." He walked into the lounge and stood in front of the inglenook fireplace. "Dragoș," he called out. "You reckon we could get this woodburner out? It's Scandinavian. Those things are worth a fortune but it's gotta weigh half a tonne at least."

"We try," said the big man, rubbing his chin and staring at it.

"Let's do it then," said Art. "I'm just going out the back. There has to be a workshop here somewhere. There's probably some tools and God knows what else there."

"Wait a minute," said Petru. "Don't you think we should say prayer or something for this people? I mean, we just come in and raids their house. Seems, how you say, disrespectful?"

"You're right, my man," said Art. "Where's a freaking Christian when you need one? Jago? He's a Sunday school boy." He shouted out Jago's name several times but there was no reply. "Zippo? Get in here and help lift this," he shouted, but there was still no reply from outside. "What happened to those two dolts? I'll go and get 'em."

Art turned and walked out of the house swinging the shotgun in his left hand. But he didn't get far. He could see the other two by the car on the drive. Something didn't seem right. They were sitting sheepishly on the gravel, back to back, and it looked like they were holding hands. He didn't have much time to think about it.

"Drop the weapon and get down," screamed the soldier. Art fell to his knees in shock and raised his hands. "Caught you red-handed you bleeding Johnny," he snarled.

Art looked up at him. He was young, clean-cut, and his trembling hands held a service pistol that was pointed directly at Art's face. "We was just checking up on these folks," murmured Art. "Turns out they don't need no more help where they've gone."

"Bullshit," snapped the soldier. "You were robbing, plain and simple. I heard you."

"We was merely liberating what was no longer needed, that others—that is, those of us still with a pulse—might make use of it so as to keep said pulse going on a bit longer."

"Shut up!" yelled the soldier back at Art. "You were robbing, and by the looks of you I wouldn't mind betting you'll be passing whatever you find straight onto Barleycorn and his scum."

Art stared at the soldier as if nonplussed, and then his face creased into a smile. "Oh come on, surely you don't believe all that crap do you? Did you not go to school before you joined the Army? You believe that, you'll believe anything." He looked up at the young soldier, who still looked nervous and had shaking hands. The man's eyes glanced to the side. "John Barleycorn, my arse!" said Art contemptuously.

"Do it, Barney!" yelled the soldier.

"What?" Art managed to half turn his head just in time to see another soldier step out from behind a rhododendron bush. The rifle butt connected with the base of Art's skull and as he went down he was enveloped by blackness.

"Nice one," said the first soldier to the second as they stood over Art's unconscious body, grinning. "Are there any others?"

21

~ The Mournful Tale of Rose O'Keefe ~

Following my interrogation by the woman with the plastic smile I was taken in a minibus to the campus of a university somewhere in the city. It wasn't just me in the bus—there were at least a dozen others and they all seemed as young and shaken-up as I was. I assumed that they had been selected to work for the Ministry in the same manner as me and for that reason I didn't trust any of them. I was still carrying my bag, which contained not much more than a change of clothes, some toiletries and my laptop computer. I hugged it to myself as we drove along—it felt like the only link I had between my old life and whatever new life I was being tossed into.

At the university there were scenes of chaos. I remember seeing students milling around and being herded onto buses. The others and myself were led into what must have been the students' halls of residence and allocated a room each. My room still contained the possessions of its former tenant, and there were books on shelves, clothes in the wardrobe and posters on the walls. I sat on the bed and wondered what was going on. Outside in the corridor there was shouting and raised voices and after a while the door opened and some men came into the room. One of them said "Alright darling?" to me and winked. "Don't mind us, we're just doing what we've been told to do. It shouldn't take a minute." They ripped down the posters from the walls and picked up all the books and clothes, stuffing the lot into black plastic bags and dragging them out into the corridor. Once they were done, the room looked like a prison cell.

The next few weeks were probably the most boring of my entire life. The university was emptied of students and the halls gradually filled up with people who had been enlisted to help out at the Ministry. At least, that is what they kept telling us. In a way, we were all different, but there were many ways in which we were all the same. For a start, we were all young. Most of us were shell-shocked and apprehensive of one another to begin with. Our phones and computers didn't work and there was only a very weak electrical voltage in the residential halls most of the time—enough for the lights to work but not much else. We didn't know what we were supposed to be doing, and so we spent much of the time sitting in the canteen playing cards, drinking weak instant coffee and talking. People missed their families and their friends and I remember a lot of tears. Some ran off and did not return, while others were sulky and moody, refusing to talk to anyone. I quickly realised that my profile and background did not match those of my colleagues. For a start, many of them were quite privileged. They spoke with upperclass accents and talked about things I had little conception of. Common amongst them was a real hatred of people from the lower social classes—of which I counted myself as a member. I didn't let on about my background, but I need not have worried as most of their bile was reserved for "John Barleycorns," meaning anyone on whom they could pin the blame for shattering their world.

We knew about "John Barleycorn" from the newspaper *Fortitude*. It was full of articles about explosions and sabotage and we all consumed it each week with great relish as there was precious little else to read. The university library had been locked up, so there was no way we could get books out. From *Fortitude* we learned that large parts of the country were blacked out, and that many areas in the cities had erupted in rioting and looting. The Army had restored order, we were told, but were maintaining a high presence to prevent further looting. I kept my mouth shut about what I had seen with my own eyes in Tottenham, and nodded as if I agreed when people expressed their opinions about what should be done to quell the riots. "They should just drop bombs on the inner cities and be done with it," seemed to be the general consensus.

In those early weeks and months the food they gave us was truly awful. Mostly it was tinned stuff: watery meat pies, mushy pale vegetables and fried fritters of spam. That was the thing that people complained about the most. Many of them were used to eating in expensive restaurants, or shopping at the kind of huge stores where thousands of different foodstuffs were sold, and so being reduced to eating such a meagre diet was a real shock to them. I alone ate better than the rest. You see, the university was set in extensive parkland and I spent much of my time exploring it and seeking out its hidden corners. There were trees with nuts on them, hedges covered with blackberries, a gnarled old apple tree hidden behind a wall and plenty more besides. Of course, I kept all this to myself, as I had no desire to share with anyone else. There was a birch tree in this park and I was drawn to it for some reason. I loved its silvery bark and the gentle beauty of its golden leaves as they fell to the grass. As I watched those leaves float down I wondered about my parents and my family, and I wondered where Robin was, because I felt like he was the only person I could trust. For some reason, even though I was sad and confused, when I sat beneath that tree I felt comforted in some way. It was as if that tree somehow sensed my sorrow and wanted to reach out and console me.

After a few weeks our lives became more organised. One day we were led into a large sports hall that was to be our place of work. It had been refitted as a vast open office with rows of desks and seats. On each desk there was a computer, some writing materials and a buzzer. When we were all seated at these desks—as if we were about to sit some kind of exam—we were told to keep quiet. After some moments a man was ushered into the hall and stood before us on a raised stage at the front. He was exceptionally skinny and the skin on his head was as shiny as a snooker ball. I recognised him from the newspapers and remembered seeing him at the press conference I had been to. Some of the others clapped and cheered as he took his position at the microphone, as clearly they knew who he was and respected him a great deal.

He gave us a pep talk and outlined our roles. We were eager to help out in any way, so that normality would return and we could get back to our old lives. What's more, we had been bored out of our minds for weeks, and so were relishing the chance to engage our brains at long last. The skinny man compared us to the code breakers of the Second World War. He said that while the men were away fighting, it was the efforts of these code breakers that had really paid off and helped us to win the war. In the same way, he said, we had a chance to help repair the damage done by John Barleycorn and his ilk and get the country back on its feet again. When he spoke he had a peculiarly jerky way of delivery. He waved his arms around a lot and he had a strange accent, if my memory serves me. Every now and again he had to stop talking as people clapped. When he said our job was to help "root out the perps and bring them to justice," there were whoops from some.

Over the next week we were given basic training. Every one of us was given a pile of tickets at the start of each day with the name of a single person on it and a code to access their data. Using the computers we were able to look at every email those people had ever sent, everything they had ever bought using a credit card, their movements as recorded by their mobile phones and every post and comment they had ever put on the type of electronic discussion groups that were then termed "social media." They gave us lectures on how to identify suspicious behaviour or seditious comments, and trained us on how to spot networks and affiliations. In most cases, people had nothing to hide. They put pictures on their computers of their kids and pets, told one another of their holidays and what meals they were eating, and bought the latest fashionable clothes, books or consumer items. These people were given ticks beside their names in green ink and, at the end of each working day the stony-faced supervisors gathered them up and took them away.

But for every ten or twenty green ticks there was one who warranted further investigation. Usually these people had been "pre-identified," meaning that computers had already singled them out and put them in a category named "Further inquiry." It could have been that they had used listed trigger words on their emails or social media, or it could be that they had bought books or watched online videos that were on a list. Maybe they just had a strong correlation to known subversives in their networks. There were a thousand or more things that we had to check, and it was usually a case of narrowing it down.

If you identified a JB—that's what we called them, it stood for "John Barleycorn"—you pressed the buzzer on your desk and a supervisor would come over and take the ticket from you. These tickets were taken to a higher administrative level where they were checked out in greater depth. If we correctly identified a JB1—i.e. a prime suspect—we would get a reward in the form of a voucher. This could then be traded in for better food or some other reimbursement. Other allurements on offer included new clothing, better food, or—occasionally—alcohol. Identifying a JB2- i.e. someone who had engaged in seditious behaviour of a less serious nature—earned you a seat at the cinema. Each Friday night they put on films for those that had earned it, although usually the films were not to my taste. The JB2s might have, for example, criticised a trade pact, signed an online petition, or bought a book from an author on a disapproved list. It was low-level stuff (and I can't have been the only one wondering about our own records) but people were keen to build up their collection of entitlement vouchers. Apart from the rewards we were all assured that we would be paid at double the national minimum wage for our efforts, with our earnings stored on computers for the day when our job finished, which we were told would be 'no longer than six months away'.

Of course, doing this job put me in a terrible dilemma. I knew that what we were doing was wrong, and I knew that I was only there because I had managed to fake my feelings under interrogation. And *What role did Robin have in all of this?* I wondered. I figured that he and his friends had hacked into a computer system and got me included on a list of people to work for the Ministry, but I didn't know how or why. It felt dreadfully wrong to be poring over a stranger's personal life and assigning them a green tick or a red cross based on what I could uncover. But what other choice did I have? We were under strict orders and I don't know of anyone who disobeyed them. What would happen to the people marked down as JB1s, I fretted. Sometimes, in my pile of tickets, I would discover someone who should certainly be a JB1 according to the criteria by which we were ordered to abide, but I would feel ashamed of myself and give them a green tick instead. Maybe it were a single mother organising a boycott of a company that experimented on animals, or perhaps it was just a young student doing something to try to make the world a better place. The choice was painful. Even with the cases where I felt little sense of empathy, I dug deeper into their electronic profiles to discover some aspect of their character which might absolve me of my guilt. Maybe it was a JB1 who also liked looking at degrading and exploitative forms of pornography. In that case I'd give him a red cross. If I couldn't find anything I tended to give them the benefit of the doubt and got out my green pen. But who was I to make such decisions? I was not God. I had no right to decide people's fate.

And yet, if I saved too many it would raise the suspicions with the supervisors. I had to keep my tally respectable, otherwise I myself would be investigated and some of the JB1s I had let slip through the net might be given a second look. What would happen to me? I doubted very much that I would have escaped with a light slap on the wrist.

This work continued for months and during that time I neither left the campus of the university nor spoke with anyone I trusted. One evening in December I slipped out of my room and walked the grounds in the dark. I loved walking at night as it gave me a sense of freedom after the claustrophobic atmosphere of the university. It was a cold evening and it really felt like winter. I located the birch tree—leafless now against the stars—and sat beneath it. And, like on so many other visits to this tree, I wept. I wept for what I had lost; I wept because I was afraid; and I wept because I felt lost and I didn't know which way to go.

"Don't cry."

It was a soft voice and I looked up, startled. Had the tree just spoken to me? I remained frozen, unable to move a muscle.

And then he appeared. Robin moved out of the shadows towards me. "You," I gasped. There were no words. He moved forwards and embraced me. He looked much the same as when I had seen him the first time, with his leather jacket and his cropped hair. In the moonlight his face appeared ghostly and white, like some kind of night spirit. I buried my face in his chest and continued to cry. He soothed me, stroking my hair and holding me firmly to him. After some time I looked up at him. His face looked so kind, and there was understanding and warmth in his eyes—things I hadn't seen for a long time.

"What's happening out there?" I asked. "I have to get away from this place. I can't go on here."

"I'm sorry I wasn't here sooner," he said. "Other business kept me away, but I am here now." He looked down at me with his dark brown eyes, one of his hands still resting on my hair. "Things are worse than you think out there. Chaos is running free."

"What shall we do?" I said. "Can you get me out? Take me back home?" I implored him. I didn't know what power he had or if he could truly help me.

He looked at me in a strange way for a moment before speaking. I thought I could see compassion in his eyes. "You have no home now, Rose. You must do as I say and in return I will try to protect you. Do you understand?"

I nodded, trying to take in what he had just said. "*You have no home now, Rose.*" I felt shocked. What did he mean? But I was even more shocked when he leaned forward and kissed my lips. I recoiled, but his hand was still around my back and I couldn't go far. I could see his eyes glinting in the moonlight and he moved forwards once more. This time I did not recoil. As our lips touched I felt a connection between us —it was as if two lost souls were suddenly joined together.

I had never kissed a man before. In fact I had assumed I would probably never kiss a man. But here I was. It was as if this man could see deep down inside me to observe my naked soul and my fears. I don't know how long that kiss lasted but there was a crack nearby, like the sound of a twig breaking. We both looked up and I saw the silhouette of someone darting away into the night. Robin looked at me. "We were being watched," he said. "I must go."

"Don't go," I begged him.

"For both of our safety I must," he said, already retreating to the shadows. "I will contact you again. And soon."

"How soon?" I asked. "And how will you contact me?"

"You will see," was all he said. And then he was gone, leaving me standing there in the cold moonlight, my face still streaked with tears. I felt puzzled and anxious. But I also felt elated: soon I would leave this place.

22

A faint wisp of steam rose from the coffee cup on the leather-topped desk as a man with fingers like sausages flicked through a set of papers set before him. Occasionally the man would sigh and emit faint curses under his breath as he scribbled notes down in the margins of the papers. A buzzer rang and a woman's voice informed him he had a visitor. "Who is it?" said the PM wearily.

"It's *him*," came the reply.

The PM rolled his eyes before replying. "Give me two minutes, Clara."

"Okay," said the woman.

This is it, thought the PM. I'm going to put that weasel in his place once and for all. He took a sip of coffee, relishing the sweet black liquid, and then stood up. Standing in front of the mirror above the ornate marble fireplace he corrected his tie and looked into the eyes of the face reflected back at him. *Steely*, he thought. *Man of steel.*

He slipped one hand into his trouser pocket where it encountered a smooth pebble. It was a pebble he had been carrying around wherever he went of late, having picked it up on a beach on the Isle of Skye. They'd been up there at his sister-in-law's holiday cottage for Easter. It had been the therapist's suggestion that he find some kind of talisman to relieve the chronic stress he had been suffering from—and the amazing thing was, it actually seemed to work. He fingered the Scottish pebble between his thumb and index finger, feeling its sublime texture and unyielding hardness. *Be like the stone, smooth and hard and unyielding.* He closed his eyes and allowed himself a moment to picture the beach in his mind's eye. It was all so perfect; the distant mountains, the salty smell of the kelp on the shore, the brisk wind whipping up the little waves on the dark blue sea. He flared his nostrils and breathed in deeply. *This is where I will go when this whole business is over.*

There was a faint knock at the door and the PM's eyes snapped open. "Come in," he said. When Pope entered the room he saw the Prime Minister standing beside the fireplace in a relaxed manner with his right elbow on the mantle and his left hand placed casually in the trouser pocket.

"So good of you to make it," said the PM. "Please, take a seat, will you."

Pope looked thinner than ever. The dark pinstripe suit he was wearing hung off his frame in stiff folds making him appear famished and weak. He pulled out the seat at the PM's desk and sat down, folding one leg over the other in a somewhat effeminate manner. Pope placed the briefcase he had been carrying on the desk in front of him. He coughed a little and looked up at the PM. "You have heard about Madrid, I take it?"

"Yes," said the PM. "Dreadful isn't it?"

Pope didn't reply but simply looked down at the plush ministerial carpet.

"Of course," he carried on, "I've sent my condolences, promised help catching the perpetrators, said we must defend freedom at all costs, yadda yadda yadda."

Pope meekly looked up at the PM as if expecting some kind of outburst.

"It never changes does it, Pope?"

The PM seemed to be in an unusual mood today. Pope wondered if he had been drinking. "How so?" he muttered, feigning surprise.

"How was Iceland? You seem to be very fond of the place."

"I don't rate it myself," replied Pope. "I was brought up on the African plains. Give me sun and heat any day over darkness and cold. Dreadful place for a think tank, if you ask me."

"And that's what it is, is it? A think tank?"

"The North Atlantic Centre for Strategic Studies, Sir. It's a collection of the best minds..."

"Don't bullshit me, Pope!" cut in the PM. He moved over from the fireplace to his side of the desk and leaned forward on his fists. "A little bird told me about what you and your friends get up to there, so don't try and deny it."

Pope's mind raced. How could this have happened? The World Patriots meetings were so well guarded and secretive that even he barely knew what was going on. How had this oaf of a man come into such knowledge?

"I'm sorry," he managed to stutter. "Deny what exactly?"

The PM eyeballed him for a few seconds longer before relaxing and sitting down in his chair. "Look, Pope. I'm an open-minded kind of chap. Personally I couldn't care less what you and your friends get up to. But if news of this gets out I'm going to have to drop you faster than a hot lump of Satan's shit."

"News of what, exactly?" said Pope.

The PM leaned forward once more and hissed, "Do I need to spell it out?"

Pope squirmed. "I think you'd better had."

"For Christ's sake Pope, don't you think there are more pressing matters at the moment than attending to your... needs? As I said, I don't care where you park your piston—however distasteful and perverted I might personally find your type—but if you implicate me in a child sex scandal I won't forgive you in a hurry."

It didn't often happen that Ignatius Pope was lost for words but this was one of those moments. He quickly weighed up the situation from all conceivable angles before crafting a quick reply to the effect that he would be as discrete as he possibly could.

"Good," said the PM. "In case you hadn't noticed, we've got a lot of work to do, and we can't have you swanning off at every moment to indulge in your... unnatural hobby."

Pope, still stunned by this turn of events, affected an air of guilt and looked down at the carpet once more. "It's not what you think," he said sulkily. "If some NACSS members find pleasure in ways you might consider unusual..."

"Nah, nah, nah," said the PM, putting his hands over his ears and screwing his eyes shut. "Just be quiet, Pope! I don't want to hear any more about it. Got it?"

"Okay," said Pope.

"Good," said the PM, opening his eyes and removing his hands from the side of his head. "Now let's get on with business."

"Indeed," said Pope.

"You see all this here?" said the PM clutching the sheaf of papers and waving them in the air, "you know what it is?"

Pope peered at the papers over the rims of his spectacles. "They appear to be current affairs briefs," he replied.

"Mayhem!" said the PM slamming them down on the desk so hard the coffee cup jolted. "There's mayhem going on everywhere Pope, and quite frankly, it scares the shit out of me."

"How so, boss?"

By way of reply the PM began to leaf through the news briefings, reading out the headlines. "Stocks meltdown in Asia Pacific; wildfires sweep across Siberia; Islamist groups resurgent in MENA; subprime auto and energy loans shake US economy; Greenland icecap melting six times faster than previously thought; refugees drowning in record numbers... need I go on?"

There was an uncomfortable silence for a few moments before Pope cleared his throat a little and replied. "And your point is, Prime Minister? I hope you are not holding me in some way accountable for these tragedies?"

"Indeed I am not, Pope. But let's have a look at this headline. It's from the Washington Post. '*At least half of all British citizens malnourished and economy in free-fall as energy and terror crisis grinds on*'. Would you not agree that you bear some responsibility for *that* headline?"

"You can't believe everything you read in the papers, boss. You should know that of all people."

"What am I supposed to believe?" raged the PM. "I don't *know* what to believe any more. On the one hand, I've got the UN saying it's a humanitarian disaster, I've got the Red Cross breathing down our necks and demanding unfettered access to the regions and furthermore I've got my own two eyes telling me that this ship is sinking faster than the Titanic. But then, on the other hand, I've got happy-clappy ministerial aides telling me the whole situation seems worse than it is, I've got you emailing me spreadsheets and charts left right and centre which I have neither the time nor the inclination to understand, and I've got..."

"Did you not enjoy the visit to Milton Keynes with the UN envoy last week, Sir?" cut in Pope.

"That..." stuttered the PM, his eyes bulging in disbelief. "That was a setup—nothing more than a Potemkin village. Where did you even get those actors from?"

"They weren't actors, Prime Minister. They were just ordinary citizens thankful that the threat of terrorism was being erased. You'll find people are very grateful and compliant if treated well."

"But the cars... the shops... the so-called people! Everything was so bloody clean and organised and efficient! You do realise it never looked like that in the first place, don't you?"

"Then you could say the process is working, Sir. If it *appears* to be clean and neat and efficient, and we *say* it is, then one could argue that it's a new *reality* we have indeed created."

The PM searched Pope's face for signs that he was joking. "Oh come on! It's fake and you know it. Neither you nor I can go around creating reality. Reality is what it is."

"Then perhaps, with respect, you are the wrong man for the role."

"What did you say?" snapped the PM. "How dare you talk to me like that! Tell me, how many people have you actually got rid of outside of these fake reality centres?"

Pope was silent for a moment, his eyes closed as if in meditation. "Between five and eight percent so far, Sir, as far as we can tell. Another four percent have left the country, which is more or less in line with the model's projections."

"The model's projections..." said the PM, searching Pope's face once more.

"The yield would have been higher if the Red Cross had not intervened. Our relief effort algorithm had no baseline data to work with, but we're learning fast. And we didn't count on a certain tenaciousness among the population, growing their own food and helping one another, that kind of thing. It appears that our human behaviour module was also a little off-target—we'd based it on an American model—but this too has now been updated. These have caused negative feedbacks to occur and so various parameters have had to be adjusted and certain feedback loop-breaking catalysts may need to be introduced into the mix. Nevertheless, despite these setbacks we should be on target for reaching the twenty-five percent milestone by early next summer."

"Early next summer..." repeated the PM as if in a daze.

"To be honest, Sir," continued Pope, "all these other things going on in the world are working to our advantage."

"How so?"

"Well, for a start, they direct attention elsewhere. But more substantially, given that we're the only major industrialised nation seriously taking the painful but necessary streamlining steps, we should be excellently placed to be among the leaders of the pack in the medium-to-long term. It's basic game theory, Sir."

"Game theory... is that all this is to you?" said the PM, his voice quiet and low.

"And that's not even counting the bounceback effect. Both Germany and Japan—the two countries most destroyed by the last war—went on to become world leaders in industry and innovation. We can expect the same, Sir. The more physical and psychological damage we inflict on the people now, the greater will be the recovery afterwards."

"But what about all the people dying out there right now? Do they mean nothing to you?"

"With all due respect, Sir, your party's austerity policies were simply a means to achieve the same end, but over a longer timescale. This method is swifter, and therefore kinder. Indeed, the model calculates that your policies would have taken some twenty-five years to accomplish what can be done in three years with our method. That's twenty-two years of needless suffering avoided, Prime Minister."

The PM stared at Pope's bony cranium and a feeling of deep contempt suddenly came over him. His heart began to race and he felt a constricting sensation in his throat. Every feature in the room faded away and the only thing he could see was Pope's head, with two burning eyes staring at him. A complete terror grasped him by the heart and started to squeeze.

"Are you okay, Sir?" mouthed Pope. "You seem a little... off."

The PM gasped for air, his lips moving like a landed fish. He saw a skeletal arm move, saw a claw-like hand touch his own and it was as if a bolt of electricity shot into the back of his hand where he had touched it, burning the skin.

The PM screamed, withdrawing his hand from the desk. Air returned to his lungs. "Don't touch me!" he gasped. "Why did you touch me? I won't have it!"

"You seemed a bit unwell, Prime Minster," said Pope, seeming concerned. "Perhaps our project is too ambitious for you? The last thing I would want to do is cause you any harm. Of course, if you'd like to call the whole thing off, turn the power back on, then maybe that's the best thing to do under the circumstances. You are my boss, after all."

The room began to come back into focus and the PM's heart rate slowed. Pope continued. "There'd be a very thorough enquiry but we could scupper it long enough so that we'd outlive it. I'd have to move somewhere without an extradition treaty and you'd retire early to a golf course in Florida. Things could get back to normal with international help, I'm sure of that. There'll always be some new crisis for people to dwell on."

Pope's proposal hung in the air between them. The two men remained looking at one another in total silence for a full minute, the only sound in the room coming from a carriage clock up on a shelf. The PM felt overwhelmed by sadness. It welled up inside him and his red sleep-deprived eyes filled with tears. He spoke fitfully, between sobs. "Do it," he mouthed. "Turn the power back on. I don't want any more to do with this horror show."

Pope considered the large man slumped in the chair across the desk from him. He cut a pitiful figure: an over-stuffed teddy bear in a suit, out of his depth and out of his tiny mind. "As you wish, Prime Minister." He stood up to leave. As he reached the door he turned to the PM as if he had forgotten something.

"There was one thing, Sir."

"What?"

"It's just to say, Sir, although you already know it, of course..."

"Spit it out Pope and then get out of my life."

"That you are a weak loser, and a coward."

The PM's eyes jerked upwards. "What did you say?"

"That you're a weak loser, Sir. Admit you're a cowardly traitor who would do anything to appear strong and I'll turn the power back on. Our 313 Plan will be halted in its tracks and it will all appear as a bad dream to you. It's very simple."

The fat man began to tremble. "I will never say such a thing!"

"Fine," replied Pope. "Then you will be a weak loser who killed forty million innocent people. It's on your head, Sir." He began to turn the polished brass door handle.

"Wait!" cried the PM, leaping up. "Come back here. Sit down."

Pope complied, slowly walking back to the desk and taking his seat. The PM too sat down once more, tear tracks streaming down his chubby cheeks. "Look at me," said Pope quietly, leaning forwards and staring directly into his eyes.

The PM tried to break away from his gaze but couldn't. "What are you doing?" he shrieked. "Stop it!" There were other words that tried to escape but they welled up in his constricted throat and the best he could do was emit a kind of strangled squeak. The room dissolved once again and all he could see were Pope's eyes, burning red in an enclosing darkness. The last thing he felt as the darkness closed in on him was a warm sensation running down his left leg.

When Clara came into his office two hours later to check why the meeting with Pope was taking so long, what she discovered shocked her. Having heard nothing of the two men talking, she had listened in at the door only to hear a tinny-squealing sound, punctuated by male grunting noises. She had knocked, of course, but nobody had opened the door, just as nobody had picked up the phone when she had buzzed him. When she eventually plucked up the courage to open the door she found the Prime Minister slumped backwards in his seat with his mouth open. His trousers and underwear were around his ankles and a half-empty bottle of Johnny Walker sat open on the desk beside the coffee cup from earlier. Also on the desk in front of him, the PM's laptop was open and showing a video of a man engaged in an act with a pig that made Clara gasp and slam the thing shut. Beside it, a number of torn-open packets of painkillers littered the desk's surface, and between the PM's chubby knuckles was clasped a fat cigar butt which she could see had burned the back of his hand. "Oh my goodness," she said under her breath as she hurriedly tidied up the desk, "not again."

"Mr Pope," she called out. "Are you here?" This was most puzzling, for although she had been at her desk outside the PM's private office all morning and there was no other way out of the room, of Pope there was no sign.

23

Pope sat on the edge of the bed in a north/south orienta-
tion and closed his eyes. It was only a few moments before he
entered a strange and blurry world of grey shadows and
buzzing energy. The shadows seemed to be alive and some of
them lingered and regarded him, whereas others seemed unaware of his presence. The ones that communicated did so in
whispering voices using a strange language that Pope somehow understood. He waited patiently for his friend to appear.
Years of practice had honed Pope's abilities in this respect
and usually he didn't have to wait for long. As he waited, he
recalled with clarity the first time he had slipped into this
world. It had been at boarding school in Pretoria—a boys-
only institution of cross-country runs, Chinese burns and
roaming tutors. "I'll make a success of you if it kills me,"
Pope's father had said to his effeminate son. A wealthy law-
yer turned politico in de Klerk's government, his father had
pulled strings to get his boy into St Paul's Oratory. And, in a
way, he had been right—the boy had turned out successful—
although not in the manner his father might have imagined.

It had happened in the showers after games. Being too
scrawny to play rugby, Pope had been put on Mr Phelps'

hockey team. It was fagging week for Pope and he'd been told to clean the mud off the hockey sticks and put the goals away in the pavilion. By the time he was ready for his shower the other boys had already left for prep and he was alone in the block. Mr Phelps had come up behind him as he was shampooing his hair. Nothing could have prepared him for the pain he had felt, his face pressed against the cold white tiles of the shower block. "Welcome to the club," laughed Phelps when he had finished. "I'll kill you if you tell anyone."

It had entered the thirteen-year-old boy's dreams that very night after he had fallen asleep, fervently praying for forgiveness. "What do you desire?" it had asked. The next morning, when he awoke, Pope had been stunned to look in the mirror and see his acne condition has vanished overnight.

The following night the voice spoke to him once again and asked him the same question: "What do you most desire?" He didn't dare tell it what he *most* desired. Not yet, at least.

It was around then that Pope's life turned around. He began to turn in straight A's on his papers. The PE teacher marvelled at how this six stone weakling was suddenly able to command the hockey field. A friend's mother started giving him the eye.

This was all unusual and unexpected, but it wasn't the whole story: people around him started to die.

George Paphitis, a bully who had made Pope's life a misery for years, got savaged by a lion on a half-term family vacation in Kruger and died shortly afterwards; Mr Phelps, who wore soft-soled Hush Puppies as he stalked the boys' dorms at night, contracted a wasting disease that reduced him to a skeleton in a little less than three months. When he finally died he was rumoured to weigh so little the pallbearers had to check that he was actually inside the coffin. And Pope's own father found himself in an ambush on a visit to a township near Cape Town, and died a fiery death with a burning tyre around his neck.

"See what I have done for you?" the shape had whispered to the boy in a dream. "But you must let me live inside you if I am to continue." And so Pope had let it in to his life. From then on circumstances had seemed to favour Pope's every move. Opportunities presented themselves, tiresome people and obstacles went away, and over the course of the next few years the shy and gangling young man grew into a fêted young political mover, easily able to find the footholds and climb the ladders of the structures of power, albeit in a behind-the-scenes manner. Pope had given his helper a name—Baal—and as his professional stature and power grew, so too did Baal's. They were confidantes, and whispered to one another like secretive lovers. Pope trusted no one except the grey presence that came to him inside the privacy of his mind.

"Bear is ready to receive y'all in the Eden area on the spa level," came a female voice from a speaker hidden in a wall. Pope opened his eyes and returned to physical reality. He was already dressed in a towelled robe and was wearing his slippers. Rising from the bed he walked across the heated slate floor and pressed the button that opened the door.

Big Bear—known to readers of *Fortune* magazine as Theodore "Teddy" Whitman—had a favourite place in his compound. If—and when—the world ended for the bulk of humanity, this was the one place he planned to sit it out in comfort and watch it all on a giant flatscreen. The Eden zone was an immense mock-up of a Palaeolithic scene, complete with bubbling pools of hot water, spiky tropical palms and a continuous background soundtrack of deep rumbling groans and piercing shrieks that made one feel as if dinosaurs roamed nearby and the skies were filled with pterodactyls. Clusters of white leatherette sofas were positioned like mushrooms around this diorama, some of them half-submerged in pools of hot water, and it was in one of these clusters that Pope now sat with the other eleven core Patriots.

Big Bear's rules for Eden meetings were simple and direct: no electronics, no clothing, no bullshit. In fact, the only man-made objects the Texas billionaire allowed into Eden were the Stradivarius cigars that were handed out, cut and lit by a toga-wearing servant boy called Dawud.

The big man puffed on the cigar as Dawud held a flame to the end. When it was going (nobody else had accepted one) he let the silky white smoke pour slowly out from his mouth, his eyes closed as if in rapture, and leaned back. After some moments in this state he slowly leaned forward, opened his eyes and addressed the assembled men.

"Bothers," he began. "Let us first give thanks to the Lord for giving us His guidance and delivering us in safety to this place of refuge. May His wisdom lead us to make the right decisions and to bring about the transformation of this vale of tears unto an earthly paradise. Ay-men."

There was a muttered scattering of "amens" amongst the men. Some chose not to indulge Bear in his evangelising, but it was an unwritten rule of the World Patriots that whoever was hosting got to chair that particular gathering, and that due respect for their beliefs should be accorded. Pope looked around at the others. Apart from Big Bear, who was in his mid sixties, Pope was the second youngest. The only one younger than himself was an equally lithe-looking man known as Beaver, who had built up an Internet empire from scratch and seemed permanently surprised by his success. Other than Beaver and Oryx, the scale was tipped towards the more senior end of the age spectrum. Between these twelve men rested a good proportion—although by no means all—of the oligarchic power and wealth in the world. To join the Brethren each man had had to undergo an initiation ceremony, swear an oath of allegiance and adopt the name of an animal native to the bioregion in which he was born. Thus Pope had been named Oryx, the Internet billionaire from New York was named Beaver, and the media mogul from Australia was named Koala.

Pope considered the initiation and the naming to be puerile and childish, and yet it was precisely Big Bear's puerility and childishness that held sway over the group. This was something that Baal had suggested was a weakness he could one day exploit, and so Pope humoured it silently, as did the others. Collectively these twelve naked men sitting on the white circular leatherette sofas controlled oil companies, central banks, mining operations, patented seed corporations and much of the technostructure that kept the modern world functioning as it did. They had shadow armies at their finger-tips, used intelligence agencies for their own ends and, although none of them held public office, each decided who held the power in their respective countries and dictated how that power was used.

And yet, despite all of this power at their disposal, or perhaps because of it, most members of the Brethren were of modest character, often self-effacing and usually charming. For in truth, at the centre of each man there existed a kind of childish bewilderment. To a man, they had followed a relatively simple set of rules to realize their ambitions, and having now reached commanding heights they had found them to be hollow and unsatisfactory. Their innermost fear was that fate had somehow cheated them of glory, and their forever-yearning hearts remained dissatisfied, despite having hoarded so much wealth and power.

And now, with the World Patriots, these twelve men strove to reach out and take something from beyond the boundary of what is ordinarily available for mortal souls. As such, each considered himself to have been chosen in some way to cleanse the race of its imperfections and open the gateway for the next stage of human consciousness. Their only fears in life were death and each other.

Pope was the only member of Big Bear's inner circle who did not command a vast fortune. With only Beaver to look down upon in terms of seniority, he nevertheless commanded the respect of his elders on account of his visionary ideas. For although the wider circle of the Patriots included some ninety-nine men and one woman, many, if not most, possessed minds that were becoming fogged by old age and senility. Tortoise was forever promising them the gift of physical immortality, but had yet to deliver on this promise, causing some of the older Patriots to lose hope of being present to witness the final judgment. By contrast with these grey heads, Pope's clarity of mind, his zeal for success and his bold ambition were qualities that the other members could relate to, and for that he was accorded acceptance into the group.

The meetings were a chance to meet up and detail the current state of affairs under each man's particular zone of influence. Although nothing was ever written down or recorded, each member ran through their recent efforts towards attaining the goal of the Patriots. And that goal was nothing less than to bring about a new order of purity to the world, although details of what this would look like in practice varied from one member to the next. When it was Pope's turn to speak he cleared his throat and stood up. The others looked at him expectantly, for Pope was really the reason they were there.

"So tell us how it's going down in Limeyland," prompted Bear, a smirk playing on the corners of his mouth.

Pope detailed the progress that had been made since the last meeting. Although he was without his laptop, and was something of a nervous speaker, he had memorised a few key statistics to feed them. He told them about the population targets, and how these were being met, and about the preparation work that was being done ahead of the next stage.

"Remind us again what the next stage involves," said Big Bear, jabbing his cigar in Pope's general direction.

"Well, when we've broken the back of the population overburden—which will likely be in the next three to four months, over winter—there will be a phased powering up again, of much of the second level architecture, albeit at a much reduced capacity. We knew that we'd only be able to get away with a year at most of monetary substitution—and what I mean by that, as I'm sure you all know, is propping up the economy simply using monetary tools—without destroying our long-term competitiveness. So we're going to have to restore power in a gradual manner and monitor local situations before proceeding. There are still a lot of systems that will need to be in place for when that occurs."

"Such as?" said Koala, whose scaly skin and sunken chest suggested to Pope a more apt name might have been "Crocodile."

"As you know, gentlemen, to maintain an advanced economy, we need a class of skilled knowledge workers to generate wealth. Before our intervention, our whole project was threatened by the drain being placed on this class, not just by the underclass but also by too many middlemen taking cuts. We are now about eighty percent complete with our database, meaning that those whom we might call 'middle class' will be in a state of capture when the economy becomes operational once more."

"Capture?" said Panda. "I like the sound of that."

"We've named it 'capture'—internally, of course—because they effectively will not be free until they have paid off their debts to society, these debts being both physical monetary debt, but also social debt, in the form of paying back what they previously had assumed was for free. As we all agree, socialism is simply spending other people's money, and we want to erase the whole concept of it if we are to have a productive and free society in the longer term. There will of

197

course be a basic level of income and food security guaranteed to anyone who complies with this system, but anyone who does not will be excluded, and will remain outside the green zones."

"How will you enforce this?" asked Big Bear.

"As I mentioned last time I was here, we're still establishing these green zones that will be physical places of safety for lawful citizens. Barriers will be erected to prevent osmosis occurring between those on the inside and those on the outside. Our models indicate that within the next year the population overburden on the outside will fall enough that the productive land can begin to be re-taken and efficiently managed. That's where you come in White Squirrel," said Pope, looking at a hollow-eyed man with almost no body hair.

White Squirrel looked at Pope for a moment and then replied, "But it's too compact over there. We need wide open spaces with no people at all. Security is a concern. Bring in these new robot planters, drone surveillance and security we got cooked up... you mix that up with too many folks on the ground and you've got big problems. It just ain't gonna fly, 'less we starve 'em out first."

There was silence among the gathered men as they sat around the bubbling pool. In the distance a triceratops shrieked, as it did precisely every forty-five minutes, and a few moments later the boy Dawud appeared. "What is it, boy?" said Big Bear, placing a heavy paw on the boy's narrow shoulder.

"Sorry to disturb you, Sirs," said the boy haltingly, "I've to inform you that dinner is now being served in the restaurant."

The big Texan looked at the boy, squeezed his shoulder a little, and then raised his face to the others. "Let's do it boys," he said, rubbing his vast belly. "All of this talk of starvin' 'em out has made me hungry."

As they filed away to dinner Pope sidled up to White Squirrel. "I don't suppose you've made any progress with the bottles, have you?"

"Bottles?" blinked the man. "Oh, you mean the whisky! Yes, of course, it's all finished and ready to ship. Twenty million bottles already loaded up and floating your way, Sir."

"Twenty million," replied Pope. "That's really excellent. Thank you, Squirrel. Of course, we may need another load in a few months. We've had a few problems with resilience among the population—your whisky should help fix that."

"Consider it an honour to help, Sir," replied the owner of the world's largest chemical and gene conglomerate. "Might I add that we had some real fun testing that stuff out!"

Having spoken with Squirrel about the whisky, Pope sought out Panda. "Guns," said Pope, walking alongside the diminutive man.

"Guns?" he replied. "How many?"

"About five million," replied Pope. "Revolvers. Shoddiest quality you can—I want these things to blow up in people's faces half the time when they pull the trigger."

"He, he," chuckled Panda. "You got some sick ideas Mr Oryx. And I mean that as a complement."

24

~ The Mournful Tale of Rose O'Keefe ~

They kept us on a short leash at the university, always looking over our shoulders and prying into what we were doing. My stats were not good. Others had two or three times as many hits as I did when it came to identifying potential subversives. One day I was called into a session with a supervisor and told to explain myself. "We have been looking through some of the cases you rejected," said the woman "and we can see that you have failed to identify even obviously subversive activity. How do you account for this?"

I didn't know what to say to this accusation, and I just broke down. Really, I was a bag of nerves at that time so it didn't take much. I explained that I was anxious; that I missed my family and couldn't sleep. The work was boring, I said, and its repetitive nature was causing me to miss some of the important details. The woman, looking at some report cards, didn't seem very impressed with my complaints. "We must all do our best if we are to smoke out the enemy within and get the country back on its feet," she said. "If we let too many slip through the net we shall be back to square one before we know it."

I didn't know the wider picture back then, of course, but what myself and the others were doing was winnowing. Someone, somewhere, had decided that only a select portion of the population was to be deemed worthy of carrying on with their easy middle-class lives, and everyone else was to be left to their fate in the hunger-stricken hinterlands. There were other winnowers besides us, I later learned, and they had their own criteria for selection. Wealth, family connections, old school ties, an indispensable job role, academic usefulness, fame and simple good luck could get you onto the list of the saved. But even then there were too many for the boat. Anyone who was outspoken or difficult in some manner would get tossed into the same pit as the poor and the physically or mentally unwell, and would have to scrabble for survival. What's more, across the country, the doors to the prisons had been flung open and all manner of violent and criminally insane men and women had been unleashed upon the hapless population. A great many people had perished or gone missing during the first few months of the crisis, but the better-connected ones had generally survived and were keen to hold onto what they owned. Most of them had been summoned by the government to work in London and a couple of other "Green Zones," but most of these brought along family, friends and other contacts, and it was a morass of complexity figuring out who met the criteria and who did not.

Of all of this I knew nothing. I would only begin to build up a picture of this reality because of the words I uttered next to that cold-faced supervisor: "But I'm not a student—I'm a journalist," I blurted. "Isn't there some other job I could do?"

She considered me for what seemed like a long time before speaking. "I trust you are familiar with the newspaper *Fortitude*? They are currently seeking reporters... it's a Green

Zone job." She spoke carefully and concisely. "If I were to put you in for a transfer, would I be able to reassure them that you are made of the right material?"

"What do you mean?" I said. "Didn't I pass the tests?"

"Don't think that we haven't been watching you. Who was that man you met?"

"Man?" I said, trying to sound innocent.

The woman stared at me and I felt her eyes drilling into me. Her hair was done up in a tight bun on top of her head, and she wore a formless grey uniform. I hated her, and I knew that she knew I was lying about meeting Robin, but all the same, I hoped that she might have some mercy in her heart. "We shall see where you end up," was all she said before slamming my file shut and dismissing me.

I worked in the social media pool at the university for a few more weeks. Christmas came and went. It was a dismal affair with a lunch of boiled vegetables and tins of fried spam. But wine was given out freely and it seemed that everyone got drunk—even the supervisors. For a few hours all was merriment and reminiscing, and there was even singing and dancing. I slipped out and left them to it. By the tree under a full moon, just as I had done on many a night, I waited for Robin. I worried that something might have happened to him. Hadn't he promised to come back? The question went round and round in my mind. I forced myself to believe that he knew what he was doing and that everything would be all right. When he didn't show up yet again I returned to my room and fell asleep thinking of Christmas by the fire in my aunt's living room. A few days later a letter was slipped under my door. It bore the crest and hallmark of the Ministry of Information and advised me that I was being transferred to work at *Fortitude* with immediate effect. I should pack my belongings forthwith, it stated, and not speak to anyone about my posting.

Later that day a black taxi arrived and took me across the city to my new residence and new life. It had been months since I had set foot outside the university campus, which was set in parkland on the outskirts of London, and I was shocked to see how much things had changed. For a start, there were very few cars on the road, even though it was a working day. Many shops and offices were closed and boarded up and the icy streets were covered with litter. We drove through an area thick with smoke and I could see people draped in blankets and standing huddled around oil drums as they held their hands out towards the flames. And there were shopping trolleys everywhere, most of them filled with dirty-looking clothes, blankets and other possessions. People pushed their trolleys around listlessly, plodding slowly as though they had nowhere to go.

The taxi driver, a balding middle-aged white man, saw my look of shock. "If you think this is bad, you ain't seen nothing. Where they've 'ad them riots it's all gone."

I asked him what he meant by "gone." How could sections of a city disappear?

"Burned down the lot," he replied. "Whole streets gutted. They're pullin' 'em down as we speak."

"What about Tottenham?" I said. "That's where I used to live. Is it okay there?"

"Tottenham?" chuckled the driver. "Yeah, you could say that. Tottenham, Edmonton, Wood Green, Ponders End—all just big piles of rubble now, and the better for it if you ask me."

"But what about the people?" I asked. "Where are they?"

He just shrugged at my question and then glanced at me over his shoulder. "You don't believe me? I'll show you." We swung off the main route and turned down a side street. For a while it was all residential buildings, yet the streets were still filled with desperate and dispirited looking people trying to keep warm and shuffling around with their trolleys. At a junction a woman approached the car and began banging on the window and holding out her hand. She was pleading with the driver and pointing at what looked like a bundle of rags lying on the nearby pavement. To my horror I suddenly saw that it was not a bundle of clothes but a small child. The child's breath condensed in the frosty air like little puffs of smoke. The taxi driver yelled at the woman and she shrank away, a frightened look on her dirty face. "Bleedin' cockroaches."

We carried on driving, passing the burned out concrete shell of a shopping centre that I recognised as being near to my old bedsit. As we turned around the corner I expected to see the familiar street where the kids used to hang around and where the wannabe gangsters used to drive and play their loud rap music. But it was gone. Instead of the closely packed houses, the red buses and the London plane trees, there was a great open expanse with nothing but huge smoking mounds of rubble and the blackened stumps of trees. People moved over the rubble, passing armfuls of bricks to one another, while yellow bulldozers piled up more building debris, along with mangled cars and the twisted branches of dead trees. "There's Tottenham for you," said the driver with what sounded like glee. "But then I always was an Arsenal man myself."

Filling this open wound in the city, there now stretched a wall. Only half-built, it looked to be made of tall, prefabricated slabs of concrete erected in a deep trench. Up ahead of us a tall brick watchtower was under construction and it was here that the slow-moving people were depositing piles of bricks from the destroyed houses. Dozens of men were running to and fro with barrows filled with cement, and soldiers, with their weapons pointed at the ground, stood with feet apart in the mud. Seeing my look of horror the taxi driver explained: "I suppose you've been inside that university place for so long you 'aven't got a clue what's been going on in the real world. There's been riots out here, people been running wild. Every night it was, shootings and burnings and looting. They had to put up a barrier to stop it spreading inwards and it's worked so far. All they're doing now is building it a bit higher to keep the troublemakers on the outside away from the folks on the inside Should've been done years ago, if you ask me."

I tried to take this scene in, wanted to ask him more, but we were coming up to some kind of checkpoint. "You got your ID, love?" he said, looking at me in the rear view mirror.

I took out my ID card and passed it to the driver, who passed it through the window to a guard sitting in a cubicle behind a sheet of bulletproof glass. He looked at it, handed it back, and we carried on our journey. On the other side of the barrier the taxi moved along at walking pace. You could hardly call it a road—it was more like a muddy track strewn with bricks and debris. Bulldozers and cranes were at work everywhere, some of them battering buildings with huge wrecking balls, and others lifting concrete slabs into place for the barrier. "Buffer zone," said the taxi driver.

As on the outside, men and women carried piles of bricks and pieces of tangled metal in their arms and deposited them in heaps to be sorted through by others. Soldiers and yellow-hatted foremen strutted among them, speaking into walkie-talkies and directing them. As for the labourers, I had never seen people looking more downtrodden. The driver, once again, read my feelings. "Those are the lucky ones," he said. "Desperate times call for desperate measures, but there's work for all who want it." There was a clunk and scraping noise as we drove over a piece of rubble. "Bugger," said the driver. "The sooner they get this finished the better—I've gone through four oil filters in as many days."

"How long does the wall go on for?" I asked.

"All the way round, love. No point 'avin a wall if it doesn't go all the way is there?"

That was when I learned that a huge swathe of inner London—stretching from the financial district in the east to the wealthy residential areas and royal palaces in the west—was being enclosed inside a giant concrete wall.

There came another checkpoint at what was obviously the inner barrier, but this time we were just waved through. A moment later we were inside the city that was being turned into a fortress, and the difference was remarkable. All in all, it appeared little different to how I remembered it before the crisis. Other than the black cabs there was very little car traffic, but to make up for it many people rode bicycles or mopeds. Our taxi threaded its way down roads lined with shops, the windows of which spilled out light onto the streets. There were cafés too, and restaurants filled with people enjoying lunch. People strolled with bags of shopping and spoke into mobile phones. "Are the phones working again?" I asked the driver incredulously. "I thought they were still down."

He chuckled once more. "Yeah, they work just fine inside the Green Zone, just so long as it's not long-distance." I mused on this, wondering if it would finally be possible to get in touch with my parents. It wasn't long before we slowed and then came to a stop outside a Georgian terraced house with black iron railings. The driver consulted a small device on his lap. "This is the one, darling. Number 22, your new home." He opened the glove box and took out a package which he passed to me through the Perspex screen that separated his cab from the passenger area. "This is for you, I believe."

I took the package and ripped it open there and then. In it were a set of keys and some printed instructions detailing basic information about the house I was being assigned. There was also a credit card with my name embossed on it and some documents relating to my position as a reporter for *Fortitude*. "Make yourself at home and there'll be someone round tomorrow morning at eight sharp to take you to your new job," said a cover note.

I opened the taxi door and stepped out into the cold January air.

"Listen, love, just one other thing," said the taxi driver winding down the window. "You've got plenty to learn about how things work in here, so don't go messing it up." He lowered his voice and indicated that I should bend down a little to hear what he was saying. "I'm just doing my job—taking people in and sometimes taking them out again. You watch your step in 'ere, play by their rules, and don't ruffle no feathers, otherwise you'll find yourself out there again." He jerked his thumb over his shoulder and there was no question about where "out there" might be.

"Thanks," I said. "I'll be careful." The taxi driver gave me a wink and then pulled away, leaving me standing on the curb outside the house with the keys in my hand. My heart was sinking. It was not just because I had seen what was being done to the city, nor was it what had become of the people who had lived there. No, it was because I knew, deep down and with a cast-iron certainty, that I would end up on the outside myself. All that remained was to see how long I could survive in this Green Zone. How long could I keep up this pretence? I stepped up to the house, turned the key in the lock and slowly opened the door.

25

Art opened his eyes and then quickly shut them again. Was he dreaming? He could see that he was in his cottage and lying on the bed but what was *she* doing there? *Perhaps it's a nightmare,* he thought. He lay and listened with his eyes shut. There was the occasional crackle of a log burning in the hearth and outside someone was banging with a hammer. The minutes passed and he opened his eyes a crack once more. Janey Wilde sat in a wicker chair near the foot of the bed reading something. Art examined her through half-shut eyes. She was wearing a flimsy tie-dyed chiffon blouse, black jeans and a pair of scuffed Doc Martens that went halfway up her calves. She'd had her hair cut short but still had the nose ring that sat in the centre of a face which was considerably slimmer than the last time he'd seen it. Her eyes flicked up from the book and in the same moment Art realised his ex-girlfriend was reading his confidential plans for Twin Oaks Farm.

"Get yer eyes off of that!" he said, flying up from the bed in an instant.

"Whoa!" said Janey, jerking the exercise book away from his reach. "Looks like you've woken up at last."

"Give," he continued, reaching over her and pulling the lined A4 exercise book from her. "That's not for your prying eyes."

"Take it," she said dismissively. "It gets kind of boring sitting here looking at you for half the day—what's a girl to do to amuse herself?"

Art felt a soreness at the back of his head which stretched down his neck and upper spine. "Bloody hell," he said, reaching a hand back and rubbing it. This caused a further sharp spasm of pain, this time in his hand, and it was then he realised his right forearm and hand was wrapped up in bandages. It felt as if it was on fire. "What happened?" he cried.

"Seems like Arthek Gwavas got himself into a scrape. Lucky to have got him out of it alive, says the others."

Art looked puzzled as he tried to recall events. He remembered going to the house, finding the bodies and the gun, going outside. Then he recalled the soldier. "I remember there was a soldier. Bleddy idiot he was, saying we was thievin'."

"Which you was. And, yes, that's the one you saw. The one you didn't see was the one that did the damage, though it was his last act in this vale of tears, by all accounts."

"Heh?" said Art, looking into Janey's large round eyes ringed with black eyeliner. "What do you mean? What's 'appened to him then?"

"Smacked him good and proper, didn't he, your Romanian feller. Nearly took his feckin' head off his shoulders with a sledgehammer. From behind. Right old mess, they says. They'll be after you now, you bloody nincompoop."

Art stared at Janey, letting the words sink in. Had they really gone and killed a soldier? If so there would be hell to pay if they found them. "When did this happen?"

"Yesterday morning. Just so happened I was walking along running an errand for Mum when I sees this blue pickup truck speeding along towards me. 'Hello,' I says to myself. 'If it isn't that no-good layabout Arthek Gwavas—'im who'd happily spend someone else's wages all on himself and leave his fiancée dressed up and sittin' alone at the Five Bells on her birthday while he goes off gallivanting with his mates down the Dolphin.'"

Art rolled his eyes. "I've said I was sorry about two hundred bloody times woman..." he protested. "I was going through some stuff at the time and..." but Janey held a finger up and cut him off.

"And so it turns out is *was* him, but not in the manner I expected to encounter him. Turns out there's some emmet driving and what I initially thought to be two slaughtered lambs in the back turns out to be Mr Considerate himself and poor old Jago, who Molly always fancied though I couldn't see it myself. Luckily for Mr Considerate, it turns out, the former was in considerably less pain than the latter."

"Jago?" said Art. "What's happened to him?"

"Bullet wounds. One in the leg and one somewhere up near his neck. Sounds like he took 'em for you too—that your soldier friend had it in his mind to give 'em to you once he'd seen his friend go down. Just so happened that he was already pointing it at you and if young Jago hadn't sprung on him—handcuffed and all—you might not be looking so lively right now. I always said you had the luck of the devil, and so it was that you managed to go and get shot at by a soldier who couldn't hit the side of a barn."

"What of him? And what about the soldier?" said Art, fearing the worst.

Janey stared at him. She'd meant to put the frighteners on him; still hadn't forgiven him for the breakup. It seemed to be working—Art looked terrified.

"Soldier unloads his gun at you. First shot goes into the ground next to your head, then you caught the next one in your hand. The last two went into poor old Jago as he tried to save your sorry arse. Turns out he isn't made of Kevlar. That's when the rest of your mates turn up and jump your bad shot soldier and give him a beating he won't forget in a hurry. There was a struggle. He got away, gun and all. The rest of them didn't hang around long after that—not with that fella's head lying there on the ground."

Art stared at Janey in horror; this hadn't been in the plan. "As for Jago," she continued, "he's had a tough time of it. A bottle of gin helped as they got out the bullets and since then he's been rolling around with a fever down in that cabin over by the woodshed. They've been boiling water for him and keeping him as clean as can be, and Linda's been putting all manner of herbs and potions on his wounds. There's a vet out Helston way who's rumoured to have some proper medicine, but nobody's been able to find him yet."

Art held up his bandaged hand and stared at it. "What am I supposed to do with this?" he said. He thought of all the projects that needed his urgent attention. Winter was here and he wanted to get some coppicing done in the woods. There was more building to do—there was always building to do. And how was he supposed to drive? Or write his plans? He groaned, lay back on the bed and went to run his hand through his hair, as he always did when he was stressed.

"Argh!" he cried. "What's happened to my hair? Where's it gone?"

"We thought it best to change your appearance, given what's happened."

"So you cut my hair off?" said Art, feeling his stubbly head with the fingers of his left hand. "There's six years of growing gone into that and you just come in here and cut me dreads off..."

"Army could've traced your car and turned up at any minute, couldn't they? Good job you've got someone to look after you, isn't it?" said Janey, winking at him. "Car's hidden as well. Parked it well out of the way and covered it in branches, we have."

"You?" said Art, knowing what was coming next. "I know what you're trying to do. You can't stay here. We haven't got any room for freeloaders and we're already running low on food."

"Oh come on now," said Janey. "You could do with a couple more women round here—it's a dump."

"It's a very functional dump, I'll have you know, and it's managed to keep us alive thus far. And what do you mean a *couple* of women?"

"Well, I can't very well leave Mum on her own now can I? What she doesn't know about gardening you could write on the back of a stamp. And she was a midwife back in the day. You could use someone with her skills. In any case, she likes you, which is more than could be said of most women."

"She doesn't like me—she hates me!" said Art hotly, recalling the time when Maureen Wilde had discovered him hiding in her daughter's wardrobe when they had been teenage lovers. It had been all downhill from there. "Last thing she said to me, I recall, was to stay away from you, if you don't remember. Called me a pot-smoking scarecrow."

"Oh, she didn't mean it. You know what she's like—she was just playing hard to get on my behalf. Truth be told, she's always secretly admired you. Anyway, you need her. She's got Mo's Ark."

"Mo's Ark? What you on about?"

"Don't you remember? She was involved with that seed bank thingy with Transition Cornwall? I know you thought they were all a bunch of middle class twits, but the fact of the matter is she's sitting on a few thousand heritage variety seeds. You could plant up a whole market garden with what she's got stashed away."

Art stared at her blinking. The idea of his once-almost-mother-in-law living with them was a dispiriting prospect. In his opinion she was one of those busybodies who always poke their noses into everyone's business and always seem to be doing charity work without seeming to ever have a proper job. She was pious and she was into choral ensembles and flower arranging competitions and dog grooming and she was, frankly, irritating in a dozen different ways. But she *did* have those seeds. Perhaps he could steal them, he considered. That would be a whole lot easier than having her here at the farm. Janey got up from the wicker chair and sat down beside him on the bed. Placing her hand on his head, she began to stroke his stubbly scalp. "Of course," she said soothingly, seeming to read his thoughts, "Mum's seeds have been put in a *very* safe place away from any little mice that might want to nibble them."

Art recoiled from her touch. How was it that she could read him like a book? His cultivated air of aloofness that worked so well on others had no effect on her whatsoever. "What about you?" he snapped. "What can *you* bring? There's no room here for any more people who can't do anything useful. I mean it. One hundred and fifty—that's the maximum number of folks that are ever going to live here, and each one of them's gotta bring something to the table."

"Oh, come on now," cooed Janey. "You know you need me. I'll look after you until you're better at least." She looked at him with the kind of tender look in her eyes that she knew could win him over—that is to say, it had always worked in the past. "And besides, I can help you with your little Project Bacon."

Art gnashed his teeth when he heard this. He hadn't revealed Project Bacon to anyone. But, of course, she had been reading his plans all day long.

"We can get rid of that nasty old pig together," she said, resuming the stroking of his stubbly head once more.

"How?" said Art. "How can we get rid of Peck? He'll shop us to the Army the moment he gets wind of what's happened. We're already running out of booze and food to feed him—

soon there'll be no reason at all why he should put up with us."

Janey looked at him and leaned forwards, placing her lips near his ear. "Poison, darling. We'll poison Mr Pig and then we'll bury him somewhere up on the top field and nobody will ever find out about it. And then you and I will move into the house and all will be good, just you see."

He stared at Janey. The plan had merit. Just the thought of Peck clutching his stomach and writhing around in pain made him feel better already. Of course, she was mad, of that there was no doubt. But that's why he had been attracted to her in the first place. He allowed a smile to form on his lips. "I think you might just have earned yourself a place at Twin Oaks," he said.

"And Mummy?" she replied, batting her eyelids.

"Tell her to come up here when she's ready. But not without her seeds; no seeds, no entry."

* * *

Coincidentally, at the same moment that Art and Janey were plotting his demise, Peck was plotting ways in which to get rid of them. Looking down from the first floor bedroom window he could make out the hastily-erected buildings, parked caravans and vehicles of all the uninvited guests on his farm. Now the leaves had come off the trees it was all clearly visible. *Shanty town*, he thought. *They've built themselves a muddy little refugee camp on my retirement fund.*

He caught his reflection in the windowpane. A gaunt and haunted face stared back at him. It was the first day he had been sober in months, and it was not an experience he was enjoying. These days the paranoia had become too great and he never left the farmhouse. The boy brought him his whiskey and some food without fail, but yesterday he hadn't showed up.

This sobriety was almost too much to bear. Not only was there the withdrawal to deal with, but as the blurring effects of the alcohol had dissipated, the dismal situation in which he lived had come into sharp focus. The house was a total mess, with clothes and dishes and mouldy food spread over the floors. The kitchen was unusable and the bathroom unspeakable.

It was all *his* fault.

He stared down at the mess *he'd* made of the land. He'd make him pay. He'd trap that rat. As he gazed at the small community spread out below he indulged in a fantasy. He imagined holding a flamethrower, feeling the pressure on his trigger finger. How they would run screaming from their burning shacks and how he would cut them down. As the filthy *Untermenschen* ran away in terror, white phosphorus would rain down on them, frying their flesh as they squirmed in the mud and screamed in agony. Napalm death—a cleansing of the Earth!

Peck drew in a deep breath and savoured his fantasy. Of course, it was impossible. But if only he could get the boy... surely the others would then leave. Kill the king rat and the others would scatter. He'd get the Army in, plant something incriminating. They'd be dealt with swiftly. He chuckled at his ingenuity.

The crisis would be over soon enough. The power would come back on again and the banks would be working again. Any week now, it would be. By spring everything would be completely back to normal and come summer he'd be on the Costa del Sol and all of this would be behind him. He closed his eyes and imagined the sun on his face. Yes, the realisation of his dream was growing near—all he had to do was deal with the boy and the rest would fall into place.

26

Jack felt one of the trolling lines go taut. At first it was a gentle, inquisitive pull but it quickly became more strident as the fish took the bait. It pulled the kayak around so that it faced leeward into the rocky shallows around the mount and caused Jack a small measure of alarm as he wondered what was on the end of the line. A stiff morning breeze was blowing out of the east and making for some choppy conditions that buffeted the small vessel around in the otherwise sheltered waters of the cove. Jack used the paddle to stabilise himself before shoving it hastily into the plastic securing clips on the deck and twisting his body round to grab the rod. As he did so his cold hands fumbled it and he almost dropped it into the water. The fish gave another sharp tug and he allowed the line to slacken momentarily, reeling it in before pulling it back sharply towards his body.

It had been a good morning so far and Jack had landed twenty or more mackerel in a little over an hour and a half. Art had said the runs wouldn't start until April or so but Art, Jack had learned, didn't know everything. This, however, didn't feel like a mackerel. Its pull was far too strong, for a start, and it was causing the kayak to veer off course. Jack let out a quiet curse and reached forward, pulling down the central skeg to give him more stability. He hoped it wasn't a shark. *What the hell would I do if it was a shark? It'll pull me out of the kayak and make a meal of me.* He let this panicky thought rise and fall within him for a few seconds. *It's not a shark,* he reassured himself. *Sharks don't go for worms on hooks.*

With both hands on the rod, he began to reel in whatever it was he had managed to hook. It didn't give up the battle easily, pulling Jack and his small vessel in quite close to the rocks at the base of the mount before wearily accepting defeat and allowing itself to be scooped up into a net. He hauled it onto the deck, his heart pounding from the exertion. He needn't have worried about it being a shark. Nevertheless it *was* a large fish, perhaps a ten pounder, he thought. The cosh he'd whittled from a piece of oak was tied by a short chord to a nylon rope that ran around the inner edge of the decking. As the fish gulped for oxygen he clubbed it over the head and watched until it stopped moving. He held it there for some moments, admiring its inert silver body and the blue iridescence of its back that seemed to fade before his eyes. It was a sea bass, Jack was pretty certain of that, although he'd only ever seen them on display platters in restaurants. He took a canvas bag out of a screw top compartment in the bulkhead and carefully placed his catch inside. It was too large for the bag and he had to pull the drawstring tight, leaving the tail of the fish poking out.

The sun was by now high enough in the eastern sky to have made a golden ladder leading across the sea. Gulls swirled on the morning air currents over the small greyish island poking through the water as a group of cormorants, silhouetted against the morning sky, sat on a seaweed-plastered rock and gazed out to sea like old fishermen. Atop the rock sat a granite fortress, just as it had for centuries, although God only knew where the occupants had disappeared to: no flag flew above it these days and people said the whole place was boarded up. *Spring is in the air*, thought Jack as he pulled up the skeg and paddled towards the island. *The rest of the world can go swivel, as far as I'm concerned.* The tide was low but already turning and there was barely enough depth to make it between the harbour walls. He pushed off the sandy seabed with the paddle and brought the kayak to rest on a muddy little beach beneath a row of stone cottages. A be-whiskered old man sat in a deck chair outside one of these cottages, sipping something steaming in a mug and puffing on a pipe. Next to him, on a strip of carpet laid out on the cold cobbles, there rested an old one-eyed bull terrier with brindle fur. Jack pulled the kayak up out of the water and loaded it onto a small trolley with large rubber wheels. The old man looked up and called out to him.

"Wasson Jack? Any luck out there?" The dog, upon hearing his master address someone, opened its one eye and looked disinterestedly at Jack as he pulled the kayak over the muddy beach and up onto the quay.

"There's more and more mackerel coming in," replied Jack, slightly out of breath. "Here," he said, fumbling to open the bulkhead and remove the canvas bag containing his catch.

"What's that you've got there?" said the man eyeing the tail of the bass poking out. "Get 'er out and we'll have a look."

Jack carefully removed the large fish and held it up. If he'd caught such a fish a year before he would have been getting someone to take a picture of it and put it on Facebook. But now there was no Facebook, as far as he was aware, and such thoughts seemed frivolous and even crazy. Gordon, the old man, let out an admiring whistle. "She's a whopper, for sure," he said, "haven't seen one that big for a good few years. Since them trawlers disappeared seems like these old beauties feel safe enough to come back."

At the sight of the fish the dog rose to a sitting position, put up its crooked ears and moved its head to one side. "This one's mine Brutus," said Jack with a grin. "Get your beady eye off it!"

"Course it is son, you'd better get it home and cooked to feed up that lassie of yours. Must be any day now, right?"

"Still a couple of weeks to go, we reckon," said Jack, slipping the sea bass back into the bag. "Here," he said, "I caught these for your breakfast." He proffered four mackerel to the old man who took them wordlessly and rose to deliver them inside the cottage. The dog trotted inside after his owner leaving Jack alone on the quay. He went over to a mountain bike that was locked to some metal railings. Releasing it, he then secured the kayak in the same manner, turning it upside down and chaining it to the metal railings using the bike lock. There was a small trailer hitched onto the back of the bicycle and into this he placed the bag of fish, along with the rods, a bait box and a his buoyancy vest. There was already a plastic bag in there filled with a collection of limpets and mussels Jack had found at low tide on the rocks on the far side of the mount, as well as another bag bursting with fresh seaweed. To top it all a half dozen razorfish were bundled together with a rubber band (Art had shown him a trick to catching them which involved pouring salt down the holes they made in the sand and then grabbing them as they shot out).

The old man in the cottage looked after people's boats and was happy to get paid in fish, but Jack didn't want to take a chance leaving his fishing gear lying around and always took it back to the farm with him at the conclusion of his fishing trips. He glanced up at the causeway and, seeing that it would soon be covered by the incoming tide, he went over to the cottage and put his head through the door. Already the stove was lit and some eggs hissed and crackled in an iron skillet atop it. The old man's wife, Trudy, was standing over the sink and gutting the mackerel with a sharp paring knife but when she saw Jack she quickly put down the knife and waved him in.

"Good morning my lovely. Thank you for these fine fish."

"Uh, you're welcome," said Jack. "I'll probably not come over tomorrow. Got some work to do over at the farm that can't be put off any longer."

"Now just you hold on a minute young man," said Trudy, bustling off into another room. "Got something for you, I have," she called from the darkness of the little fisherman's cottage. Jack thrummed his fingers on the doorframe and waited. Presently she reappeared bearing something. "Here," she said. "A little something for you and Cat."

It was a small woollen blanket. "Just a little something to keep the new arrival warm, when he or she decides to make an appearance. Gave me a little project this past week as well," said the old woman with a twinkle in her eye.

Jack was abashed, didn't know how to reply. "Thank you," he eventually said. "It will really mean a lot to us." He bent down to give Trudy an awkward kiss on the cheek, causing her to titter with laughter.

"Away with you, before the causeway disappears otherwise you'll be stuck here all day and you two will end up knocking back drams of that whisky Gordon found. They're saying a big cargo ship went down in one of the January storms. There's whisky washing up all along the coast, says some, just like in that film."

Jack left the old couple to their breakfast and began to push the bike with its trailer down the ramp onto the stone causeway. Already the water was washing up around some of the larger rocks and he considered whether he might spend a couple of minutes looking for some crabs to add to his haul. Eventually deciding against it (*they'll be too small, better to focus on getting some proper crab pots down for the summer*, he thought) he continued along the raised stony path, just as people had done for countless centuries before him. Up ahead stretched a sandy beach and Jack could already see a person moving towards him like a ghostly waif. This was the part he hated the most about his fishing trips.

A sound distracted him and made him look down at his feet. In a small rock pool off to the side of the causeway something was bobbing around. Jack put the bike on its stand and bent down to examine it closer. *Well, I'll be damned!* Three plastic liquor bottles were bobbing around in the surf. *Well what do you know!* He held one of the bottles up and looked at the label. Laughing Chinaman 44% ABV. *Never heard of it,* thought Jack, *but Art will be pleased.* He fished out the bottles and shoved them into the trailer.

As soon as Jack set a booted foot on the firm sand a woman began to sprint towards him. Thin, almost skeletal, her loose clothing flapped as she ran, her arms huddled around her midriff as if she were trying to keep warm. He recognised most of the beggars by now, knew them to be more or less harmless, but they unnerved him nevertheless and he wanted to avoid any aggravation. During the first couple of encounters he'd given them a few fish and even sat with them awhile, but that had only seemed to encourage them and they had become strident in their demands. Two weeks ago one had pushed his bike over and tried to run off with the catch, and now Jack was not taking any chances. "I've got nothing for you today except seaweed," he shouted at the woman. She stopped in her tracks and seemed to simply stand there on the beach, head lowered in despondence. Others, sitting further away around a driftwood campfire shouted out curses which carried over the sands. He felt pity for them but there was nothing he could do. If he gave them fish he would simply be taking it out of the mouths of himself and his friends.

Jack broke into a fast walk and pushed the bike up a concrete ramp which led to the road running through the village. When he got to the empty tarmac road he allowed himself to turn around and look at the people on the beach to check that none were following him. None were. Wondering why they were not coming over, he saw then that most of them were holding bottles like the ones he'd just discovered. He smiled. *That should keep them happy for a while*, he thought. Satisfying himself that they wouldn't be chasing him today he mounted the bike and set off to the farm.

27

~ The Mournful Tale of Rose O'Keefe ~

Rose O'Keefe put down her pen. The last of three candles was beginning to gutter, casting jumpy shadows on the walls as it fought to stay alive. The light bulb had given out hours ago, reminding the old woman that the night was well advanced. How long had she been sitting there scribbling her story? She looked at the yellowing pad filled with her cramped and untidy handwriting. More than half of the pages were now used. *And I haven't even got to the interesting part,* she said to herself. No matter, she was tired now. She decided she would sleep until first light and then continue writing.

Outside, an Atlantic storm was gathering—she had grown aware of the branches of a fig tree scraping against the window as they swayed in the wind. She put her hands on her knees and rose slowly to her feet. Crossing the room—for her sturdy little house comprised of only a single room—she opened the wooden door and stepped outside. It was a dark night. The stars blazed bright in the skies above, but otherwise all was inky blackness. Rose closed her eyes and felt the force of the wind on her face. There came the sound of the stable door rattling on its hinges and, from within, her horse Frodo snorted uneasily. It was unusual to feel such a strong wind blowing on a clear night like this. Perhaps there was a deeper meaning in this, a warning perhaps. She decided to check. Keeping her eyes closed, she sought some reassurance by opening up to the other reality she had grown to know so well. Opening up her inner eye, she looked out over the expanse of moor and sea, now lit up by some unearthly luminosity. She could see the wind rushing towards her, could see the multitudes of tiny elementals with their frenetic energy dashing here and there. They carried a message. "Danger!" they all cried out. "Time is of the essence!"

Startled by their message, Rose opened her physical eyes and stared once more into the darkness. *So this is how it ends.* She felt a small frisson of fear run down her spine. "I hope it will not hurt too much," she said out loud to the night. How had she missed this? Perhaps it was because she had felt preoccupied of late with other thoughts—how long had it been since she had last tuned in to the other side? And then she began to chuckle. She had no fear of death itself, for she knew that it was merely the transmutation of one form of being to another. Indeed, she had died once before; the experience was not new to her. But on the other hand she hated pain, and she hated the uncertainty of not knowing what form her passing would take. She returned inside again and secured the door behind her with all three locks before lying down on the bed tucked into an alcove beside the wood burner. *I shan't miss these tired old bones,* she thought.

In an instant she was asleep and the sound of her soft snores sang a duet with the wind as it whistled around the shingles on the washroom door. After only ten minutes her eyes flicked open again and she sat up and yawned. Busying herself, she rekindled the embers in the fire and added some fresh sticks to get a good blaze going. She placed the old iron teapot atop the stove and, as it began to warm, she searched through another drawer, muttering to herself and tossing things aside. "This is the one I need," she said to no one in particular as she took out a packet of powdered herbs, sprinkled them into the teapot and waited for it to brew.

When she had drunk the tea and lit another candle, she settled herself at the table, picked up the pen and stared at the pad of paper once again. *Time is of the essence*, she thought.

* * *

What can I say about my time inside the Green Zone in which I found myself? I was given a house, a job, and a chance to live a normal life. I stayed there for two whole years, at first keeping my head down like the taxi driver had advised me and simply trying to make the best of a bad situation. There's no point in going into all the details of those two years, so I shall describe the things that stick out the most in my memory.

To begin with, I was taken to my new job as a junior staff writer for that strange newspaper called *Fortitude*. There was a great irony in this, because it turned out that the newspaper's headquarters was the very same building from which *The Shield* had been run! There were even a few old colleagues whom I recognised, still sitting at the same desks as if nothing had happened, and the editor was still there too, doing the same job in the same office.

For the first few months my job was to make up silly little propaganda stories. There would be a number of pictures circulated among us each morning and we would pick one and then make up a story to accompany it. So, for example, I might get a picture of a woman standing on a pile of rubble and handing a cat to a soldier. My imagination would get to work and I would think up a story to accompany the image. Our team was given the remit of PSIS, which stood for Positive, Sentimental and Inspiring Stories—although it was a joke between ourselves that we should swap the order of Sentimental and Inspiring. We were told that these stories were the equivalent of "little white lies" to keep people's spirits up during the crises they faced. There was no harm in it, the editors told us, and our little stories were a kind of tonic to people feeling down. And so I would think up a story about a woman setting up a campaign to save pets with the help of a kindly Army officer. That was the kind of thing we were encouraged to dream up.

The more senior journalists wrote stories about counterterrorism operations, and there were usually pictures of dead bodies lying in pools of blood to accompany these stories. One day they wrote their most important story to date. There had been whisperings of it in the staff canteen all week, but I'll never forget the shock I felt when the story was splashed across the front page under the simple headline "GOT HIM." The main picture showed a young bearded man lying dead on the ground with a grinning soldier resting his foot on his lifeless face accompanied by the caption "John Barleycorn Killed During Eight Hour Shootout." The reason for my shock was because I recognised the dead man: he was one of the canteen cooks who had just served me lunch. My initial thought was that he must have had a twin brother. Then I wondered if perhaps it was the cook, and he'd been living a double life all this time. Those were my thoughts, but the very next day he was back serving mashed potato and sausages again in the canteen and joking with the senior journalists about reincarnation. Oh how naive I was back then! It was only a couple of months later when a colleague asked me if I wanted to see something "awesome" and took me down to the basement of the building. It was like a big studio filled with theatrical props, camera equipment and lights. "I thought you knew about all this," she whispered when she saw my amazement.

At that point my faith in pretty much everything had been shattered. It was as if all of what we took for granted had turned out to be fake, but that nobody wanted to mention it. For example, on the couple of occasions I expressed out loud my concern that my parents were okay and that I hoped I could soon go and visit them, people gave a nervous laugh and changed the subject. My colleague—the one who had shown me the basement—told me later I should "Learn to shut up, or you'll end up on the outside." And so I became mute. I turned up for work, made up my little white lie stories, went home again in the evenings and never said or did anything out of line. I learned to suppress my feelings and my natural curiosity simply in order to survive. And of course, I missed Robin; just where had he gone?

I might have been in what they called the main Green Zone (I later learned that there were several), but life was far from normal compared to the old days. I had a job, a house and a reason for getting up in the morning, but everything else seemed to be in a state of permanent flux. Indeed, it was a crazy time. The electricity was unstable; food was sometimes abundant and at other times hardly available at all; transport was unreliable and people acted erratically. A lot of my colleagues took a drug called "shine" every evening and pretty soon there was an epidemic of drug abuse across the city. And then, all of a sudden, shine became unavailable and there was anger and discord everywhere. People went mad and threw themselves in front of taxis and the authorities didn't seem to know how to deal with it.

Eventually a new drug came along—this new one was called "smile"—and tranquillity was restored. In between bouts of doing drugs and partying, people talked of nothing at all apart from entertainment, celebrities ("celebrities" were random people who had been artificially made famous by media organisations) and sports. Yes, there were still some sports going on, but the bulk of it consisted of foreign football matches beamed into homes via satellite. People talked of little else and I noticed after a while that everyone had begun to smile all the time as if they were permanently happy. I don't know—maybe it was the drug they were on that was making them do it, but if you didn't walk around with a smile on your face people asked you why you looked so miserable. I didn't take the drug myself; if someone offered me a smile pill I would pretend to take it, but secretly spit it out at the first opportunity, but it meant I had to affect a kind of half-smile in public, which hurt my face. Yet in reality it was as if we were all living in some kind of giant laboratory and being experimented upon—and we were never allowed to forget that we were the lucky ones on the *inside*! It was sheer madness, and the only way to remain sane was to reject it all and think of escape.

I buried myself in books. There were still libraries and bookshops, and so this wasn't hard to do. My job paid me reasonably well, and there wasn't an awful lot you could spend money on anyway, so I spent most of it on books and eating out. At night you could hear distant gunfire and loud earth-shaking bangs from beyond the walls of the Green Zone, and I shuddered in my bed.

And then Robin appeared in my life once again. He was sitting there one night in the darkness when I got home from work. At first I didn't recognise him. His hair had grown longer and he was much skinnier than the last time I had seen him. The clothes on his body were all dirty and stained and his eyes looked haunted. "I have been on the outside," was the first thing he said to me. And then, "I need you to shelter me."

We lived together, like husband and wife, for a while. There were some things I never found out about Robin, and some things that will remain a secret to all but us, but let me tell you this: before the crisis, Robin had been a software developer. He had been so gifted that even as a teenager he was approached by the government's secret service and assigned to their cyber security division. This was necessary in those days as people had created systems of such stupendous technological complexity that even those who had created them had lost the ability to understand how they functioned. Because of this weakness, these systems had become vulnerable to attack by anyone who could find a way into them. Very few people recognised this weakness until it was too late. You have to remember that the worship of technology was a kind of religion back then, because that is the only way you can understand people's irrationality in this regard. And nobody understood this complexity and irrationality better than Robin, perhaps along with a handful of others. They could see through it all, and what scared them was the fact that the safety of whole nations was being placed in the hands of people like them. It was like the technocrats had created a Frankenstein's monster, and didn't know what to do with it.

Robin had worked for them in secret, but he had a cover job as a newspaper photographer. There were plenty of things he knew about what was going on behind the scenes of our new reality, and over the course of the next few nights—after he had cleaned himself up and I had cut his hair—he told me everything he thought I had a right to know.

It was a lot to take in, but I had already figured out half of it for myself. I simply couldn't understand how it had been allowed to happen. "Why?" I asked Robin innocently. He just shrugged and said "Too much trust, too much stupidity and greed. It's just human nature, I suppose."

But Robin was in trouble. Something had happened and he couldn't tell me what it was for fear of implicating me. He had been on the outside for several months, moving around and gathering information. I had grown to love him, and could hardly bear to be away from him during the working day. But on the fifth evening after he returned he turned to me and said the words that I will never forget as long as I live.

"Rosie," he said, "your entire family is dead."

I didn't want to believe it. I cried and cried and told him he must be mistaken. But he was certain. "Your parents did not have enough food to last out. I sought them out, thought that I could bring them to safety just as I did you, but it was too late. I have seen their bodies," was all he would tell me. "Here," he said, taking something from his pocket and handing it to me. "Your mother had it on the bedside table next to her when she died." I took it from him. It was a crumpled photo of our family. I was six years old in it, beaming at the camera with my gappy mouth. We were all beaming at the camera, all of us unaware of the future that awaited us.

"But what about my siblings and my aunt?" I managed to ask when I had stopped crying. "Did you find out what happened to them?" Robin shook his head slowly. There was sorrow in his deep brown eyes and I knew he didn't want to cause me distress.

"All is not lost," he said later that night. "A resistance has been seeded and it is gathering in strength. There are a lot of angry young men and women out there and they are receiving assistance in terms of weaponry, food and organisational training. They give us hope."

"Help?" I said. "Where are they getting help from?"

"I can't tell you. But know that there are other forces out there who are fully aware of what is happening and have an interest in bringing it to an end. The ones who have set this in motion are the lowest, most despicable human beings in the world. They are not even human beings at all, in my opinion, for they lack the gene of empathy. I have seen things that have convinced me evil is afoot in this land and beyond."

"Like what?" I asked, perhaps preferring not to know.

"They are clearing the land. I have seen plans with vast zones demarcated on them. Mostly, this is happening in the north, but also in other areas. Ships are arriving at Bristol Docks. Huge ships filled with giant machines, drilling rigs, containers filled with steel pipe. Convoys of trucks are moving across the country, bringing this equipment to where it is to be used."

I stared at him in horror. "And my family just happened to live on top of one of these zones?"

"I'm sorry," he said. "These areas have already been written off. They're going after the oil and gas, and the people just got in the way. Drilling has already started."

He told me he would have to lie low for several months. I would need to shelter him, feed him, and bring him information. He looked into my eyes and told me it would be dangerous and urged me to think deeply about it. "We may die," he added. "In fact, it is a likelihood."

"I don't care," I said. "I don't care if I die."

And I meant it.

28

The farm lay about four miles inland amidst a patchwork of fields and woods at the base of a rounded hill. Getting there from the beach usually took Jack the best part of an hour, given the load he was pulling and his proclivity for stopping every so often to pick a wildflower or fish a useful-looking plastic bottle or Coke can out of a ditch. It was a slow grind but Jack was in no hurry. The spring air meant it was no longer necessary to wear gloves as he rode and daffodils and wild ransoms were popping up here and there from roadside verges adding splashes of colour to the greyish green landscape.

Jack stopped the bike and put it on its stand. He was in the middle of a dual carriageway that would have been busy with cars, trucks and vans just a year before, and yet now he had this entire stretch of tarmac to himself. He knelt down by the roadside and pulled up a few ransoms, savouring their rich garlicky smell. They would go well with the fish, he thought, and shoved them into a coat pocket. He was about to get on his bike again but an idea seemed to strike him. He wandered back to the verge and picked a few daffodils, taking care not to damage the stems too much as he did so.

These he tied to the handlebars of the bike with a spare elastic band, and then he was on his way once more.

His route meant that he had to skirt Penzance before turning inland. He didn't like to venture too far into the town on his bike; past experience had not been kind to him. Aside from the beggars imploring him for fish there were still soldiers patrolling, and everyone at the farm tried to avoid the Army in case the connection was ever made with the earlier incident. Following that, young Jago, who had suffered gunshot wounds, had hovered near death for the best part of a month before somehow finding the strength to pull through. Nobody at the farm would easily forget his screams during the operation to remove the bullets from his body, and each prayed that they themselves would never need to undergo an operation without anaesthetic. As for their Romanian friend who'd bashed in a soldier's head with a sledgehammer, he and his kinsmen were long gone, and had set off back to their homeland in search of a better life. *And who would blame them?*

Everyone at the farm had spent the entire winter shivering together in their thin-walled shacks and caravans. Food was getting scarce, the wood pile was all damp and tempers were getting frayed. The spirit of bonhomie that had united them after Cat's feast (as it had become known) had slowly been eroded away by months of heavy rain, chilly weather and bad tidings. As the reality of their situation had sunk in, many of them at the farm had become melancholy and depressed. And then the Romanians had left, taking their musical instruments with them and leaving the native Britons to spend their evenings in darkness and silence. People had nightmares. Some broke down and left, two people committed suicide and another died from carbon monoxide poisoning. Jack had helped dig the graves in one of the lower fields, shovelling mud in the rain and wondering how many more holes they'd have to dig before the ordeal would be over.

And yet, despite the misery and the cold and the fear, there were always more people turning up and wanting to stay. Art always said the same thing to these people. He asked them what they could bring to the farm, what their skills were, and why they should be permitted to stay. If they claimed to have a useful skill he would ask them to demonstrate it on the spot. If they passed this test they were put on a month's trial period to see if they fitted in. Most did, but those who tried to stir up trouble found themselves being marched off the land with a shotgun pointed at them. They never came back. "150," Art kept repeating, "give or take a few."

Jack was not immune to the weariness and the melancholy that was sweeping their camp. But for the most part he brushed it aside and concentrated on survival—his own and Cat's—as well as the imminent arrival of their child. *What kind of world are we bringing this kid into?* he sometimes asked himself, tossing and turning in the small hours of the night. *Who knows?* answered his more optimistic side. *Perhaps one that is better in some ways than the old one.*

Whatever Jack's thoughts were about the way the world was going, he was at least happy not to have ended up like the people he was now passing in the vast car park outside the newly constructed but already decrepit supermarket on the outskirts of town. These were the car people. Hundreds of them were living in vehicles or else sleeping in pop-up tents pitched on the tarmac. They sat around on deckchairs and cooked scraps of food on weakly smouldering piles of trash, looking for all the world as if they were waiting for normality to be restored and their old lives to be restarted. The men wore ragged leisurewear and were bearded, the women were hollow-eyed and wore shapeless clothes or were wrapped in blankets. There was an Army truck there right now, and Jack saw them lining up to receive morsels of food and bowls of soup from the soldiers. Most of them had been holidaymakers, caught out when the lights went off, the fuel stopped flowing and the roads were closed. He shuddered to think how close he could have been to ending up among them. Running into Art that evening might just have saved his life, he considered, because no matter how bad he thought the conditions were on the farm right now, the hope of what spring would bring staved off his fear and made his life more bearable.

He turned inland, passing the supermarket with its pitiful leisurewear refugees, and began the slow ascent to the farm. *It is all so weird*, he thought to himself, not for the first time. Presently he passed through a small village with a squat Norman church and graveyard. The cottages in the village all had their curtains drawn and there was almost no sign of life within. Roses were coming into flower around the doorways and the village pub looked just as it had for hundreds of years, albeit without the wooden furniture in the beer garden, which had long since been burned as firewood.

He passed on through and continued up narrow lanes enclosed by stone walls bristling with a profusion of spring flowers. About a mile from the farm he had to cross a small stone bridge spanning what the locals called a river, but was in fact more like a large stream. Having crossed it earlier in the day from the other direction, he had failed to notice a ramshackle construction made from old packing pallets and tarps which someone had built for themselves under the protective arch of the bridge. *What a stupid place to build a shelter*, thought Jack. One sudden downpour on the moors and the whole thing would be washed away in a torrent. He stopped the bike for a moment, partly to catch his breath but also to take a closer look at the structure under the bridge. On closer inspection, leaning over the side of the bridge, Jack noticed that there was a foot poking out from the crude shelter. It was wearing a dirty-looking tennis shoe and didn't appear to be wearing a sock. All of a sudden it moved and a voice cried out.

"Who are you?" It was an angry voice and Jack had no time to react before the man jumped out of the shelter and stood there glaring at him. He was quite tall and skinny with a bewhiskered, sour-looking face that was pockmarked with zit scabs. He was also holding a handgun and pointing it at Jack. "Come any closer and I'll put six holes in you," he growled.

Jack stuttered a response. "Sorry mate. Calm down, I was just seeing if you were all right. I'm just passing on over, on the way up to Twin Oaks Farm, that's all."

The sour-faced man scanned Jack for clues as to whether he was being honest. "Why should I believe that? How do I know you aren't one of them?"

"One of who?" said Jack.

"One of *them!*" shouted the man.

"I don't know what you're on about. Are you hungry?"

The man squinted at Jack, unsure whether to trust him. "Might be," he said. "Why?"

"I've got fish. You like fish?"

"Yeah, I like fish," said the man, his hunger clearly getting the better of him. He looked up at Jack and lowered the gun. "Got no fire though. Matches are all wet."

Jack considered his situation. Was this man dangerous? Probably not. Could he be useful in some way? Maybe. Perhaps he could be an extra pair of eyes for them. He could find out for the price of a fish. "Here," he said as he clambered down the bank to where the man was stood. "I hope you like mackerel."

The man started at the fish and then grabbed it from Jack's hand. After examining it for the briefest of moments he sat down on his haunches and bit hungrily into its side. Jack stood there and watched and it wasn't long before all that was left was the head and the bones, the guts having been pulled out and tossed into the stream. "Sorry about this," said the man with an impish grin and Jack watched as he sucked out the eyes of the fish before cracking open its skull with his teeth and poking his tongue into the cavity. He turned away. "Don't know why," said the scab-faced man when he was finished "but when you're starving hungry you just get this taste for the eyes. Vitamins, I reckon. Weird innit?"

"Yes, weird," replied Jack. "I'm Jack, by the way. From London, but the Midlands originally. Got caught down here when the power went off and stayed ever since. What about yourself?"

The man stifled a small belch and wiped his dirty fingers on his trousers before reaching out a bony hand. "Erik. I escaped from London and got here on that," he nodded in the direction of the bridge and Jack saw one wheel of a bicycle poking out from behind the shelter. "Would go further if I could to get away from those fuckers, but I ain't got no boat. Yet."

Hearing that the man was from London, Jack was full of questions. "What's going on there?" was all he could manage to say, "We've got a flat near Hyde Park. Is it safe around there?"

Erik scoffed. "Safe? Ha! There's nothing safe about London. Nothing safe about anywhere right now. Three hundred miles I came on that bike, probably more like five hundred if you count all the detours. At night too. You want to know what its like to ride a bike five hundred miles in the dark with no lights? I'll tell you..."

"Tell me about London," cut in Jack. "Tell me what's going on, I want to know."

And so Erik told him all about London. He told him about the riots and about thousands of people pouring in pulling suitcases and thousands more pouring out with just the clothes on their backs. He said they had started pulling down houses in the area where the rioting was going on, said they were planning to build a wall. "Those lizard-brained shits ain't gonna imprison Erik inside their wall!"

"Lizard brains?" said Jack.

"You mean you don't know?" said Erik, his eyes widening. "I think you'd better sit down."

Jack did so and for the next hour and a half Erik regaled him with his theories of what had happened and how life was now nothing more than an epic battle against them. He told Jack that the Illuminati had taken control, that they were all being experimented on like rats in a laboratory ("They've been spraying us for years from planes!"), that global warming was a hoax perpetuated to achieve a One World Government and that the End Times were near, although he planned to escape them too. "Jesus comes anywhere near me I'll put a cap in his arse too!" he said, patting the revolver tucked into his waistband. "I ain't got no time for peacenik hippies, I don't care who they say they are."

"But isn't this all one big conspiracy theory?" said Jack, who had never been one for such things. "I mean, people have been saying these things for years and they have never proved anything. Think about 9/11: people said that was a conspiracy, but there's no proof. I saw a programme about it once on the BBC..."

This was a bad move on Jack's part because Erik instantly became animated and began to leap about with wild abandon, spitting profanities. "BBC? BB fucking C? You know who owns that? You're even more of a stupid shit than you look!"

When he had calmed down enough he put his face right up in Jack's and spoke quietly with a kind of fervent passion. "Come on man, think! The easiest way to get away with this kind of plan is to make it look like all the conspiracy theorists are mad. Well, listen matey, don't call me a conspiracy theorist. You don't think they're planning world war three right now? Six months from now, unless we get off this toxic dog turd of an island, we'll all be shadows and cinders.

Cinders! If you can't handle the truth then you'd better get out of my face and leave me alone!"

"Whoa," said Jack. "I'm sorry. I didn't mean to offend you, I was just raising a point."

"Well, fuck off and raise your dumb points somewhere else. Maybe you've got a flock of sheeple up at that farm of yours who'll listen," said Erik as he turned away and skulked back inside his shelter. Jack could still hear him cursing to himself under his breath as he rummaged around. "BB pigging C... ha!" All of a sudden the sour-faced Erik poked his head out and gave Jack a big toothy grin. "So long, brother. Oh, and thanks for all the fish."

"So long," Jack called out meekly. He then scrambled back up the bank and got on his bike, vowing to get home without any more distractions. Pretty soon the stone bridge and its angry guardian were far behind him. *What a strange morning I'm having*, he thought as he climbed the last section of road that led to the small farm. The sun was out in full force now and sweat was running down his back. Up above a skylark sang in the clear blue sky and the silvery sea glinted in the distance. *What if he is right?* thought Jack. *What if he is only half-right? Even a quarter-right would be bad enough.*

29

The members of the 16th Air Assault Brigade stood to attention as a light but bitterly cold rain fell around them on the training quad. A man in a long black overcoat walked along the lines, pausing at every third or fourth man to utter a pleasantry or make a quip. The man, who was accompanied by a brigadier walking stiffly beside him, seemed in a hurry to get the inspection over with. There was a certain fluidity in his movements that hinted at a great bulk hidden beneath the tailored folds of the overcoat and might unkindly be described as a rolling waddle; a movement that was at odds with the sharp jerky steps of the brigadier. And although his demeanour betrayed nothing but authority a close observer may have noticed that the drops of moisture on his face were not rain, and the whitish pallor of his skin was steadily turning to a light shade of grey. "How many of these men have seen action?" asked the PM.

"All of them, Sir." The brigadier's Adam's apple rose and fell in his throat as he expanded on his reply. "A lot of them have been dropped right next to rebel enclaves and have fought hand to hand with the enemy. Many more are currently deployed in the field as we speak."

"Remarkable," muttered the PM unenthusiastically as he finished the line. In his head he was counting down the seconds until he could get back to the ministerial car. "Just remarkable." He turned to look at the assembled soldiers, and their hard expressionless faces stared back at him. Just the look of them caused his anxiety level to jump. He had no illusions that most of them hated him on a deep-down level and would gladly tear him to pieces if given the order to do so. He cleared his throat. "I want you to know that your efforts and sacrifices are not going unnoticed, and neither will they go unrewarded. I'm sure that many of you will have had grandparents or great grandparents who fought against the threat of the Nazis in the Second World War. The challenge of our times is no less grave. I just want you to know that as Prime Minister I will sincerely..."

The PM paused mid sentence. His mind had gone blank. He had given this speech, or something similar, a thousand times before and normally he didn't even have to think about the words. But this time they just seemed to have deserted him. Frozen. His fists opened and closed in the coat pockets. "I will sincerely..." he started out for a second time. The panic was rising. Barbiturates. If I could just get back to the car. He had to have some more barbiturates now otherwise. Otherwise...

"Sir," cried the brigadier. He was too late to catch the falling man. There was an awful sound like a coconut being hit with a hammer as the PM's head hit the asphalt. A few of the soldiers allowed themselves to glance down, although none of them rushed to give first aid. "Medical!" barked the brigadier, and two men wearing green tunics rushed from a nearby building. The PM's own security detail remained standing by a military prefab over in a corner of the quad. One of them pulled a coat lapel closer to his mouth and spoke some words into the microphone that was clipped there. "Get me Pope," he said. "There's been an incident."

Two thousand miles away a stick figure was running across a frozen landscape beneath a sawblade horizon of black and white peaks. The stick man was utterly alone in this wilderness, with not even an animal or a bird to lend him company. He was running across the rock and ice face of a huge glacier—a mere microbe against the vastness of the panorama. As he ran, his feet crunched on the frozen snow, causing little puffs of ice crystals to fly up in his wake and glint in the low sun as they settled. Pope's phone buzzed and he stopped, his breath hanging like steam in the frozen air. A message flashed across the tiny screen: "PM down. Hospital. Request immediate guidance."

Despite the cold, Pope's bald head glistened with sweat as he steadied his breathing. He stuffed the phone back into the pocket of a Lycra jacket and stood there looking at the distant shape of the Grímsvötn volcano. A thin smile spread across his lips.

30

~ The Mournful Tale of Rose O'Keefe ~

We lived together on the top floor of the house. It was quite a stately house, a Georgian terrace with iron railings on a wide street that led into a leafy city square. Before it had been allocated to me, it must have been two separate flats, because there were two kitchens on different floors and two entrances. The paperwork said the property belonged to the government but, just like my room in the halls at the university, it bore the imprint of past lives that had been suddenly uprooted. Sometimes I wondered who had lived there and what had happened to them. I searched for clues (part of me wondered if they might show up on the doorstep again) but could find nothing. Well, almost nothing. Moving the fridge one day to retrieve a pen I found a printed photograph of a young couple that had slipped down the back. They seemed to be in their late twenties, and she was strikingly beautiful in a Latin kind of way. He was also quite good looking, and had a dreamy kind of look on his face. I knew immediately that either she or both of them had lived here because the picture had clearly been taken in the kitchen where I now stood. Perhaps it had been taken with one of those cameras that printed out pictures immediately, I don't know. I scrutinised the picture looking for clues as to who they were or what might have become of them. But the picture revealed no clues and so I stuck it to the fridge as a kind of homage to the pair, hoping that, wherever they were now, they were doing okay.

There was no way we could risk anyone finding out that Robin was living there. The upstairs blinds were kept drawn at all times and I brought him takeaway food and leftovers from the staff canteen. I also did my best to get hold of books and clothes, although people everywhere were very suspicious of one another and *Fortitude* was forever printing articles about spies and criminals hiding out in people's basements. Sometimes he went out at night to meet "friends" and came back again before dawn. "Where do you go to?" I asked him, but he would never tell me. It was for my own good, he said.

One night he came home with a computer and some kind of radio equipment. "And now we are connected to the world once again!" he said gleefully. That's when my real education began. I have so much to be thankful to Robin for, because he opened my eyes and showed me my position within the swirling maelstrom of this reality. Without a good map it is not possible to navigate a complex world, and at that moment the world was more complex than it had ever been, or would ever be again.

On that first evening, I remember, we ate a Chinese takeaway meal and opened a bottle of red wine. Having checked that all the blinds were secure and the doors locked, we turned on Robin's little laptop computer and watched our first news release together. At first it was eerie. There was a man wearing a golden mask sitting at a desk and reading out news reports. His voice was digitally distorted and a caption underneath said "Today's *NewZ* is read by Sir X." It was always read by "Sir X," I was to discover, whoever he might be. "Don't worry," laughed Robin when he saw the expression on my face, "they are good guys, really, but they have to hide their identity."

The programme lasted about an hour, and showed reports from around the world. You have to understand that there were no real news programmes on television any more at that time, and although we had all grown up using the Internet, a lot of it had become "dark" and inaccessible. In other words, there was almost no way that people anywhere in the whole country could find out what was happening in the wider world without resorting to illegal downloads like the one we were watching.

At first the news reports were full of confusing words and concepts that meant nothing to me. They talked about conceptual things from the word of finance, about climate systems and about political and terrorist organisations I had never heard of. I had always hidden in my little world of astrophysics, and had little interest in what I had decided was the narrow and limited world of people and their doings. But now, under Robin's tutelage, I began to build up a picture of the world in which we were living, of the various actors and agencies, and how they were messing it up so badly. Unlike the kind of "feel good" news stories that I invented in my day job, stories on the *NewZ* were almost always hard-hitting, if not downright terrifying. They showed cities being blitzed in the Middle East, thousands of people starving in Africa, European politicians being shot at point blank range and the lifeless bodies of brown-skinned children poking from piles of rubble. Periodically, Robin would reach forward and press the space bar to pause the video and ask me if I understood the relevance of whatever we had just seen, and invariably I would shake my head. I had never felt so dumb or stupid.

But with his patience and his calm manner, Robin began to construct in my head a model of how the world worked.

Night after night we would sit and watch the *NewZ*, or read well-thumbed books and magazines he had brought back from his friends. Robin was a truly excellent teacher. Whenever I struggled to relate one concept to another or failed to understand how an event could happen, he would lean in and with a wry smile repeat, "Follow the money, girl. And if you can't follow the money, follow the energy—either path will lead you to the toad squatting at the heart of this mess."

And in this way I got to learn about the forces shaping the world. I had, for the last year or so, assumed that everywhere else in the world was in better shape than Britain. It was not so, I learned. Other countries seemed to be following the same path. First it had been Italy, quickly followed by Spain, Portugal and Greece. In each case it was the same story: a sudden loss of electrical power blamed on a small band of domestic insurgents or Russian hackers, followed by rioting, starvation and chaos while the richest cities and provinces sealed themselves off from the rest. France soon followed, as did a handful of other countries across Europe, Asia and South America. Currency exchanges and national finances were in chaos everywhere, but stock markets were somehow still rising. I learned all about hyperinflation, bond market meltdowns, derivatives bloodbaths and debt defaults. It was a steep learning curve. "Why do humans have to make everything so complicated?" I said.

And it seemed we were at war too. Although even the *NewZ* never actually came out and called it World War III, Britain, France, the United States, Israel and about a dozen other rich countries seemed to be locked in endless rounds of bombing smaller—usually dustier—countries. The various actors in all of this were an alphabet soup of ever-changing acronyms, Arabic names and government agencies—it was almost impossible to get a handle on it all! Even Robin's great powers of explanation couldn't make me understand all the ins and outs of what was going on, and he said that I'd need to read a lot of history books to truly understand it. "But that's not important," he said. When I asked him why, he simply smiled and repeated his mantra: "Just follow the energy." I must have looked puzzled, so he explained what he meant in this case. "Look, the world has run out of cheap fossil fuels. Most of what remains of the easy-to-get stuff with a high net energy yield is still in the Middle East and North Africa, hence the bombs, the revolutions, the terrorist groups and all the foreign meddling. Oil is the most dangerous drug that mankind has ever been hooked on. We'll do anything to get our fix of it, even if it kills us all."

"But why?" I asked. "We don't need oil, we can get by just fine with renewables. We can power our cars on hydrogen, we can fly planes using biofuels, and they are working on a new generation of nuclear reactors that are safe and don't produce any waste. And even if we have messed up here, we can always start new colonies on other planets—and don't tell me we can't because *I'm* the expert in astrophysics on this sofa, and not you! I've read up a lot on it. Chinese scientists are working on bioforming, and what can't be grown can simply be 3D printed when we get there."

When I said all this Robin stared at me for a moment and then began to roar with laughter. He fell back on the sofa, wiping away tears of mirth while I stared at him in annoyance. "I love your optimism, Rosie," he said, "but careful it doesn't get you killed."

As the seasons rolled by the remaining scales fell from my eyes. Winter turned to spring and then summer, and then autumn came around again. It had been almost two and a half years since the country had been shaken to its foundations, although so much had happened that it felt like many years had passed. One November morning, after days of fierce storms, I woke up and saw the street outside had turned into a brown and muddy river. "This city's days are

251

numbered," said Robin, looking down through a chink in the blind. Of course, when I eventually got to work that day, having to wade through knee-deep water, people said it was all the fault of Abdulla al-Hamas, who had blown up a cargo boat as it was passing near the Thames Barrier.

"Who was Abdulla al-Hamas?" you might ask. Well, he was the new John Barleycorn. When we reported that the latter had been "killed" in a gunfight, there was a great party across London and everyone was given the week off work. The PM had declared victory against the eco-terrorists and said that he was ready to lift the state of emergency and start sending people home again. The centre of London had thronged with many thousands of jubilant people in what was being called the biggest party of the century. And then the Trafalgar Square bomb had gone off. Hundreds had died, and not just in the initial blast: many also perished as Nelson's Column had come crashing down on top of them. The state of emergency was not lifted—instead it was heightened and Parliament was finally put into a state of "temporary" dissolution, from which it never emerged. Everyone agreed that these measures were necessary security steps—well, almost everyone.

Abdulla al-Hamas's face was displayed on every wall, taxi and computer screen—and if you ever came to the offices of *Fortitude* and stared a little too closely at one of the office cleaners, you might even see it there too. After the floods that day, when I had had to wade through water to get to work, the PM—who was getting fatter and more wild-eyed every year—came into the newspaper office wearing a set of fishing waders and was escorted to the basement and made to stand in front of a green screen. I snuck down into the basement on the pretext of delivering a message to the editor, who was busy writing a script for the PM, and lingered a while to watch them filming. That evening his rousing speech was on the evening television news and was the top trending video on the only YouTube channel that wasn't blocked for us. The video showed the PM standing atop the twisted metal ruins of the Thames Barrier, with a smouldering half-sunk cargo ship in the background. In his speech he lambasted this new terrorist atrocity and promised more funds to make the city walls stronger and the flood barriers more watertight.

When I got home that evening, I was eager to tell Robin about this latest episode of propaganda which I had seen in the making. I had even managed, on this occasion, to use a smartphone to discreetly snap a picture of the PM in front of the green screen having his makeup touched up. I had gleaned from Robin that on his nightly missions he would download short bursts of digital transmission on his short-wave radio equipment, which he would then decode using the laptop. The information was usually the latest episode of the *NewZ* podcast but also could contain thousands of web pages from servers that were blocked in London.

But Robin didn't always just download information: sometimes he would upload it too. It seemed that he was a point of contact for many others in the resistance movement, and they would bring him data and messages on computer chips that he would compile, encrypt and broadcast for them. Robin had told me that this was a game of cat and mouse with the authorities, which could detect the bursts of radio transmission, pinpoint the location from which they were transmitted and would often be at the scene within minutes. Since I was someone who worked inside *Fortitude*, obviously I was a pretty big source of information for Robin and his friends. He had been reluctant at first to allow me to be drawn into his web, but my insistence, as well as the desire to avenge my family, proved too powerful in the end. I knew that I was playing a dangerous game, and I knew that we'd be caught one day. I just didn't know when.

Maybe it sounds strange for you to read this, but I was very much enjoying my life at the time. Yes, I might have been living in what was effectively a psychological war zone within my own country, but I was living life on the edge with the first and last man I ever loved. We were crazy, brave and courageous, but we were never reckless. And so I was shocked to come home that November evening, bursting to tell Robin about the PM and the green screen and a hundred other things, only to find the house empty. I looked all over, but of Robin there was no trace. A window had been left open on the top floor—the window we had half-joked we would flee through if cornered—and his computer and radio equipment were missing. A cold fear spread inside me and I returned downstairs and slumped on the sofa. I sat there for some time in the dark, my head spinning with possibilities. And then I remembered the code.

Should something bad happen to him while he was alone in the house he would leave a discreet message to indicate he was okay. It was the picture of the couple—the one I had found down the back of the fridge. We had placed it as a bookmark in a well-worn copy Robin's favourite book—*For Whom the Bell Tolls*—and left it on the floor beside the top window. If Robin had to flee, but was in no immediate danger, he would turn the picture upside down and replace it. If the picture was upside down and back to front it meant I was in danger too and should leave the house immediately and call a number he had made me memorise. If the bookmark was undisturbed it could mean he had not had time to adjust it, for whatever reason, which should be taken as the worst possible omen.

I walked up the stairs to the top floor once again and opened the door to the dark room. The window was still open and a faint breeze caused the blind to sway slightly. I walked over to it and looked out. Normally I would have been able to see the green of the park, but now all was glassy water over which hung a pale yellow moon. The book was at my feet and I stooped down to pick it up. I opened it at page 100, my heart in my mouth. The pieces of the photograph fell to my feet like confetti and I was left staring at the whiteness of the pages. Over the text someone had taken a black marker pen and drawn a smiley winking face. Below it they had written a simple message.

It said: "You're next."

31

Save for the roar of the occasional F16 fighter jet tearing a hole in the sky above them, spring was a peaceful—if hungry—time at Twin Oaks Farm. When winter rains finally gave way to drier and sunnier days, the sticky mud that had blighted the lives of the settlers began to dry up and crumble and was soon obscured by foxgloves and primroses spreading a green carpet over the land. Verges, and other places not torn up by the boots and wheels of the settlers, burst forth with wild garlic and alexanders and the dry stone walls, built by hands from another era, erupted in a riot of colour and life. Small lizards sunned themselves on rocks amongst the toadflax, and bumblebees emerged sleepily from crevices, while the enamelled bodies of slow worms oozed between the snowdrops and the daffodils.

The return of the sun and the flowers brought much cheer to the settlers and made their deprivations seem more manageable. Food was running low and it seemed that every week brought with it the exhaustion of one thing or another from their store of pillaged goods. The rice and dried pulses were almost all gone, as was the once huge pile of budget packet spaghetti that had provided so many calories and allowed so much work to be done. The last cup of coffee had been drunk sometime around Christmas, and bread, sugar and chocolate were all but a distant memory. Furthermore, the farm was now unwillingly a dry farm, with the wine, beer and other alcohol having been drunk down to the last drop.

Art, as usual, was worried. He worried about running out of food, and he worried about soldiers and thugs turning up with guns, and he worried about Peck. The old bastard had gone unusually quiet of late and Art felt that he was planning something nasty. He still provided him with a box of provisions each week, but these days instead of it being a heavy box filled with tins of food and bottles of drink, it consisted merely of whatever scavenged scraps they could find. There was fish and cabbages and wild plants and, very occasionally, a wood pigeon or a pheasant. The box, left on the doorstep each week, would be taken in and then reappear empty, so Art knew that the old codger was still alive. But the man in the farmhouse kept the curtains drawn closed and people generally kept well clear of the place. Perhaps they could gradually starve him to death, thought Art, not for the first time. Janey wanted to kill him outright, but Art wouldn't agree to it. The last thing he wanted on his conscience was outright murder.

He sighed and got out his exercise book. It was filled with scribbled lists of food plans, pencil drawings of field designs and the occasional missive or poem penned late at night by candlelight. He turned to the list of people he had once drawn up and ran his eyes down it before reaching for a pen and crossing another couple off. The crossed-off names had the reason for leaving beside them, which in most cases was "CHI" which was Art's shorthand for "couldn't hack it." Six simply said "disappeared" and one had "expelled for theft and laziness" written beside it. The two suicides—a man and a woman who had thrown themselves off some cliffs—said RIP beside them, as did the girl who'd mistaken water hemlock for wild carrots.

Thinking about losing people, what the hell had happened last night? Jack had turned up a few days ago with three bottles of whisky he'd found on the beach. They'd opened them after dinner and passed them round and everyone who'd drunk more than a mouthful had ended up completely paralytic. They'd gone from being merry to being violently drunk in a matter of minutes. A mass brawl had broken out for no good reason, and the newly-built dining area had been badly damaged as a result. Two normally sheepish men had decided to fight one another with chunks of wood, a woman had run around trying to smash windows with a broom handle and another had to be restrained and bound up with rope after trying to throw herself on the campfire. Art himself had taken a slug and had felt the whisky seize his brain like the one and only time he'd experimented with injecting heroin. Having more tolerance to mind-altering substances than the others, he had quickly realised then that something wasn't right and had pried the bottles from their hands (not an easy thing) and poured out the contents. Even after a single mouthful of Laughing Chinaman whisky he felt hung over today. He ripped a page out of the exercise book and wrote on it in large black letters.

ANYONE DRINKING LAUGHING CHINAMAN WHISKY WILL BE EXPELLED FROM TWIN OAKS AT GUNPOINT. I MEAN IT. AG

That should dissuade them, he thought. *What will the evil feckers think of next?*

He tossed the book aside and looked around at the mess inside his cottage. Everything that had been coated in mud— the floor, the skirting and even the bed—was now coated in powdery brown dust. He looked at the sleeping figure of Janey, who was not much more than a lump under the duvet with a single foot poking out near the headboard. Buster, his old and black and white cat, lay curled up like a pretzel atop the sleeping figure. *This place needs a spring clean*, he thought, *I'll put it to her when she wakes up.*

Art put on a pair of tatty, mud-caked boots and the leather fur-lined cap he had taken to wearing since his hair had been cut short. He picked up the silver hash pipe from the bedside table and placed it in his pocket thinking that he might have a toke on it when he went to relieve Jago from rabbit-watching duty. He then clomped out into the cobbled courtyard to sniff at the morning air and stretch his body. This was the way he began most mornings, with an inspection of the farm, and today would be no different in that respect. First off he would take a peek inside a shed put up from hammered-together pallets and corrugated steel that he jokingly called 'Ye Olde Cider Barn'. Inside it, three large oak barrels sat on piles of old tyres, the airlocks bubbling quietly. Art would tap the sides of each barrel with a knuckle, savouring the solid sound of forty gallons of cider within. *It won't be long now until it's ready*, he thought with some satisfaction. *Whitsun. We'll have a big party at Whitsun.* The apples had come from the abandoned garden orchards and lone trees that dotted the area, and it had been Art's personal crusade to get as many of them as possible by hook or by crook. Times could be hard, he considered, but they were always less hard when you had a glass of scrumpy cider in one hand and a fat spliff of home grown in the other.

Once he had inspected the cider barn he would walk past the various sheds, caravans, yurts and campers which comprised the small community, pausing here and there to chat with people brewing tea over fires or frying up some fish and herbs for breakfast. But this morning, being a Sunday, nobody was up and Art carried on through the bluebell-filled copse that ran beside the stream, climbed over a stile and walked up the path that led to the fields.

The lower fields had begun to take on the chaotic and haphazard appearance of urban allotments. Everyone had been apportioned a section of land and was allowed to do with it what they liked. As a result there were now half a dozen polytunnels stitched together using PVC piping and clear packaging plastic, a smattering of glass greenhouses, some water butts, raised beds and small patches of bare soil in which grew neat rows of cabbages and leeks. Winding paths led here and there and the first-time visitor might have been alarmed to see a dozen sentinel-like figures standing erect and motionless around the plot. These smooth-skinned, bald-headed aliens had sparkly black skin and from each one dangled flashing circular disks on lengths of string. There were no faces to animate their bald heads, save for the occasional monsterish parody of an expression executed in lipstick and spray paint. It had been Cat's idea to ram-raid New Look and make off with their mannequins. Giving them a new lease on life as scarecrows had greatly appealed to Art's warped sense of anarchic humour and the CDs added an element of movement to scare off hungry birds and lend the scene a surreal dimension.

Art walked over to a patch of cabbages and bent down. Pulling back a lower leaf he spotted a fair-sized slug, causing him to tut. "Sorry mate, you're not welcome here," he said plucking the hapless gastropod from the leaf and grinding it into the path with the heel of his boot. The winter had been wet and warm: ideal survival conditions for slugs. *Toads*, he thought, setting out once more. *We need to find some spawn and get some toads on the go round here.* As he walked he racked his brains trying to think of where he might have seen a pond with breeding toads in it. There had to be one somewhere. *This year we'll have to dig more ponds ourselves*, he thought.

The top field, which sat on the brow of the hill, looked as if thousands of arrows had rained down onto it from an attacking army. But they weren't arrows, rather they were goat willow withies. It had been quite an effort during the winter to convert a seven-acre field from being a chemical-soaked cabbage patch and turn it into a nascent coppice woodland. The twigs were cut offs from some mature trees that grew down in the marshy pasture by the stream, and they were stuck six inches into the ground and spaced a foot apart. Assuming the majority of them survived, the fast-growing willows would be an abundant source of firewood and charcoal in years to come. They would act as windbreaks too, allowing for the back-planting of oak and sweet chestnut further into the future. Art had demonstrated how to build and use a rocket stove out of the most basic of materials, and the others had already begun constructing their own. Future winters would be so much more bearable with reliable heating.

At the centre of the field there was a circular area about thirty feet in diameter where no willow had been planted. This, in Art's mind at least, was where a charcoal burner's hut would be built. He imagined the occupant, hands black from handling his product, sitting outside it and gazing at the surrounding woodland. But at present there was no charcoal burner's hut, just a figure wrapped in a blanket, slumped on a deckchair and snoring. A .22 air rifle was propped up beside him as he slept.

"Wake up ya' lazy fecker," said Art, aiming a muddy boot at the young man's calf. Jago's eyes shot open, startled at this rude awakening. "Those rabbits won't shoot themselves will they?"

"I'm sorry," mumbled Jago. "Must have just drifted off for a couple of minutes."

"Couple of hours more like," laughed Art. "Here, let me take over while you go get yourself some brekky. Bit of a cold one last night wasn't it?"

"Sure was," said the young man, stifling a yawn and wrapping the blanket more closely around himself as he stood up. "I'll see you dreckly."

Art settled himself into the deckchair and rested the air gun on his lap as he watched Jago limp away from the field. They'd had a terrible time with Jago, what with the injuries he'd sustained at the hands of the soldier. For quite a while it had been touch and go, but the young Cornishman had been born tough and he had pulled through in the end, though he'd have scars to show for the rest of his days. It was people such as Jago that Art was trying to encourage at the farm. Sooner or later they'd have to fight for this land—Art felt sure of that—and he'd need as many Jagos as he could get hold of. People didn't simply give away their land: there would come a day when title deeds and business contracts would rise again, as if from the dead. Chaos had reigned for a while, but the chaos wouldn't last forever and one day someone would want this land back and Art and his 150 settlers would be evicted.

Evicted from my own land!

Art felt the anger and indignation flutter in his chest once more. In the beginning, when the lights had gone out and the country had been plunged back into the 18th century, Art had felt so sure that this was their chance to take back what was rightfully theirs. But now, after all the worry and the hardship, the mud and the meagre food and the depression that had fallen over the farm, it was difficult to keep that dream alive. He sighed and looked out over the landscape to the east, squinting against the sun. *What shall I do now?*

To a great extent he'd lost interest in what was going on in the wider world. The burdens of making a liveable homestead and simply trying to survive were of enough concern to him and the others. There seemed precious little to be gained by speculating on theories about what was going on far away and why it was happening. Of course, people would turn up at the farm bringing stories with them, and the radio news from France, which they could pick up on a clear day, was occasionally listened to. Cat, who understood French, would translate for the rest of them. So they had a fair idea what was going on as reported across the Channel, but not much of it seemed relevant to their situation. The world had suddenly become a lot bigger, and for some reason they felt the safer for it. Most of them were simply too tired to pay much attention to things not immediately relevant to them.

The winter hadn't helped with the gnawing feeling of despondency and fatigue, and each one of them yearned for the hungry gap to end. Art had not paid attention to this fact in his plans, and he chastised himself for the oversight. *Fat,* he thought. *We need more fat and less protein next winter.* He pondered how they might be able to get the balance right. They'd eaten their fill of fish and rabbits, to be sure, but man cannot survive by rabbit and fish alone. Now there weren't even that many rabbits around—although enough remained to cause serious damage to the willow coppice if they were given half a chance. *Pigs,* he thought. *We'll use the old piggery and start breeding them. There will be whole herds of them—great big fat pigs. We'll have bacon and pork chops and sausages* (at this thought his mouth began to water). *We'll fatten them up on... and there lies the problem.* What to fatten a pig on when every available scrap of food was going directly to the humans? He thought for a moment. *Acorns! We can feed them acorns - but where would we get so many from?* Now he had something else to worry about.

These were the thoughts that occupied the head of Arthek Gwavas—a lowly farm hand whose name would be remembered for generations to come—as he sat on that lonely hill one spring morning and pondered the uncertain fate of his little settlement. Indeed, so deep in thought was he that he did not hear the soft footsteps creeping up behind him, only realising that someone was there as the shadow of a raised arm briefly flickered across his face and the cricket bat came crashing down on his already dented head.

32

All was quiet in the PM's private medical suite when he awoke on what would be the last day of his life. A faint mechanical hum was the only sound in the room—a room so white in its every detail that the awakening man wondered momentarily if he had already passed over to the afterlife. He struggled to sit up and pulled back the covers, swinging his feet over onto the carpeted floor. Something tugged on his arm and he looked down at it. An IV line was taped to his forearm. He followed the line and, seeing that it emerged from the machine that was making the faint sound, he ripped off the tape and pulled out the needle and left it to dangle against the cool white linen, upon which it deposited little spots of blood.

"Nurse," he half-shouted, but nobody replied. There was a drawer in the small bedside table and he pulled it open. In it was a set of keys, his iPhone and the Scottish pebble he kept in his pocket. He grabbed for the phone and turned it on. "6:09am on Wednesday," it said. "Wednesday," thought the PM, I've been out for two whole days. The messages on his phone confirmed this: 76 text messages, 12 voice messages and a slew of emails, both personal and official. He had no desire to read or engage with any of the messages and simply tossed the phone onto the bed.

The PM rose unsteadily to his feet and walked over to a large window. Outside lay an expanse of manicured gardens of the type found in stately homes and royal palaces. He allowed his eye to follow a row of topiary to a high brick wall upon which yellow roses grew on trellises. There was an antique cast iron greenhouse filled with what looked like tropical ferns, and a neat oblong pond bustling with pink lily flowers. He stood there for several minutes taking in the scene, which was glistening in the early-morning sun as if a light rain shower had just fallen. For the first time in many years the PM felt a sense of tranquillity and peace. He was surprised to discover he had tears in his eyes and then, quite suddenly, his body was racked by great sobs.

What have I done? The PM staggered backwards and collapsed into a sitting position on the bed. He grabbed his face with his hands and began to sob silently. He was still crying when the door quietly opened and his wife walked in and sat softly down beside him. She held his hand and he looked up at her, tears still streaming down his cheeks. "Anne?"

"I was so worried about you, Dave. We thought we might lose you."

"Where are we?" he said.

"Scotland," she replied, still stroking his hand. "Or near as dammit—somewhere in the Borders. They said you'd need to stay here until you recover."

Her husband absorbed this information for a moment. "We've got to get away," he said in a cracked voice. "I expect they've already got a replacement for me, haven't they? It's Pope—it's all a game to him." Anne looked at him blankly. "We can still get out of this. Pope will move on to someone else: he's sucked me dry and broken my body, but he hasn't got my soul. Where are the kids?"

His wife looked shocked. "Away? Where to, hon? The kids are on their way here right now. We didn't know if you'd come round today but the doctors gave you a blood transfusion and something to stop you shaking. We feared the worst..."

"Costa Rica," said the PM. "Or maybe Brazil. Somewhere that doesn't feature in Pope's plans. We could defect."

"Defect, honey? What do you mean? We can't just fly away—the people need a leader."

"I'm the Prime Minister," bellowed the man suddenly, "I don't run this country, *they* do."

Anne, startled by his outburst, searched her husband's face. "Dave," she said sternly, "I wanted to break this to you gently but you're not the PM any more. It's Pope. He's been brought in as caretaker until you get better. You're supposed to stay here while you recover."

She watched the effect her words had on her husband. His mouth opened and closed like a fish and he stared at her; two small red-rimmed eyes engulfed in a puffy white face. "But it can't be him," croaked the PM, "he's not even an elected member for Christ's sake. Who authorised this?" Perhaps he was having a psychotic episode, she considered. The doctors had warned of all sorts of possible side effects from the drugs he was coming off and the drugs he was coming onto. What her husband needed, she thought, was rest. Rest and recuperation should do the trick and stop any crazy talk of running away to the other side of the world. After all, there was no way she was willing to give up the their place beside Regents Park or the lunches at the Ritz to which she'd become accustomed. And then there was the kids' schools to think about; the pied-à-terre near Piccadilly where she met her lover twice a week; the galas at the Equestrian Society... no, there was no way she was giving any of that up. She decided she had better humour him until his mental balance was restored.

"I'll tell you what," she began, "let's take off to my sister's place for a week or two. We can walk on the beach and talk and make plans. You always loved that place, didn't you?"

"Yes," he stuttered. "You're always right Anne, you know that?" He reached into the bedside drawer and took out the pebble. Holding it up between the two of them he addressed it in a hammy Scots accent "We'd better get this wee laddie back where he belongs." Anne tittered and leaned forward, kissing her husband lightly on the forehead.

"We'll be alright Dave, I know we will be."

Later that morning, when the children arrived, pulling their small suitcases behind them, they found their father pacing nervously around the room. "Ah, there you are my darlings," he said, getting down on his haunches to give the two children a hug. Nathan, six, and Lucy, eight, were excited to be away from prep school and prattled about their helicopter flight up from London. "Daddy, we saw a big fire in a city," said Nathan, his eyes wide with excitement.

"And some little planes going really fast," added his sister. "The man in the helicopter said they were not our friends and we had to get away from them. I want to have a helicopter when I'm big."

"Really?" said their father, his incredulity only half-faked. He shot a glance at his wife's impassive face. *What the hell was going on out there?*

Neither of the children had seen their father for over a month and both were eager to regale him with tales of what they had been up to at boarding school. "There'll be time for all this talk when we get to your aunt's place," said their father, rubbing them each on the head and turning to Anne. "We need to get a car," he said. "Is Nick here?" Nick was his most trusted security guard. She nodded. "Can you call him up here?"

A few minutes later the security man stood in the room with the family. "Nick, we need to get to Skye. What are our options?"

Nick, a bull-necked man who wore the permanent crease of a frown on his brow, sucked in his breath like a plumber with bad news. "The roads are dodgy but doable. We'd need to get a couple of support vehicles and take the armoured car."

"What about a 'copter? Why can't we use one of them?"

The security man winced. "I'd have to get it cleared, Sir. The one the kids came in has buggered off again." He looked down at the floor, almost shamefully. "Thing is, Sir, I've got orders to keep you here. Obviously, we go way back and I'll help you out. But air transport is out of the question."

Dave regarded Nick in the silence that followed. His phone buzzed and the text from Pope hovered on the screen for a moment. It read "Welcome back. Glad to hear you are feeling better. Big developments. Will be there after lunch."

The ex-PM looked at his security man again. "How soon can we leave?"

* * *

The three-vehicle convoy sped along the M74 motorway. By mid-afternoon they were skirting Glasgow and heading towards the Highlands. Dave was driving the bulletproof Range Rover with blacked-out windows, his wife sitting in the passenger seat beside him with Mitzy, the Chihuahua she took with her everywhere, the two kids in the back. The two armoured Humvees that accompanied them carried six police officers and Nick. One of the vehicles pulled a trailer loaded with fuel and mechanical spares in case of breakdown. Driving along the motorway was slow going on account of the numerous burned-out and abandoned cars and trucks which littered it. There were people, too, walking along the tarmacked surface and pushing their possessions in shopping trolleys. "Slow down, Dave, you might hit someone," said Anne.

"Can't slow down," said her husband. "We have to stay in convoy." She sighed and his phone buzzed again. He took it from the dashboard and looked at it. It was Pope again. "Where R U?" This was the fifth message from him. Dave fiddled with the phone and turned it off.

"Keep your eyes on the road, dear," said his wife.

By the time they reached the Highlands, they were in need of refuelling. They stopped at a mountain pass and put down the windows while two officers filled the Range Rover's tank. "Smell that air, kids—that's the smell of freedom!"

"Why are we going to Auntie Meg's?" asked Lucy. "Can we have pizza for dinner?"

Nick leaned in at the window. "I've radioed ahead, Sir. I think it's best to lose our friends here and I've arranged to change cars at the bridge. I'll send these boys back now and will accompany you as far as the bridge. Of course, I'll have to retain an extra driver, but we're past the main danger zone."

"Danger zone?" said Anne. "Why should we be in any danger?"

"That'll be fine, Nick. Thanks!" said the ex-PM.

By the time they had passed Fort William and traversed Loch Lochy the weather had taken a turn for the worse. Clouds the colour of gunmetal filled the skies and shrouded the snow-covered peaks. "Are we there yet?" asked Lucy.

It was early evening when the two cars reached the Kyle of Lochalsh and crossed the bridge over the sea to Skye. All around them a landscape of sea and mountains stretched out. "Is this where the Loch Ness Monster lives, Daddy?" asked Nathan.

They pulled up in the forecourt of a deserted petrol station and cut the engine. A shiny black Audi was parked there, waiting for them. The security man got out of his car and came over to the others. "It's just a single skin I'm afraid," he said. "But you shouldn't have much trouble up here. There's no tracking on it and I would disable your phone if I were you, Sir, if you want peace and quiet. I could accompany you all the way but I'm guessing you want your privacy."

"Damned right, Nick," said Dave, fixing the security guard with his eye. "Thanks for all you have done for us. I'll repay you when I get the chance."

"Take care, Sir," replied the hard-faced man. "The key's in the ignition and there's a full tank. I'll transfer your luggage."

Five minutes later they watched as the armoured Range Rover drove away across the bridge. A minute or two later its headlights were mere pinpricks of light in the darkening landscape. The ex-PM felt as if some invisible shackles had been removed. He stared at the car until it was gone, and then he turned the key in the ignition.

"You *do* know the way from here don't you?" asked his wife.

They drove on into the night, burrowing into the dark fissures between the mountains. The ex-PM put his foot down, relishing the growing distance between himself and Pope. "For God's sake slow down," Anne admonished her husband as he took the high-powered car careering around bends. He wasn't feeling too good. The drugs and the adrenaline rush of their escape were both beginning to wear off and his knuckles were white on the steering wheel. *There is bound to be some scotch at the place. Or vodka. Even a couple of bottles of wine will do*, he thought.

"Are you feeling okay darling?" asked Anne, her face half-lit in the dashboard light.

"Mum, I'm hungry," groaned Nathan. "You said we'd be there soon and that was *ages* ago."

"Be quiet," shouted his father. "Don't you know how hard it is to drive a car around these roads?" Mitzy growled in displeasure from his place on Anne's lap.

"Sorry," said the little boy, meekly. A long curve in the road was approaching and instead of easing up on the accelerator his father pressed down on it harder.

"I said slow down!" said Anne once again. "There are deer up here and they can jump out and ..." All of a sudden there came a maniacal electronic laugh from somewhere in the car, like one of those laugh-in-a-bag toys that had popular in the 1970s.

"What the hell...?" said the ex-PM glaring at the flashing phone sitting between the arm rests. "I turned that bloody thing off. There's no way..." He grabbed it and looked down. The screen was flashing red and there was a pixelated depiction of a laughing clown and two words flashing in block capitals: GAME OVER.

"What the f..." he started, but his words were drowned out by his wife's sudden scream as the Audi ploughed straight into the blade of the stationary military bulldozer. In the moments after the collision the only sound to be heard came from a hydraulic hose somewhere in the twisted mess of the vehicle, accompanied by the some faint sobbing. When the hissing and sobbing eventually subsided a powerful light came on, illuminating the ghastly scene. A man stepped down out from behind some boulders lying to the side of the road and walked twice around the wrecked car, pointing a standard issue military handgun into its interior. When he was satisfied with what he had seen he climbed up into the cab of the bulldozer and turned on the engine. There came the sound of metal scraping against tarmac as the wreck was shunted off the side of the road. The car fell into space, before crashing into a promontory rock and then landing upright in a dark peaty pool below.

By dawn there was nothing to be seen of the car or its occupants, and even the broken glass and shattered plastic on the road above had been swept away. Two hundred feet below the road, the only tell-tale sign of the incident was an iridescent patch of oil on the surface of an otherwise pristine bog. Only a tiny group of people knew what had really happened on that fateful night and, as it happened, they would soon take this secret with them to their own graves.

33

~ The Mournful Tale of Rose O'Keefe ~

Rose O'Keefe put down her pen for a moment and rubbed her eyes. She had reached the most unusual part of her narrative and wondered, for a moment, if she should perhaps skip over it and just stick to the physical details. There were some painful memories in there too—memories she didn't like to dredge up. What's more, she worried that future people might think she was crazy and that this would discredit the rest of her story. And the story, she had decided, would form the first part of the teachings she had so meticulously detailed over the years, and which were now bound in a green leather jacket and stowed in the bottom drawer of her desk. Outside, the wind had unlatched the wooden gate on her small vegetable garden, causing it to bang wildly against its post. She wondered whether she should go and close it. Given half a chance the rabbits would be in there at first light and that would be the end of the winter greens. No, she thought, it would be better to press on. First light was not far off and her tale was not yet complete. The gods only knew what harrows the dawn would bring with it, although she had no fear. She picked up her pen and continued.

* * *

It is getting more difficult to lay down my account. My challenge lies not simply in recording the turbulent events that broke my heart, but also in explaining how the world was back then to those who today can scarcely imagine it. Almost nobody at that time could have imagined how suddenly their lives were going to change. It seemed that one minute we were happily going about our everyday business and the next we were fighting for survival as the forces of chaos were let loose and the hubris of foolish men rent our society asunder. How could this be? Could nobody have foreseen how events would unfold? Oh, there were some, Robin told me, but their voices of caution were drowned out by those who were unwilling to face this darkness. It was as if our minds had been hijacked on purpose. People back then were too busy to think much about the wider world. They were overwhelmed with work and trivial matters and relationships—there was no time to think. There was so much information we were expected to parse—so many choices confronted us in our daily lives. Most people were overwhelmed and unable to think clearly—too wrapped up in their own lives to see the wood from the trees. There was so much entertainment back then and it was easy to lose yourself in the made-up fantasy worlds they showed on television, or the ones you created for yourself inside your own head or on a computer screen. Is it any wonder why so few people had any idea of what was to strike them? I had been no different in this respect.

The moment I found Robin was missing, I understood that my own chances of survival were slim. At first I just sat there in a state of fear, like a deer frozen in a hunter's lamplight. When my mind cleared and I regained my senses, I felt as if I was being toyed with. Would an attempt to escape be futile? I felt so. Nevertheless, I rushed around the house throwing my most important belongings into my small bag—the one I had left home with in the first place. Robin's computer was gone, as was the radio transceiver. I left the house after dark and hurried through the streets with my head down. I remember that it was a rainy evening, and as I walked aimlessly through the streets of London my clothes soon became wet all the way through. Never had I felt so alone and scared. I didn't know what I was going to do or where I was going. There was no plan. I still had the work phone in my pocket—the one I had used to take a picture of the PM earlier that day. My hand clutched at it inside my coat pocket and I wondered if it was safe to use it to call the number I had memorised. But the battery was almost dead, so if I was going to call on it I would have to do it soon.

It was late at night by the time I ended up at Waterloo Bridge. I stared at the black waters passing beneath me. The reflected lights of the city were stretched and distorted by the movement of the river, and I stared at them, mesmerised, for some time. Perhaps I would throw myself in, I considered. I imagined my body being pulled under the surface—a watery end to an unsatisfactory and irrelevant life. I had loved and lost, and now I felt that there was little left to live for. These are the thoughts that moved languidly through my mind as I contemplated my end. But there was another thought. What if Robin was still alive? What if they had taken him somewhere—somewhere deep and shadowy where screams went unheard? I knew such places existed, had heard the testimony of people interviewed on the NewZ. I could rescue him. With him freed we could get far away from this place of nightmares and live the rest of our natural lives somewhere free from intimidation and coercion. But first I would need to make contact with his network. I could not rescue him alone.

I pulled the phone from my pocket and called the number. It rang several times before a voice answered. "Yes," it said. It was a man, sleepy sounding, and the connection was crackly.

"This is Matilda," I said, remembering what I had been told to say. "I am going walkabout. John is not with me."

I waited for a response. But instead there was a click and the line went dead. I tried the number again and it rang out, giving me the option to leave a message. "No!" I shouted at the phone, and flung it down into the river below. I stood staring at the waters, a feeling of panic in my chest. Had I been tricked or just abandoned? I had no way of telling. Presently I made my decision. I made my peace with the world and climbed on top of the balustrade that kept pedestrians from falling. I was about to jump when I heard a voice cry out "Rose!" There were two men running towards me. For a moment, I thought I might be saved, that they would take me somewhere safe and warm and dry. But then I saw their black leather jackets, the resolve on their humourless faces and the clear, purposeful way in which they ran. They were no friends of mine. Before they could reach me, I jumped. There was a terrible feeling of falling followed by a sudden smack as I hit the water. I think I must have momentarily blacked out and then come to again because I remember looking up and seeing a powerful torchlight shining into my face from above. There were cracking noises and I remember thinking that fireworks must be going off somewhere, and then I felt myself sinking into the waters.

The cold was the thing I remember most about dying, and then the way that it slowly became warm again. The current must have pulled me under, but I didn't care. I breathed the cold, black water into my lungs, hoping to make my death a speedy one. It was.

And now, dear reader, the story of who I became really begins. Please bear with me as I explain what happened after my fall from the bridge. If you choose not to believe me then that's okay, but please try and retain an open mind as you read my words. Remember, I am a scientist by learning: only true experience has taught me what I know today.

Down in those murky depths of the river my life force left my body. All of a sudden I felt myself rising up and floating above the whole sorry scene. I could see the poor lifeless body of Rose O'Keefe turning round and round in those dirty waters like a rag doll in a washing machine. And just as clearly I could see those two men on the bridge firing their pistols into the dark river, and to me they seemed like children with toy guns. Everywhere I looked seemed infused with the strangest kind of light. It was a type of light that I had never seen before, nor can adequately explain. I felt giddy, excited even, to be leaving this weary realm.

Above me in the sky it seemed as if there were an even stronger light and I felt compelled to travel towards it. As I rose it seemed as if millions of people below me were crying out in sadness. Except they were not people, all of them. They were trees, foxes, dandelions, potted plants in offices, elephants in faraway Africa and a million other types of plant, animal and even mineral. Even the grass in Hyde Park seemed to be weeping, and I felt overcome with embarrassment! "Are you really sad for little insignificant me?" I called out—although I didn't use words, I just thought these things and it seemed as if my thoughts were transmitted—and they all seemed to answer "Yes!" in unison. My heart felt ready to burst with love, for want of a better word. Yes, it really was the strangest and nicest sensation I had ever felt.

I travelled up through a shifting cloud-like tunnel towards the light above me. When I got there I couldn't tell whether weeks or even months had passed, or perhaps it was just seconds—it is hard to explain. During the trip I had been floating around in a state of what can only be called ecstasy. I had no idea such feelings were possible. Stranger still, time had ceased to exist in the state that I was used to. It didn't seem to matter if things took seconds or years—it was all the same thing. I arrived at a place that seemed like a beach. It was, I recall, a very beautiful natural beach with powdery soft sand on the edge of a very calm sea that shone in colours I had never before seen. On the beach—joy of joys!—there hovered some balls of light which I instantly recognised. It was my family—and Robin was there too. How strange it is of me to describe balls of light as my family and Robin, but that is exactly what they were. There were others too. They were people I recognised and loved from somewhere else, but had somehow forgotten about until now. They all greeted me with great tenderness and we all expanded into one another in a way that is not really possible to describe in physical terms.

How long was I on that beach with my loved ones? Again, I cannot say, for all time had disappeared. A minute? A hundred years? Both and neither—all I know is that they were happy to see me. They all told me the sorry stories of how they had died, although they related the tales in a detached way that made them sound more interesting than sad. It seemed that it was only my death which was of concern to them. "You are here too soon," said the sphere of light who was my father in this life. "That is why we have come here on this beach to meet you." Another light had appeared and it came over to me and spoke directly into my essence. I couldn't tell if it was a man or a woman, because it seemed simply to be just pure energy. "Dear Rose," it said. "It is so heartening to see you so well, but your life container has been damaged and is now in for repair."

Yes, it really said "in for repair"!

I was flabbergasted. "Are you God?" I asked, and all of my loved ones began to laugh.

"No, not exactly," it said. "Although I am just as much a part of the Great Spirit as you are."

Next, I was made aware of what looked like a pile of old clothes that had washed up on the shore. As I got nearer I realised with some shock that it was me. I was lying there looking all bedraggled and soaked, and there were holes all over my body. "It's me!" I cried in surprise. "I've been shot."

Again the others chuckled, although I didn't see anything funny about it. "It's not 'you', as such," explained one of them. "Do you wish to truly see yourself?"

"Yes," I replied, a little apprehensively.

"Then look into the water," said the light sphere that was Robin.

I went over to the perfectly still sea and gazed into it to see my reflection. For a second time I was shocked—I appeared to be nothing more than a wrinkly gossamer thin tube that looked not entirely unlike a used contraceptive. The others saw my reaction and laughed gently. "Don't worry, dear," said my mother. "We all look like that upon arrival, but it's just a temporary state."

"I see," I said.

I looked over at the body of the young woman lying by the water's edge. Several more balls of energy had appeared and were hovering over "me." They pulsed different colours and I knew they were healing my body.

"Your vessel is almost ready," said the one whom I had mistakenly called God. "You must leave soon and continue on your mission."

"My mission?" I said, puzzled. "I didn't know I had a mission."

"How easily you will forget it when you enter the density of the Earth realm!" it said. "But continue it you must."

There was no sadness as I left Robin and my family. "I will be back soon," I said, knowing this to be true, as did they. We all pulsed in unison one more time, entering one another's essences and vibrating together. That's the only way I can describe it. "You make us all so proud," said my mother.

The being who seemed to be in charge led me over to my body. "Try not to damage it again," it said. "This time you will have many allies who will help you and guide you in your mission. You must make the best of your free will and remember that we are with you at all times."

And with that I seemed to slip back into my body. In an instant I felt the cold return. I opened my eyes, discerning a gloomy half-light. I was lying down on something soft and wet and my mouth was full of mud. I spat it out and struggled into an upright position. For a few moments I was disorientated. My head was woozy and I felt sick to the stomach. I appeared to be on a mud flat beside a wide brown river and I felt puzzled as to why that nice warm sea and sand had suddenly disappeared. All of a sudden I began to retch. River water gushed out of my mouth and nose, leaving me gasping for air like some primordial fish coming onto land for the first time.

When I had finished puking up the river water I stood up and looked around. In one direction I could see a great flat expanse of slate-grey sea that filled the horizon. In the other I could make out the dim low form of a city with clusters of familiar-looking skyscrapers jutting up. They were far enough away to look like studded growths of crystals jutting up into a pale sky. London, I thought.

And then what had happened to me previous night came flooding back. The last thing I could remember was jumping, and then the feeling of sinking and the sound of firecrackers. Clearly, by some miracle, I had survived the river and been spat out into the estuarine wastelands where the Thames meets the sea. *Had all the rest been a hallucination?*—I wondered—*the ravings of an imaginative mind as the cerebral cortex fades to black?* I began to retch once more, my empty stomach straining out the last drops of muddy water and river weed.

"Feeling sick?" said a voice.

I spun around to see who it was, but there was nobody there.

"Try a bit of me," it said. "I promise you'll feel better in no time."

There was still nobody there. In fact there was nobody to be seen in any direction as far as the eye could see. "Down here," said the voice.

I squatted down next to a clump of green leaves with purplish flower heads that was giving off a raw, minty smell. "That's right," said the voice. "Just a few of my leaves. Chew them and you'll feel much better."

"Well, thank you," I said, feeling more than a bit silly talking to a plant.

"No problem," said the mint. "Just don't eat all of me."

I sat and chewed on the leaves. And it was true! I did feel better in just a short time. "I told you so," said the plant.

"I think I have gone insane," I replied.

And that, dear reader, is how I stepped out of one reality and into another—one that I could scarcely have believed were possible.

34

Cat had been awake since before the dawn. She heard Jack leave on his morning fishing tour and laid on her side staring at the blank wall of the van. Something didn't feel right. The baby was still kicking just as it had done over the past few months but she sensed some kind of change happening. Perhaps it would be today. The thought frightened her and she sat upright in the cramped bed.

What am I doing here?

She tried to quell a rising sense of panic. How had she come to end up in this position? She was twenty-six years old, living in a damp and rusty camper van beside a stream and almost nine months pregnant. Jack, the clean-shaven boy she had met in London, was now a bearded fisherman, and seemed way too happy in this role. She had not spoken to her friends or family since the fateful day when the power cuts had started, and now she faced giving birth on a dirty farm aided only by an old woman who claimed to have worked as a midwife in the 1960s.

Breathe.

Cat shut here eyes and made a conscious effort to control her breathing. Her pulse was racing and she felt hot shivers run up and down the skin on her legs. A thought occurred to her. She tried to block it out but it came back again.

No, I mustn't even think of it.

But the thought wouldn't go away. How long would it take to get back to London? She had seen soldiers drive past in military vehicles. Jack had said there were plenty more on the main roads. She could walk. Yes, she could still walk even with the baby inside her. How long would it take to walk to the town? *Maybe only a couple of hours if I take things easy.* The soldiers would look after her. She could use her charms: they had worked in the past, why wouldn't they work now? The soldiers must have convoys going around the country. They could deliver her to safety.

I still have my golden credit card.

She plunged her hand down the sides of the cushions on the bed, feeling around for it. Her fingers found it, taped against the underside of a plywood seat for safekeeping. She ripped it off and pulled it out. It was a golden ticket that could take her back to the world she once knew. Why hadn't she thought about it until now? Why had she needlessly put herself through so much misery? She gazed at it, recalling the day her father had handed it to her. "Just for you, *mi preciosa.*" It was for emergencies.

This was an emergency.

What if the hippies were liars? They said that nothing was working. They said the whole country had gone back to the Middle Ages. What if they *wanted* nothing to work? What if they *wanted* to live in the Middle Ages? They said there were no trains or buses or planes any more. They said that the banks were closed, that everything has crashed and the TV screens had gone black and the computers had stopped working. *But what if that was what they had wanted all along?* Why do *they* think they know anything about what is going on in the rest of the country?

Because they listen to that idiot!

286

Art says this, Art says that. What if Art was lying? What if he just wants us here on this farm living like serfs and doing his bidding? What is this—some kind of homage to *The Heart of Darkness*? What if things were broken down here in Cornwall but everywhere else was fine? How would we know if he was telling the truth? Cat sat up sharply, astonished by this new thought. But what about the radio in French? Hadn't that told us about all the turmoil that was happening? She considered this for a moment, her mind prodding this uncomfortable thought, checking it for signs of falsehood. If they had radio in France then France must be okay. She could get to France. From France she could get anywhere. Argentina would be okay. We have had hard times before and we know how to live through them, unlike these English pansies! The plastic card cut into her hand and she realised she was gripping it far too tightly.

"*Just for you, mi preciosa.*"

She began to shake. It was not just herself she had to consider any more. Soon she would become two. Yes, there would be the shame of turning up back home as an unmarried mother. There would be disappointment all round. But she could live with that. Wasn't this the 21st century in any case? *But what about Jack?* She thought about this for a moment, pictured his boyish face in her mind. He would be all right. He would always be all right—that was one of the problems with men.

I could be in London by tonight.

She stuffed some clothes into a small rucksack. There was no time to think. Thinking things through was a luxury she could not afford. She was running on instinct now—the instinct to survive. *Bribery.* How much would she need to offer to get her on a plane to Buenos Aires? She would call her father and he would sort it out. Are the phones working in London? She felt certain that they would be. What about the little problem of her being eight months pregnant and on a

287

plane flying over the Atlantic? Not an issue when you have a gold credit card and a father who can move and shake. She imagined being met at the airport by him. "*Mi preciosa!*" She would be the prodigal daughter. He would sacrifice the fatted calf. The yearning to escape grew stronger.

"I must leave right away."

She followed the path that led through a small woodland beside the stream. The bluebells dripped with early morning dew and the birds sang the dawn chorus, although she didn't notice any of this. There was no sign of life inside the shacks and caravans she quietly passed.

"If anyone sees me, then, so what?"

She didn't speak to most of them anyway and they didn't speak to her. The path began to rise and she slowed accordingly. Every now and again she had to pause to catch her breath. It was during one such pause that she heard someone coming. At first she thought it was some kind of animal. It was grunting and breathing heavily and there was a rustling noise as if the beast was dragging itself along the path. Maybe it was injured. She decided she had better get out of its way, whatever it was, and removed herself from the path as fast as she was able.

Squatting down behind the burgeoning greenery of an elder bush she remained as still as possible. After a few moments she saw the shambling figure of a man appear. He had wild white hair and was dressed in dirty-looking tweeds. Cat hadn't seen Peck in a long time, and he'd lost a lot of weight, but it was certainly him. He appeared to be struggling with something, and at first she thought he was dragging along a sack of potatoes or turnips. It was only when he was almost level with her on the path that she could see what it was. The unmistakeably scrawny body of Arthek Gwavas was being dragged along feet-first with both arms flailing behind him. Peck was so close now that Cat could smell the sour reek of his body odour. She closed her eyes and mouthed several Hail

Mary's in quick succession. When she opened them again she found herself looking directly into the eyes of Arthek Gwavas. She gasped a little and put her hand up to her mouth in horror.

"Was he dead? Had Peck killed him?"

The eyes were heavy-lidded and dopey. Not unusual for him, she thought, but he didn't look dead. Unconscious perhaps, but not dead. Peck groaned and carried on staggering along the path. A minute later he had disappeared around a bend and the last thing Cat saw of them was Art's shaved head bumping on a stone that protruded from the path. When she was sure they had passed she stood up and looked around in case any more dangers lurked in amongst the trees.

"I can be back at home in a week."

She emerged from the bushes and along the path that led out of the farm onto the road that would take her to the sol-diers and safety.

35

Every time he considered the new PM, Pope sighed inwardly. Victoria Steele, a blue-eyed power-dresser, had been singled out as an excellent choice, but she was proving harder to tame than her predecessor. Full of bombastic intention and an unshakeable belief that she could raise a phoenix from the ashes, Steele, who, politically speaking, had come out of nowhere, had been in office for barely a month before she started issuing threats against other nations. The thirty-six-year-old daughter of a Hampstead doctor, Steele wore her hair in a tight bun atop her head and promised to launch a nuclear attack on Russia after accusing them of providing aid and support to the groups of rebels who were launching increasingly bold offensives outside the Green Zones.

And as if that were not bad enough, she was furthermore threatening to round up profiteers, place a moratorium on foreign energy and agricultural firms—which she termed the 'enemy within'—and had devised a five-year plan to get the nation back on its feet. She said she aimed to reopen Parliament "at the earliest opportunity" and set up a truth and reconciliation committee to find out what had gone so wrong and who was to blame. Those found guilty of high-level wrongdoing would walk the steps to the gallows, she had said. Furthermore, she had commandeered *Fortitude* to write screed-like editorials about land reform and reparations to citizens affected by the events of the past two years. Unsurprisingly, she was wildly popular.

Big Bear was livid.

"What the hell were you thinking, Oryx? What was wrong with that other guy? You know, the fat one with the pill habit and the dizzy wife? All you had to do was get him a bit of Medicare and he'd have been good for another five years. Instead, you go and bump him off and install this..." he searched for the right words, "this crazy bitch that doesn't play by the rules. Dammit, man, she's even getting the Russkies involved in all this, and they are seriously not playing ball. So tell us, what the *hell* were you thinking?"

Pope visibly shrivelled under the verbal onslaught. The eyes of all the Patriots were upon him as he squirmed. It was bad enough that he was being put under such scrutiny, but worse yet that it was happening at the annual World Patriot Convocation—the time of the year when they should have been toasting their success. But there was nothing he could say; Big Bear was right. Steele threatened their entire project. She was a loose canon. Unhinged. She would have to be removed at the earliest opportunity. "I'm sorry," he managed to say. "She'll be gone as soon as I've got a suitable replacement."

"Better make it soon," Bear growled. "She's already kicked up a hot fuss—it'll be difficult to deflate *that* balloon."

After this dressing down, Pope returned to his room and sat on the bed in a state of dejection. Why had Baal advised him so badly? Was it some kind of test, or had Pope done something to offend his guide? He closed his eyes and silently hummed the incantation that usually summoned him. Often he would take the form of a pulsating ball of light, only occasionally morphing into humanoid form, but today there was nothing. Pope continued calling for a few minutes but was left only with a dark void. *Has he abandoned me?* The thought panicked him for a moment. What if he had? Without Baal's help he was powerless.

And then it came. The familiar sense of Baal's presence flooded Pope's senses.

"What do you want?"

The entity seemed angry. It had happened like that before but he could always be placated. Pope transmitted pure thought forms to him. "I am puzzled, O Great One. You said that Steele was the right one and yet she has brought nothing but trouble for us. Why did you advise me thus?"

"There are factors that are not easy for you to understand. Do you question my guidance?" came the reply.

"No, of course not," Pope replied. "I only wish to understand why you put forward one who is so unmanageable. Could it be that you made a mistake and had meant to suggest another?"

There were a few seconds of silence and then the ball of light began to pulsate quickly.

"You dare to question me? You, a mere mortal human—as ephemeral as a wave breaking on a beach or a leaf in autumn—dares to question the great and almighty Baal who has existed for uncounted aeons and will exist until the end of time?"

Pope gulped and got down off the bed onto his knees. "I'm sorry... I didn't mean..." he began but was interrupted by a knock at the door. Pope opened his eyes, losing the connection. "What is it?" he hissed. It was just Dawud, the young refugee boy Big Bear used as his personal servant. He was holding a tray with a cup of green tea on it.

"Afternoon tea, Sir."

"Just put it over there," snapped Pope, angry at being disturbed.

"Thank you," said Dawud, placing the tray on a table on the far side of the room. The door clicked quietly closed behind him. Pope stared at the young boy from behind, anger still coursing through his veins at being interrupted. Something about the boy irritated him. Perhaps it was his helplessness. He hated helpless people, hated their pathetic nature—like the girl in the park with the puppy. All of a sudden he found himself leaping up and seizing Dawud by the shoulders.

"Sir?" the boy shouted. "What are you doing?"

Pope was brutal and showed the boy no mercy. "Please, Sir, stop it!" shouted Dawud. But Pope did not stop until he was done, and then he went over to the bed and collapsed on it.

Dawud, sobbing on the floor, pulled his clothes back on. He picked up the teacup, which had fallen off the table during Pope's assault, and placed it back on the tray. Standing up to leave with the tray in his hands Dawud suddenly stopped sobbing.

Pope, his bald head drenched in sweat, opened an eye and looked up at the boy. "What now?" he said impatiently. "Get out of here you little hussy before you tempt me again."

But Dawud just stood there; his eyes wide open as if he had seen a ghost. Pope stared at him. "Get out!" he shouted, leaping up and yanking the door open himself. This had the effect of further startling the young boy, who issued a small yelp and suddenly ran out of the door, dropping the tray in the process. The door slammed shut behind him. "Imbecile," muttered Pope under his breath. It took him a full five minutes to get his breathing back to normal and achieve a state of calm once again. "Master," he called inwardly. "Master, I'm sorry. I had to get it out but I am ready now."

But there was no voice in reply, only silence.

36

~ The Mournful Tale of Rose O'Keefe ~

I didn't know where I was or where I should go, but I felt compelled to walk away from the city in the distance. For two days I struggled through mud and marshland, wading across ditches filled with brackish water and tearing my clothes on barbed wire and thorny bushes. The landscape was forlorn and threadbare and I felt as if I were the lone survivor of an apocalypse that had rendered everyone else missing. Often I stumbled across the skeletons of cattle and horses in the fields, and it seemed like the only other living creatures around were the crows and ravens which sat on fence posts and regarded me with interest as I passed.

On the third day of wading along the muddy banks of that great estuary I spied a structure silhouetted starkly against the skyline. As I got closer it became evident that it was an old cement block and brick tower sitting in the shallows. Clearly abandoned long ago, I sat on the shore and waited for the tide to recede so that I could get to it. Inside it was dank and musty and many of the walls had been sprayed with graffiti. Yet, wet and exhausted as I was, I felt that this abandoned tower could offer me some protection against the elements. I sat there, huddled up in the darkness inside the building's cavernous belly, wishing I had the means to light a fire.

That night was the worst night of my life. The tide came in again at dusk, cutting me off from the land, and darkness fell quickly across the cloud-choked skies. Lying on the floor and shivering, I soon became aware of a terrible presence that seemed to infest the space around me. The building creaked and groaned on its concrete legs and all night long the slop and sluice of the water below me was complemented by a high and thin wailing sound as the easterly wind whipped over the marshlands and whistled through the forlorn tower. All night long it seemed as if the tormented spirits of men and women swirled around me, testing me and urging me to join them. The night seemed to last forever, but when dawn finally came I could not get out of that accursed tower fast enough. Having not managed a wink of sleep, I left at first light and headed for a thicket of thorny bushes on a distant rise of the mud bank.

To be away from that strange barnacle-encrusted tower immediately lifted my spirits, and I found a hidden reserve of energy to take me as far away from it as my legs would carry me. I was weary, to be sure, but so far on my journey I hadn't lacked for food. My days of foraging the parks and streets of London had stood me in good stead, and I was easily able to find sufficient quantities of berries and nuts as I made my way across that soggy and vacant landscape. But I knew that to survive I would need to build a shelter.

I began by clearing a patch of boggy ground with a view to making some kind of shack from the driftwood and debris that littered the shore. Almost immediately a voice seemed to tell me I was doing something wrong. "Look at me," it said, "water halfway up my trunk a dozen times a year and still I survive where no human could." I looked. It was a tree—a willow with gnarled and wind-stunted branches dripping green moss. "Thank you, old tree," I said and left the space to look for somewhere safer. I walked a little further inland to find somewhere more suitable. I didn't want to go too far inland as intuition told me there would be roads and villages and desperate people. Out here, amongst the bog plants and the stunted trees, in a world of water and mud, was where I felt safest. I picked a little spot on a grassy bank half-surrounded by rose bushes. Perfect, I said to myself, a Rose among roses.

My first attempt at building a shelter would not have impressed anyone. I rammed some sticks into the ground and made a crude roof out of a piece of muddy silage plastic I found stuck to a thorn bush. But at least it kept me dry while I scavenged other building materials over the coming days. It rained heavily that night and I was able to collect rainwater in a soft drink can, so at least I had that to be thankful for. Over the next few days I found packing crates by the dozen washed up on the shore. They were heavy and waterlogged but I dragged them up to my shelter—which I had called the 'Rose Garden'—and made a kind of shed out of them. It was spacious enough for me but I still needed more materials for the roof if I wasn't to live beneath a constant stream of drips. But more than this I needed fire, and I knew that to get it I would have to go inland in search of it.

I set off at dawn after a meagre breakfast of sea buckthorn berries, rose hips and sloes. In the distance I could see a small stone church, and so I headed towards it through scrubland that eventually gave way to fields. I had only been walking for a short while when I came across a country road. There was a small lay-by with a car parked in it. The car was obviously abandoned, as its tyres were flat and the cap on the fuel tank had been pried off. I wondered if there might be someone inside but a quick rub of the window with my sleeve revealed it to be empty. There was nobody around—in fact I hadn't seen another living soul since I had come to on the riverbank the week before—and so I took a large stone from a field and smashed it through the side window. I opened the door and rummaged around inside the car to see if I could find anything interesting or useful. One of the first things I did was try the cigarette lighter to see if it worked. But of course the car's battery had died long ago and there was no electrical charge to light it up. Nothing overly useful was immediately obvious inside the car. It just contained some CDs, a few child's stuffed toys and a blanket, which I took. I pulled out the back shelf to see if there was anything in the boot, and it turned out there was. I could see some tent poles with a piece of canvas tarpaulin and a black donkey jacket which I immediately put on. Digging my cold hands into the pockets I found a half empty packet of cigarettes, a ticket to a music festival and—joy—a lighter. Looking in the boot again, I uncovered a plastic bag with packets of dried soup, some dehydrated noodles and a sticky black mess that might once have been a banana. I struck the lighter a couple of times just to make sure it worked and then picked up the tent, the food and the blanket to take back to my little camp.

As I slammed the car door shut its mirror suddenly reflected a face back at me. It took me a moment to realise it was my own. My face and hair were encrusted with dirt and mud and if it hadn't been for my eyes, I don't think I would have recognised myself at all. I used the rock to smash off the wing mirror, and stuck it in my pocket. You never know when you might need a mirror, even if you live on a mud flat.

That night was as good as a night in a five star hotel as far as I was concerned. I lit a fire at the entrance to the shack using some small sticks I had been drying out for days, and used it to cook the noodles and a packet of soup in a tin can. I piled on more sticks and broken pallet slats and soon there was a roaring blaze that dried everything around it, myself included. After I had eaten, I lay back on the blanket and listened to the rain falling on the canvas I had stretched across the roof of my rickety shelter. With my stomach full, the warmth from the fire and the softness of the blanket and the jacket to keep the chills away, I felt about as happy as I could be—under the circumstances.

That's how I first came to be living in a shack on the muddy bank of a tidal estuary. It was to be my home for the next twenty-two years, right up until the day when Mother Nature reclaimed the land for the sea. I lived on the margins of the human world, only really interacting with it when there was a need to do so. My companions were the marshland plants and the animals and birds that came and went. Of course, in those early days, people sometimes came and went too. There were villages inland, and people survived as best they could. Once I had been noticed, they became curious and approached me. In time I simply became part of the landscape—just another person eking out a subsistence in a dismal time. One day some children came by and called me names like "Mad Rose" and shouted out that I was a witch. They threw stones at my little shack, but ran off when I came out and threatened to turn them into newts.

The plants showed me the way. I learned how to tune in to their strange languages and ask them the right questions. "How do I do this?" or "What would cure that?" And more often than not they would tell me their secrets in a way that I could understand, and I would write these things down. At first I experimented on myself, making compounds and tinctures from what they offered me. I began to build up a large collection of glass jars—you could find them all over the place in those days—and I filled them with the raw ingredients given to me by my friends in the plant world. There were strips of bark from willows, the desiccated leaves of elders, dried feathery roots, berries and nuts aplenty, as well as dozens of different varieties of seeds. Once, an old man came limping by, and I asked him what ailed him. "It's my feet," he said. I took a look at them and saw how swollen and deformed they were and so I put a poultice on them and told him to rest awhile. The next day he was fully cured of his curse and was thankful beyond words.

Word of this "miracle" soon got around, and it wasn't long before the parents of the stone-throwing children turned up, sheepishly enquiring whether I might have a cure for their various afflictions. I wrote down their symptoms and asked them to come back in a week, during which time I conversed with the plants and made up concoctions I hoped would ease their suffering. When the parents came back, I was ready with my various medicines. In most cases the cures worked, and the people were speechless with gratitude. In a few cases the people refused to be helped, and no matter how much plant medicine I gave them, their insistence that I was playing some kind of trick on them made it impossible for their bodies to be receptive to the curatives. Mainly, however, people were thankful. They stopped calling me a witch and would often leave gifts of food and other needful things. This is how they repaid me, as nobody had seen money for a long while by then. One night I recalled how I had drowned and the being I had met who had told me I had a mission to undertake, and I now realised the form of this mission. For to become a healer is the greatest gift a person can have bestowed upon them—that is what I felt then and still feel now.

Still, despite being able to talk to plants and to heal, at heart I was still a devotee of the scientific method. I took detailed notes of all that I did, and would often run my own experiments in an attempt to validate my hypotheses. On occasion I would attempt to "trick" the plants into giving me the wrong information, or by disguising the true ailment of the patient—but my conceit was no match for the wisdom of the plants, and they often made me feel like a fool. I kept scientific notes on a laptop computer one of my grateful patients had given me (for, after a few years, my "Rose Garden" shack had matured into a nice little watertight abode with solar cells on the roof and even a little outhouse tucked away behind it), and also scrupulously copied them onto paper by hand. From these experiments I was able to begin sketching out my own theory on the nature of reality and conscious-ness, which took the better part of twenty-five years to for-mulate, and which is laid out in detail in the tome I hope will accompany this diary.

From the way I have described it, you might think that all was well and peaceful in my little world. But the truth was far from that. Although I lived on the margins, staying out of the so-called "civilised world" as much as possible, that world would often encroach on mine uninvited. It was only a couple of years after my rebirth as a mudlark that the planes started flying overhead and the distant booms of the guns grew louder with each passing week. It was nations fighting nations and citizens fighting citizens in a war of attrition, said the villagers, and fear was everywhere. Famine and dis-ease followed in the footsteps of the war, although my little muddy corner of the world was relatively unscathed by it. While the shattered remnants of the "civilised world" fought it out amongst themselves, I kept my focus on the much wider world I had encountered and was now a part of. Some-times people were brought to me with terrible disfiguring wounds from the fighting. In many cases there was nothing I could do but give them a dose of powerful mushrooms and some reassurance to ease them into the next world. Then came a great wave of people maddened by terrible cancers caused by atomic weaponry, and again there was little I could do for these poor folks. The same sort of thing happened to the people who had lived near the nuclear power station on the coast, which, it was said, had been abandoned in all the chaos. It was only years later that the Grandmother Plant Spirit (which is what I call her) showed me how it was pos-sible to teach the body to consume a cancer in a matter of days, no matter how advanced it had become. And the more I learned or was shown, the more I realised how vast the field of knowledge was and how unknowable most of it would be to a single soul, no matter how learned one might be.

But it wasn't war or pestilence that turned me out of my little marshland and forced me to take to the high road. It was something an order of magnitude more powerful. For when the great icy wastes of the world decided all of a sudden to melt away, and ocean levels jumped in a single season, there was nothing to do but get to higher ground. My allies in the plant world had warned me of what was coming, and I tried to pass on their message to others. Naturally, many people chose not to heed my words, and it was with much sadness that I set out one day in the late summer of 2040 with just my faithful horse hitched to a wagon, and went out into the wider world to spread the word of my findings and see what remained of the country I once knew. Nothing could have prepared me for what I was about to discover.

37

It was the rope cutting into his wrists that hurt Art the most as he slowly came round. He was on a hard floor, his legs stretched out in front of him and his hands tied behind his back. He was cold and could feel solid stone behind, propping him up. The next thing to hurt was his head. It ached so terribly that Art felt sure his skull was fractured, possibly in several places. Just what had happened to him? He tried to remember but drew a blank. He had no idea whether it was day or night, and could not remember anything much beyond the fact that he lived on a farm. It was dark, but not completely. Some light was coming in through the walls and it looked to him as if he was in some kind of draughty outbuilding that had had the windows blacked out. A rich musty smell added to this suspicion and he sat there puzzling for some time, straining to remember what had happened and how he had got there.

Time passed. He could hear birds calling to one another outside. His mouth was caked and dry and in his semi-dazed state he began to wonder if this was some kind of purgatory. If it was, he hoped it wouldn't last too long; he had been told at school that purgatory could go on for thousands of years.

He was thinking about this when there was a rattling of chains and then the sound of a door creaking open behind him. "I know the sound of the devil when I hear him," said Art.

There was the click of a switch and suddenly the place was flooded with bright light. Art groaned and quickly shut his eyes. Peck came and stood in front of him. "Come back to life again, have we? For a moment there I thought I might have cracked you one too hard. That would've spoiled our little party wouldn't it?"

Art slowly opened his eyes a slit, taking in the dim outline of the man who now stood before him. It was a bewhiskered old man in a stained tweed suit. His gaunt face had the look of one who had once been fat but was now starving, and it was topped by a greasy mop of white hair that didn't look like it had seen a comb in several months. This shabby figure looked familiar, but Art couldn't remember where he'd seen him before. "Did you say party? I'm afraid I won't be able to join you in my present condition. I've got a terrible headache tonight, plus I'm tied up, so to speak."

"Oh don't worry," replied the man. "You're the guest of honour. There can't be any party without the renowned Arthek Gwavas joining in."

Art heard Peck say his name. It rang a bell. "Arthek who?" he said. "Who's she when she's at home?"

Peck looked down at the scrawny young man trussed up against the old milking post. Perhaps he had hit him too hard. It wouldn't be much fun if he couldn't even remember who he was. He'd been planning this moment for weeks and was determined not to let the boy ruin it. He considered his options. For the past few weeks he had been busy finalising the sale of the farm. His release papers had been delivered in the form of a letter that had been handed to him by a soldier on behalf of a foreign agricultural concern he had never heard of. It had offered him the chance to sell up and clear out. On the few occasions that Peck had been out he'd met other landowners who'd had the same offer from the same firm. Most had been more than happy to accept the awful terms and the insulting prices being offered. They'd be paid in hard currency—US dollars—and there was an option to be resettled in a retirement community up country somewhere. Peck had gone for the cash only deal, which now sat in a briefcase on the kitchen table. Tomorrow night he would be gone. Gone to a new life. If he could make it to Falmouth, he was sure he'd be able to find a boat that could take him over to France. From there he could get buses and trains south. Old Fred Campbell from Botallack Farm had done the same thing three months back, and word was that it had all gone well. They'd already gone over his farm with bulldozers and all that remained of the old granite house and Cornish hedges was a big pile of rocks and tangled roots. The rest of it was surrounded by razor wire and they'd put up a big sign at the front saying "Biosynergen plc Unit 5503." Peck wished he could be around to see them turf out the squatters on his land. He imagined the bulldozers rolling over their shacks and the screams as they fled for their lives. This thought made him feel all warm and fuzzy inside.

"What you smilin' at mister?" said Art from the floor. "Fancy getting me a glass of water or something and telling me how I managed to get here?"

Peck looked down at the young man who had so blighted his life. Soon, he would be gone and all that would be left would be a pulpy mess. There would be no legal claims following him down to the Costas and he wouldn't have to worry about him getting revenge either. No, there would be no loose ends whatsoever.

The machine stood in the corner. It was primed, fuelled, and ready for action. "Water?" he said distractedly. "You don't need any water." With that he turned and left the building, switching off the lights as he did so and leaving Art trussed up against the post and more puzzled than ever.

After a while Art fell into an uneasy sleep, taunted by nightmares. Over the next few hours he awoke in agony several times. Cramps racked his arms and legs and his head throbbed as if it was about to explode. But through the pain he began to experience flashes of remembering. His mind felt like a jigsaw puzzle that had been scattered on the ground. Slowly he began to piece bits of it back together and he could at last remember who he was and what had happened over the last few months. The man, he now felt sure, was Peck, and that wasn't good news, as far as he was concerned. Not good at all.

38

One clear Arctic night under a bright waxing moon something momentous happened. Deep beneath the frozen subsoil, in a subterranean "doomstead" of a Texan oligarch, a young Syrian boy lay wide awake, terrified by what he was about to do. Beside him lay the shapeless form of a large man, emitting a low and steady stream of snores into the darkened room. He couldn't understand the feelings inside him any more than he could explain the strange voice that spoke to him inside his head. He was startled. Scared. Not as scared as he had been when a life-shattering Jihadi bomb had disintegrated his family home in Homs, killing his parents, his baby sister and the family dog; and not even as scared as during those first few months of being passed around by Big Bear's friends; no, this was an altogether different kind of fear. This particular fear was... *exhilarating.*

"What are you waiting for, boy? I have told you what to do."

Dawud gulped. There it was again, speaking to him. "Why should I?" the boy mouthed silently in the darkness.

"You do want revenge, do you not? Remember what they did to your sister. Remember how she called out to you for

307

help and how they just laughed and carried on having their way—and you, powerless to help her. Will you not do it for her?"

"But how will I know what to do? What if I get it wrong?"

"Just do as I direct you and nothing can go wrong. Men such as these have had their time in this world. They have served their purpose, but now they must be eradicated. It is a simple task, and you will not go wrong. I have foreseen these events. Now do it."

Dawud screwed his eyes up tight. There were tears in the corners. His Anger at Pope had caused Bear to beat him tonight. He had got himself drunk on rye whisky and left the party early, taking Dawud with him. Behind the sound-proofed doors of Bear's suite the man's violence had been unleashed, and the boy had had to plead for mercy for the second time that day. If the voice had not been there, consoling him and giving him strength through it all, he was not sure he could have survived Bear's onslaught.

"Trust me."

The boy opened his eyes again and slipped quietly from the bed, padding across the carpet to the dresser. He put on his clothes and stood looking down at the bed. Big Bear always slept with a gun within clutching distance of his right hand. It was in a concealed compartment in the side of the bed that would spring open when the ever-listening security system recognised his voice crying out. He had seen it spring open accidentally on several occasions before, usually when the Texan was enjoying Dawud, or some of the other children who were often flown in for a night's entertainment.

"You know what to do."

Dawud went over to the wardrobe and felt around for the door handle. A small recessed light illuminated the interior and allowed him to see the box of toys. From it he removed the pair of handcuffs and opened them. Big Bear usually slept on his back with his mouth wide open and arms flat beside him, and tonight was no different. The dim bulb in the wardrobe gave him enough light to see as he gently lifted up one arm, moving the man's heavy paw onto his hairy belly and allowing it to rest there. Next, reaching over the man's girth, he took the other arm and did the same before slipping on the handcuffs and locking them tight. The heavy man grunted and stopped snoring for a moment, and Dawud's heart seemed to flutter in his mouth. After a few moments the snoring resumed and Dawud could breathe once again. He took a length of silk from the box and tied one end around the chain of the cuffs, securing the other to the post diagon-ally opposite at the foot of the bed. It wasn't the best knot or the tightest fit but it would buy him a few vital seconds.

"Do it now before he wakes up!"

The marble lamp was heavy as he lifted it up above his head, but Dawud was strong for a ten-year-old. He held it there for a few seconds, said a silent prayer for his family, and then brought it crashing down on the sleeping man's ex-posed groin. Big Bear cried out in pain, awakening with a screaming string of expletives. The cabinet sprung open and the Magnum .44 popped out, presented handle-forwards on a cushioned metal arm, loaded and ready to be fired. Big Bear immediately tried to grab it but found himself in a state of bondage. Dawud leapt forwards and grabbed the gun, back-ing off and levelling it at the dark, heaving shape trying to get up off the bed. "I'll kill you," yelled Big Bear, recognising the boy in the half-light.

Dawud's hands trembled as he tried to point the gun and feel for the trigger. The weapon had been made for someone with much bigger hands than his and he found he had to hold it against his chest, putting his left hand around the neck of the long black barrel to steady it. Big Bear lashed out at him with a foot, kicking him backwards towards the wardrobe. The boy regained his balance and aimed the gun at the thrashing shape. He squeezed the trigger. There was a loud bang, even with the silencer, and he was flung backwards against a cupboard and the gun flew out of his hands. Moments later there came a deep groaning noise from the bed and a soft gurgling sound. Dawud stood up and backed away towards the door. He reached for the dimmer and turned up the light, fearing for what he would see.

Big Bear lay on the bed with a great open wound in his belly like a heavily lipsticked mouth. From the parted lips pink entrails splayed out across the blood-spattered sheets and yellowish bile oozed out from the sides. His belly burst open, the billionaire lay there moaning quietly with his fists spasming open and closed as he rode the waves of agonising pain. Dawud spied the gun on the carpet and picked it up again. He held it steady and straight this time and walked over to the injured man. Seeing the boy approach, Big Bear turned his head and looked at him with bloodshot eyes. "I'll give you anything—anything you want in the whole world," he managed to mouth. "You name it, you got it." But the boy's face remained impassive. "Please, I beg you," pleaded Bear, and he lifted his hands over his head and onto the bed behind him as if in surrender, the silk rope having been severed by the blast.

"I want my father back, you son of a bitch!" Dawud said, quoting a line from one of his favourite movies, his voice shaky and creaking with emotion.

Bear's fingers crawled around behind the pillows feeling for the panic button. He felt around for its smooth, rounded outline and was about to press it when Dawud fired his second shot. The hollow-point expanding bullet hit Bear in the middle of his face and burst open inside his skull, causing his head to explode like a water balloon. In the space of half a second all that remained of the head of one of America's richest and most powerful men was a flap of skin and a wall covered in fragments of skull, blood and brain matter. Dawud stared at the mess for a second and dropped to his knees in shock.

In his mind he could hear the soothing voice.

"Good. I told you there would be no problem. Now for the second part."

Dawud stood up. There was no going back now. He picked up Bear's suit jacket, which had been tossed on the floor, and rummaged in the pocket for his cigar cutter.

"The index finger. Just cut off the index finger. Soon you'll be free as a bird."

39

Dawud stood in the half-lit room holding his tormentor's index finger in his right hand. It had been a job to remove it with the cigar cutter and the young boy had eventually resorted to placing the whole hand on the bedside table and bringing the marble lamp down with some force on the miniature guillotine. The finger had then come off cleanly just above the knuckle, revealing a cross section of white bone encased in red flesh.

"Perfect. Well done."

Glancing round at the room and pausing to gather himself together, Dawud thought that he had better get his coat on. There was a drawer in the wardrobe that contained his belongings, and from it he pulled out a blue parka with a fur-lined hood. He was putting it on when the first tremor came. For a second it seemed as if the room had turned to liquid and Dawud had to grab hold of the wardrobe door to steady himself. The illusion of solidity in this underground fortress momentarily dissolved and the boy experienced a curious feeling of sudden vulnerability. In a moment it was over. Such tremors were not uncommon, but there was something in the amplitude and persistence of this one that hinted at worse to come, and it sent a shiver down his spine.

"Quickly, my friend, it is coming!"

Dawud placed the bloodied finger in the pocket of the coat and sat on the bed as he pulled on his boots. Beside him, on the blood-soaked sheets, lay the cooling mass of Theodore Whitman. The brain that *Fortune* had once described as "the best business brain on the planet" was now little more than a spray of congealed jelly, the larger chunks of it slowly sliding down the wall above the bed. The boy felt no remorse for what he had done. Perhaps he was in a state of shock, or had flipped into survival mode, but for the most part he considered the man's death the responsibility of someone else; he himself had merely pulled the trigger. Having finished lacing up his boots, he took one final look at the mess on the bed, stood up and went out into the corridor. After a moment he paused and re-entered the room. He emerged a few seconds later tucking the pistol into a large pouch on the front of his parka.

Living underground for so long meant that Dawud had lost track of the meaning of time as it was experienced on the surface, in the world above. To avoid disrupting the circadian rhythms of its inhabitants, the bunker had been outfitted with an ambient lighting system that closely matched the above ground light levels. In addition, hallways had been fitted with large LCD screens that relayed real-time feeds from hidden cameras outside, giving the effect of an outdoors stroll, though without the benefit of fresh air. It was almost three in the morning and the lights were turned down low. Glancing at one of the screens, Dawud could see that the moon was high in the sky, casting a luminescent pallor over an empty landscape in which coldly glowing mountains could be discerned in the far distance. He padded up the hallway to the elevator that would take him from level five up to level one, where the control centre was located. He knew that his every step would be monitored, but it didn't matter any more. Another tremor shuddered through the surrounding rock as he walked.

"Hurry up boy—walk faster!"

The elevator took him upwards towards the surface. But it didn't go all the way up to the first floor. At level three it slowed and stopped, the doors sliding open. This was the Eden level and it was where tonight's party was still in full swing. Around a hundred of the world's most well-connected and respectable psychopaths had been in attendance at the annual convocation—along with a couple of hundred other rising power players hoping to join their exclusive club—and Big Bear had spared no expense to make this year's bash the most extravagant one yet. Aside from the dining, which had featured a course from every continent—including stuffed Siberian sturgeon, pulled panda and an entire roasted big horn sheep on an enormous platter—there had been a live show put on by a famous geriatric rock star, a series of wittily self-deprecating speeches from various heads of state and a procession of newly created genetically engineered animals, including a glow-in-the-dark goat that was ridden around by a realistic-looking naked female robot. The wine had flowed like a river, and everyone in attendance felt that such an extravagant party could only mean one thing: that the good times were here to stay.

The elevator door glided open to reveal an incapacitated man leaning against a brushed steel pillar. There was vomit down the front of his dinner jacket, and as he looked up Dawud recognised him as the head of the NGO that had delivered him into the clutches of Big Bear. The drunken man looked up at Dawud with watery eyes that were still smarting from the hilarious speech given by someone code-named Monkey. By then Dawud had become quite comfortable handling the big gun; the bullet hit the man in the centre of the chest, exploding inside his chest cavity and ejecting his insides backwards onto the carpet. Dawud lowered the gun and pressed the lift button again. When the door next opened it did so upon a cavernous space dotted with statues from ancient Greece and Rome. Directly ahead, only a few paces from the elevator shaft, there was a control nest, in which sat a bald man wearing headphones and staring at a bank of screens. Most of the screens showed empty corridors but one had plenty of animation in it. Dawud recognised it immediately as the Joy Division on level seven. This was the screen the man was staring at intently and he looked up on Dawud's approach in annoyance at being disturbed. He pulled one headphone away from an ear and glared at the boy. "What are you doing up here at this time of night?" he snapped.

"Sorry, Sir. No time to explain," said Dawud as he raised the gun and fired at the man. The recoil from the shot knocked the gun out of his hands, just as it had done with Big Bear, and it fell to the floor. There was a sound like wet laundry being slapped against a rock and the man disappeared below Dawud's line of sight. After scrambling to pick up the gun, the boy quickly ran around the desk to locate him with a view to finishing the job. But he need not have worried, for the man was in no state to cause him any trouble: all that remained of his cranium was a shattered mess, still wearing headphones. Where a face had once been, all that could be seen now was a large hole showing a section of mosaic floor. Dawud glanced around at the various computers and instruments of the control centre. Under the desk was a large computer with a multitude of flashing lights on it. Its size and proximity to the dead man lent it importance in Dawud's view and so he raised the gun and aimed it squarely at it.

"No!" the voice shouted in Dawud's head.

"You will be entombed down here with the rest if you destroy that one. Here, relax your arm and allow me."

Dawud did as the voice said and was surprised to find his arm moving of its own volition. The gun came around to point at a small but solid-looking electrical box up on the ceiling. His finger didn't even need to squeeze the trigger before the box flew into a thousand parts. In an instant the room filled with cold air.

"Now leave."

"But there is one bullet left," said Dawud out loud. "Shouldn't I use it?"

"Save your last bullet. Now get out of here. It will be any moment."

Dawud ran over across the room to the elevator. This was the sole remaining means of getting either into or out of Bear's "doomstead." It was large enough to serve as a freight elevator, and only those with top-level clearance could operate it. Dawud punched the button marked "Up" and a soft female robotic voice asked him to present security clearance. He pulled the severed finger out of his pocket and held the fingerprint down against the glass sensor, praying that it would work. After a few seconds the voice said "doors closing." Dawud tossed the dead man's finger though the closing gap and wiped the blood that covered his own fingers on his trousers.

Quite a few metres of solid rock separated the control room from the surface above. When the doors opened, Dawud was inside a neat little room that was concealed within a building that to the outside world appeared to be a wooden shepherd's hut. The ground lurched once again as he stepped out. Set into a metal panel beside the elevator was the control panel for its operation. Dawud raised the gun at it and stepped back. "I know what to do," he said calmly.

"There is no need. The ice dam is broken. It will be a matter of minutes now. You have done everything you needed to do and you will now be allowed to leave."

Dawud lowered the gun. "What is an ice dam?" he wondered. The boy had no conception of such a thing. He stared at the control panel, on which blinked a green light. He had seen how the electrical box had exploded below—the

317

box that controlled the ventilation system—and he wanted to do the same to this controller box. Big Bear had let him watch movies on his time off and one of his favourites had been *Star Wars*. He wanted to be Han Solo in the Death Star, shooting the control panel and rescuing the princess. This is what he had prayed for.

He raised the gun and fired. As before, the box exploded into pieces, leaving the whiff of ionised electricity and burning wire casings in the air of the shepherd's hut.

"As you wish. Now it is time for us to wish goodbye to one another."

There were no more bullets. Dawud pulled the trigger one last time just to be sure. The elevator was now dark and broken and he backed away from it, feeling his way out of the door. He stepped out into the night air. It was extremely cold.

"Drop the gun!" screamed a man. Dawud looked up and saw three or four heavily armoured men pointing weapons at him. Behind them, and around them, stretched a sea of flashing lights revealing dozens of helicopters, armoured vehicles and SUVs. Dawud dropped the gun and slowly put up his hands and the man pointing the gun lunged forward and pushed him to the ground. He felt the heavy man sitting on top of him, and heard several more screaming at the top of their lungs. "Check him for explosives!"

Dawud let his body go limp as the men rifled through his clothing. "All clear," one of them said. They turned him over onto his back and began yelling at him. The ruckus attracted more attention and within moments he was surrounded by men in combat uniforms screaming at him and pointing weapons. "He had a gun," one of them was shouting over and over, "the kid had a fucking gun." He looked up at the sky. Shifting curtains of light danced against the inky blackness of the universe. He watched as they moved across the stage of the stars, pulsating with eerie beauty as though they were alive. The ground beneath him began to rumble. It wasn't the tremulous shudders of earlier, but instead a low and steady rumble that was growing louder and more pronounced with every passing moment. Dawud lay and stared up at the celestial performance in the sky above him once more. The sound of the screaming angry men began to fade away and all of a sudden he felt as if he was no longer alone. Love and warmth flooded into him and a smile broke across his face. He stared up in astonishment, tears of joy welling up in the corners of his eyes.

"Mother, father!" he cried out. "I'm here!"

* * *

The flood hit with the power of ten thousand locomotives. Boulders were hurled about by the spewing icy waters and an unholy wind howled across the plains. The short life of Dawud was extinguished in an instant. Hours later, when the scene was illuminated by the rising sun, all that was visible as far as the eye could see were giant rocks, mud and the battered remains of vehicles. Dawn brought with it helicopters with more men equipped with GPS units and sniffer dogs. They secured the area against nobody in particular, holding their machine guns at the ready, and dug around frantically in the debris, calling out but getting no reply. By midday the men had located a shaft which, at first, had appeared to be a muddy well.

Eventually another helicopter arrived, this one carrying frogmen outfitted with dry suits. One man dove down into the shaft and came right back up, then another one, then a third. Eventually, they held a discussion. "Nothing to report" was the consensus conclusion. Then the men got back in their helicopters and disappeared into the darkening skies. There would be no memorial raised to the dead. The place had never officially existed, and nobody had been there. Explanations as to why so many members of the global elite had simply disappeared, complete with an assortment of conspiracy theories to suit every political leaning and taste, were carefully crafted and widely distributed, but the true story of what had happened to them persisted only in hushed whisperings and spoken words, until it too passed into folklore. For centuries to come the plain below the Grímsvötn volcano was reputed to be haunted by the tormented souls of evil spirits, and it was said that if you put your ear to the ground on a certain night of the year you could still hear them wailing in a hell of their own making.

40

~ The Last Testament of Rose O'Keefe ~

There I was, forty-two years old and setting out to explore what had become of my country. The waters were rising around me and I could feel their approach through the ground beneath my feet. In all the years I had been living on the margins of the swamp I called home, I had rarely ventured out for more than a few miles. It is true that I had journeyed far in that time, further than most people could possibly ever imagine, but in the physical world I had remained more or less in one place. Now that was all about to change.

I guided my trusty horse Frodo along roads leading west. He was of the type they call a Shire horse, chestnut brown and with a huge, powerful body; he'd been gifted to me by a breeder whose daughter I had cured of a terrible mouth abscess. I had fashioned a type of gypsy caravan from an old ambulance, and this was packed with my books, gadgets and other belongings. That old van was cumbersome and stubborn on the hills, but Frodo was strong and we were never in any kind of hurry. Sometimes I guided him along the ways, but he was a clever horse and there was usually no need on some of the straighter roads. And so I was able to sit inside the vehicle, singing to myself and knitting as we travelled. Of course, the road system as I remembered it was still there, but there were no cars now. The roads themselves were potholed and turning to gravel, but many of the signs were still up and they made a mockery of the motor age that had passed. "60 miles per hour zone", they might say, as we trundled along at less than one tenth of that speed, or "Traffic queues likely ahead," even though the traffic had now for the most part turned into rusting pieces of junk sitting in roadside ditches.

It was summer when we set out. We had only been gone for three days when the ground shook. The first time it did so was in the early morning. I was making tea over a little fire and Frodo was grazing on some grass in the middle of a traffic roundabout. Birds flew up from the trees and my little billycan fell over onto the fire, causing it to steam and hiss. "There it is," I said to Frodo, who looked as startled as the birds. "That's what they had warned us about."

There were other such tremors, but the really big one came about a week later. We were passing to the south of London at the time, and could clearly see the little that was left of the city's outline on the horizon. It reminded me of when I had woken up on the riverbank all those years ago, having been flushed out of the metropolis, and how I had come to and looked up to see the distant skyscrapers. I had known even then that it was a place that was doomed and that I should never return. When the quake came, it was as if the surface of the Earth was a loose skin on an old drum that was being beaten by the gods. Everything jumped and shook and crashed about, and when I next looked up the London skyline was no longer there at all. A great dust cloud rose up where it had once stood. I felt a great loss. It was as if a huge stone had been flung at the great web of life, leaving it holed and tattered. I had borne witness to the death of a city and it took my breath away. "Quick," I said to Frodo, "we must get to higher ground as fast as we can."

Even before nightfall the sea had started to come rushing in. We had made it to a range of hills to the south that were high enough to ensure our survival. We were not the only ones—there were many wanderers on the roads in those days. Mostly they were broken and dispirited people, rattling around the countryside begging for food or looking for opportunities to work. After the big quake we all scrambled for higher ground. Maybe we humans haven't lost the memories of cataclysms encoded into our ancestral genes, because something inside us all knew what was coming next. The skies darkened and a low, howling wind rose up in the east—it was enough to chill your blood! From our vantage point high up on that hill we could see the tsunami rolling across the land like a moving wall of white water. We knew it must be moving fast, but from up there its progress seemed slow and languid. People wailed and wept, believing that the apocalypse was at hand.

Two or three days later the skies cleared and the winds died down. The sun came out and the people dispersed across the lowlands once again, unsure of what they would find there. But something kept me from leaving and I lingered in those chalk hills for a year or more. I could sense here that there was some kind of ancient energy which spoke to me, and when I told others about it some of them became interested and asked to hear about my work. Having grown used to being alone for so long, I at first found it difficult to accept the company of others. But they were friendly and interested in my work, and it was in fact a relief to be able to talk openly about my experiences and what I had learned. Every day and every evening I spoke, and they listened and took notes. All were young and most of them were women. They had been born after the great crises had begun, and had no experience of the "time before." There was nothing too unusual about most of them being women, as the country had lost most of its men, both young and old, to war. Those that had survived the war often took to drinking anything they could ferment, and many more men were lost in this way. These young women were like the fresh, green shoots that come up after a long, hard winter. They were hardy and pioneering and eager to make things work again. Among those that listened to me, each had her own particular interest, and I encouraged them to conduct their own lines of research into some of the areas I had opened up for them.

Three of the women, in particular, I came to think of as my star pupils. Sonya, a wide-eyed and waif-like woman local to the area, was fond of flowers and their wisdom. Reika, a stubborn young lass with a northern accent, found herself drawn to the language of birds and the creatures of the forest. And then there was Meta, who had travelled from the Scandinavian lands across the sea in a boat she had built herself. Meta was the hardiest and most adventurous of the three, and her particular calling was the ocean and all the life that lived within it. When I got to know Meta we discovered that we could journey together in hidden worlds, as well as speak to one another in our dreams.

When I felt the time was right for me to leave, I said farewell to these three "sisters" and urged them to go out into the world and spread the knowledge they had learned. "You are all at the beginning of a journey that has no end," I told them.

Frodo and I set off once more. At first we travelled to the north, skirting the remains of London wherever the now permanent floodwaters allowed our onward passage. So much had been drowned! For miles we travelled on the high roads that were once motorways, looking out across expanses of land where trees and houses poked out of the putrid muck. For almost thirty years I roamed, half of it with Frodo. I sold cures to people and I continued my writing and my research.

"*I am a scientist as much as I am a healer. There is a rational explanation for every phenomenon and yet there are many thing in this life we will never understand scientifically.*" That was my standard reply to those who called me a crazy witch. Inevitably, just like my star pupil sisters had wanted to, there were a few others who wished to learn more. I began to tell them what they wanted hear, and word soon spread about the strange woman who could talk to plants and heal people and their animals. The first lecture I ever gave was beneath the spreading limbs of a huge beech tree not far from the city of York. I was amazed that over two dozen people turned up, some of them having travelled through the night to get there. They were a ragtag mixture of people, and the only thing they held in common was a curious mind and a desire to create something new from the wreckage and failure of the past. That was when I realised there might be an audience for my work.

In those three decades I travelled all over these islands. I saw the woeful state many places had been left in after years of war and neglect, and yet I also saw something of an awakening of the human spirit from its deep slumber. There were whole towns reduced to rubble, poisoned lakes filled with deadly chemicals and beaches where it was hard to see the sand below the detritus of our ravaged civilisation. People came to me with blistering open sores, or festering tumours and gangrenous limbs, and I would do my best to soothe them and oftentimes managed to cure them. No doubt about it, those were times of woe. And yet, for all the poisoned lands and the damage done, there were happy children, and there were flowers in the spring, and there was the song of the skylark over the ruined motorways that were once full of the roar of countless engines. In the quiet hour before dawn it was possible to sense the rebirth of a fresh new world.

Others felt it too, and perhaps that was why my lectures became so popular. There was a hunger for something new. It occurred to me that I might have something important to say —something that might be of some use in this new world, and so I began to do less healing and instead focused my thoughts on writing a book that would crystallise my teachings in a way that would be understandable by everyone who could read.

But I needed peace to think and to write. At over seventy, I was no spring chicken, and my popularity had become more of a burden than a blessing. I needed a place to escape to—somewhere where I would be left more or less undisturbed—and that is why I decided to point my wagon in the direction of one of the few places in these isles I had never been to: the kingdom of Kernow. At this point it had been over thirty years since the leader of the rebellion had been cut down by the English. But as everyone knows, the victory had been pyrrhic and the New English were soon drowned like rats following the tsunami, leaving what had been Cornwall free to rule itself and restore its true name. People said that it was still a dangerous place, filled with mentally damaged war veterans, vagabonds and bandits, but I knew how to look after myself and took no notice of their warnings.

I travelled there without major incident, unless you count my meeting with a bunch of scallywags on Bodmin Moor who stole the wheels off my caravan as I slept one night. They even tried to steal Bilbo, my new horse, but he had a good kick on him and sent them on their way. Having bartered a new set of wheels from a travelling mechanic, I was on my way again. I headed as far west as I could without falling off the end of Britain into the sea, and my first impressions of Kernow are still vivid. It was a land of strong light and ancient granite. Unusually bright flowers decorated the stone walls and the roads were lined with tall palms that welcomed me like an old friend. Most of the people spoke

English with a strange accent and many of them were staunch veterans of the vicious conflict they had lived though. There were others—the Mebyon—a tough folk who refused to speak anything but their own indecipherable language, and I never got very far with them. I reached Land's End late one evening and set up camp in the ruins of a grand old hotel on the cliffs. It felt like I was home, and I got a curious feeling of déjà vu, like I mentioned at the start of this narrative.

But living on a wind-blasted clifftop would not do for an old lady, so the next morning I doubled back and looked for somewhere a bit more sheltered. I found it in a bend in the road not far above the fishing village of Mowzel. And that, dear reader, is where I left off at the start of this meandering tale.

It has been some fifteen or more years now since I arrived, and yet now I must end my story. As you can see, I have led an interesting life through tumultuous times, though many have lived through far worse. I have witnessed the end of an old civilisation, and perhaps the first contractions of the birth of a new one. I am but one old soul amongst millions on this planet of ours. And yet, now, I must go.

* * *

Rose O'Keefe abruptly shut the book in which she had been writing. For a moment she allowed her old fingers to feel the leather skin of its cover. The tiredness was almost overwhelming and she stifled a yawn. *Just a couple more things to do and then I can rest.* She rummaged in a drawer and pulled out some red ribbon, which she proceeded to tie around the book until it was bound. She then reached into a lower drawer and pulled out a thick book similarly bound, and placed the two volumes in a very faded and crinkled plastic bag on which the words "Sainsbury's Bag for Life" could just be discerned. Lastly, she took out a slip of paper and wrote a short note.

Dearest Bran,

I'm afraid this is the end. Please take care of these books until the right person comes and asks for them. You will know who she is when she arrives. Also, please take good care of Bilbo. I doubt they will take him—nobody would harm or steal a witch's horse. He is an old and loyal friend with a strong spirit—just like me, you might say!

Do not mourn for me. I am fine.

Your old friend,

Rosie. xxx

She opened the plastic bag again and slipped the note inside it. Standing up, she stretched her back, yawned once more, then walked over to the front door with the bag in her hand. Outside, the wind had died down and the first signs of a greyish light were beginning to illuminate the sea to the east. Something caught her eye. Down in the ebony blackness where the village lay in shadow there were lights. Several of these flickering lights moved in a line. They were moving along the steep road that led out of the village to her house. Rose looked at them and sighed. So this is how it ends!

Rose O'Keefe walked around the back of the small house and felt around at ground level. Pulling on a rope, she lifted up a trapdoor. She removed a dirty hessian sack and into it she carefully placed the plastic bag containing her writings. This was then restored to its place under the trapdoor, which was closed behind it. Next she went over to the stable and opened the door. Inside, Bilbo lay on a bed of straw in the way that horses do, with his legs folded up beneath him. He lifted his head as Rose walked in and looked at her with his large shining eyes. She went over to him and crouched down. Placing her arms around his neck she nuzzled against him so that her wild grey hair tangled together with the black hair of his mane. She whispered something in his ear. *Goodbye, dear friend.* Tears welled up in her eyes. *Goodbye.*

41

Cat stumbled on through the heather, her surroundings a blur, as she focused on placing one foot in front of the other. She was breathing heavily and her long dark hair had become plastered to her face, causing her to stop and brush it away with the palm of her hand every now and then. Butterflies and bees flew up at her unsteady approach. Suddenly she stopped, panting and leaning forward, with her hands on her knees. It was coming—she knew it was coming! The pain welled up in her abdomen, spreading round to her lower back like lightning. She tried to cry out but only a stifled sound managed to escape her lips. For a few moments she was paralysed. The spasm of pain was like nothing she had ever felt before and she remained frozen, terrified of moving for fear the agony would get worse, if that were even possible. How long had it been since the last one? She had been trying to count but she couldn't be sure she was doing it right. Time seemed to have slowed down as the pain intensified and her sense of being in control felt shakier with each new contraction.

"*Hijo de puta*," Cat managed to gasp as it began to subside. She fell forwards onto her knees and closed her eyes as the pain ebbed away. When she opened them again the world around her appeared different. The colour seemed to have drained out of everything and things seemed to have a sepia tint. Below the moor she could see a line of pine trees and, in the distance, the sea. *Where am I?* Her mind struggled to make sense of her surroundings. Only a moment ago she had been sure that she was walking across the Pampas, but now something told her this was not the case. The trees, the plants, even the insects—everything felt so different to how she remembered it. Was this some kind of cruel trick someone was playing on her? If it was, she thought, it was simply not funny and she wasn't going to fall for it. She shifted her weight and moved into a sitting position. There she sat, cross-legged, with her hands resting on her belly, and felt the breeze on her face. "I won't fall for it!" she shouted out. "You must think I'm stupid!" Her voice got lost in the breeze and the sun beat down on her face, leaving the heavy drone of a bumble bee the only sound. "*¡Mierda!*" she said quietly.

The baby. There was a baby inside her and trying to get out, but where had it come from? Cat's mind groped around in the dark for answers. What if it wasn't a baby at all? What if it was a giant serpent that would come out and devour her? A fluttering panic rose up inside her. *I must get to Papa. Papa would know what to do, not like dumb, stupid judgemental Mama.* A thought came into her head. Soldiers. That's who she was looking for. Yes, the soldiers would take her to Papa. She scanned the trees and the shoreline, feeling sure they were there, hidden, watching her from afar with their binoculars. Maybe this was their trick! She laughed an abrupt, mirthless laugh. *How funny boys can be!* Yes, that must be it.

Her hand registered pain. It was not a terrible, agonising pain like the contractions, but a sore, uncomfortable pain. She opened it up and saw the gold card. By clutching it so tight it had cut into the skin. Cat gazed at it unsteadily, studying the name that was embossed on it and recognising it as her own. There was blood around the edge of the card where it had cut into her palm. Yes, that was her name all right. But at the same time it was not her name. For a brief moment something in reality diverged and she saw herself as two separate people with both a before and an after version. Looking down at her body she saw the stretched and dirty frock pulled tight across her protruding belly. On it rested a dirty hand with bitten-off fingernails and protruding knucklebones. How had she allowed this strange transformation to occur? Not too long ago she had been the girl about town, knocking them dead with her killer smile and her smoky eyes. More cruel trickery! Why was she being punished like this? "Jesus," she cried out, reaching for the cross that dangled against the loose fabric of her blouse. "Please... please!" Tears began to well up in her eyes. "Make it stop. Make it stop. I've had enough."

But instead of stopping, the pain came again. The contractions were becoming closer together now. How long had it been?

* * *

Jack returned from his early morning fishing trip to find Cat gone. The door had been left open and the backpack she habitually took around with her was full of clothes and lying on the grass ten yards away. Nobody had seen her or heard her go and, to add to the mystery, Art had vanished too. By nine that morning half the residents were gathered in the communal space around the fire pit. Various possible scenarios were hashed out. "Perhaps her waters broke and he took off to that doctor fellow down in Sancreed," said someone. But Art's car was still there, with the tank still empty and still camouflaged with branches in case any soldiers came by. "Or could be they've gone into town together to fetch some supplies," said someone else, although it didn't seem likely as the two hardly ever spoke.

"More likely she hit him on the head with a frying pan and is off burying the body," joked another, although nobody laughed.

"I saw him not three hours ago," said Jago, appearing in their midst. "I was up all night on watch and he took over up on the top field. Anyone checked up there?" At this, two of the quickest runners set off in that direction.

Art's girlfriend Janey sat on a rocking chair wearing a look of neutrality. "It wouldn't be the first time he's disappeared without so much as a..." she said. "Better concentrate on finding the girl if you ask me. Art can look after himself, but I wouldn't fancy her chances, given the state she's in." In the back of her mind there prowled an uneasy thought. All this talk of Art and babies and disappearing together was making her feel uneasy. *If I find out he's...* although she didn't dare finish the thought.

The others stood around looking pensive. Although nobody said it, Jack could guess what they were thinking. Cat had often been observed wandering alone and talking to herself. Of late she had taken to wearing a large crucifix around her neck and it wasn't unusual to see her sitting by the stream and holding it, seeming to talk to it. Jack suddenly felt like the outsider and had the urge to get away from them all. He turned and walked away calling out to them as he left. "I'm going to search the lanes on the bike." There was a communal murmur that amounted to "good idea," and then he was gone. When he had left the others began to drift away too. The uneasy thought that none had dared give voice to was spoken by a girl by the name of Sara. "Cut my wrists, that's how I'd do it," she said in a low voice. "Who'd want to bring a kid into this world?"

"Rope," replied her friend. "Anyone noticed any missing?"

"Will you lot just shut up?" said Linda, the young nurse who was good with herbals. She had been helping Cat through her pregnancy and knew more than most about the state of mind Cat could have fallen into. "Why don't you make yourselves useful and be off looking for her. She can't be far away. Even if she left three hours ago she couldn't have made it more than a mile or two in her condition."

And so it was decided that they would fan out in groups of two. It was only when they had all disappeared that Linda, just to be sure, went up to the two old oaks that stood on top of the hill above the farm. Upon finding nothing there she set off down the hill again and it was then that she noticed something glinting on the path. Linda bent down to pick it up and found herself holding a small silver dragon with a slim, scaly body that finished in an open mouth. She recognised it immediately as Art's hash pipe. Standing up again, she turned the pipe over in her hands, marvelling at the intricate metalwork. There was something else on the ground and she picked that up too. A broken chain. She threaded it through the hole in the pipe, considered it a moment longer and then set off down the hill at a half-run. Something felt wrong—very wrong.

42

The chains on the door rattled, waking Art up with a start, and some rusty hinges creaked as light filled the room. "Get in you great brute," said a familiar voice. Peck spoke quietly as if he were talking to an accomplice. There came the sound of shuffling feet and then the door swung closed again and the room became half dark. A few moments later the old landowner was in Art's field of vision. He was still dressed in the shabby tweed jacket from earlier but now he also carried a pair of elbow-length rubber gauntlets of the type used by vets to examine cows. In one hand he was carry-ing a black plastic fuel canister and in the other was a bulky canvas bag. Art watched him as he went over to a metal workbench and dumped the bag on it. He then unscrewed the cap on the petrol can and added a few glugs of engine oil be-fore screwing it back on and shaking it vigorously. He began to whistle tunelessly in the way that men of a certain age are prone to do while carrying out routine tasks. As Peck went about his business he didn't pay the trussed-up Art the slightest bit of attention. He retrieved metal toolbox from under the bench, and from it withdrew a number of hand tools, including a Stanley knife and a hammer.

"What are you doing?" said Art, his voice croaking and raspy from lack of fluids.

Peck continued to ignore him, moving once again to the side and out of his field of vision. There came the sound of something large and heavy being dragged across the floor and a metallic clang that Art identified as a wheelbarrow being banged against a wall. There was another sound too, a deep throated animal noise. Art was wondering what this might be when all of a sudden there was a rope put around his neck from behind. The whistling stopped. "Ha-ha," said Peck, "just keep still a minute will you." Art struggled but his hands and body were bound and all he could do was shake his head from side to side and kick out with his feet.

"What're you doing you feckin' tuss?" he managed to say before the rope tightened around his oesophagus. As he shook his head from side to side his peripheral vision could make out Peck's hands twisting a stick round and round as the rope tightened. His eyes bulged and the blood vessels in his temples felt like they were about to explode. As he struggled for breath he could once again hear Peck whistling tunelessly—as if he were polishing windows or edging a lawn rather than garrotting a man. There was air trapped in Art's lungs that couldn't get out. He thrashed his head around and made a gurgling sound, but that was the extent of the actions available to him. After a while he stopped making even this sound and his body began to relax. *Viva España,* flashed across his mind; it's *Viva España.* And then, thankfully, he passed out.

As Art fell into unconsciousness he suddenly felt himself flying free. "*Oh,*" he thought, "*this is strange.*" He appeared to be hovering up near the ceiling in what was certainly one of the old pig sheds down in the lower reaches of the farm near the old barn. Below him was the slumped body of a young man tied to a post and the hunched figure of a man holding a stick behind his head. Next to them, tethered to a metal ring in the wall, was an emaciated but large black-spotted pig. After a while the man relaxed the stick and began to twist it in an anti-clockwise direction. Art perceived a longing to go back into the body of the young man but in his new state of weightlessness curiosity got the better of him and he allowed himself to float higher. He was soon through the roof of the building and looking down on the scene from above. A few hundred yards away a group of people were standing around a smouldering campfire and Art got the feeling they were concerned about something—perhaps it had something to do with the young man sitting up against the pillar. The faces of some of them looked familiar but he couldn't put his finger on how or why he knew them. Then, something far off attracted his attention and he allowed himself to float towards it. It was a young woman, crouched on all fours in a field of purple flowers and moaning in pain. Again Art had the feeling that he should know who this was, but it was like being in a dream where people and their identities shifted and changed from moment to moment. As he floated over towards the young woman, he suddenly felt that he was not alone. A flimsy see-through presence darted past him in the air, earthbound. It said something to him as it passed, making him laugh out loud. "I'm late, I'm late," it said, or something like that. And now there were two figures in the field of purple clover. One of them was very small and was crying. Art felt he should do something to help. He saw other figures blundering around aimlessly in the landscape and directed some thought energy towards them. "*Over there*," he thought, and on doing so the figures changed direction and began to run towards the woman and the baby.

"*How strange this all is,*" Art thought to himself once more. "*And which way shall I go?*" He felt a strong desire to carry on floating upwards. To do so would be so good, he felt. "This way lies bliss," something seemed to say. But on the other hand he felt as if there were some unfinished business that had to be taken care of and that bliss should probably wait until later. He drifted downwards again, floating over field and forest and farm until he found himself once again over the grey pre-fabricated roof of the old piggery. From beneath the roof there issued a tremendous racket of machinery in motion and Art, despite his ethereal form, felt a heavy sense of foreboding. He tried to float upwards again but his feet had begun to take on mass and were pulling him down and he found himself being pulled back through the roof as if he were sinking in quicksand. The metallic clanging grew louder and he could see now that it was the farm's old log chipper in action. The body of the young man was now stretched out rigid on a wooden scaffolding plank and bound tightly about the legs and waist with rope. Both the plank and the young man were resting on a set of wooden trestles with the young man pointed feet-first towards the open mouth of the chipper. The chipper's waste outlet had been positioned above a rusty metal wheelbarrow and the tethered pig was regarding the machinery and wheelbarrow with interest. The old man was standing at the bench, squinting at some papers that were spread out on its surface.

Art tried to flap his arms like a bird but a force was pulling him inexorably towards the body on the plank. The pig looked up at him with a half-interested expression on its face. "I'm sorry," it seemed to be saying. "Nothing personal but I haven't eaten in days." He was sinking fast now, too fast to stop falling back into the body. As he sunk into the body he screamed out loud causing Peck to spin around.

"Ah, you're back with us again," shouted the old man above the din of the machinery. "Ready to meet your maker yet?" Art squirmed on the plank in horror, testing the bonds. His legs and feet were tied up good and proper, and his hands were bound together at the wrist beneath him on the other side of the scaffolding plank.

"Let me go," he yelled. "Why are you doing this to me?"

"Wassat?" said Peck, cupping an ear. "You trying to say something?"

"Turn it off," shouted Art in terror. "Let me go and you'll never see me again, I swear. You can have your farm back—I'll make the others leave."

Peck grinned again and looked down at the pig. "What do you say Benjy? I know you're hungry but shall we let him in on our little secret?" The pig stared back at him, nonplussed. "Oh, all right then," said Peck. "This'll be priceless—you mark my words." With that, Peck moved over to the machine and flicked a switch, causing it to fall quiet in an instant. Art's ears rang in the silence.

"Now then, now then," said Peck. "I've a boat to catch so we'll make this as quick as." He moved over to the table and picked up the sheaf of papers he had been reading a moment before. Art looked at him with fevered eyes as he cleared his throat and began to read. "Donald Peck, I know you got my last letter as I saw you crossing the street to avoid me last Tuesday outside Boots..."

Peck stopped reading and tutted. "No, that's not the one." He rifled through the sheets in his hand. Art could see that they were letters, written in dark ink on cheap A4 lined paper. "Hmm," said Peck. "Here we are. You ready to hear this boy?"

"Stop calling me that," snarled Art. "You untie me now or you won't see sunrise tomorrow, you hear?"

Peck snorted a little and began to read the letter. "Dear Donny. I have been awake all night thinking about our little argument and how we can sort this out. What you told me about Brenda is just terrible. I wouldn't wish that on my worst enemy and I'm sorry that you both have to go through it." Peck paused, waving the letter in the air. "You remember my wife Brenda don't you? She was quite fond of you, although she wouldn't have been if she'd known the half of it."

"Known what?" spat Art. "What are you on about?"

"Patience," said the old man, "I'm just getting to that. Right, here it is." Peck, eyed the letter. "She goes on a bit about some personal stuff you don't need to know about and then we get to this bit: I'm telling you Donny, it is definitely yours and you'll have to pay for it. I would hate it for Brenda to find out about it—and she doesn't need to—it can be our little secret and no one needs to know."

Peck shuffled again and selected another letter. "I can't cope any more. He just screams all the time. I haven't had any sleep for three nights and unless I get what you promised me I'm going to have to tell all. Don't get me wrong, I don't want to do it, I've got to. You understand me, don't you?"

Art glared at Peck. "Untie me now, you mental case. I don't care about your bleeding love letters or whatever they are. Just let me go."

Peck lowered his gaze to the paper again and continued reading. "All I want is the best for me and our son. Yours, Tracey." He looked up again at Art, who was now glaring at him, a stunned look on his face.

"Hmm," said Peck, addressing the pig once again. "Anyone in here ever heard of someone by the name of Tracey?"

"Shut your mouth you filthy swine," shouted Art. "You're lying."

"Nope, it's all true," said Peck, "I *assure* you it's all true. I'd have happily had you drowned at birth—or preferably before—but your mother was quite the blackmailing whore, wasn't she." He held up the sheaf of papers and waved them in the air in front of Art's shocked face. "Wouldn't take a knitting needle and instead ended up making me sign a legal agreement to provide for you in the event of anything... unfortunate... happening to her. Such as stepping in front of a train."

"You bastard," whispered Art. "You complete bastard."

"What's that?" said Peck. "You can explain it all to her when you meet her in a couple of minutes, assuming you're going down to the same place as her."

And with that Peck folded up the letters and stuffed them into the pocket on the front of Art's shirt. "Right, Mr Benjamin, are you ready for some supper?" The pig looked up at Peck expectantly as he strolled over to the chipper and pushed the button. The machine spun up and again filled the room with its mechanical clatter, drowning out the screams of Art as he rocked to and fro on the plank in a desperate attempt to break free.

"Let's just have a test run shall we? Make sure everything's working like it should be." Peck went over to the black holdall on the bench and took something out. Moving over to Art he held it up so he could see. "Say goodbye," laughed Peck. Art's old cat Buster was strapped firmly to a two-foot log with polythene cable ties. He gazed at Art, half in recognition, half in sadness, as if an extra sense had told him what was coming next.

"No!" screamed Art. "Put Buster down you evil twisted fecker!"

But Peck did no such thing, instead holding the poor cat in the mouth of the chipper as it hissed and yowled. "Heads or tails?" smirked Peck. "Heads it is." For five or six seconds the mechanical clanging and thumping of the machine increased in volume, complemented by a tinny clattering sound as the bloody pulp was spat out into the wheelbarrow. The pig strained at his tether, squealing in anticipation. "Wait a minute Benjamin," said Peck. "That's just the starter, the main course is coming up next."

Art continued to scream obscenities at Peck. "Be quiet, son!" laughed the old man. "It'll all be over in a moment." He moved carefully around to the foot end of the plank and lifted it up so that it was resting on the lip of the chipper just inches away from the mechanical gnashing of the bladed teeth. Art went silent, and ceased his struggling. Peck then moved gingerly around to the head end and began to lift it up into position so that it could be slid forwards. He looked down into Art's impassive eyes. "You know, making you with your mother was a lot of fun, but I'm going to enjoy unmaking you even more. You got any last words?"

Art looked at Peck blankly. "Yes," he said. "Just one thing."

"What's that?"

"You forgot something about my mother," said Art. "Something important."

Peck looked puzzled. "Heh?"

"Something that made her good at her job..." he added.

Peck put on a large grin, revealing a row of rotted black teeth. "She was a whore and a pole dancer, son," he laughed. "There was plenty of things she was good at, but not many that a father could honestly talk about with his son. She could bend over backwards and tie herself up in knots like a Bangkok bargirl."

"Exactly!" said Art, and with one swift movement brought both of his arms up underneath him, dislocating both of them momentarily at the shoulder, and reached around the back of Peck's head with his bonded hands. With the old man's head firmly stuck Art yanked his arms forwards with all his might. Peck went face first into the top edge of the plank, losing most of his teeth in the process and breaking his nose into the bargain. With him stunned for the moment, Art brought both hands up over his own head and sat upright on the plank as Peck staggered backwards clutching his face. He threw his bodyweight sideways, unbalancing the plank and causing both it and himself to come crashing to the floor. He tried to get his wrists free of the plastic baling twine that was tied around them, but quickly realised it was too tight and so tried to untie the rope around his legs instead. Peck was cursing loudly and staggering around behind him with a mouth full of blood and broken teeth. Art discovered the rope around his legs was not properly tied and by pulling at the end and wriggling he managed to loosen it a little. In the meantime Peck had gone over to the workbench and was rummaging in the holdall. Art picked and pulled at the rope in desperation. It was coming looser but he was still bound by it when Peck loomed over him holding a monkey wrench in his hand. He swung it once, but Art dodged and it hit the side of the chipper. Peck steadied himself and raised it above his head—this time he was sure he would not miss.

Art pulled and pulled at the rope but could not loosen it enough to pull free from it in time. Peck readied himself to bring the wrench down on his head. "Time to say goodbye you little bastard," he shouted. Art looked up, wincing, waiting for the wrench to fall and for his life to end. But instead something entirely different happened. There was a sudden brightening in the room and Peck looked up momentarily at the space behind Art. His tweed jacket seemed to flutter slightly, as if from a sudden breeze, and then a large dark patch spread out on his chest. He gazed down at this patch for a moment and then his legs went out from under him and the monkey wrench fell to the ground. As he fell, he reached out as if to steady himself on something, but instead of finding the firmness of a bench or a chair it found the open maw of the chipper. There was an audible change of pitch as the whirring teeth gained purchase and the old man was yanked sideways. What followed was a momentary mechanical grinding as flesh and bone were ground and chipped, but the sideways angle at which Peck had stumbled into the machine had prevented the whole of him from being pulled in. It had him up to the left shoulder and was busy ripping off his clothes as he wailed and screamed. He tried to pull out what was left of his upper arm, but the machine was stronger and dragged him in sideways at the shoulder. Pecks head was momentarily squashed into the side of the machine and he just had time to make a noise that sounded like "nggghhhhh," before it was yanked into the machine. Peck went into the chipper headfirst and neither Art nor Jack, who was standing in the doorway holding the smoking shotgun, would ever forget the high-pitched grinding noise that ensued, nor the thud as the overfilled wheelbarrow tipped sideways and spilled out its contents onto the floor at the pig's feet.

When it was over Art slumped back on the plank and shut his eyes. Jack rushed over to the machine and turned it off as others ran in. Janey was at his side, bending down over him and sobbing. "You bleeding idiot," she said between sobs. "You stupid bleeding idiot."

43

~ The End of Rose O'Keefe ~

Later that day the old willow charcoal man was making his rounds. He knew something was wrong even before he got to the crooked old cottage by the bend in the road. The gate was off its hinges and lying on the ground, and there was the stinging smell of burning plastic in the air. When he got to it he found a smouldering pile of ashes and twisted metal outside the front door, which stood ajar. He could hear scuffling noises coming from within, revealing that someone was inside. "Rosie," he called out, but there was no reply. Bran opened the door. Inside the small house everything was turned over. Drawers were pulled out, crockery smashed and furniture was on its side. The faintest movement behind the desk caught his eye. He leaned over and grabbed the intruder by the ear.

"Don't hurt me," shrieked the young boy. It was Tom Trevean, son of Tam Trevean, a Mowzel fisherman and local dispenser of rough justice.

"What's going on here? Where's the old lady gone?" bellowed Bran.

"Drownded," squeaked the boy. "My dad and his crew took her down to the beach this morning and drownded her like what you're supposed to do with them English witches."

Bran let go of the boy and fell back into a sitting position in shock. "What did you say?"

The boy continued. "Tied her 'ands up they did, chained her to the ring in the rock and let the tide take her. She didn't even whimper or nothing—I sawed it with my own eyes. Mister Bairns the magistrate says good riddance and now she's dead all the kids' hair will grow back. Said she'd put a curse on 'em. We burnded all of 'er stuff too. All them plastic gadgees full of spells went pop and there was green flames and everything. Just goes to prove she was a witch, says my mum."

The old man stared at the boy, who was now quivering with fear. "Get out," he said softly, and the boy took off at a pace, running out of the house and through the broken garden gate. Bran sat there for some time, taking in what had happened. Although Rose had been over twenty years his senior, the two of them had become great friends almost from the first moment she had arrived. The idea that she could have been killed by a bunch of stupid, superstitious villagers was beyond belief. He sat there and allowed tears of grief to flow.

After a while he heard a noise coming from somewhere outside. Bilbo, he thought. He got up and went out. Bilbo was standing in the garden, snorting and stomping one hoof on the ground. Bran went over and soothed the horse, who was clearly agitated. "I'm sorry old boy," he said. "I'm sorry." He stroked the soft fur on the end of the Bilbo's nose wondered what to do with Rose's old horse.

Bilbo ignored the old man and stamped his foot once more. He was stamping on a wooden trapdoor; the lid for the cold store and charcoal scuttle where Bran would normally replace the used sacks with full ones. Seeing that he had the old man's attention, Bilbo stepped to one side.

"What's that?" said Bran, reaching down for the rope handle. "What are you trying to tell me?"

Bran pulled open the trap door and looked down. There was a sack and inside the sack there was something heavy. He opened it, and removed the plastic bag. "Well, I'll be damned," he said under his breath. "Will you just look at that."

44

In the southwestern lands of Britain, atop a hill, by the sea, the patch of land once called Twin Oaks Farm bristled with the spirit of survival and resilience. Arthek Gwavas had found himself as the legal inheritor of the farm, and even though the age when such legalities seemed meaningful was drawing to a close, he established himself as the titled owner of the land and the head of the small clan of settlers who lived there. Although he was a benevolent and enlightened chief, he was afflicted by a fiery indignity that ran through him like a seam of tin running through the granite below his feet. It was this passion for justice, coupled with a certain recklessness, that saw others flock to his side when a corporate army deploying guns and armed drones invaded the farm. The Battle of Coppice Hill, as it was later known, went down as the signal event in the western land of Kernow. An initial skirmish, which saw several of the settlers gunned down in cold blood, led to a long standoff that claimed many other lives. Art Gwavas, the story goes, dressed up as an old woman and escaped, returning a month later with a large band of men and women who swarmed upon the lightly armed security guards and their bulldozers, driving them away. Over the period of the next year three more raids were attempted, but in each case the private militiamen were driven away by the fortitude and guile of the locals. Wanderers, hearing about the standoff, came from afar to join on the side of the rebels until events further afield, which were never fully explained or understood in those parts, saw the corporations dissolve and the militiaman give up their posts and flee. News of this victory spread far and wide, and others became emboldened to retake their own land.

That was back in the times before the seas rose and the farm and the lands around it had become an island. Years of strife followed, and the initial shock of losing the modern world never wore off for those who had experienced it. Gwavas almost made it to old age, but his life was cut short by a killbot thought to have been sent by an English provocateur in an attempt to sow discord among the Cornish. But the assassin's bullet only served to strengthen the bonds within the breakaway territory, with thousands journeying on foot or on horseback to pay their respects to the fallen rebel. The chronicle recorded that crowds watched in awed silence as the body of Gwavas was carried to a high beacon and cremated as the sun set into the Western Sea on Midsummer's Eve in the year 2040.

But the death of Gwavas was not the end, for his life was merely the prelude. The people, so long given over to despair and hopelessness, had found a reason to regroup and rebuild. In the years before he was struck down by the assassin's bullet, Gwavas had written his book *Revolution on Planet Earth*, which set out practical ways in which man could live in a more or less harmonious way without destroying the land he depended on for survival. It was with relish and fervour that the people set about rebuilding their lives in accordance with these Gwavian principles. In time, a kind of balance returned and the people's horror of losing their convictions and their faith dissolved into the joy of finding meaning in the smallest of things once more. Thus, in one small part of the world, hope blossomed like a waterlily opening on the oily, debris-strewn surface of a polluted lake, and contentment slowly returned to the hearts of the people.

AFTERWORD

By the time industrial wood chippers could no longer be conceived of, the story of Arthek Gwavas' encounter with one morphed into the myth of a man named Arthur and a dragon, and a valiant archer who had slain the ogre who commanded the dragon with a single shot. And then the dragon turned on the ogre. Another myth told the story of the archer's son, born to a woman from a far off land, who grew up a simple charcoal burner, but who would later—along with a pale-skinned woman from the cold north—help spread the word of the Rosokifians far and wide across the land and beyond, teaching people how to ask questions of plants and animals, and how to interpret the answers. That story will have to wait for another day, in another time.

Jason Heppenstall is a writer and editor living in the UK. Over his varied career he has worked at the heart of the British civil service, as an energy trader and as a correspondent for The Guardian. He now lives by the sea in deepest Cornwall, growing woodland mushrooms and writing. He blogs at

http://www.22BillionEnergySlaves.blogspot.com

This story was originally published chapter by chapter as part of an online blog and I would like to thank those who took the time to read it and leave comments in the form of constructive feedback. I would also like to thank my family for supporting me over the time it took me to write this book. Seat of Mars is a work of fiction and any resemblance to persons living or dead is entirely deliberate— you know who you are...